Ar

Carrie pointing Melody and Ed guardians of person and her estate. In Carrie's mind, the Buckleys' unexpected visit to her office and Melody's clearly agitated frame of mind could mean only one thing: Katherine had now passed away and the family wanted Carrie's help in closing out her legal affairs. The thought that Katherine was pregnant was just too grotesque to contemplate.

"How did it happen?" Carrie stammered, her green eyes wide with astonishment and disbelief.

"We have no idea," Ed Buckley replied bitterly. "Believe me, if I had any inkling who the filthy bastard was who did this to my daughter, I would tear him to pieces with my bare hands."

**Praise for Nancy Kopp's debut novel,
*Acts & Omissions***

"Suspenseful. . . . What sets this book apart . . . is the strong development of the characters."
—*The Capital Times*

ABSENT WITNESS

Nancy Kopp

AN ONYX BOOK

ONYX
Published by New American Library, a division of
Penguin Putnam Inc., 375 Hudson Street,
New York, New York 10014, U.S.A.
Penguin Books Ltd, 27 Wrights Lane,
London W8 5TZ, England
Penguin Books Australia Ltd, Ringwood,
Victoria, Australia
Penguin Books Canada Ltd, 10 Alcorn Avenue,
Toronto, Ontario, Canada M4V 3B2
Penguin Books (N.Z.) Ltd, 182–190 Wairau Road,
Auckland 10, New Zealand

Penguin Books Ltd, Registered Offices:
Harmondsworth, Middlesex, England

First published by Onyx, an imprint of New American Library,
a division of Penguin Putnam Inc.

First Printing, October 1999
10 9 8 7 6 5 4 3 2 1

REGISTERED TRADEMARK—MARCA REGISTRADA

Printed in the United States of America

PUBLISHER'S NOTE
This is a work of fiction. Names, characters, places, and incidents either are the
product of the author's imagination or are used fictitiously, and any resemblance
to actual persons, living or dead, events, or locales is entirely coincidental.

To
Loretta Barrett,
Hilary Ross,
and Joan Sanger

Many of my friends and colleagues generously
offered encouragement, suggestions,
and in some cases the use of their names
to enhance this novel. I salute you all.
Keep the clever ideas coming!
Special thanks go out to Adrienne Thomas
for proofreading this manuscript.

Prologue

The well-dressed middle-aged man opened the morning edition of the *Chicago Tribune* and perused the small news item on page three:

Local Hospital Named to National List
By Gail Wolfe, *Chicago Tribune* Staff Writer

Jackson Memorial Hospital, Evanston, has been named as one of the nation's top mental health treatment centers in the newly published edition of *The Best Hospitals in America*. This marks the hospital's third consecutive listing in the annually published directory.

"We are extremely gratified to have once again earned a spot on *The Best Hospitals* list," said Werner Von Slaten, Jackson Memorial's administrator. "We have a staff of highly respected medical professionals who pride themselves on offering patients an ideal mix of state-of-the-art medical technology and old-fashioned TLC."

Von Slaten went on, "The Midwest is sometimes incorrectly viewed as having a dearth of first-rate health care, particularly in the area of mental health. Jackson Memorial is firmly committed to providing the best care available, and we are obviously very pleased to be honored alongside much larger and older facilities."

Jackson Memorial is a private hospital that was founded in 1980. It currently serves about 600 patients and has over 50 physicians on staff. The hospital treats patients suffering from both psychological and neurological disorders, such as those who have sustained head trauma injuries.

Other hospitals listed in the mental health category of *The Best Hospitals in America* include the UCLA Medical Center and the Hospital of the University of Pennsylvania.

As he finished reading the article, Werner Von Slaten indulged in a self-satisfied nod. In his five-year tenure as the hospital's administrator, Jackson Memorial had gone from being regarded as a strictly middle-of-the-road facility to recognition as one of national prominence.

Good job, Von Slaten complimented himself as he folded the paper and placed it on his desk. His plans for the hospital were right on target. And best of all, this latest accolade should not only increase the hospital's reputation, it should also garner him a hefty year-end bonus.

Part I

Chapter 1

"Oh, Carrie, the most horrible thing has happened!" The stylishly dressed middle-aged woman had barely taken a seat across the desk from Carrie Nelson when she suddenly burst into tears and covered her face with her hands. The woman's husband, who was seated beside her, immediately reached over and patted his wife gently on the back.

Carrie, a Chicago attorney in her early thirties, spoke soothingly to her distraught client. "What is it, Melody?" Carrie asked, pushing her shoulder-length blond hair back off the collar of her black wool suit. "Has something happened to Katherine? Has she taken a turn for the worse?"

While Melody Buckley made a whimpering sound, Ed Buckley angrily spat out the response. "She's pregnant!"

Carrie was a partner at Ramquist and Dowd, a thirty-lawyer firm with offices on the thirty-third floor of a high-rise building on Wabash Street in downtown Chicago. She had arrived at Ramquist eighteen months earlier, after having come to an abrupt and acrimonious parting of the ways with the management committee at her former office.

For a long moment after hearing Ed Buckley's news, Carrie sat mutely across from her clients with her mouth agape. As she fought to clear her head, she glanced down and focused on the blue-and-cream Oriental carpet on the floor of her comfortable office. Then her gaze shifted back to the petite redhead and the lanky, dark-haired man sitting in front of her.

Eight months earlier, the Buckleys' attractive and vivacious twenty-two-year-old daughter had been a University of Chicago senior majoring in art history. Then, on a rainy spring evening, a pickup truck lost control on a busy highway, crossed the center line, and slammed head-on into Katherine's small sports car. The vehicle had been instantly demolished and its lone occupant critically injured.

Although Katherine had no pulse or respiration at the scene, fast-acting paramedics had performed CPR and managed to bring her back from the dead. Several procedures to relieve intercranial bleeding had spared her life. Tragically, however, the young woman had never regained consciousness and remained in what doctors termed a "twilight" condition, giving no sign that she had any perception of events around her.

Although Katherine was not brain-dead, there had been no change in her condition since shortly after the accident, and the doctors' prognosis was bleak. In addition to the neurological trauma, the incident had left Katherine's immune system in an extremely fragile state, and twice she had nearly succumbed to bouts of pneumonia.

The Buckley family had been utterly devastated by the accident. Melody and Ed were both around fifty, but they appeared to have aged ten years in the past eight months. They visited Katherine in her bright, cheerful room at Jackson Memorial Hospital every day. They played her favorite music, read her cherished poems, and prayed for a miracle that would restore their youngest child to them. Sadly, with every week that passed, chances of that miracle grew increasingly dim.

Carrie, who had been the college roommate of Katherine's cousin Amanda and had known Katherine since she was in elementary school, had handled the legal formalities appointing Melody and Ed guardians of Katherine's person and her estate. Now, in Carrie's mind, the Buckleys' unexpected visit to her office and Melody's clearly agitated frame of mind could mean only one thing: Katherine had passed away and the family wanted Carrie's help in settling her legal affairs. The thought that Katherine was pregnant was just too grotesque to contemplate.

"How did it happen?" Carrie stammered, her green eyes wide with astonishment and disbelief.

"We have no idea," Ed Buckley replied bitterly. "Believe me, if I had any inkling who the filthy bastard was that did this to my daughter, I would tear him to pieces with my bare hands."

Such gruff language was atypical of Ed, but under the circumstances Carrie fully understood his anger.

"When did you find out about the pregnancy?" Carrie asked, finally focusing on the stunning news sufficiently to pose a coherent query.

"Yesterday morning," Melody replied. She had now regained her composure and was sitting there sedately in her chic powder-blue suit, her hands folded in her lap. "Katherine's internist called and said it was important that we come in to see her right away. Katherine had been running another low-grade fever, and I was afraid maybe she had developed pneumonia again. Ed was already at work, so I called him and we met at the hospital about forty minutes later. That's when we found out—" Her voice trailed off.

Ed picked up the narrative. "Because Katherine was showing signs of a new infection, the internist had ordered a full blood workup. As a matter of course, that includes a pregnancy screen. When the results came back, the internist thought there must be a mistake, so she ordered another test. The result was the same: positive. Then she did a pelvic exam and that confirmed it. Katherine is about twelve weeks pregnant."

"Did you talk to anyone else at the hospital?" Carrie asked.

"You're damn right we did," Ed replied. "I told the internist to call the chief of staff. I was informed that he was in Europe presenting a paper. Then I said I wanted to talk to whoever the hell was in charge, so they sent us down to see the hospital's administrator, a guy named Von Slaten."

Carrie jotted the name on a yellow legal pad. "Is he a doctor?"

Ed shook his head. "No, he's more of a numbers cruncher. I think he might be a lawyer."

"What did Von Slaten say? Had he already heard about Katherine's condition?"

"Yes," Melody answered. "The internist had informed him prior to calling us."

"And what was his reaction to the situation?" Carrie asked.

"Damn little," Ed replied bitterly. "He said it was very unfortunate but he simply couldn't believe that anyone on his staff was responsible. I told him since it was highly doubtful that a second Immaculate Conception had been visited on our daughter, somebody on his staff obviously must have been responsible."

"What did he say to that?" Carrie inquired.

"He again expressed his sympathy and suggested we speak to our attorney. That's why we're here."

Carrie pursed her lips and shook her head. "This is unbelievable. Jackson Memorial is a highly regarded hospital. Didn't they just win some sort of national award?"

"Oh, sure, Von Slaten has two or three plaques on his wall proclaiming how great the place is," Ed said. "I felt like ripping them down and beating the guy senseless with them."

"The first thing you need to do is move Katherine to another hospital," Carrie counseled.

"It's already done," Melody said. "We transferred her to Converse Medical Center this morning."

"Is that the one in Winnetka?" Carrie asked.

Melody nodded. "It seems like a very nice facility, and the doctors were most kind to us. I think they'll take good care of Katherine there."

"That's great," Carrie said. "Now, I'm assuming you'd like me to handle the dealings with Jackson Memorial from here on in."

"You're damn right," Ed said adamantly. "Those people must be held fully accountable for what happened to Katherine. We need to know the truth, and I don't care what you have to do to get it. Threaten them. Sue them. Whatever it takes. Just don't let them get away with this."

Carrie nodded and jotted a few more notes. "Have you talked to the police?"

Melody seemed a bit taken aback by this suggestion. "No. Do you think we should?"

"Absolutely," Carrie replied. "Having sexual relations with a person who is unable to give consent is a serious felony. We should get the police involved right away. Their investigation could be very helpful in ferreting out the truth."

"Then do it," Ed instructed without hesitation. "We trust your judgment completely. We know you'll do right by Katherine."

Carrie scribbled some more notes on her legal pad. "I'll contact the police and set up a meeting with Von Slaten as soon as I can."

"I want those miserable bastards to pay for what they did," Ed said, his voice cracking. "I'm not even necessarily referring to money—although if we could squeeze some of that out of them, so much the better. But the thought that something like this could happen to our daughter while she was under their care—" His voice cracked, then he recovered himself. "I want you to show them no mercy."

"We'll make them accountable," Carrie promised. She glanced at a calendar on her desk and did some rough calculations. "It's early February. If they say Katherine is about twelve weeks along, then the assault must have occurred in early November. Did either of you notice anything unusual about her condition at that time?"

Melody shook her head. "No. Her second round of pneumonia was in late October, but within a week she'd bounced back."

"I'll want to go over Katherine's complete medical records and see if anyone on staff noted anything out of the ordinary going on with her around that time." She leaned forward and addressed her clients. "As far as how I will be proceeding with this, the firm has a policy that all new cases have to be vetted by all of the partners."

"Do you mean you might not be able to help us?" Melody asked with concern. "We were so counting on you."

"Don't worry," Carrie assured the Buckleys. "It's just a formality. The managing partners like everyone in the firm to know about the new business we're taking on. It often proves very helpful because lots of times someone else in the office will have had previous experience in handling a similar type of case and can offer good advice. So I'll run the facts of Katherine's case by the partnership tomorrow morning and by tomorrow afternoon I can be officially under way with my representation."

"Sounds good," Ed said.

Carrie leaned forward. "Have you told Matt and Cynthia yet?" she asked, referring to the Buckleys' two older children.

"Not yet," Ed replied. "It's been such a shock that we've sort of been operating on autopilot. Our first priority was to get Katherine out of Jackson Memorial and our second was to talk to you. I guess we'll have to call the kids tonight." He swallowed hard. "I don't relish doing it. They're going to be so upset, and they've already been through so much."

"I'm sure they'll be a wonderful source of support," Carrie predicted. She paused a moment before making a more delicate inquiry. "Have you thought about what this is going to mean for Katherine?"

"In what way?" Melody asked.

"Well," Carrie said carefully, "have you given thought as to whether or not the pregnancy should be allowed to continue?"

"Of course it will continue," Ed replied at once. "Melody and I are opposed to abortion."

"Oh," Carrie said, trying to hide her surprise. "Are you Catholic?"

"No," Ed answered. "We just don't personally believe in it."

"I see. But do the doctors think Katherine is physically strong enough to carry a pregnancy to term?" Carrie asked with concern. "I thought you were told that even a cold could be potentially fatal to her."

"Her new team of doctors will be performing a complete

physical examination over the next couple of days," Ed answered. "But aborting our grandchild is simply not an option."

"Even though you don't know who the father might be," Carrie said pointedly.

Ed shook his head. "That baby deserves a chance to be born, regardless of who his or her father is."

"And you agree with this decision, Melody?" Carrie asked. "Even if the pregnancy might be dangerous for Katherine?"

"Yes, I agree completely," Melody replied resolutely. "I believe it would be wrong to take this innocent child's life."

Carrie had a feeling of great unease about this plan, but the decision was obviously the Buckleys' to make. "All right, then," Carrie said. "I'll have my secretary prepare medical releases that will allow me to obtain copies of Katherine's medical records and to speak to all of her caregivers, both at Jackson Memorial and at her new hospital."

"Thank you so much, Carrie," Melody said softly.

"Yes, thanks, Carrie," Ed said. "It eases our mind to know you'll be looking out for us."

Carrie got up from her chair and came around the desk to give Melody and Ed each a big hug. "It's my pleasure," she said. "Your family has always been very special to me. Now you wait here just a minute while I get those releases. Once they're signed, you can be on your way. I'll call you tomorrow afternoon to let you know how things went at the partners' meeting and with Von Slaten." She walked over to the door, then turned back and added, "Believe me, I intend to get right on this and do whatever I can to find out just exactly what happened to Katherine at Jackson Memorial."

Chapter 2

After graduating at the top of her University of Chicago Law School class, Carrie Nelson had spent seven years toiling away as an associate in the litigation division of Henley, Schuman, and Kloss, a legal behemoth that employed eight hundred lawyers in six offices nationwide. The firm's main office in Chicago accounted for three hundred attorneys and occupied seven floors of a sparkling new glass-and-granite building just west of Lake Shore Drive. The posh quarters featured inlaid Italian marble columns and floors, ballroom-size conference rooms adorned with Oriental carpets, and four working fireplaces.

During her tenure at Henley, Schuman, Carrie had worked long hours honing her trial skills on numerous high-profile cases. Only a year and a half away from being considered for partnership—every associate's Holy Grail—Carrie found herself in the enviable position of being appointed lead attorney on a pharmaceutical patent infringement case after the partner who had been handling the matter was suddenly stricken with a life-threatening illness.

Taking the pressure in stride, Carrie stepped up to first chair. Her client was Ronson Drug Company, the plaintiff in the suit. Ronson claimed that a larger competitor, Sodderholm Industries, had stolen its formula for a generic antihistamine tablet. Carrie had evaluated the case to be worth a minimum of fifteen million dollars. With trial less than two months off, Sodderholm had offered a paltry four-million-dollar settlement, so there was no doubt in Carrie's mind that the trial would go forward.

Henley, Schuman's management committee saw things differently.

One hot summer afternoon, Carrie found herself summoned to the penthouse office of J. Richard Toussant, one of the firm's six management committee members. Toussant was roughly the size of an NBA player, and everything about his office matched his larger-than-life scale. The fifteen-hundred-square-foot space featured floor-to-ceiling windows on two sides and a ten-foot-high waterfall on a third wall. A series of shelves on the fourth wall displayed his vast collection of priceless antique inkwells.

Carrie settled into a leather chair in front of Toussant's boat-size desk and declined the partner's offer of a beverage.

"I see the Ronson Drug case is coming up for trial," Toussant said, rubbing two well-manicured fingers over his graying moustache.

"Yes, the week after Labor Day," Carrie replied.

"Where do you stand on settlement negotiations?"

"Sodderholm Industries made a four-million-dollar settlement offer shortly after we filed suit. Since then they've refused to budge one iota, and since that figure is clearly inadequate, a settlement appears to be out of the question."

"The client is aware of the outstanding settlement offer?"

"Of course," Carrie replied. "They're not interested. I've told them we have a very good case and I expect a jury to award them at least twelve million."

"We want you to take the four million," Toussant said nonchalantly.

"What?" Carrie's head snapped up. "Who wants me to take it?"

"The management committee."

"But why? We have an extremely strong case. A jury could award as much as eighteen or twenty."

"And it could also award nothing," Toussant countered. "Let me be frank with you, Carrie," he said, bending his large frame forward in a paternal gesture. "The firm is not having a stellar year. Several large clients have bailed out on us, and we have lost a number of big trials in cases we'd taken on a contingent fee basis. Year-to-date revenues are down significantly. In an effort to avoid further losses, the management committee has reviewed all pending files and identified those cases where we feel we're vulnerable. The Ronson Drug case is one of those. As a result, we have targeted that case for settlement."

Seeing Carrie's frown, Toussant added quickly, "Now I'm not saying that I disagree with you that four million is a bit low. But I'd be willing to bet that if you approached Sodderholm's counsel with an offer of six or seven, they'd take it in a flash. That way Ronson will be assured of getting something; the firm will receive a much-needed influx of cash, and everyone can go home happy."

"Ronson won't settle for six or seven," Carrie said, tapping her right foot on the floor in irritation.

"They will if you tell them to," Toussant said confidently. "I understand they have enormous respect for you."

Carrie's face was flushed with anger. "They respect me because I've always been honest with them," she shot back. "And that's why I would never recommend that they consider accepting such a low settlement. It would be malpractice to even suggest such a thing."

Toussant's face hardened. "You have done outstanding work for us over the years, Carrie," he said, his jaw clenched. "I believe you have a bright future here. But you are not yet a partner and you are not calling the shots on this. So if I tell you to settle a case, you'll settle it."

In the next thirty seconds every negative aspect of Carrie's career at Henley, Schuman flashed before her eyes. She thought of the long hours`she'd put in to meet the firm's exorbitant billable-hour expectation; the theater and symphony tickets that had gone to waste because of last-minute crises at the office; the constant kowtowing to the partners' every whim; the lack of control over her own destiny.

Like every associate, she had thought of leaving, of chucking it all in order to do something different with her life, something better. But she had never seriously consid-

ered acting on those urges. Until now. Somehow, staring
across the desk at the smug expression on Toussant's face
made all of Carrie's unrealized dreams for the future co-
alesce, and in that instant she knew what she had to do.

Without giving herself time to reconsider her decision,
Carrie leapt out of her chair and shouted, "I will not tell
my client to take a shitty settlement offer just because the
firm is running a little low on filthy lucre this month. As
far as I'm concerned, you can take your proposed settlement offer and shove it. I quit! I refuse to be part of a firm
that puts its income stream ahead of its clients' best
interests."

She spun around and marched out the door before Toussant had any chance to retort. Thirty minutes later she had
packed her personal belongings into three banker's boxes
and was in her car making the short ten-minute drive to
her town house in nearby Lincoln Park.

It wasn't until she was seated in the kitchen at her round
oak table drinking a cold beer that she realized what she'd
just jettisoned. The backing and prestige of one of the nation's largest law firms. The opportunity to work on cutting-
edge legal issues. A virtually unlimited expense account. A
six-figure salary. All gone in the time it had taken her to
shoot off her big mouth.

Rather than allowing panic to set in, Carrie immediately
got on the phone and began to network about new job
possibilities. By the end of the next day she had come up
with several concrete prospects. The most promising of
these seemed to be at Ramquist and Dowd.

Burt Ramquist and Christopher Dowd were both in their
late forties. Ten years earlier they had walked away from
their partnership slots at a national firm and set out to
start their own business. Since then their office had grown
steadily. R&D selected their new recruits carefully. They
were interested only in attorneys with stellar records who
had been in practice at least six or seven years.

"We haven't got time to change anyone's diapers, or
teach them how to take a deposition or make a court appearance," Ramquist liked to comment when asked what

the firm was looking for in new attorneys. "We have more business than we can handle, and we want people who can hit the ground running." While Ramquist was outgoing and a brilliant legal tactician, Dowd was quieter and handled more of the administrative side of the firm.

In the course of her afternoon's phone call marathon, Carrie connected up with Pat Grove, a family law practitioner she had met on a number of occasions at Chicago Women Lawyers Association gatherings. Like most of the firm's lawyers, Pat had arrived at Ramquist and Dowd after reaching the end of her tether with her large firm's "take no prisoners" tactics.

Pat was not one to shy away from hard work, but when a partner had ordered her, at eight and a half months pregnant, to drop everything and fly to Paris to interview a potential divorce client, she knew it was time to draw the line. By the time Carrie was job hunting, Pat had been at R&D three years and was able to limit her practice to four days a week in order to allow her to spend more time at home with her banker husband and two young daughters.

"I think you'd really like it here," Pat said encouragingly after Carrie explained her situation. "We all work hard, but by most standards the place is pretty laid-back. No one has a big ego, and everyone is genuinely interested in putting the clients first. And you couldn't be calling at a better time. We just had a litigator leave. Her husband is an insurance company exec and he got transferred out east."

Twenty-four hours later Carrie found herself being ushered into Burt Ramquist's office. Ramquist was tall and stocky and had graying hair that he wore a bit longer than was currently in vogue. But as Carrie took a seat in a maroon-leather side chair, she found it hard to focus her attention on him because of the highly unusual decor of his office. It was a virtual shrine to Elvis.

The walls were covered with posters from Elvis's movies. A two-piece wall clock behind Ramquist's desk featured the King swiveling his hips. Elvis music wafted out from a hidden sound system. Carrie couldn't imagine why Pat Grove hadn't mentioned this quirk. This guy was a brilliant litigator? Carrie was incredulous. It seemed like maybe he would be better suited being a tour guide at Graceland.

To Carrie's surprise the forty-five-minute interview was businesslike and pleasant, and the lawyer's obvious infatuation with the Big E was never mentioned. Ramquist had clearly done his homework—he seemed to know about every major case Carrie had worked on. He asked numerous questions about the strategies she had employed in different situations, how she thought her ideas had worked out, what she might do differently next time. Any nervousness she might have felt quickly evaporated, and she found herself slipping easily into conversation with this unusual character.

"So you came to a parting of the ways with Henley, Schuman," Ramquist observed. "What seemed to be the problem?"

In a straightforward manner, Carrie explained her meeting with Toussant. "I'd been living with that patent case for two years. I learned every nuance of the client's product and the defendant's imitation. There was no doubt in my mind that I could prove a clear-cut case of patent infringement and that a jury would award substantial damages. I would sooner turn in my license to practice law than force a client to take a settlement that I felt to be inequitable."

"So you walked out."

"Yes."

A smile played about Ramquist's lips. "With no further discussion or acrimony."

"Well—" Carrie hesitated a moment, then boldly said, "I don't know if you'd consider it acrimonious, but I did tell Toussant what he could do with his settlement offer."

Ramquist threw back his head and let out a loud guffaw. "Good for you. I'd say J. Richard got off lightly. So tell me, what were they paying you at Henley?"

Carrie told him.

Ramquist picked up a pen and began scribbling rapidly on a piece of paper. Carrie knew that Henley, Schuman's salaries were some of the highest in the country and she wondered if she should say that she wouldn't mind taking a pay cut. But before she could get the words out of her mouth, Ramquist threw down his pen and said, "What if we were to offer you a salary of twenty thousand more than that for your first year with us?"

Carrie's mouth dropped open.

"After a year we would expect to make you a partner, at which time you would share in the partnership draw," Ramquist went on. "How does that sound?"

"It sounds wonderful!" Carrie exclaimed. "When do I start?"

"How about tomorrow?" Ramquist suggested.

"Thank you so much," Carrie said, as she shook hands warmly with her new employer.

Ramquist gave her a thumbs up gesture and a wink. "Well let me tell you, darlin'," he said, slipping easily into an Elvis-like drawl, "we're mighty glad to have you here takin' care of business with us. Just don't be cruel and change your mind, now you hear?"

Carrie was at a loss to know how to respond, so she merely said brightly, "See you tomorrow," as she let herself out.

For a long moment she stood outside Ramquist's door feeling slightly dazed. There was no getting around the fact that the head of the firm was eccentric. But with the deal she'd just been offered, she frankly didn't care if he dressed up like Tiny Tim, strummed a ukelele, and crooned "Tiptoe Through the Tulips" all day long.

Carrie was still standing there reflecting on her good fortune when she heard a friendly voice ask, "Can I help you with something?"

Carrie started and looked up to see Dona Winkler, Ramquist's secretary, standing next to her. "Ah, no, I'm fine," she replied to the dark-haired, buxom young woman. "In fact, I'm going to be working here, starting tomorrow."

"Oh, good. You said yes," Dona said, giving Carrie a big smile. "Burt was really hoping you would. He told me how impressed he was with your credentials. If I can ever answer any questions or help you with anything, just let me know. My office is right there," she said, motioning to her left.

"Thanks," Carrie replied. "I am a bit curious—" she began but then found herself at a loss as to how to politely inquire about the boss's Elvis fetish.

Dona nodded knowingly. "You mean the Elvis thing?"

Carrie nodded dumbly.

Dona waved her hand dismissively. "It's harmless. He's just been a lifelong, die-hard fan. Believe me, after a while you won't even give it any thought. It's just part of his personality. Besides, it's not his only eccentricity."

Carrie raised her eyebrows. "You mean there's more?"

Dona laughed. "Nothing sinister. He rides a recumbent bicycle seven miles to work every day, and he's learning how to play the accordion." As Carrie's mouth fell open, Dona went on, "But he is a very good lawyer and a wonderful, warm human being. There is an endearing, almost childlike quality about him that's very refreshing. I think you'll find this is a great place to work."

"I hope you're right," Carrie said, beginning to wonder what she'd gotten herself into.

Her fears were unfounded. Carrie soon discovered that she fit in perfectly at Ramquist and Dowd. And in a delicious bit of irony, two weeks after she settled in at her new job, Ronson Drug, her old patent infringement client, came calling. Incensed with J. Richard Toussant's curt announcement that Carrie had left the firm and would they kindly agree to settle their case at once, Ronson had told J. Richard to go screw himself, demanded immediate return of their file, and hightailed it over to R&D to beg Carrie to continue working on the case.

Aided by a yeomans' effort on the part of her new colleagues, Carrie tried the case and won a verdict of nineteen million dollars. R&D had named her a partner in the firm the next day.

Revenge was sweet indeed.

Chapter 3

When Carrie arrived at the office the morning after her meeting with the Buckleys, she asked her secretary, Tammy Hennick, if the time for the partnership meeting at which she would seek approval to handle Katherine's case had been confirmed.

"Yes," the tall, slender, auburn-haired woman replied. "Dona just E-mailed me that Burt set it up for nine-thirty in conference room two."

"Good," Carrie said. "I want to get moving on this as quickly as I can."

"If you find out who's responsible, they ought to be shot—or at least castrated," Tammy said, making a face. "Having sex with a woman in a coma has got to be the grossest thing I've ever heard of."

"I agree," Carrie said. As she walked into her office and shrugged out of her red wool coat, Tammy followed her to put some phone messages on the desk.

"You aren't in the market for another cat, are you?" Tammy asked conversationally. "Doug and I found the cutest brown tabby last night."

In their spare time Tammy and her husband, who were about Carrie's age, scoured the city rescuing abandoned and abused animals. Their home was a makeshift sanctuary for cats, dogs, rabbits, squirrels, and the occasional raccoon. Tammy good-naturedly badgered everyone at Ramquist and Dowd into adopting at least one pet. Soon after Carrie's arrival she had been induced to take in a scrawny white kitten. The stray had quickly ballooned into a fifteen-pound dynamo named Muffin who reigned over Carrie's home like a corpulent monarch.

"I don't think I'm ready for another cat just yet," Carrie laughed. "But if you and Doug ever come across a nice single, straight man in his thirties, let me know. I might be interested in adopting him. God knows I don't seem to be having much luck locating any decent guys on my own."

"What happened to the stockbroker you met at Pat Grove's New Year's Eve party?" Tammy asked.

"Borrrring," Carrie replied, rolling her eyes. "His idea of a good time was discussing options and hog futures."

"What about the dentist?" Tammy inquired.

"He went back to his old girlfriend," Carrie replied.

"And the accountant?"

Carrie grimaced. "The last I heard, he was having some gender identity problems." She pulled a mirror and comb out of her purse and made a quick run through her hair. "I'm getting tired of spending every night alone. So I'm serious. If you get wind of a nice guy coming on the market, keep me in mind."

"You're better off sticking with pets," Tammy said sagely.

"How can you say that?" Carrie asked as she sat down in her chair. "You have a great husband."

"Yeah," Tammy agreed as she turned back toward her own work station. "But I think he was one of the last good ones. Take my advice. Animals are much less trouble in the long run."

"Maybe so," Carrie called after her, "but it's embarrassing trying to take them to the movies or out to dinner."

The partnership meeting began promptly at the appointed hour in the firm's biggest conference room. The large rectangular space was decorated in soothing pastel shades. Seventeen of the firm's twenty-three partners were seated around a huge walnut table. Since lawyers typically are not known for having pint-sized egos, Ramquist and Dowd did have its occasional internal scuffles. However, the firm had managed to avoid any large fracases, and there was a genuine camaraderie among its members.

As always, Burt Ramquist chaired the meeting. After straightening his Elvis necktie, which was adorned with a TCB (Taking Care of Business) tie tack, Burt called on Carrie, who was seated next to him, to make the presentation about her new case. She explained her history with the Buckley family and what she knew about the situation so far.

"I'd never heard of anything so despicable as a sexual assault on a comatose woman," Carrie said, "but I did a little research last night and discovered that in the last five years there have been at least a dozen similar assaults reported nationwide. So I guess there are more sickos out there than I realized."

"You have to figure that there are probably quite a few more than that, since not all incidents will be discovered, and of those that are, not all will be reported," Terry Payne, a fresh-faced young partner, put in. "Some families might well prefer to keep such sordid events hidden."

"That's a good point," Carrie agreed.

"Did any of the other assaults you came across result in pregnancies?" Pat Grove inquired.

"Two, as far as I could tell," Carrie replied. "In one case the woman's doctors were able to perform a C-section. The baby was delivered healthy, and the woman continued on in a coma. In the other case the woman died in her fifth month, before the fetus was viable."

"Has anyone had any experience with Jackson Memorial or know anyone on staff there?" Ramquist asked.

"No, but if this is any indication of the kind of treatment they provide, I guess we'll have to find someplace else to send you when you finally go off the deep end," Chris Dowd said drolly. The room erupted in laughter. The firm's founder was a sandy-haired, low-key man who delighted in taking little jabs at his old friend and colleague.

"Thank you so much for the vote of confidence, Christopher," Ramquist said, trying to feign a wounded look. "So no one knows anything about the place, good or bad?" He looked around the table. Hearing no response, he addressed Carrie. "What's your game plan going to be?"

"I plan to meet with the hospital's administrator this afternoon." She referred to her notes. "His name is Werner Von Slaten. I want to pin him down as to what he feels the hospital's liability is, and I'm also going to throw out a sky-high settlement figure and see how he reacts."

"Something tells me he won't just pull out the checkbook," Bob Mulcahy, a corporate lawyer, chortled.

"I'm sure he won't," Carrie agreed. "But from his response I should be able to gauge what he thinks of our case and how difficult he's going to make things. Then I want to speak to Katherine's internist." She again referred to her notes. "Dr. Dawn Redding. She's the one who discovered the pregnancy, through a routine blood test. Katherine had a team of doctors attending her at Jackson Memorial, but Dr. Redding was the one responsible for coordinating her day-to-day care, so she might be able to provide some valuable insights into who might be responsible for the pregnancy."

"I assume you're also going to contact the police," Terry Payne said.

"Absolutely. Right after my visit to the hospital."

"Isn't there some merit in going to the police first?" Ramquist suggested.

"Not necessarily," Carrie replied. "I'd rather talk to the hospital administrator first and get a feel for where he's coming from."

"And if he acts like an asshole, you can tell him you're going directly to the police and you can threaten to have him brought up on charges personally for gross negligence in running his lousy excuse for a hospital," Payne suggested.

Carrie smiled. "That might work, although I'm not sure I'd put it in quite those terms."

"Have you thought about contacting the Illinois Hospital Licensing Board?" Madree Williams, an attractive black woman in her forties, inquired.

Carrie shook her head. "No, I hadn't."

"That could prove useful," Madree went on. "The more pressure you can put on the hospital, from as many sources as possible, the better your chances of getting a favorable settlement. If they think they're in danger of having their license pulled, they might be much more willing to cooperate with you to make the problem go away."

"That's a great idea," Carrie said, jotting herself a note. "I'll add that to my To Do list."

"Assuming they don't settle easily—which is probably a given—and you have to file suit, what causes of action do you envision?" asked Ann Muchin, one of the firm's top producers and its appellate practice specialist.

"It's a little hard to speculate until I know more facts," Carrie replied, "but for starters I'm thinking of battery, negligent disregard for patient safety, and negligent hiring and supervision of staff members. If anyone thinks of anything else I might be able to throw in, let me know. The more claims, the merrier."

"Is there any indication that Katherine has any awareness of what's happening to her?" Ann asked. "I'm wondering if you have a claim for conscious pain and suffering. Obviously that would greatly enhance the value of the case."

"I don't think anyone knows for sure if Katherine has any cognitive processes," Carrie replied. "She does apparently react to some painful stimuli. For example, if she's poked with a pin, there is some physical response. But it's impossible to judge whether that's just an involuntary muscular response or whether she actually has some appreciation for what's happening. I do plan to make a claim for conscious pain and suffering, and I don't think I'll have any trouble finding a medical expert who will testify that it's possible that at some level Katherine has some comprehension of what's going on. I realize the hospital will be able to trot out a witness who will say the opposite, but assuming the case goes to a jury, I have to believe that Katherine's situation is so sympathetic that there will be a substantial verdict."

"Does anyone else have any suggestions for Carrie?" Ramquist asked.

Don Templeton, a black lawyer in his late forties, raised

his hand. "Assuming you do have to file suit, I'd suggest demanding that the case be put on a fast-track disposition. I can see the hospital trying to drag things out, hoping that Katherine dies during the pendency of the case, thereby potentially diminishing the damages."

Carrie jotted a note to herself about Templeton's suggestion. "That's an excellent point," she said. "Thanks, Don."

"Are Katherine's parents going to terminate the pregnancy?" Pat Grove asked.

Carrie shook her head. "I brought that issue up yesterday, and they were adamant that they want the pregnancy to proceed."

"Even though the baby's father is very likely a sadistic pervert?" Pat asked, aghast.

"They made their position very clear," Carrie replied. "They said their grandchild deserves a chance at life."

"But surely the odds of Katherine's body being strong enough to carry the child to term are minuscule," Ann Muchin put in. "How will her parents feel if they lose both her and the baby?"

"I can't answer that," Carrie said. "I agree with you that their plan seems foolhardy, but it's not my place to judge them. They said Katherine's new doctors are going to be doing a complete physical exam over the next couple of days. Maybe if the Buckleys are told that continuing the pregnancy could prove fatal to Katherine, they might change their minds."

"Does Katherine have any realistic chance of recovery?" Madree Williams asked.

Carrie pursed her lips. "Unfortunately, it's highly unlikely," she said. "While there have been cases where patients who have been in comas for years miraculously wake up, the odds of that happening are probably a billion to one." Carrie paused a moment. Looking around the table, she saw expressions of sympathy on many faces. "No matter how you slice it, this whole situation sucks."

"Does anyone else have anything to add?" Ramquist asked. "If not, I assume we are all in agreement that this is a case we want Carrie to pursue."

All partners' heads bobbed up and down in assent.

Turning to Carrie, Ramquist said, "Refresh me on what your schedule is like for the next few months. I know you have that medical malpractice case coming to trial."

"That's scheduled for June first," Carrie replied, "but we're getting closer to settlement, so it may resolve itself. I have a couple of cases that might try at the end of the year. The most pressing thing I have going right now is the case that was referred in by the Legal Action Coalition."

"The black families that are being evicted from public housing because a couple of their kids got themselves arrested?" Burt asked.

Carrie nodded. "Right. The criminal activity leading to the arrests did not occur on the rental property, and the kids are currently in juvenile facilities, so there's no threat to the property or the other tenants, but the landlord has it in his head that one bad kid taints an entire family. In other words, it's pure guilt by association, which is illegal as hell."

"Where are you on the case?" Ramquist inquired.

"I'm still trying to negotiate. I have a meeting with the landlord and a Fair Housing Board facilitator the first of next week. If we're unable to resolve it and the landlord proceeds with the eviction, I'm planning to file a preemptive strike lawsuit alleging violations of my clients' civil rights."

"Sounds interesting," Ramquist said. "Keep us posted on that. Now, assuming that Jackson Memorial doesn't roll over and play dead, it sounds like things might start happening fast and furious on the Buckley case. Do we have any volunteers to help Carrie out, as needed?"

Carrie looked around the table. For a moment there appeared to be no takers. Then Will Rollston, the firm's newest partner, raised his hand. "Since my wrongful-death case just settled in the middle of trial, it looks like I'll have some time available. I'd be happy to help Carrie out."

Carrie gave Will a smile and said, "Thanks. I appreciate it." Rollston, who was in his mid-thirties, had arrived at R&D three months earlier, after the dissolution of his old firm, and he brought a number of substantial cases with him.

Carrie knew Will had a sterling reputation. She had also heard via the office grapevine that the tall, sandy-haired attorney with the athletic build was single and had recently broken up with a longtime girlfriend. So far, Carrie had had little chance to talk to him, but she had to admit that on more than one occasion she had thought she might like to get better acquainted.

"Thank you, Mr. Rollston," Ramquist said. "By your chivalrous act of volunteering, you prove once again that you are a gentleman and a scholar. Is there any other business to come before this meeting?" He looked around the table one last time. "Hearing none, we stand adjourned. Good luck with the case, Carrie, and remember, never be afraid to hit 'em where it hurts."

As the partners headed back to their offices, Will came over to Carrie. "This sounds like a very interesting case. Let me know what I can do to help."

Carrie nodded and looked up at him. Will's eyes were deep blue, like a lake on a clear summer day. "Why don't we talk as soon as I've finished my initial meetings with the hospital and the police?" she said.

"Sounds like a plan. I'll look forward to hearing from you." Will gave her a friendly pat on the arm, then turned and left the room.

As Carrie watched Will's tall form move fluidly down the hall, she smiled to herself. Maybe the case wouldn't be totally depressing after all. She scooped up her file and hurried back to her office to prepare to launch the opening volley in *Buckley v. Jackson Memorial*.

Chapter 4

Jackson Memorial Hospital sat atop a tree-lined hillside in Evanston, a short drive north of downtown Chicago. The majestic red-brick building had once housed a tuberculosis sanitorium. While the patient wings had been modernized, the exterior and grounds retained the elegance of a bygone era.

As Carrie got out of her car and walked toward the main entrance, she imagined patients taking leisurely walks on the vast expanse of lawn on warm summer days. But a moment later, as a brisk gust of wind caused her to pull her red-and-navy cashmere scarf tighter around her neck, Carrie remembered that summer was months off, and it was unlikely that mental patients were allowed to cavort on the grassy hillsides wearing loose-fitting white clothing and carrying parasols like a scene from a romantic historical movie.

This was not Carrie's first visit to Jackson Memorial. Twice in the past eight months she had joined her former roommate Amanda Buckley in visiting Katherine here. Carrie hated to admit it, but she had found the experience of being in a mental hospital somewhat disquieting.

Although the facility was tastefully decorated, there was just something about the atmosphere that left Carrie feeling a bit spooked. She paused and took a deep breath before she stepped through the front door. Since it was likely she was going to be making a fair number of return trips here over the coming months, she would have to get used to the place.

Carrie had called ahead and informed Werner Von Slaten that she was representing the Buckleys and that she would be paying him a visit. In that brief phone conversation, Von Slaten had sounded reserved but polite. Carrie wondered if the hospital's administrator was at all nervous about the meeting. If he wasn't, he should be.

The administrative wing of the hospital, on the building's first floor, retained its turn-of-the-century character. A polite, well-dressed young receptionist showed Carrie to Von Slaten's office. His suite boasted high ceilings and hand-rubbed oak woodwork. The hospital's administrator was seated behind a large antique oak desk. He stood up as Carrie entered and cordially offered his hand. "Ms. Nelson? How do you do? Werner Von Slaten."

Carrie extended her own hand, and the two exchanged a firm handshake.

"May I take your coat?" Von Slaten asked.

Carrie set her briefcase on the floor, removed her coat and scarf, and handed them to Von Slaten, who hung them on an old-fashioned oak coatrack.

"Please have a seat," Van Slaten said. "Would you care for some coffee or tea?"

"No, thank you," Carrie replied. As she settled herself into a brown-leather armchair and Von Slaten returned to his own seat, Carrie gave the office and its occupant a quick once-over. Von Slaten appeared to be in his mid-forties. He was taller than average, had a medium build, and short razor-cut brown hair. He wore a hand-tailored charcoal suit. Carrie rated him as reasonably attractive.

The man's desk was piled high with paperwork. A pair of reading glasses had been laid on top of a spiral-bound book. The wall behind the desk was covered with framed documents. Without obviously staring, Carrie was able to make out a law school diploma from Stanford and an M.B.A from Harvard. The guy had great credentials. Out of the corner of her eye, Carrie also spotted plaques denoting the various awards the hospital had won. On the surface at least, both the hospital and its administrator appeared to be class acts. But judging by what had happened to Katherine, in Jackson Memorial's case beauty was only skin deep.

"Thank you for taking the time to see me today," Carrie said pleasantly as she opened her briefcase and pulled out a legal pad and her file on the *Buckley* case. "I'm sure you must be very busy, so I'll try to make this meeting brief."

Von Slaten motioned at the papers piled on his desk. "Yes, somehow things always have a way of piling up. I'm sure it's the same in your line of work."

Carrie cut to the chase. "As you know, Katherine Buckley, who was a patient in this hospital for the past eight months, is approximately twelve weeks pregnant."

Von Slaten nodded. "Yes. I received that unfortunate news yesterday."

"I'm sure you can appreciate the fact that Katherine's pregnancy has come as a stunning blow to the Buckleys, and I assume you are as eager as they are to learn the cause of her condition."

Von Slaten raised one eyebrow. "I assume there is very little doubt about the *cause* of Katherine's condition," he said with just a hint of sarcasm.

Carrie frowned. The jerk had barely let her get started before making a snide remark. This did not bode well for the rest of the meeting. "I was referring, of course, to learning the identity of the person responsible for impregnating Katherine," Carrie said.

"Of course," Von Slaten said evenly.

"How long have you been the administrator here at Jackson Memorial?"

"Just over five years."

"During your tenure, have there been any other sexual assaults on patients?"

"On rare occasion we have had patients engage in consensual sex," Von Slaten replied. "After all, the fact that patients might have some mental disturbances does not mean that their other bodily urges and functions are not in proper working order. But other than those very limited instances, I am aware of no assaults."

"Then how do you explain Katherine Buckley's current condition?" Carrie asked pointedly.

"I can't explain it," Von Slaten responded simply. "Can you?"

"In part I can, yes," Carrie said, sticking out her chin. "Security is obviously lax here, and someone who should not have had access to a comatose patient obtained that access and perpetrated a heinous assault on her."

"What proof do you have that our security is lax?" Von Slaten demanded, his voice taking on an edge.

"Do you mean to tell me that you think there's nothing wrong with someone sneaking into a patient's room and having sex with him or her without consent?"

"How can you be so sure that's what happened?" Von Slaten said.

"Come now, Mr. Von Slaten," Carrie said in an exasperated tone. "How else do you suppose Katherine became pregnant? Through some sort of sperm migration?"

"Comatose or not, Katherine Buckley was a very popular patient," Von Slaten said. "I checked the visitors' log. There was a steady stream of people going in and out of her room. How can you be so certain that one of them didn't assault her?"

Carrie's head snapped up. "You are accusing one of Katherine's *visitors* of assaulting her?" she demanded, her voice rising. "Do you actually expect anyone to believe that someone she knew did this? That is patently absurd!"

"Why do you find it absurd that someone she knew violated her and at the same time find it completely plausible that an unknown person who sneaked past my security people did so?" Von Slaten volleyed back.

Carrie was fuming now. "If you truly cannot appreciate how abhorrent it is for someone to have sex with a woman in a coma, then you should not be running a mental hospital."

Von Slaten's jaw clenched at the insult, and he glared at Carrie.

Carrie reached into her file, pulled out several pieces of paper, and slapped them down on the desk in front of Von

Slaten. There was clearly no point wasting any more time with this asshole. "Here are releases signed by Mr. and Mrs. Buckley authorizing Jackson Memorial to release all of Katherine Buckley's medical records," she said curtly. "Today is Wednesday. I expect a complete copy of Katherine's records by Friday, along with a comprehensive list of everyone you've had on staff over the past year, from doctors all the way down to dishwashers, with their titles and dates of employment," Carrie said briskly.

"I would also like copies of any logs kept by your security people for the past four months," she went on. "You will note that the medical authorizations also permit me to speak to anyone on your staff who might have had contact with Katherine. I will want to start interviewing people as soon as possible."

"I will see that you have the written materials you've requested by Friday," Von Slaten said evenly. "As to staff interviews, I would request that you coordinate those with me before talking to anyone. Give me a list of people you want to speak to. I will set the meetings up, and I will sit in on the interviews. Is there anything else?" He looked at Carrie expectantly.

Carrie took a deep breath and said as calmly as she could, "When I drove up here this afternoon, I thought to myself that we could do this the easy way or we could do it the hard way. The easy way would be for you to say you're sorry about what happened to Katherine and then make some effort to cooperate with me. You have clearly demonstrated, however, that you prefer to do things the hard way." She paused and looked the man squarely in the eye.

"Which is?" Von Slaten prompted as he returned her stare.

"Which is that I sue your hospital for every cent it's got," Carrie said vehemently. "I comb through every piece of paper in this place and interview every live body. I subpoena your board of directors and all your investors. I conduct endless rounds of discovery and depositions. And last, but not least, I send in a team of detectives to investigate the criminal wrong that was done to my client, and I request the Hospital Licensing Board to review your licensing status. And that's just for openers," Carrie said brashly as she got up from her chair and walked over to the coatrack. "When I am finished, sir, you will regret that you didn't choose the easy way."

"Is that a threat, Ms. Nelson?" Von Slaten demanded.

Carrie reached up to get her coat and found it was stuck on the hook. She gave a furious tug and though the coat came free, the coatrack toppled over onto Von Slaten's desk, causing papers to scatter all over the room. "No, that is not a threat, Mr. Von Slaten," Carrie said sweetly as she headed for the door with her coat and scarf over her arm. "*That* is a promise."

Carrie stormed out the hospital's main entrance, then slipped into her coat. But instead of going back to her car, she followed the sidewalk to the left. So Von Slaten wanted to schedule and sit in on all the staff interviews, did he? Well, Carrie wasn't in the habit of taking orders from anyone, particularly not from pricks like him. She was a firm believer in self-help, and if she could find another accessible entrance to the building, she was going to practice what she preached.

After a hundred feet or so, she came to a side door. She thought it was probably locked, but when she gave it a tug it opened easily. She smiled. So security at Jackson Memorial wasn't lax, eh? In an instant she was back inside the hospital.

From her previous visits with Amanda, she recalled that Katherine had been in a wing on the third floor, on the west side of the building. That should be right above where she was now standing. Carrie took a few steps to the right and came to a stairway. *Up we go,* she thought, as she clutched her briefcase close and began climbing.

She arrived at the third floor slightly winded. Damn it. Her colleague Ann Muchin was always harping at her to get more exercise. If she was going to make a habit of this sort of clandestine activity, it might not hurt to get in better shape. Pausing a moment to catch her breath, she opened the door a crack and peered inside. Off to the right she could see a nurses' station. That looked familiar. She must be in the right place.

Carrie strode confidently down the hall toward the station. As she walked, she found herself looking into the rooms she passed, trying to remember which one Katherine had been in. They all looked the same, and she couldn't recall the room number.

A pretty young nurse sat behind a desk, making entries in a computer. Her name tag read "Jenny Kowalski."

"Excuse me, Ms. Kowalski," Carrie said pleasantly. "My name is Carrie Nelson. I was looking for Dr. Dawn Redding. Would you happen to know if she's in this afternoon?"

"Yes, she is," Jenny replied. "She's in her office. Go straight down this hall, then take the first left and it's the second door on the right."

"Thanks for your help," Carrie said, giving the nurse a smile.

When Carrie arrived at Dr. Redding's office, she gave the door a short rap.

"Come in," a woman's voice called.

Carrie opened the door and stepped inside. A very attractive dark-haired woman in her mid-thirties was seated at a desk, going over some charts.

"Dr. Redding?" Carrie asked.

The woman nodded.

"I'm Carrie Nelson. I'm an attorney, and I represent Katherine Buckley and her family."

At the mention of Katherine's name, a shadow fell over Dr. Redding's face and she swallowed hard. "Please have a seat," she said. As Carrie sat down and unbuttoned her coat, the doctor added, "I am so very sorry about what happened to Katherine. Her parents are wonderful people, and she was one of my favorite patients."

Carrie nodded. "Thank you. The Buckleys speak very highly of you, too." The doctor seemed unsure of what to say next, so Carrie pressed on. "The Buckleys have retained me to find out what happened to Katherine. By my calculations, if she's now about twelve weeks pregnant, the assault must have occurred in early November."

Dr. Redding nodded.

"Do you recall anything unusual about Katherine's condition at that time?"

The doctor shook her head. "No. I looked through her chart and my notes for the entire month of November, and I could find nothing. She did have pneumonia at the end of October and was very sick. We almost lost her, in fact. But a week later she was doing much better."

"Do you have any idea who could have done something like this to her?" Carrie asked, looking earnestly into the doctor's face.

Dr. Redding met Carrie's gaze and again shook her head.

"Any hunches, any gut feelings?" Carrie prompted.

"No, I'm sorry. I've been racking my brain for the past two days, and I keep coming up empty."

"Does the hospital run two or three shifts for its staff?" Carrie asked.

"It varies a bit," Dr. Redding replied. "Most departments generally run three shifts—seven a.m. to three p.m., three to eleven, and eleven to seven. But during vacation periods and at some other times some departments will be down to two shifts, seven to seven."

"Does the hospital have set visiting hours?"

"We're very lenient about that. Unless there are special circumstances, visitors are not allowed after ten p.m. or before seven a.m. But other than that, we encourage lots of visitors, provided it doesn't interfere with therapy sessions or medical treatment times."

"I am a friend of Katherine's cousin, so I was here a couple of times, but I'm afraid I'm a little disoriented. Would you mind showing me Katherine's room?"

"I'd be happy to," Dr. Redding said, getting up from her chair. "It's right this way."

Carrie followed the doctor back down the hall, past the nurses' station, toward the stairway by which she had come. Dr. Redding stopped at room 309, the second from the end.

"Here it is," she said. "It's not been filled yet. Would you like to go inside?"

Carrie nodded.

"Go ahead," the doctor said. "I need to check on a patient next door. I'll be right back."

Carrie stepped into the room and looked around. The hospital bed had been made up, ready for a new occupant. The monitors that had charted Katherine's vital signs stood dark and silent. Carrie closed her eyes for a moment, imagining Katherine's presence, somehow trying to capture her aura, urging her spirit to communicate who had violated her. Carrie remained lost for a few moments in her private thoughts, then suddenly felt a hand gripping her right arm.

"Hi!" a man's high-pitched voice announced. "Who are you?"

Carrie's eyes flew open and she pulled her arm free from the hand, which belonged to an elderly male patient. He was dressed in severely wrinkled pajamas, a brown robe, and tan deerskin slippers.

"Who are you?" the old man asked again, taking a step closer to her.

Carrie swallowed hard and moved toward the door. Where did Dr. Redding say she'd gone? "I'm Carrie," she replied in a shaky voice. "Who are you?"

"I'm Bob," the old man replied cheerfully. He looked at Carrie carefully, then said, "You're pretty."

"Thank you," Carrie said, moving closer to the door.

Just then Dr. Redding appeared.

"What are you doing in here, Bob?" the doctor scolded. "You know you aren't supposed to go into other people's rooms."

"I didn't think there was anybody in this room," Bob replied contritely. "I'm sorry. Don't be mad at me."

"I'm not mad at you," Dr. Redding said, giving him a reassuring pat on the arm. "You run along now."

"Okay," the old man said. Addressing Carrie again, he said, "You're a nice person," before shuffling off.

Seeing the look on Carrie's face, Dr. Redding asked, "Did he scare you?"

"A little bit, yes," Carrie admitted.

"He's perfectly harmless. His name is Bob Brakefield. He's seventy-five years old. He's mildly schizophrenic, has early symptoms of Alzheimer's, and has had some mild strokes. His wife's physical health is frail, and she could no longer take care of him at home."

"Is his room near here?" Carrie asked.

Dr. Redding shook her head. "No, he's on the fourth floor, but docile patients like Bob are able to wander around pretty much at will, so long as they don't bother anyone."

"Are many patients here able to leave their own wards?" Carrie asked. It suddenly occurred to her that perhaps another patient could have been responsible for attacking Katherine.

"Quite a few are," Dr. Redding replied. Seeing Carrie's frown, she asked, "Are you thinking that a patient might have assaulted Katherine?"

Carrie nodded.

"I would seriously doubt it," Dr. Redding said. "Our patients are monitored closely, and anyone showing any sign of aggression is not allowed to mingle with the rest of the population."

"Still, it's something to consider," Carrie mused. She was just about to ask Dr. Redding to elaborate on the types of illnesses treated at Jackson Memorial when she saw Von Slaten storming down the hall toward them. From the set of his jaw and his long strides, she could tell he was not in a good mood.

"Ms. Nelson!" the administrator spat. "I thought I made myself clear that *I* would be the one to set up meetings with staff. What are you doing up here?"

"I wanted to see the scene of the crime," Carrie replied curtly. Addressing Dr. Redding, she said, "Thank you for showing me Katherine's room."

"It was my pleasure," Dr. Redding replied. "Please give my regards to Katherine's parents."

"I will," Carrie promised. "Good-bye."

"Good-bye," the doctor replied.

As Carrie turned and headed toward the stairway, Von Slaten called after her, "A word of caution, Ms. Nelson. If you're ever again caught talking to anyone in this hospital without clearing it with me first, Security will escort you out of the building. Do I make myself clear?"

Carrie kept walking. It was only through the greatest strength of will that she refrained from turning around and giving the guy the finger. *Some first-class mental hospital this is,* Carrie fumed as she reached the first floor and headed back out into the cold. From what she'd seen so far, the man running the place was crazier than the patients.

Chapter 5

Carrie drove directly from the hospital to the police station. She had no real experience in dealing with the police. Neither her old firm nor Ramquist and Dowd handled criminal matters, and outside of occasionally having officers testify about their investigation of an automobile accident scene, she'd had virtually no contact with law enforcement officers.

Still seething from her confrontation with Von Slaten, Carrie walked into the station expecting—or at least hoping—that once she explained what had happened to Katherine Buckley, hordes of squad cars would descend on Jackson Memorial and immediately begin interrogating every conscious human being in the place until they ferreted out the identity of the person who had attacked Katherine. It didn't take much more than thirty seconds for Carrie to realize that that was all a pipe dream.

Once inside the nondescript two-story building, Carrie marched resolutely up to a reception desk manned by a slightly overweight uniformed cop. His name tag read "Spangler."

Carrie pulled a business card out of her pocket and handed it to the policeman. "I'd like to speak to a detective," she announced in a decisive tone.

Officer Spangler raised one eyebrow. "What's this in regard to?" he asked in a slow drawl.

"I want to report a crime," Carrie replied.

Officer Spangler looked Carrie carefully up and down. "What kind of a crime?"

Carrie bristled but replied, "A sexual assault."

As Spangler's visual inspection became decidedly more intimate, Carrie suppressed a shiver. "This would be something that happened to you personally?" Spangler asked, in what sounded like a hopeful tone.

"No, it's something that happened to a client of mine," Carrie replied, trying hard to keep her voice even. "Now, if you'd please be so kind as to summon a detective, Officer Spangler, I will relate the entire story to him or her."

"It's *Sergeant* Spangler," the man stated, scrutinizing Carrie's business card and giving her another long glance. "Look, Ms. Nelson, I guess I must be missing something here. Why can't your client report this crime herself?"

"Because she's been in a coma for the past eight months," Carrie exploded. "That makes it just a tiny bit difficult for her to bop on down here and make small talk with you. Now are you going to get me a detective, *Sergeant* Spangler, or am I going to have to take this matter up with your supervisor?"

The shock value of hearing about the client in a coma, coupled with Carrie's obvious obstinancy, finally seemed to energize the portly sergeant. He turned his back on Carrie, picked up the phone, punched in a couple of numbers, and spoke quietly to the person on the other end. Then he replaced the receiver and turned back to Carrie. "A detective will be right with you, ma'am. I apologize for the delay."

"Thank you *so* much, Sergeant," Carrie said in a syrupy-sweet tone. She took a few steps to one side of the man's desk to await the detective's arrival.

Within two minutes a tall, slender man in his early forties wearing dark-gray slacks, a white shirt, and a Jerry Garcia tie strode quickly out of a back office. "Whatcha got for me, John?" he asked Spangler.

The sergeant motioned toward Carrie and offered her business card. "This lady says she has a client in a coma who's been sexually assaulted."

The new arrival took Carrie's card, glanced at it, then stepped over and offered his hand. "Ms. Nelson? Detective David Clauff." As they shook hands, the detective said,

"Why don't we step into one of the interview rooms and you can fill me in on the situation?"

Carrie followed Clauff back the way he had come, and they entered a small room furnished with a soda machine, a file cabinet, a gray metal table, and three metal chairs.

"Please have a seat," Clauff said.

As Carrie sat down, she gave a quick glance around her. There were dust bunnies under the table, and the walls looked as if they hadn't been painted since the Nixon administration. No wonder cops were always so crotchety. Who wouldn't be in such depressing surroundings?

Clauff opened the top drawer of the file cabinet, pulled out a yellow pad, took a pen out of his shirt pocket, and sat down across from Carrie. "All right, tell me what you believe happened to your client."

Carrie explained about Katherine's accident, her tenure at Jackson Memorial, and the recent discovery of her pregnancy. Detective Clauff took copious notes and interrupted frequently with questions.

"You say the hospital has been put on notice of the pregnancy?" Clauff asked.

Carrie nodded. "Apparently Katherine's condition was confirmed the day before yesterday. The Buckleys learned about it yesterday morning. They spoke to the hospital's administrator, Werner Von Slaten, immediately afterward."

"And what was his reaction?"

"He basically blew them off. I talked to him myself, right before I came here, and I got the same treatment."

Clauff stopped writing and looked up. "How can he blow this thing off? There's no question but that the girl is pregnant, right?"

Carrie shook her head. "She's about twelve weeks along."

"And she hasn't been out of the hospital since late May?"

"Not until yesterday, when she was transferred to Converse Medical Center."

Clauff scratched his head with the pen. "Then obviously

the pregnancy is the result of a sexual act that occurred at Jackson Memorial."

"That's right."

"But this Von Slaten still denies that the hospital has any responsibility?"

"He tried to claim that one of Katherine's visitors probably assaulted her."

Clauff looked at Carrie intently. "And you don't think there's any possibility it happened that way?"

"That's a preposterous notion!" Carrie exclaimed. "The Buckleys are an upstanding, upper-middle-class family. The idea that anyone who knows them would rape a woman in a coma is ludicrous."

Clauff gave a small shudder. "I've been with the department fifteen years and I've seen a lot of odd things, but I've got to admit this scenario is just plain sick."

"I agree completely."

"Give me the Buckleys' full names and their address."

"Edward and Melody Buckley, 2239 Serra Drive, Glencoe."

"Are they employed?"

"Ed is an analyst at Morgan Stanley Dean Witter. Melody doesn't work outside the home."

"The Buckleys are Katherine's legal guardians?"

"Yes. I handled the guardianship for them. I can get you a copy of the order appointing them if you'd like."

Clauff waved his hand. "That won't be necessary, at least not right now. What's the name of the doctor who was treating Katherine at Jackson Memorial?"

"She had a team of doctors, but the internist who discovered the pregnancy is named Dawn Redding. I spoke to her briefly—before Von Slaten ordered me off the premises—and she seems like a competent doctor as well as a nice person. I think she'll cooperate in any way she can."

"Do you know the name of Katherine's new doctor at Converse?"

"Just a minute. I think I have it." Carrie dug through her bag and pulled out a scrap of paper. "The Buckleys gave me two names. Carl Hillhouse and Kaylee Flanagan."

"Has Katherine ever been conscious since the accident?"

"No."

"No signs of cognition at all?"

"No."

"And the doctors don't expect her to ever wake up?"

Carrie shook her head sadly. "Barring a miracle, no."

"Do the Buckleys have any thoughts at all on who might have done this?"

"None whatsoever."

"Do you have any ideas?"

Carrie thought for a moment. "Not specifically, but from my brief visit there today it's clear that security is pretty lax. I was able to go in a side door and up to the third floor, where Katherine's room was, without being observed or stopped. And while I was in Katherine's room, an elderly patient walked right in on me."

"What's his name and what was he doing there?" Clauff asked.

"His name is Bob Brakefield, and he was just wandering around," Carrie replied. "Dr. Redding assured me he's harmless, but he scared me to death. And it got me to thinking that there are probably lots of other patients who also wander around at will. I'd be willing to bet that some of them are young and strong and could pose a serious threat to a comatose young woman."

"So you think a patient is responsible?"

"Not necessarily, but it just seems like this is a unique situation involving a unique cast of characters, and we shouldn't rule anyone out."

"I assume Jackson Memorial treats people with all sorts of mental problems, sexual deviations, and so on. They don't let people like that just roam the halls at will, do they?"

Carrie shrugged. "I don't know. Dr. Redding said they make sure that patients who might be dangerous are kept confined."

Clauff put the pen down. "All right. I think I have enough information for starters. I'll take a drive up to the hospital this afternoon, and I'll let you know if we find out anything."

"Thank you," Carrie said gratefully, finally feeling that someone was showing appropriate concern for Katherine Buckley. "Is there any reason why I can't proceed with my civil lawsuit against the hospital while the criminal investigation is pending?"

Clauff shrugged. "It shouldn't make any difference on our end. But can you sue without having more facts?"

"This is America," Carrie replied. "Where you can sue now and get the facts later." Seeing the surprised look on Clauff's face, she explained. "I don't mean to make light of the situation, but in many cases it's advantageous to file the lawsuit first and fill in the blanks with the details as you go. You see, you don't need a lot of information to file a complaint; only enough to put the adverse party on notice as to what the case is about.

"Once you've filed, the rules of civil procedure give you very broad access to all sorts of information about your adversary. I didn't exactly hit it off with Mr. Von Slaten today, and unless I file a lawsuit, I'm sure the hospital won't tell me squat—and they'd be under no obligation to do so. But if they've been named a defendant and refuse to furnish documents or make potential witnesses available, I can get a judge to order them to cooperate or they'll risk being found in contempt. So I'm going to want to file as soon as I can."

"File away," Clauff said encouragingly. "It sounds like they deserve whatever happens to them." He stood up and held out his hand. "It's been nice meeting you. Good luck to your clients, and I'll be in touch."

"Thank you very much," Carrie said, grasping his hand firmly. "It will mean a lot to the Buckleys to know that someone is looking out for Katherine's interests."

Chapter 6

Carrie arrived back at the office late in the afternoon, ready to begin developing a battle plan for the *Buckley* case. As she breezed past her secretary's desk, Tammy announced ominously, "The Queen was here looking for you. She wants you to call her right away."

"The Queen" was the lawyers' affectionate nickname for Sheryl Gervasi, the firm's fiscal officer and purchasing agent. A brash, confident woman in her forties with a wicked sense of humor, Sheryl made it her life's work to make sure that the paperwork connected with the firm's finances was done correctly and on time. Partners who didn't bat an eye at the thought of engaging in a court battle with the meanest lawyers in the city would get weak in the knees when they had to face the Queen's wrath.

Carrie groaned. "What did I forget to do now?"

"She didn't say," Tammy replied. "How did the meeting at the hospital go?"

"Lousy," Carrie replied. "I'll tell you about it later." She went into her office, threw her coat across a chair, and immediately dialed Sheryl's extension.

"Yeah," a curt voice answered.

"Hi, Sheryl, it's Carrie Nelson."

"What day is this?" Sheryl demanded.

"It's February fourth," Carrie replied pleasantly.

"And what day was the January expense account and billing information due?"

"Ah . . . I don't remember exactly. Yesterday?" Carrie answered hopefully.

"It was due a week ago," Sheryl growled. "What happens to people who don't get their expense and billing info to me on time?"

Carrie was a veteran of this drill. "No partnership draw for the month," she replied.

"Correct," Sheryl growled. "No money in your pocket, which means no kitty food for little Fatso. Now what are you going to do before you leave the office today?"

"I'm going to finish up my expense accounts and billings for January," Carrie answered contritely.

"Good girl! You get a gold star. Don't forget—I'll be waiting."

Carrie disconnected that call with a slight shudder, then dialed Will Rollston's number. His secretary, Karen Hundley, picked up. "Karen, it's Carrie Nelson. Is Will in?"

"He's on the phone," Karen replied pleasantly.

"Would you ask him to come down to my office in about fifteen minutes so we can discuss the *Buckley* case?"

"Sure thing," Karen said.

Next, Carrie placed a call to Jackie Crabb, one of the firm's paralegals. After identifying herself, she said, "I need some quick work done on a case I'm going to be filing in about ten days. Have you got any time for me?"

"Is this the case with the comatose woman who got raped?" Jackie asked.

Carrie replied that it was.

"Count me in," Jackie said. "I'd love to work on it."

Carrie asked the paralegal to join her and Will for their meeting.

While she waited for Will and Jackie to arrive, Carrie phoned the Buckleys to let them know that the firm had approved her taking their case. She also filled them in on her visits to the hospital and the police.

"Your description of Werner Von Slaten was certainly accurate," Carrie said ruefully to Ed Buckley after she'd described the futile meeting with the hospital's administrator. "What a despicable human being! I am going to relish suing his hospital."

"When do you plan to file the lawsuit?" Ed asked.

"Hopefully within a couple of weeks," Carrie replied. "I

want to move on it as quickly as possible, but it's going to take some time to do the legal research to pin down our causes of action."

Melody Buckley had taken the phone from her husband. "Do you think the police will be of any assistance?" she asked anxiously.

"We'll have to wait and see," Carrie replied. "But I hope so."

Ed came back on the line. "We appreciate all you're doing, Carrie."

"I know you do," Carrie responded. "I want you two to hang in there. I'll keep in touch."

A short time later Carrie, Will Rollston, and Jackie Crabb were seated around the small round table near the window in Carrie's office. Carrie gave the other two a quick rundown on her visit to the hospital and her talk with Detective Clauff.

"That Von Slaten must have ice water running through his veins," Carrie said, bristling with anger again as she recalled her meeting with the man. "He made it very clear he's going to fight us every step of the way, so I think we need to really come out swinging." She looked at a calendar. "Today's the fourth. If it's at all possible, I'd like to be ready to file our lawsuit on Monday the sixteenth."

"That's not allowing yourself much time," Will commented dryly.

"I realize that," Carrie replied, "but time is of the essence and we're going to get zero cooperation from Von Slaten until the hospital has actually been named a defendant." Seeing Will's skeptical look, she said, "I know it's a stretch, but let's shoot for the sixteenth. If we're truly not ready to file then, we can always postpone it a few days."

Turning to Jackie, Carrie said, "I'd like you to dig up as much information as you can about Jackson Memorial. Who owns the controlling financial interest in the place. Who's on the board of directors. I know it's privately owned, but can we get access to any financial statements? Has the hospital ever been sued before? Pull up all the news clippings you can find for the past ten years."

Jackie, a cheerful dark-haired woman in her mid-thirties, scribbled furiously on a yellow legal pad as Carrie talked.

Addressing Will, Carrie said, "Being accosted by that old mental patient made me realize that the other patients could be a valuable source of information for us. I don't necessarily think a patient attacked Katherine, although I guess that's possible. But if there are patients who can wander around without supervision, maybe one of them saw something."

Will frowned. "Do you actually think a mental patient could be a useful witness?"

Carrie shrugged her shoulders. "There are many degrees of mental illness. Surely not everyone in the place is a raving lunatic. Some of them are probably fairly lucid. Anyway, how will we know unless we talk to them?"

"And how do you propose we talk to them?" Will inquired. "I assume most of them have been committed involuntarily and are not capable of giving consent to speak to us. That would mean we'd have to get permission from their guardians."

"You're probably right," Carrie agreed. "I'll admit I haven't exactly thought through the logistics of this."

Will pondered the problem a moment, running his hand over his chin. "I think we're caught in sort of a catch-22 here. We need permission from the guardians in order to talk to the patients, but we can't very well get the guardians' permission unless we know the names of the patients, which Von Slaten is not about to give us."

"What if we ask the court to order Von Slaten to turn over a list of names of all patients who have been at the hospital during the time Katherine was there?" Carrie suggested, thinking out loud. "We could file a motion and brief in support at the same time we file our complaint."

"The hospital's going to claim doctor-patient privilege or patient confidentiality," Will countered. "How are we going to get around that?"

"Necessity," Carrie shot back.

Will raised one eyebrow.

"The best-evidence rule?" Carrie tried again. "Oh, hell,

I'm sure you'll think of something," Carrie said, waving her hand dismissively.

"*I'll* think of something?" Will repeated drolly. "I take it that means you'd like *me* to prepare the motion and brief on the patient list."

Carrie smiled, thinking how attractive Will was. "Is that a problem?"

Will shook his head. "No, I guess not. I've always enjoyed creative writing."

Turning back to Jackie, Carrie said, "While you're digging up dirt on the hospital, see if you can find out what law firm they've used in the past. I always like to know who my adversary might be."

Jackie added the task to her To Do list.

"Can either of you think of anything else?" Carrie asked. "I'm getting really psyched about this. Von Slaten was such a jerk that I'd love to rub his nose in it."

"What about the idea that was mentioned at the partners' meeting this morning about asking the court to put the case on a fast track?" Will suggested. "We have to assume that the longer the pregnancy continues, the more dangerous it's going to be to Katherine's own health. Since she's already twelve weeks along, I was thinking we should ask the court for an expedited schedule that would give us a trial date within six months."

Carrie considered the idea. "That's awfully fast, considering that we're starting out cold. I like the fast-track idea, but we don't want to box ourselves into a corner. After all, we're the ones who are going to have the burden of proving that the hospital was negligent. Can we really put the case together in that short a time?"

"I think we can," Will replied confidently. "I'll draft a motion on that as well." Seeing Carrie's worried look, he said, "Who knows if the court will even consider it? But if it will, I think it'll work out to our advantage."

"Okay," Carrie said, nodding. "Let's go for it. Anything else?"

"I did think of one other thing," Will said.

"Shoot," Carrie replied.

Will pulled a piece of paper out from the back of his legal pad. "I did a tiny bit of research after the meeting this morning and I pulled this off of the *Tribune*'s Web site." He handed Carrie the paper.

Carrie briefly scanned the document, which was a copy of an article announcing that Jackson Memorial had been named to the *Best Hospitals in America* list. She looked at Will expectantly. "So what's your suggestion?"

"Jackson Memorial is a private hospital, so I'm assuming it relies heavily on word of mouth and referrals to get new patients. I was just thinking that it would probably put a lot of pressure on them if the press were to get wind of the fact that a comatose patient at that facility had been raped."

Carrie pondered the idea for a moment, then grinned. "That's very devious. I love it! Who should we leak the story to?"

"Why not the same reporter who wrote this laudatory piece?" Will suggested. "Katherine's story is a reporter's dream. Whoever Gail Wolfe is, I'll bet she'd love to sink her teeth into it. This could be Pulitzer material."

Carrie nodded. "That's a great idea. Let me run it by the Buckleys first. I have to make sure they have no objection to going public, but I'm sure that once I explain our objective they'll agree. Any other suggestions?"

Both Will and Jackie shook their heads.

"Then let's man the battle stations. We'll touch base the day after tomorrow to see how things are going."

Jackie immediately got up and went back to her office. Carrie and Will lingered for a few moments, tossing around various other ideas about the case. As the two of them were standing in the door of the office, Tammy got up from her desk and approached them. "You've never responded to any of my E-mails about adopting a pet," she scolded Will.

Will looked a bit taken aback. "I guess I didn't think the timing was right for me to get a pet," he replied somewhat sheepishly.

"The timing is always right for a pet," Tammy countered. "Where do you live?"

"In Skokie."

"In a house or an apartment?" Tammy went on.

Will looked at Carrie for reassurance, but she merely smiled. "Ah . . . I have a house," Will replied.

"With a yard?" Tammy asked, continuing the interrogation.

"Yeah."

"Fenced?"

"Yes."

"Do you like to walk or run for exercise?"

"Well," Will answered hesitantly, "I do try to run three or four mornings a week."

"Perfect!" Tammy exclaimed. "You're a dog person, and it just so happens I have a wonderful dog for you."

"I don't know if I want a dog," Will protested.

"Wait till you see him. Hold on just a minute. I have a picture." She scurried back to her desk.

"What's with her?" Will asked Carrie. "Is she running a one-woman ASPCA or something?"

Carrie laughed. "No, she and her husband are just batty over animals. They work with a local veterinarian who runs a no-kill shelter. Doug—her husband—is even more vigilant than she is. He's a road-test examiner, and a couple years ago he got reprimanded because he made a guy stop on the Dan Ryan in the middle of a road test so he could rescue an injured dog."

"And he only got a reprimand?" Will asked incredulously.

"As it turned out, the head of the Illinois Department of Transportation heard about the story and ended up adopting the dog, so Doug's supervisors couldn't very well come down very hard on him."

"Unbelievable," Will said, shaking his head.

Tammy returned, clutching a photo in her hand. "Here he is," she said, holding it out to Will. "He's a ten-month-old Weimaraner, and his name is Floyd."

Will took the photo and frowned. "He looks pretty big. How much does he weigh?"

"I'm not exactly sure," Tammy hedged, "but I don't think he weighs much more than a hundred pounds."

"He's ten months old and he weighs a hundred pounds!" Will exclaimed. "That's not a dog—that's a baby elephant."

"I'm sure he's done growing," Tammy hurried on. "Look, I'll make you an offer you can't refuse. You can take him on a trial basis. Doug and I will drop him off at your house on Friday night. We'll also bring enough dog food for the weekend. If it really doesn't work out, we'll pick him up again on Monday, no strings attached. How's that?" She looked at Will expectantly.

Will turned to Carrie.

"Don't look at me!" Carrie laughed. "Tammy knows she's got a live one, and she's not about to take no for an answer."

"Oh, all right," Will said. "I'll try him out for the weekend. But I'm not making any promises about keeping him permanently."

"Great!" Tammy exclaimed. "You can give me directions to your house and we'll set up a time to drop him off." She went back to her desk.

Seeing Carrie's smirk, Will said, "Well, I felt sorry for her, so I thought I'd give it a try. After all, she says they'll take him back, so what have I got to lose?"

"With a hundred-pound puppy, probably most of your earthly possessions," Carrie murmured under her breath.

"What was that?" Will asked, frowning.

"Nothing," Carrie said quickly. "I'd better go try to call the Buckleys to ask if they mind our leaking their story to the press." She turned away quickly so Will wouldn't see her face contort with laughter. The Tammy Hennick Pet Patrol had just scored another victim.

Chapter 7

After working nearly nonstop for three days to prepare a draft of the complaint in the *Buckley* case, Carrie allowed herself the luxury of sleeping late on Sunday morning. After showering, she threw on a pair of jeans and a sweater, then had a bagel and coffee while leisurely perusing the Sunday *Tribune*. Around noon she drove down to the office to put in a few hours on the next day's meeting in her housing discrimination case. She tried hard to make working on weekends the exception rather than the rule, but sometimes it was unavoidable. Work piled up, deadlines loomed, and there simply wasn't enough time to get it all done during the week.

In the middle of the afternoon she ran into Will Rollston in the firm's law library. Like Carrie, he was dressed casually, sporting a pair of jeans and a Chicago Bulls sweatshirt.

"What are you doing here on a Sunday?" Carrie asked pleasantly as she looked up from her seat at a small corner carrel of the library.

"I have a hearing on a summary judgment motion in a wrongful dealership termination case tomorrow morning, and I thought I'd better make sure none of the cases I cited in my brief have been overruled," Will explained, leaning casually against a bookcase. "Judge Watkins is a real stickler on that. I've heard that he personally checks every single case cited in every brief to make sure nothing has been overruled. How about you?"

Carrie gave him a brief rundown of her case.

"I remember Burt mentioning that at the partners' meeting the other day," Will recalled. "I can't imagine the landlord would have a ghost of a chance of evicting tenants based on what their children did off the premises. It sounds like a no-brainer to me."

"That's the problem," Carrie groused. "This particular landlord is well known for having no brain. I'm hoping the Fair Housing mediator will be able to talk some sense into him. Unfortunately," she said, motioning at a stack of soft-cover books in front of her, "I've discovered that a couple of courts in eastern states have allowed tenants to be evicted on similar grounds. Those cases are currently on appeal, but for the moment they do provide a precedent for what my guy is doing, so if we can't reach an agreement tomorrow, I'm afraid we're headed for court."

"It still sounds like you'll win in the end," Will said confidently. "Public policy is definitely on your side. Oh, by the way, I finally connected up with that *Tribune* reporter yesterday. I'd been wondering why she hadn't returned my call, but she'd been out of town on assignment for a few days. I told her about Katherine and the goings-on at Jackson Memorial, and she sounded very interested. She said she'd do some checking and get back to me in a day or two."

"Great," Carrie said, smiling. "I think some carefully placed news blurbs coinciding with our filing of the lawsuit will be just the ticket to throw a chill into my buddy Von Slaten and the powers that be at the hospital."

"I haven't gotten very far on the motions yet," Will said apologetically. "It turned out that I had some fires to put out in a few other cases the last couple of days, but I promise I'll get to them tomorrow right after my hearing."

"Don't worry about it," Carrie said. "I'm not making much headway on the complaint, either. We'll still shoot for the sixteenth as our target date for filing, but if we have to postpone for a few days, so be it. I don't want to sacrifice quality for speed. Even though Katherine's condition does put us in a time crunch, a few days more or less won't matter much."

"Speaking of time crunches," Will glanced at his watch.

"I'd better wrap it up here and get home to let the dog out."

"That's right, you've had a weekend guest," Carrie said. "I forgot all about it. How's it going?"

Will laughed. "So far, Floyd has chewed up two pairs of shoes, two books, and the leg on a kitchen chair."

"Oh, no!" Carrie gasped.

"At least he's completely house-trained, thank God," Will went on. "But he doesn't seem to grasp the concept of walking. He's a terrific runner, but both yesterday and today I found myself being pulled down the sidewalk at top speed when I tried to take him out for a morning constitutional. The beast has absolutely boundless energy. Both times I came back totally wiped out, while he was still raring to go. When Tammy and her husband dropped him off, they said his former owners hadn't realized how big he would get or how much attention he would require. I definitely see what they meant."

Carrie smiled sympathetically. "Well, you were a Good Samaritan, trying to help Tammy out. I'm sure she won't have any hard feelings about your giving him back."

"What do you mean, giving him back?" Will retorted, clearly aghast at the thought. "Floyd is a wonderful dog. He's just going to need a little fine-tuning." He gave his watch another glance. "Well, better run. See you tomorrow."

"A little fine-tuning and probably complete replacement of your household's contents," Carrie murmured, chuckling to herself as Will departed.

Although Carrie went into Monday's housing discrimination meeting without any great expectations, the episode quickly devolved from being merely a waste of time into a virtual free-for-all.

The meeting was held in the office of a federal Fair Housing Board facilitator named Christy Thomas.

The landlord who was trying to evict Carrie's clients was a tall, thin, and balding man in his early fifties named Joe Scalerri. Scalerri owned half a dozen large apartment buildings in which the majority of tenants received some type of federal housing subsidy to help them pay their rent. He was well known in Chicago rental circles as a slumlord who did the bare minimum in upkeep on his buildings and who treated his tenants with disdain, if not outright contempt.

Carrie's clients were one Hispanic family and two black families, each of whom had a teenage boy who had recently been arrested for a felony. The matriarch of each family was present at the meeting. The three women were strong-willed and all too eager to tell their side of the story. Although Carrie had cautioned them in advance not to speak unless spoken to, it soon became apparent that her advice had fallen on deaf ears. Scalerri's brash smugness and the proud indignation of Carrie's clients mixed like oil and water.

Christy Thomas, a tall woman in her thirties with brown hair, started off by asking Scalerri to briefly explain his position.

Before answering, Scalerri took a handkerchief out of his pocket and loudly blew his nose, as if to show how little he thought of Carrie's clients and the entire legal system. When he had finished, he made a show of setting the soiled hanky on the table in front of him.

"Each of these three families got a son who committed serious crimes," Scalerri said in a gruff voice laced with a heavy southside accent. "Juan Garcia got busted for armed robbery. Jamal Washington got it for rape. Sammy Johnson for drugs. Behavior like that can't be tolerated in my buildings. I got a duty to my other tenants to provide them a safe place to live. The leases that each of these people signed gives me the right to terminate based on criminal activity." He threw up his hands. "I rest my case."

Carrie, who was seated across the table from Scalerri, could sense Eureka Washington, who was on her right, bristling at Scalerri's remarks. Carrie unobtrusively put a hand on the woman's arm in a signal to remain calm.

Christy Thomas turned to Carrie. "Ms. Nelson, would you like to respond to Mr. Scalerri's statement?"

"Yes, I would," Carrie replied. "My clients do not deny that their children were involved in criminal wrongdoing, and in no way are they trying to downplay the seriousness of those offenses. But there is a proper time and place for that conduct to be redressed, and that is through the court system. Mr. Scalerri seems to imply that kicking the families of those three boys out of their apartments will somehow help punish the boys or serve as a deterrent to keep other children from committing similar acts. I assure you it will not. The only thing that evicting my clients will accomplish is to put twelve completely blameless people out on the street."

"They shoulda thought of that before they got into trouble," Scalerri groused. "Troublemakers ain't welcome in my buildings."

"I can understand that," Carrie said smoothly, "but the boys are no longer living in your building. They have been in the custody of juvenile authorities since their arrests, and it is extremely unlikely that they will be released until they turn eighteen." Carrie leaned forward a bit, toward Christy Thomas. "We have offered to stipulate that none of the three boys will ever return to Mr. Scalerri's building, but that is not enough for him. Instead, he has apparently appointed himself judge and jury not just over the three boys but over their families as well."

"A bad apple never falls far from the tree," Scalerri said in an effort to wax philosophical.

Carrie scowled at him.

Christy Thomas shuffled through her file. "When are the leases up?" she asked.

"The Washingtons' in five months, the Garcias' and Johnsons' in seven," Carrie replied.

Thomas nodded and jotted some notes. Addressing Scalerri, she asked, "Is there any way we can reach an accommodation here?"

Scalerri shook his head. "I wish I could help these people out. I really do," he said, feigning sympathy. "But the truth of the matter is, some of my other tenants have threatened to break their leases if I don't get them outa the building. I just can't afford to lose good renters in order to keep bad ones."

Carrie seized on this patently false statement. "What other tenants? What are their names?"

"I can't remember offhand," Scalerri replied lamely. "I didn't bring my notes with me."

"Where are your notes?" Carrie followed up.

"Back at the office," Scalerri answered.

"Well, then, when you get back to the office, would you please be so kind as to fax or mail me a list of the names of the tenants you've referred to?"

"What for?" Scalerri asked warily.

"So I can contact them," Carrie replied sweetly. "I'm sure if I explain the situation to these other families, they will understand my clients' position and will withdraw any objections they have to my clients' remaining in the building."

"That sounds like a reasonable request," Christy Thomas said. "Mr. Scalerri, can you furnish Ms. Nelson with such a list in the next couple of days?"

"Ah . . ." Scalerri was clearly trying to think of a way out of the hole he'd dug for himself. "I can't."

"You can't because there is no such list!" Carrie exclaimed triumphantly.

"No, I can't give it to you because it would be an invasion of those other tenants' privacy," Scalerri retorted. "See, they told me they were afraid of retaliation if their names ever got out." He sat back in his chair and smiled, clearly pleased with his cleverness.

"Retaliation by whom?" Carrie asked. She was quickly losing her patience with this stupid, arrogant man. She wished he had brought his attorney with him. Perhaps she could have reasoned with another lawyer. But Scalerri was a notorious cheapskate who tried to handle the bulk of his legal work himself. He obviously didn't appreciate the old maxim that a person who represents himself has a fool for a client.

"Why in the world would anyone fear retaliation?" Carrie persisted. "Have you forgotten that the three boys involved in the criminal conduct are all securely locked in juvenile detention?"

"Yeah, but there's other kids in each of those families," Scalerri replied. "One of them might be violent."

"ENOUGH!" Eureka Washington shocked everyone present by booming out her comment. Turning to Christy Thomas, she said in a calm but firm voice, "I have heard all I can stomach out of that man. I took off work today to come here. So did Miz Garcia and Miz Johnson. We came to show our good faith and all we get is ridicule." Her dark eyes flashed in anger. "Who do you think is gonna do other tenants harm now that our boys is in lockup?" she demanded, looking Scalerri square in the eye. "My seven-year-old Billy? Or maybe Miz Garcia's nine-year-old Sasha?"

"I didn't come here to listen to you mouth off," Scalerri said coldly.

"No, you came here to belittle all of us, to keep us in what you think is our place," Eureka shot back. "Just like you've done since we all moved into your lousy bug-infested building."

"If you all don't like my building, why don't you move out?" Scalerri taunted.

"And make things easy for you? I don't think so," Eureka retorted. "We know our rights and, Mister, you are violatin' 'em all to bits and we ain't gonna stand for it. So you just try to put us out, 'cos we ain't goin' without a fight." She nodded her head firmly to punctuate her declaration.

Carrie gave her client a small wink. She couldn't have said it better herself.

Christy Thomas shifted in her chair. "It appears we are at an impasse," she said regretfully. "Does anyone have anything else to add before we adjourn?"

"No, I'm all through talkin' to these hens," Scalerri said, pushing his chair back from the table and getting to his feet. "I'll be gettin' out the eviction papers shortly," he said to Carrie. Then, directing one last sneer at her clients, he added, "I'll see you all in court."

As the landlord began to head toward the door, Carrie called after him in a loud voice. "You're right about that,

Mr. Scalerri. You will see us in court. But it will be in our court, on our terms."

Scalerri turned back and glared at Carrie. She had clearly piqued his interest.

"You see," Carrie went on, "before you can get your eviction actions heard, I intend to sue you in federal court for a whole slew of civil rights violations. I hope you have some money set aside for legal fees, because what I have in mind is going to keep a couple of lawyers rolling in big bucks for many months to come. How do you like them apples, Mr. Scalerri?"

Scalerri made an obscene gesture, then beat a hasty retreat.

Before he was even out of earshot, Carrie's clients burst into a hearty round of applause. Eureka Washington put an arm around Carrie's shoulders. "You know, the first time I met you I was thinkin' to myself what is a skinny white woman dressed in fancy clothes ever gonna be able to do for the likes of us? But the more I see of you, the more I realize you're just another sister, only in different trappings. You go, girl!" she said enthusiastically as she leaned over and enveloped Carrie in a big hug.

"Thank you," Carrie said, grinning. "I'll do my best to earn your confidence."

Eureka loosened her grip. "Best way to earn our confidence is to whip that man's miserable bony ass. And from the sounds of that little speech you just made, I do believe you're just the person to do it."

Chapter 8

"We're pathetic," Carrie grumbled to Ann Muchin. "Speak for yourself," Ann retorted.

Ann was Carrie's best friend at Ramquist and Dowd. Although Ann worked like a fiend, occasionally she would take a day off and join Carrie on a shopping spree. While Carrie was blond and fair-skinned, Ann had dark-brown hair and flawless skin the texture of porcelain. Both women were above-average height, but as they moved into their thirties they found that each year it took a bit more diligence to keep their weight down.

They especially enjoyed trawling for unique items in Carrie's Lincoln Park neighborhood. On this sunny Saturday afternoon in February, they were walking briskly down Armitage, half a dozen blocks from Carrie's town house. It was a blustery day and they both pulled their wool scarves tighter as they made their way from one shop to the next.

"Well, how would you describe two women who are alone on Valentine's Day, if not pathetic?" Carrie demanded.

"We're not alone," Ann contradicted sweetly. "We're with each other."

Carrie reached over and slapped her friend soundly on the arm. "You know perfectly well what I mean. It's Valentine's Day and we are sans men. For the second year in a row, I might add."

"Big deal," Ann said. "Think of how many of our friends are divorced and how many women are struggling to get out of abusive relationships. Don't you think we're better off the way we are?"

Carrie clutched her black leather bag closer to her and

picked up the pace a bit as the cold penetrated her wool jacket. "Of course we're better off than most of the people on the planet," she said, raising her voice. "So what? Since when is there a law against wanting more?"

"This is just a phase," Ann said confidently. "You'll get over it." She hunched her shoulders against the cold. "I'm freezing. Let's cross the street and go to Geri's. You can buy something to cheer yourself up."

Geri's was an upscale consignment store that handled a unique mix of top designer fashions and collectible jewelry. Many of Carrie's favorite outfits had been snagged there. While Carrie and Ann could easily afford to pay retail, bargain hunting was in their blood. It was the thrill of the hunt that attracted them—a person never knew what wonderful treasures might be right around the corner.

"Hi, Geri," Ann greeted the proprietor warmly as she and Carrie walked in.

"Where have you ladies been keeping yourselves?" Geri replied jovially. The store's owner was a gregarious dark-haired woman in her late forties. "You haven't been in for a while. I suppose you've both been working like dogs again."

Ann walked up to the counter. "What have you got that's new and exciting? We could both use a little treat."

"You're in luck," Geri replied. She reached into the display case in front of her and pulled out several items. "Look. I've got two pair of Chanel sunglasses, never worn. A Fendi bag, used twice. And I just finished marking four fabulous Jil Sander suits that I'm sure would fit one of you like a glove."

Ann picked up one of the pairs of sunglasses and examined them. "These are nice. How come somebody's getting rid of them?"

Geri leaned forward and said confidentially, "Both of these girls just broke up with their boyfriends. The shades were Christmas gifts, and it's now too late to get a store refund, so they brought them here. I get lots of divine items under similar circumstances every year around this time."

Ann tried the glasses on and looked at her reflection in

the mirror. "Not bad. What do you think?" she asked, turning to Carrie.

"I think it's terribly callous to capitalize on someone else's misery," Carrie sniffed. She picked up the other pair of glasses and slipped them on.

"What's with her?" Geri asked Ann quizzically.

Ann shrugged. "She's a little PO'd that it's Valentine's Day and we don't have dates. Ignore her. It's just a phase. I like these glasses. I'll take them," she said, setting them back on the counter.

Carrie looked at herself in the mirror. The glasses were both stylish and classic. It was simply impossible to feel unattractive or depressed in Chanel. As if by magic, she felt her mood lift. "I'll take mine, too," she said, taking the glasses off again. "Now, where are those Jil Sander suits you mentioned?"

Forty minutes later, the two women continued down the street, each hefting a large bag containing their Geri's purchases. "Do you feel better now?" Ann asked.

Carrie nodded. "Yes, I do. I'm sorry I was so crabby earlier. I just have to blow off a little steam once in a while. I need to stop at the bookstore before heading back to my place. Jean called yesterday and said the books I ordered for my dad's birthday are in."

"Fine with me," Ann said.

Books and Company was one of Carrie's favorite neighborhood shops. Carrying a mixture of new and used volumes and featuring a small coffee bar in the back, it was run by an energetic retired businesswoman who had been a lifelong book lover and decided to make her avocation into a job that she could enjoy well into her golden years.

"Good afternoon, ladies," the owner said cheerfully when she spied Carrie and Ann.

"Hi, Jean," Carrie replied. "I'm here to pick up my books."

"Coming right up," Jean said. "While I run to the back room to get them, help yourselves to some coffee or hot chocolate."

"Do you suppose hot chocolate will spoil our appetites?" Carrie asked Ann.

"No chance," Ann replied as she headed toward the coffee bar. "This power shopping is hard work. I'm sure we burned off loads of calories today."

"In that case," Carrie said, "wait for me."

Several hours later Carrie and Ann were relaxing in Carrie's living room after enjoying a hearty steak-and-potato dinner. Carrie's flat occupied the first and second floors of a late-1800s townhouse in Lincoln Park. The first floor consisted of a large living room, kitchen, bath, and study. The upper floor contained two bedrooms and a second bath. Carrie enjoyed decorating and had furnished her residence with a combination of antiques and unique items of indeterminate age that she had carefully hand-selected.

"It feels really good to kick back like this once in a while," Ann said contentedly as she leaned back in a chair and sipped a glass of Merlot. With her left hand, she stroked Carrie's cat, Muffin, who was curled in her lap. "I should treat myself to days off more often."

"I've been telling you that for as long as I've known you," Carrie replied from her seat on the burgundy-and-green-striped couch. "But you never seem to listen. You work harder than anyone I know."

Ann shrugged. "I'll admit it. I've always been rather driven. It's just the way I'm built."

"So where are you off to next week?" Carrie asked.

"L.A. for three days of depositions in a wrongful-death case Terry Payne and I are handling," Ann replied. "Say," she said. "If you're looking for some male companionship, why not give Terry a call? He's a really nice guy."

"He *is* a nice guy," Carrie agreed. "But he's going through a nasty divorce, so somehow I don't think he's going to be interested in getting involved with someone else right now."

"Well, it was just a thought." Ann took another sip of wine. "What about Will Rollston?" she asked conversationally. "Since you're going to be working on the *Buckley* case with him, it will give you the chance to get to know him better."

Carrie smiled and took a sip of her own wine. "I must say I have given that possibility slightly more than passing consideration, especially in the last week. Do you know anything about him?"

Ann shrugged. "A little."

"Really?" Carrie asked with surprise.

"Yeah, I've talked to him several times when he and I have both been working late at the office."

"You never told me that," Carrie scolded.

Ann shrugged. "I never knew you were interested. What do you want to know?"

Carrie leaned forward eagerly. "Whatever you've got. I understand he lives in Skokie. Seems like sort of an odd place for a single guy who works downtown."

Ann nodded. "He inherited a house from an uncle a couple years back and he thought it might be nice to get out of the heart of the city. He says he plans to live there until he's ready to buy something fancier."

"What else?" Carrie asked, taking another sip of wine. "Do you know anything about the dearly departed girlfriend?"

Ann shook her head. "Very little. One night Will did make sort of a cryptic remark about it being the birthday of someone he used to go with and how she never liked any of the gifts he bought her anyway and always exchanged them immediately, so it was probably just as well they'd broken up."

"Interesting," Carrie said. She looked at her wineglass. It was empty. She picked the bottle up off the marble-topped coffee table and poured herself a refill. "Do you know any other tidbits?"

Ann shook her head. "Nope. I'm afraid that's it. In between working up the case, you'll have to give him the third degree and fill in the blanks yourself."

"Maybe I'll do that," Carrie said, nodding emphatically.

"Good," Ann said, leaning forward over the cat to help

herself to more wine. "So you're all set to file the complaint on Monday?"

Carrie nodded. "As ready as we'll ever be, considering we have only the bare bones of information to go on so far."

"What's happening with the police investigation?"

"It's too early to tell," Carrie replied. "I talked to the detective on Thursday. He said the investigation was proceeding and he'd let me know when he had anything definite."

"Maybe that newspaper article will shake some information loose," Ann said. In Thursday's *Tribune,* Gail Wolfe, the reporter Will had contacted, had posted a small third-page story about Katherine's assault. Jackson Memorial had declined comment.

"Nothing yet," Carrie replied. "But I expect all kinds of things to break loose once the case is actually filed."

"I think you can count on that," Ann replied sagely. "What's going on with your housing discrimination case?"

"I'm scrambling to finish up the complaint so I can file that in federal court in the next few days as well," Carrie replied. "I'm going to have to work most of the day tomorrow to put it in final form."

"Sounds like you're going to have a busy week," Ann predicted.

"I know," Carrie said, making a face. "I guess I spread myself a little thin when I thought I could get both the *Buckley* case and the tenants' suit worked up at the same time."

"It's only going to get worse once the cases are actually filed and you get into tight discovery deadlines." Ann lifted her glass. "I propose a toast: to tremendous success in both of your new cases. And a word of advice to go with it. Try to get all the rest you can now. Because something tells me this is probably the calm before the storm."

Carrie raised her glass. "What about success in the boyfriend area?" she asked mischievously.

Ann laughed. "Absolutely. May Will Rollston and/or

some other fabulous creature find you utterly ir-
resistible.''

Carrie leaned over and clinked glasses with her friend.
"I'll definitely drink to that.''

Chapter 9

On Monday, Carrie discovered the prescience of Ann's comment about the calm before the storm.

A Ramquist and Dowd messenger filed the summons, complaint, and accompanying motions in *Buckley v. Jackson Memorial Hospital* shortly before lunch. Will had alerted the *Tribune* reporter, as well as various other media representatives, that the case would be filed that day. The filing obviously piqued the media's interest, and Carrie spent most of the afternoon giving telephone interviews about the case.

"You drew Judge Rita Little," one journalist noted. "Would you care to comment on how you feel Judge Little will handle this case?"

"I have enormous respect for Judge Little," Carrie replied. "I have tried a number of major cases in her court and have always found her to be hardworking, judicious, and very well versed on the law. I think she and this case will be an excellent match."

"I notice you have filed motions to expedite the case and to require the hospital to turn over a list of its patients," another reporter commented. "Both of those requests are rather unusual. How would you assess your chances of prevailing on either of them?"

"Both requests are out of the ordinary," Carrie agreed. "But this is a unique case. As discussed at length in the briefs accompanying the motions, we believe there are compelling reasons to grant us both forms of relief."

"On what basis?" the reporter asked.

"Because of the serious nature of Ms. Buckley's medical condition," Carrie replied.

"Aren't there confidentiality problems in trying to compel the hospital to release the names of its patients?"

"It is certainly not our intent to undermine patient confidentiality in any way. As we explain in our brief, we will not attempt to interview any patient without consent from that person's guardian."

"But what basis do you have for believing you are entitled to discover the patients' names in the first place?"

"Again, Ms. Buckley's medical condition supports the request," Carrie said patiently. "She has been the victim of a grievous assault. Unfortunately, she is unable to tell us who assaulted her. As a result, it becomes imperative that we be able to speak to anyone at Jackson Memorial who might have witnessed the assault. That includes other patients at the facility."

"Do you have any idea who the perpetrator might have been?" the reporter asked.

"Not at present," Carrie admitted. "But obviously that is something we hope to learn through the discovery process."

No sooner would one reporter thank Carrie for her time and sign off than another call would be waiting. By midafternoon she was beginning to get hoarse from all the talking she had been doing. She made a quick trip to the firm's kitchen to get a bottle of mineral water and as she passed her secretary's desk on her return, Tammy called out, "That detective is on the line. He says it's important."

Carrie hurried into her office and picked up the phone. "Carrie Nelson."

"Ms. Nelson, this is Detective David Clauff."

In stark contrast to the fairly friendly tone the detective had adopted when Carrie had met him at the police station, he now sounded rather brusque. Carrie hoped this didn't mean his investigation had reached a dead end. "Hello, Detective," she replied cordially. "How are you?"

"Fine," Clauff answered curtly. "I was wondering if you

might have time to come up here this afternoon for a brief meeting."

Carrie frowned. What could this mean? "I'm afraid you've caught me at a rather bad time," she answered. "You see, we filed the Buckleys' civil suit against the hospital today, and I've been pretty busy taking calls about that. Is there any way we could handle this by phone?"

"Well—" Clauff hesitated. "I really would prefer to talk to you in person. You see, I've been investigating the assault on Ms. Buckley, and while I can't say I have enough evidence yet to make an arrest, I have identified a prime suspect. That's what I wanted to talk to you about."

Carrie could feel her pulse quicken. A suspect! What great news! "I'm very glad to hear you have a suspect," she said. "But is there really a need for us to discuss this in person? Can't you just tell me now what you've found out?"

Carrie could hear Clauff exhale loudly. "All right," the detective replied. "Suit yourself. After speaking to Mr. and Mrs. Buckley and numerous people on staff at Jackson Memorial, in my opinion the most likely person to have assaulted Katherine is—"

Carrie drew in her breath and waited eagerly.

"—her boyfriend, Todd Fleming."

Carrie dropped the phone receiver. Visions of the case she had just filed on Katherine's behalf swirling down the drain danced through her head. "I'm sorry," she said as she retrieved the phone. "What did you say?" The words would scarcely come out. She felt as though she were choking.

"It seems more likely than not that Todd Fleming assaulted Katherine," the detective replied in clipped tones. "Now perhaps you will understand why I thought it best for us to talk in person."

"Say no more," Carrie replied. "I'm on my way."

Half an hour later, Carrie was seated across from Detective Clauff in the same small, dingy room where they had

had their initial conversation. During the drive, Carrie's mood had turned from shock to anger.

While Carrie had never met Todd Fleming, she knew from conversations with the Buckleys that the young man was a third-year law student at the University of Chicago, that he was from a good family, that he and Katherine had been dating for about three years, and that they were planning to announce their engagement around the time he graduated from law school. In Carrie's opinion, the attempt to pin Katherine's assault on Todd was nothing more than an underhanded ploy on the part of the hospital to avoid taking responsibility for its own actions.

"I simply can't accept your conclusion that Katherine's boyfriend assaulted her," Carrie informed Clauff firmly.

The detective shrugged. "Accept it or not, that's where the evidence is pointing."

"What evidence?" Carrie demanded.

"The visitors' logs reveal, and the hospital staff confirms, that Todd was a frequent visitor to Ms. Buckley. In fact, he came to see her a minimum of four times a week from the time she arrived until she transferred out."

"So?" Carrie interrupted. "That doesn't prove anything."

"Please let me finish," Clauff requested.

Carrie grudgingly sat back in her chair and waited for the remainder of the detective's remarks.

"On many of those visits Mr. Fleming would be alone in Katherine's room for fairly substantial periods of time," he went on. "Apparently a nurse or nurse's aide would check in on Katherine roughly once an hour, unless she was experiencing some unusual health problem, such as her bouts with pneumonia, in which case she would receive more regular monitoring. But in the normal course of events, the nurses' checks would be fairly evenly spaced. This means that a person familiar with the routine, as Mr. Fleming clearly was, would know how much time remained until the next check and would be in a position to carry out the assault in the interim."

"The same can be said for anyone on the hospital staff," Carrie pointed out.

"That's true," Clauff agreed. "But my interviews with the staff turned up nothing unusual, whereas my interviews with Mr. Fleming and his family and friends indicated that Mr. Fleming has been extremely upset since Katherine's accident, to the point of despondency. He has been on medication off and on to ease his depression."

"Depressed people normally lack motivation," Carrie put in. "The fact that Todd Fleming was despondent and on medication is all the more reason he would be unlikely to rape Katherine."

"Mr. Fleming seems to be a good person," Clauff admitted. "I have no reason to doubt that he still loves Katherine very much, and I don't believe he intended to hurt her in any way. But I am told that people suffering from severe depression, particularly those who are on medication, sometimes do bizarre, even macabre things, to make themselves feel better."

"So you're telling me you think Katherine's boyfriend had sex with her comatose body to make himself feel better?" Carrie said coldly. "Why, that is positively sick!"

"Having sex with a comatose woman is indeed sick," Clauff agreed. "But unfortunately Mr. Fleming seems to be the most likely perpetrator."

"Did anyone see Todd Fleming assault Katherine?"

"No," the detective admitted.

"Of course they didn't, because it didn't happen." She looked the detective straight in the eye. "Tell me, who was it who first developed Mr. Fleming as a suspect? You or Werner Von Slaten?"

Detective Clauff looked at Carrie evenly and said, "No one develops suspects for me. After conducting my own investigation, I concluded that Mr. Fleming was probably the one who did it."

"Does Mr. Fleming know you consider him a suspect?" Carrie asked.

"I haven't come right out and said it in so many words,"

the detective hedged, "but I would assume he has an ink-ling of what's going on, yes. After all, he is a law student."

"But you have spoken to Mr. Von Slaten about your suspicions as to Mr. Fleming?"

"I've spoken to him on the phone several times, yes."

Carrie clenched her jaw. She could envision the mileage the hospital's attorney would get from this scenario when mounting the defense to the Buckleys' lawsuit. "Do you plan on charging Mr. Fleming with the assault?" Carrie asked.

Detective Clauff paused a moment, then replied, "A final decision hasn't been made on that. My lieutenant has been informed of the situation, and I've had a couple of discussions with the prosecuting attorney. Frankly, I'm not sure what's going to happen. All I can say at this point is no charges are imminent."

"But you feel you have enough evidence to charge him?"

Another pause. "Probably, yes."

"Are you continuing to investigate the matter?" Carrie asked.

Clauff slowly shook his head. "I have no current plans to do so."

"Why not?" Carrie demanded.

"Because I think the responsible party has been iden-tified."

"Well, I don't agree," Carrie said, raising her voice for the first time. "What I think is that you were bamboozled by the hospital's very slick administrator and as a result, an innocent young man is being railroaded for a horrible crime while the real perpetrator is getting off scot-free. That's what I think."

"I'm sorry you see it that way," Clauff said. "But even though the evidence may be circumstantial at this point, I think Todd Fleming is our man."

"Well, let me tell you that I intend to conduct my own investigation, and I intend to find out what really happened."

Detective Clauff squirmed a bit uncomfortably in his

chair as Carrie elaborated. "As I believe I mentioned to you earlier on the phone, I filed the civil suit against the hospital today," she said, getting to her feet. "Now that the case has been filed, I will be entitled to conduct all manner of discovery to find out what happened to Katherine. And when I do, you will see that you have made a dreadful mistake. I just pray that my discovery of the truth won't come too late to spare Todd Fleming and the entire Buckley family a lot of additional anguish." She turned on her heel and marched briskly out the door.

Chapter 10

The hearing on the motions to expedite the *Buckley v. Jackson Memorial* case and require the hospital to turn over a list of its patients was held four days after the case was filed.

The intervening time had flown by in a blur. The case had instantly become a media darling and had generated countless inches of newsprint and minutes of air time. The hospital had brought out the big guns, retaining the internationally known law firm of Perillo, Linholm, and Untermeyer to defend it. Owen Wellborne, a senior partner at the firm, had immediately issued a statement saying that Jackson Memorial denied all charges that had been leveled against it and looked forward to the opportunity of proving that neither it nor its employees had done Katherine Buckley any harm.

Sure, Carrie thought with disgust upon reading the statement. The hospital intended to prove its innocence by dragging poor Todd Fleming through the mud. The Buckleys had understandably been very upset at learning that Katherine's boyfriend was being painted the villain.

"I thought from the tone of some of the detective's remarks that he had it in for Todd," Ed Buckley boomed over the phone when Carrie called to report the news. "If you ask me, the police are just too damn lazy to conduct a real investigation, and Todd is a convenient scapegoat."

"It's insane to think Todd did this," Melody Buckley said. "Why, he's been like one of the family for years. He would never do such a thing."

"I guess this just means you'll have to do the investigating and show that detective he's full of crap," Ed said.

The Buckleys were holding up fairly well, but Will Rollston had gone ballistic at the hospital's attempt to frame Todd.

"Todd Fleming is Katherine's boyfriend?" Will had exclaimed incredulously. "I know him."

"How?" Carrie asked with astonishment.

"About a year and a half ago I was one of three lawyers who team-taught a trial advocacy class at the University of Chicago Law School," Will explained. "Todd was one of the two or three top students in the class. He was bright. He was eager to learn. And he was a gentleman. I think I'm a pretty good judge of character, and there is no way in hell he would do something so horrible as to assault a comatose woman. The hospital is clearly covering up for one of its employees, and by God we're not going to let them get away with it! They've got to be held responsible for what happened to Katherine."

"Amen to that," Carrie agreed.

When Carrie and Will walked into Judge Little's courtroom shortly before one-thirty on a gloomy Friday afternoon, Jackson Memorial's entourage was already present. Owen Wellborne, a tall, impeccably dressed man in his mid-fifties with salt-and-pepper hair, was accompanied by a man in his early forties and a woman who appeared to be about thirty. Werner Von Slaten was also seated at counsel table.

"I suppose it would be the polite thing to go over and say hello to them," Will said under his breath as he and Carrie walked up to their own counsel table.

"The hell with politeness," Carrie murmured back. "I don't feel like fraternizing with the enemy. Let's just sit down."

As Carrie pulled a stack of legal pads and other papers out of her briefcase, she glanced around her. The large courtroom was pretty well filled. While most lawsuits were deadly dull, there was nothing like some good old-fashioned sex and violence to pique people's interest.

Carrie poured herself a glass of water and collected her thoughts. She was tired to the bone. In addition to the stress of the *Buckley* case, on the previous day she had finalized and filed—with Madree Williams's able assistance—the housing discrimination lawsuit. With these two new cases added to her already heavy caseload, her plate was full indeed.

Within moments, Judge Little's bailiff, Adrienne Thomas, called court into session. "All rise," the tall young woman called out authoritatively. Everyone in the courtroom got to their feet.

As Adrienne spoke, Judge Little came through a door at the back of the room. "This court is now in session, the Honorable Rita Little presiding," Adrienne continued. "Your silence is commanded."

"Please be seated," the judge said as she took her seat behind the bench. Judge Little was a tall, dark-haired woman in her mid-fifties. A former prosecuting attorney, she had been appointed a judge about ten years earlier. Although in her days as a prosecutor she had been viewed as a tough-on-crime conservative, her political views had seemed to moderate somewhat since she had donned the judicial robes. She was widely regarded as intelligent, thoughtful, and fearless. As Carrie glanced up at the bench, she was once again very pleased that this was the judge they'd drawn for the case. If anyone would see to it that Katherine Buckley got a fair shake from the legal system, it would be Judge Little.

"We're here for motions in *Buckley v. Jackson Memorial*," Judge Little said, looking at the stack of papers in front of her. "May I have the appearances, please."

Carrie got to her feet. "Carrie Nelson and Will Rollston for the plaintiffs, Your Honor." She sat down again.

Wellborne stood. "Owen Wellborne, Dennis Nolden, and Charlene Bull for the defendant, Your Honor. And in addition, Werner Von Slaten, the hospital's administrator, is also present."

Judge Little nodded. "Thank you, counsel. Now let's get down to business. Ms. Nelson, you have the floor."

Carrie got to her feet once more. She was wearing one of the Jil Sander suits she had purchased from Geri's, a brown-and-cream pinstripe with a straight skirt and oversized jacket. To accessorize the outfit, she had added a vintage Chanel necklace and matching earrings.

"Your Honor, the plaintiffs have filed two motions. The first is to expedite these proceedings. While we are painfully aware of the crowded state of the court's docket, and while we don't intend our request to deprecate the importance of the many other cases the court has pending before it, we respectfully suggest that this case merits special consideration." Carrie shifted her weight to her other foot and continued.

"Katherine Buckley has been in a coma for more than eight months. In addition to her neurological condition, which has shown no improvement since her accident, her physical health is very frail and is deteriorating. In addition, her new treating physicians report that Katherine's pregnancy is likely to cause a severe strain on her health."

Carrie paused a moment and looked the judge straight in the eye. "It is very possible that Katherine Buckley might not survive this pregnancy. Whichever person at Jackson Memorial is responsible for causing Katherine's condition stripped her of her last shreds of decency. It would be the ultimate insult if Katherine passed away while the case was allowed to languish. What we are asking in our motion to expedite, which is well within the court's discretion to grant, is to level the playing field just a bit, to allow us to at least try to bring this case to a conclusion while Katherine is still with us."

Judge Little nodded. "I see you have attached a proposed timetable to your motion."

"Yes, Your Honor," Carrie replied.

"You suggest here completing discovery by July first and scheduling the trial around July fifteenth." The judge looked at Carrie keenly. "Do you really believe that is an adequate amount of time to prepare a case of this magnitude?"

"Yes, Your Honor," Carrie answered, nodding firmly.

The judge nodded to herself and scrawled a few notes on a legal pad. "And your other motion?"

Maybe it was her imagination, but Carrie felt that the judge was with her. She hurried on with her argument to sustain the momentum. "Our other motion is to require Jackson Memorial to disclose the names of all of its patients during the time Katherine Buckley resided there and also to disclose the names and addresses of each patient's legal guardian. While we understand that the hospital objects to this request on the basis of doctor-patient privilege, this case presents a highly unique situation in that the victim of the assault, who would normally be our principal witness, is unable to tell us what happened to her."

Carrie briefly glanced over at the defendant's counsel table. All three of the hospital's attorneys were furiously scribbling notes on their legal pads. "In other words," Carrie went on, "you might say that Katherine Buckley's comatose state makes her an absent witness. She was there but can't communicate about the events of the assault. It is entirely possible, however, that one or more other patients at the hospital might have witnessed something and might be able to tell us what they saw."

Carrie paused to take a small sip of water. "It is important to keep in mind the narrow scope of our request. We are not asking for access to patients' medical records. We are merely requesting a list of patients' names. Because we are aware that the majority of the patients at the hospital are not competent to make their own legal decisions, in the event we do receive a patient list, we guarantee that we will take no steps to contact any patient until we have received written authorization from that patient's legal guardian. If authorization is denied, we will not speak to that patient."

Carrie looked directly at the judge. "Believe me, Your Honor, if this weren't such an unusual case, we would not be making this unique request. But if we aren't given access to the patient list, the hospital will in effect be able to hide behind a cloak of secrecy and we will be deprived of the opportunity to do justice for Katherine Buckley. We hope

that your honor will look favorably on both our requests.
Thank you."

As Carrie sank into her chair, Will gave her arm a light
pat, indicating he thought she had done a good job. Carrie
nodded gratefully and looked up at the bench. Judge Little
was scrawling more notes. Then she looked up and said,
"Thank you, Ms. Nelson. Mr. Wellborne, it looks like it's
your turn."

The courtly lawyer got to his feet. "Your Honor, I'm
happy to report that I believe we can move things forward
here a bit."

Judge Little raised one eyebrow. "And how might we do
that, counsel?" she asked.

Wellborne smiled, showing off thousands of dollars'
worth of dental work. "I am pleased to report that the
defendant has no objection to the timetable suggested in
the plaintiffs' motion to expedite."

Carrie and Will turned to each other in amazement. The
hospital was agreeing to speed up the case? Why on earth
would it do such a thing?

"So if your honor sees fit to give us a trial date in mid-
July," Wellborne went on, "the hospital will not oppose
it." He paused and cleared his throat. "Now, I'm afraid our
position on the motion to disclose patient lists won't be
quite so collegial. As your honor is aware, the doctor-
patient privilege enjoys a long history in American jurisprudence. The theory behind it, of course, is to encourage patients to be completely frank about their condition so as to
allow a correct diagnosis and proper treatment. If patients
had to worry that what they said would be disclosed to
third parties, it would have a chilling effect on full and free
communications."

Wellborne paused to take a drink of water. "Ms. Nelson
tried to get around the privilege issue by saying she doesn't
want the patients' medical records, only their names. We
don't believe there is a meaningful difference between the
two. In addition, each of the patients at Jackson Memorial
has a right to privacy. That privacy will be violated if the
patients' names are disclosed."

Wellborne covered his mouth and gave a brief cough. "Pardon me, Your Honor," he said as he continued. "Ms. Nelson also tried to downplay the impact of her request by saying that she would not attempt to interview any patient until she had obtained consent from the patient's guardian. We submit that the unique nature of the maladies treated at Jackson Memorial is yet another reason why the plaintiffs' motion should be denied. Jackson Memorial treats patients with mental and neurological disorders. Although all illnesses can be debilitating and cause a variety of problems for the patients and their families, we believe that the sensitive nature of mental disorders oftentimes creates a special hardship for patients' families."

As Wellborne was droning on with his remarks. Carrie jotted a note on her legal pad and showed it to Will. "Does he think we're going to publish details of the patients' medical records in the *Tribune*?"

Will smiled and nodded.

"Allowing the plaintiffs to have access to patients' names and the names and addresses of their families or guardians and then allowing them to upset those families and guardians with unwanted phone calls or visits would be tantamount to cruel and unusual punishment," Wellborne went on. "The plaintiffs have no evidence that any patient at Jackson Memorial witnessed an assault on Katherine Buckley. What they are suggesting amounts to a fishing expedition that would probably yield them no benefit and in the long run could cause substantial grief to many vulnerable patients and their families. For these reasons, Your Honor, we respectfully request that you deny the motion to turn over any patient lists. Thank you." Wellborne took his seat.

"Thank you, counsel," Judge Little said, jotting down a few more notes. "I am prepared to issue my ruling at this time." She flipped through her file. "Since the defendant acquiesces in the plaintiffs' request to expedite the matter, the court hereby grants that motion." The judge addressed her bailiff, who was seated at a desk to one side of the bench. "Ms. Thomas, my calendar indicates that the weeks of July thirteenth and twentieth would be available for a jury trial. Does your master schedule confirm that?''

Adrienne Thomas consulted a brown leather book in front of her. "Yes, it does, Your Honor," she replied.

"Good," the judge said. "Then it is ordered that the proposed timetable set forth in Exhibit C of the plaintiffs' motion be adopted as the schedule in this case, with the matter set for a two-week jury trial to commence on July thirteenth."

As the judge spoke, Carrie scribbled notes reflecting the ruling.

"Turning to the second motion, for disclosure of patient names and names and addresses of each patient's guardian—this issue is obviously more problematic. There are strong legal and policy arguments on both sides. In making my ruling, I must weigh the interests in patient confidentiality against the plaintiffs' right to obtain evidence that might tend to establish the identity of the person who assaulted Ms. Buckley. After engaging in this weighing process, I have determined that the equities favor requiring the hospital to disclose the requested information."

Yes! Carrie thought joyously. She had to suck in her cheeks to avoid breaking into a grin. She looked down and tried to concentrate on making notes on her legal pad.

"It is the order of this court that Jackson Memorial Hospital furnish the information requested by one week from today, February twenty-seventh. The plaintiffs are strongly cautioned that under no circumstances are they to speak to any patient until they have obtained the written consent of that person's legal guardian." The judge paused and reviewed her notes. "I believe that concludes the matters that are before us today. Ms. Nelson, you may draft a written order for my signature."

Carrie nodded. She would take care of it as soon as she got back to the office.

"If we have no further business," the judge went on, "we stand adjourned." She rapped her gavel on the bench. "Call the next case," she instructed Adrienne Thomas.

Wellborne and his crew, apparently not in the mood for

any niceties, bolted out the door of the courtroom before Carrie and Will even had a chance to pack up their brief-cases. That was fine with Carrie. She knew she was going to be getting a bellyful of all of them before the case was over.

Carrie and Will spent the short ride back to the office congratulating each other on the outcome of the hearing. "I was surprised the hospital agreed to expedite," Carrie commented.

"I really wasn't," Will replied. "I'll bet they went along with the request just to put us through our paces. They probably think we haven't allowed ourselves enough time to adequately prepare the case and they're hoping that come July thirteenth we'll be caught short and have to drop the suit."

"Well, if they think that they obviously don't know us very well," Carrie replied, sticking out her chin.

"They sure don't," Will agreed.

As they neared their building's underground parking ga-rage, Carrie was feeling so upbeat, not only about the case but about life in general, that she decided to seize the mo-ment. She cleared her throat. "Sometimes on Fridays a bunch of us get together for drinks at O'Malley's," she commented casually. "I'm planning to stop by tonight. Would you like to join me?"

"I'd love to," Will replied, "but I'm afraid I have other plans."

Carrie's heart fell. "Oh, that's okay," she said, trying to sound blasé.

"You see, I have a date," Will went on.

Carrie's mood immediately went from merely dark to truly dismal. "You don't need to explain," she said. *Please don't elaborate any further,* she thought, grinding her teeth together. *I can't bear to hear this.*

"It's sort of an arranged deal," Will went on, clearly oblivious to Carrie's feelings. "You know, a dreaded blind date. A friend of a friend. I'm sure you've suffered through them yourself. It'll probably be boring as all getout, but I said I'd go, so I'm sort of stuck. Anyway, maybe I could take a rain check for another time." He looked over at her cheerfully.

Carrie managed an anemic grin. "Sure. No problem. I just thought I'd mention that sometimes on Fridays we go to O'Malley's."

Will pulled into his space in the parking garage. "Great job at the hearing today," he said enthusiastically. "I'm really looking forward to working with you on this case."

"Me too," Carrie replied, as she opened the car door. *And I'd be looking forward to it a lot more if you'd show a scintilla of interest in me as a woman and not just as your cocounsel,* she added silently to herself. She slammed the car door firmly behind her.

Keep your chin up, she exhorted herself as she followed Will toward the elevator. All was not lost just because the guy was going on a blind date. *Remember Scarlett O'Hara's credo: tomorrow's another day and all that rot.*

The internal pep talk failed to lift her mood. *Sure,* she thought morosely as they got on the elevator. *Tomorrow's another day, and as Dorothy Parker might have added, another day, another sock in the eye.*

Chapter 11

Carrie woke up Saturday morning feeling mildly depressed. After returning from the hearing the previous day, she had drafted an order for Judge Little's signature and sent it by messenger to the judge. Then she had resisted the impulse to go home and feel sorry for herself and had instead followed through on her plans to join her colleagues for a couple of drinks at O'Malley's, a lively Irish pub and restaurant a couple of blocks from Ramquist and Dowd's offices.

The firm was quite egalitarian, so support staff fraternized freely with partners at these impromptu after-work get-togethers. Carrie was joined by Tammy and Doug Hennick, Dona Winkler, Madree Williams, and Terry Payne. The group was already on its second round of drinks when Will Rollston's secretary, Karen Hundley, walked in.

"There's room here," Dona Winkler said, patting an empty chair next to her.

"Thanks," Karen said, squeezing into the seat. "Sorry I'm late, but Will had some correspondence he wanted to go out."

"Where is Will?" Terry Payne asked, looking around. "Is he coming?"

"He had a date," Karen replied.

Carrie took a big swallow of her pint of Bass Ale and hoped the conversation would quickly take another turn.

"A date," Terry repeated somewhat morosely. "I remember those. And who knows, if I ever make it through my divorce, I might actually go on one again."

"You will," Tammy said encouragingly.

"Congratulations on your hearing today," Karen said to Carrie. "Will said your argument was dynamite."

"I don't know if I'd go that far," Carrie replied modestly. "We're lucky to have a good judge on the case."

A waiter came over to the table and took Karen's drink order. "Would any of you like to see menus?" he asked.

"The three of us would," Tammy said, motioning at Doug and Dona.

"I'd like to stay and eat," Karen said.

"Me, too," Madree Williams put in.

"How about you, Carrie?" Dona asked.

Carrie shook her head. "I'm kind of beat," she said, finishing her ale. "Maybe some other time," she said, putting down ten dollars for her share as she got up to leave.

After she went home, Carrie ate a fat-free microwave dinner, played with Muffin, and crawled into bed around ten o'clock. Her sleep was troubled and fitful. The next morning she did some cursory housecleaning and then slipped into a pair of dressy black slacks and a blue-and-cream mohair sweater and headed north to Winnetka to visit Katherine Buckley and her parents at Converse Medical Center in Winnetka.

Carrie had been putting off this visit since she'd agreed to represent the Buckleys in their case against Jackson Memorial. The two occasions on which she had accompanied her former roommate to visit Katherine at the hospital had left her feeling edgy and depressed. Carrie hated to admit it, but she felt uncomfortable being around someone who was comatose.

In her years as an attorney, Carrie had handled any number of medical malpractice actions, and it had not fazed her to deal with people who were disfigured or terminally ill. But for some inexplicable reason, being around a person whose mind had stopped functioning normally really spooked her. She knew this reaction was probably childish, and she also knew she owed it to Ed and Melody Buckley—and perhaps most of all to Katherine herself—to overcome her queasiness and pay them a personal visit.

Shortly after noon Carrie found herself standing outside

the door of Katherine's room at Converse Medical Center. She paused for a moment, steeling herself for the sight of her client and giving herself a little pep talk that there was nothing to be nervous about. Then she took a deep breath, gave a brief knock, and walked through the door.

Katherine's room was bright and spacious. Purposely averting her eyes from the hospital bed and its occupant, Carrie saw Ed and Melody Buckley seated near the back of the room. Since she had expected Katherine's parents to be alone, Carrie was surprised to also see a tall, dark-haired young man dressed in jeans and a sweatshirt, sitting in a third chair, closer to Katherine's bed. And she was even more startled to see a tall, white-haired man dressed in clerical garb standing next to Melody. She surmised that the young man must be Todd Fleming, but she couldn't begin to guess the identity of the older man.

"Hello, Carrie," Ed Buckley said as he spied her. He got up from his chair and came forward to greet her. "It's so nice to see you." Turning to the younger man, he asked, "Have you met Todd Fleming?"

"No, I haven't," Carrie replied. She stepped forward and extended her hand. "It's nice to meet you, Todd. My colleague, Will Rollston, speaks very highly of you."

Katherine's boyfriend stood up, gravely shook her hand and then sat down again. Carrie looked at the young man closely. He was painfully thin, and his face looked tired and drawn. He had clearly been through hell, and Carrie knew if the police were to charge him with assault, his ordeal would only get worse.

"And this is our old friend, Bishop Joe Wilson," Ed went on, putting his hand on the cleric's arm. "Joe, this is our attorney, Carrie Nelson. I believe we've spoken of her."

"Carrie, it's a pleasure to meet you," the bishop said warmly as he shook her hand. "The Buckleys have told me a lot about you."

"Pleased to meet you," Carrie murmured. The bishop, who appeared to be in his early fifties, was dressed in a gray suit, purple shirt, and Roman collar. Upon looking more closely, Carrie noticed that he wore a heavy gold chain around his neck. The end of the chain appeared to be tucked into his shirt pocket. *I wonder what that's all about,* she thought, frowning slightly.

The bishop noticed Carrie's inquisitive look, then chuckled and pulled the chain out of his pocket, revealing a bejeweled pectoral cross. "The darn thing gets in the way," he explained. "So I sometimes tuck it out of sight."

Carrie's eyes grew wide at the sight of the gaudy cross. She wondered if the stones were real.

"Oh, they're real, all right," the bishop said, as if he had read her mind. "Pretty flashy, eh?"

"I'm sorry. I didn't mean to gawk," Carrie apologized, blushing profusely.

Bishop Wilson laughed. "No need to apologize. It's good for me to be reminded that I look a little goofy in this getup. Keeps me humble."

"Joe was recently elected the Suffragan Bishop of Chicago," Ed explained. "You're not Episcopalian, are you?"

Carrie shook her head.

"That means he's the Diocesan Bishop's right-hand man," Ed went on. "But our families go way back—to when Joe was the rector of our local parish."

"We've been in a gourmet food club with Joe and his wife, Joyce, for more than twenty years," Melody added. "Joe has been a great comfort to us throughout this whole ordeal."

"My new job is largely administrative," Bishop Wilson explained. "And I've been told I have some aptitude for such things. But I must admit, I miss the personal contact with parishioners."

As the Buckleys nodded at the bishop's comments and exchanged a bit more small talk with him, Carrie finally allowed herself to glance over at the slender figure tucked in the hospital bed. She knew it was now time to gather her courage and approach Katherine's bedside. But no matter how much she tried to do so, she still found she was rather nervous.

As if he could sense her apprehension, Bishop Wilson gently touched Carrie's elbow. "Why don't you come and say hello to Katherine?" he suggested. "I think she'd like that."

Carrie nodded and allowed herself to be guided over to the side of the bed opposite from where Todd was sitting.

Katherine looked as if she were napping peacefully. Although she was pale, her face was unlined and her shoulder-length brown hair was fanned out on the pillow. Since the accident, the young woman had been fed through a tube inserted in her stomach, so she had lost a significant amount of weight. Still, she didn't look sick, and it was easy to imagine that at any moment she might open her eyes and recapture her life. How tragic that, according to her doctors, that simple event would almost certainly never occur.

Staring down at the still body, in which a new life was now growing, Carrie closed her eyes and silently murmured a combination prayer and promise to find the person who had attacked Katherine. Then she opened her eyes and gently touched Katherine's cheek. Turning, she saw Bishop Wilson give her a small nod and smile. He clearly understood how difficult this visit had been for Carrie. She was touched by his concern.

The bishop reached over and squeezed Katherine's hand, then turned and said, "Well, I'd best be going. I have a late luncheon appointment. Carrie, it was a pleasure to meet you. Todd, see you soon. Ed and Melody, if I don't talk to you before then, Joyce and I will expect to see you at our house next Saturday for the gourmet club dinner."

"We wouldn't miss it," Melody replied. To Carrie she explained, "We're recreating the dinner served the night the *Titanic* went down."

"Sounds fun," Carrie said.

"Complete with period costumes," the bishop chuckled. "Wait till you see what Joyce is wearing. She's dredged up a velvet gown that belonged to her aunt. I predict it's going to be quite a memorable evening." He headed toward the door. "Good day, all."

"What a nice man," Carrie commented after the bishop had taken his leave.

"He's been a wonderful friend," Ed agreed. "Especially since—" His voice trailed off.

Todd, who up until that point had been sitting quietly at Katherine's bedside, turned and asked Carrie bluntly, "Jackson Memorial is going to try to make me the fall guy, isn't it?"

"We won't let that happen," Carrie promised him. "We'll find out who is really responsible."

Todd got up and walked over to where the other three were standing. "And what about the police? Are they going to charge me with assault?"

"The detective told me that no decision had been made," Carrie replied candidly. "Hopefully they'll soon see that they've been gravely misled and get to work finding the real perpetrator."

"I'm graduating from law school in three months," Todd explained. "I'm starting a clerkship with a federal judge in August. I felt like my life ended the night of Katherine's accident, but I've forced myself to go on because I know that's what she would have wanted. If I were to be charged with a crime, it could ruin my career."

"None of us will let anything happen to you," Ed Buckley said firmly, putting his arm around the younger man. "You know we're behind you one hundred percent. The police have allowed themselves to be taken in by that fast-talking hospital administrator. Anyone who knows you realizes you could never do what they're claiming. And now that Carrie has the case on a fast track, she'll find out the truth, and the police will see that they're wrong."

"I'll do everything I can," Carrie promised the young man.

Todd's face contorted in pain, and he turned and walked over to the window.

"What will happen next in the case?" Melody asked.

"We're starting depositions on Monday," Carrie explained. "We've got quite an ambitious schedule set up. We're starting with Dr. Dawn Redding, then moving on to the hospital's nursing supervisor and the neurosurgeon who operated on Katherine. And I've reserved an entire day for the charming Mr. Von Slaten. I must say I'm looking forward to that," she said with relish. "Then we'll be taking testimony from all of the hospital personnel mentioned in Katherine's medical records, and if other names come up in those depositions, we'll be adding more people."

"What about interviewing the other patients at the hospital?" Melody asked. "When will that start?"

"The hospital has to turn over its patient list on Friday," Carrie explained, "and as soon as we get it we'll start tracking down the patients' guardians to get permission to do interviews."

"What if some guardians won't give permission?" Ed asked.

"We're hoping the majority will," Carrie said, hedging a bit. She was a little worried that if Von Slaten got to the guardians first he could stymie her efforts to get permission, in which case Judge Little's favorable ruling wouldn't mean squat. She just had to hope the guardians were compassionate people who would listen to reason.

"What about Katherine's new doctors?" Melody asked. "Will you be taking their depositions, too? Dr. Flanagan was asking us about it this morning."

Carrie nodded. "Yes, we will want to take their depositions to document the effect the pregnancy is having on Katherine's physical state. How is she doing so far?"

"Dr. Flanagan says she's holding her own," Ed replied. He looked at Katherine lovingly. "That girl's a real fighter."

"Yes, she is," Carrie agreed, taking Ed's and Melody's hands and holding them tightly. "And she deserves to have the people around her fight just as hard on her behalf. That's why I promise you all I'll do everything I can to make sure whoever is responsible for hurting her is found and punished."

Chapter 12

When Carrie met Will Rollston early on Monday morning before the start of Dr. Dawn Redding's deposition, he seemed to be in a very good mood. "Did you have a nice weekend?" he asked jovially.

"It was fine," Carrie answered noncommittally. She wasn't about to tell him that the highlight of the past two days had been picking out a new cat toy for Muffin. Friday night's blind date must have been a rousing success for Will to be acting so upbeat. "How about you?" she asked.

"Fine," Will replied. "I took Floyd to his first obedience class on Saturday. I think it's going to do him a lot of good."

Carrie's mood took a sudden and marked upswing. The blind date couldn't have been anything *too* hot if the only part of the weekend he considered worth mentioning was the dog's obedience training.

"That's nice," Carrie said. "I'm sure Floyd enjoyed it, too."

Since the day's depositions were being taken at the behest of Carrie's clients, they were held in one of Ramquist and Dowd's conference rooms. Dennis Nolden and Charlene Bull appeared on behalf of Jackson Memorial. Owen Wellborne, being one of Perillo, Linholm, and Untermeyer's senior partners, probably didn't lower himself to attend depositions. Instead, he would likely confine himself to making strategically timed personal appearances and helping pad the bills that went out to his clients each month.

Carrie was thankful for Wellborne's absence. From his demeanor at the motions hearing in front of Judge Little, he had struck her as bombastic and just generally a pain in the ass. Actually, he had reminded her a lot of J. Richard Toussant, her old nemesis at Henley, Schuman and Kloss. She often wondered if something happened to distort peoples' brains and quadruple the size of their egos once they became senior partners at big law firms.

Unfortunately, even though Wellborne wasn't present, Jackson Memorial was still represented by its resident jackass in the person of Werner Von Slaten. As the designated client representative, Von Slaten was entitled to sit in on all proceedings in the case. Carrie truly loathed the man and hoped he would quickly tire of the tedium of civil litigation and go back to the business of mismanaging the hospital.

For the most part, Dr. Redding's deposition was uneventful. The doctor recounted Katherine's medical history during the eight months the young woman was a patient at Jackson Memorial, culminating in the blood test that had revealed the pregnancy.

"Is it fair to say you were surprised when the results of the blood test came back and you saw the positive pregnancy reading?" Carrie asked.

Dr. Redding nodded emphatically. "I was in utter disbelief," she replied. "So much so that I immediately ordered another test."

"Which also came back positive?"

"Yes."

"Doctor, do you have any opinion as to who might be the father of Katherine Buckley's baby?" Carrie asked, smoothing down the skirt of her charcoal suit.

"Objection," Charlene Bull interrupted. "Calls for speculation."

"Are you instructing the witness not to answer?" Carrie asked patiently.

"No," Charlene replied sweetly. "I am merely noting my objection for the record."

"Fine," Carrie said with mock patience. "Do you remember my question, Dr. Redding, or would you like the court reporter to read it back?"

"I remember it," the doctor replied. "And the answer is no. I haven't the slightest idea who might have fathered Katherine's baby."

"Did you ever notice any man, whether someone on the Jackson Memorial staff or otherwise, behaving strangely around Katherine?"

"No."

"Did you ever happen to come into Katherine's room and see anyone who appeared to be acting in a furtive or strange manner?"

"No."

As soon as Charlene Bull began posing her round of questions to the doctor, it became clear what the hospital's line of defense to the Buckleys' lawsuit was going to be.

"Dr. Redding, have you ever met Katherine Buckley's fiancé, Todd Fleming?"

"Yes, on many occasions," the doctor replied.

"Do you ever recall going into Katherine Buckley's room and finding Mr. Fleming there alone with Katherine?"

"Yes."

"How many times would you say you saw Mr. Fleming and Katherine alone in her room?"

Dr. Redding shrugged. "I really couldn't quantify it."

"Would you say you saw them alone more than twenty times?"

"Probably."

"Could it have been more than fifty times?" Charlene pressed on.

Dr. Redding shook her head. "I really don't know. I never paid attention."

"But Mr. Fleming was a frequent visitor to Katherine's room, was he not?"

"Yes, he was."

"Is it fair to say he visited her nearly every day?"

"I believe he did, yes."

Charlene turned toward Dennis Nolden and Werner Von Slaten and gave them a satisfied little smile. "I have no further questions, Dr. Redding," she announced sweetly.

Spare me your cutesy little act, Carrie thought disgustedly.

"I have a few more questions," she said aloud. "Doctor, on those occasions when you observed Todd Fleming alone with Katherine Buckley, was Mr. Fleming engaging in any unusual or improper behavior with Katherine?"

"No."

"When you observed Todd and Katherine alone together, do you recall what Todd would generally be doing?"

"He would usually be sitting in a chair next to Katherine's bed."

"Did you ever observe Todd touch Katherine?"

"Sometimes he would hold her hand."

"Did you ever observe Mr. Fleming touch Katherine in an indecent manner?"

"No."

"Did you ever see any other man alone with Katherine in her room?"

"Her father."

"Anyone else?"

Dr. Redding thought for a moment. "I can't say for sure, but it's certainly possible. Katherine had a lot of visitors."

"Thank you, Dr. Redding," Carrie said. "I have no further questions. You're free to go."

As Dr. Redding got up from her chair and walked toward the door of the conference room, Carrie watched Werner Von Slaten. The hospital's administrator was clearly glaring at the young doctor. Fortunately Dr. Redding did not seem to notice Von Slaten's reaction. Carrie truly liked Dr. Redding and hoped that in the near future she might consider switching her allegiance to a more congenial employer.

The next witness was Jackson Memorial's nursing supervisor, a gregarious white-haired woman named Shirley Sandow. In questioning the nurse, Carrie spent a great deal of time going over the list of Jackson Memorial's staff, which Von Slaten had previously furnished, in an effort to determine which staff members had contact with Katherine Buckley. This was a painstaking exercise that helped Carrie identify at least twenty more people who would need to

be scheduled for depositions in order to prepare the case
for trial.

As she watched her list of names steadily expanding, Carrie began to realize just how time-consuming the *Buckley*
case was going to be. For the first time she wondered if
she had made a serious mistake in pressing so hard for an
expedited trial schedule. Now she understood why Owen
Wellborne had been so quick to agree to speeding the case
along. Will had been right. This case could very well bury
not just Carrie but her entire firm. Perillo, Linholm, and
Untermeyer was probably counting on that.

Carrie sat up straighter in her chair. She could feel her
resolve strengthening. By God, she would show Owen
Wellborne and Werner Von Slaten and the whole damn lot
of them. Not only could she handle this case in double time,
she was going to win it, too. *Take that, Mr. Von Slaten,* she
thought, tossing her head.

Coming out of her private reverie, Carrie became aware
that a silence had fallen over the room. She realized that
Nurse Sandow had long since finished answering the last
question and that everyone was waiting for Carrie to pose
her next inquiry. She turned and saw Will looking at her
with obvious concern. She immediately snapped to attention and pretended to be shuffling through some papers as
she struggled to formulate a question.

"Oh, here we go," Carrie said brightly, as if she had now
located the pertinent document. "Ms. Sandow, I'd like to
change gears a bit and talk about your personal interaction
with Katherine Buckley. In an average week, how much
contact would you have with her?" As Nurse Sandow
began to reply, Carrie could feel Will visibly relax, obviously relieved that his cocounsel hadn't lost her marbles
after all.

Nurse Sandow explained that over the eight months
Katherine had spent at Jackson Memorial, she would usually see the young patient five days a week. "We all are
aware that from all outward indicators Katherine Buckley
is in a comatose state," Carrie commented. "But from your
observation of the patient, do you have an opinion as to

whether or not she has any awareness of events around her. In other words, do you believe she has any cognitive function?"

"Objection," Charlene Bull called out. "This witness is a nurse. She is not qualified to render such an opinion."

"I'm not asking for her expert medical opinion," Carrie countered. "I am merely looking for her opinion as a lay witness." Turning to Nurse Sandow, she said pleasantly, "You may answer the question—if you're able to, that is."

Nurse Sandow pursed her lips and considered the question a moment before answering. "It is impossible to answer that question with any certainty. I have been in nursing for more than thirty years and have probably treated at least fifty people in Katherine Buckley's condition. And although there is no definite proof one way or the other, it has always been my feeling that those patients are aware of what's happening around them even though they are unable to tell us so."

"On what do you base this opinion, Nurse Sandow?" Carrie asked.

"On a variety of things, such as little movements that the patients sometimes make, seemingly in response to sound or touch or smell."

"What kind of movements?"

"It varies. Sometimes a patient will move her head. Sometimes she will clench her fist or fling her arm in the air."

"Couldn't those movements be involuntary muscle spasms?" Carrie asked.

"They could be," Nurse Sandow agreed. "But I think they could also be an effort by the patient to communicate, to break through the wall of silence."

"Did you ever observe Katherine Buckley making these types of movements?"

"Yes, I did."

"And from observing these movements it is your lay opinion that Katherine Buckley has at least some awareness of events around her?"

"Yes."

In her questioning, Charlene Bull attempted to discredit Nurse Sandow's opinion that Katherine had any cognitive function.

"Have you ever taken any specialized courses dealing with brain function in comatose patients?"

"No."

"Then your opinion about what Katherine Buckley is or is not aware of is not founded on any recognized medical theory, is it?"

"I wouldn't say that," the nurse replied. "I have read a number of articles in respected medical journals indicating that comatose patients can be aware of what is going on around them, at least sporadically. I could furnish you with a list, if you'd like."

Charlene Bull's jaw dropped. This clearly was not the answer she'd been expecting. Before Charlene could decline the nurse's offer, Carrie spoke up. "I would like to have a list of those articles," she said pleasantly. To Nurse Sandow, she said, "Do you suppose you could furnish them to Ms. Bull and myself by next week?"

"Sure," the nurse responded.

"Thank you," Carrie said.

"Yes, thank you," Charlene echoed weakly. "I have no further questions. Why don't we take a short break?"

As Carrie and Will rose from their seats, out of the corner of her eye she could see Von Slaten gritting his teeth. She'd be willing to bet that poor Charlene Bull was in for a severe tongue-lashing and a reminder that you should never, ever ask a question if you don't know the answer to it.

Back in Carrie's office, Will settled into a chair and said, "I think it's going well so far. What's your opinion?"

Carrie shrugged. "It's a little early to tell, but I think so, too. At least these witnesses didn't implicate Todd, and they held open the possibility that Katherine might have experienced conscious pain and suffering." She opened her top desk drawer and pulled out half a dozen bite-size Tootsie Rolls. "I'm starving," she said, unwrapping one and popping it into her mouth. "Want some?"

"Sure," Will said, smiling. "A closet Tootsie Roll eater, eh?" he teased as he helped himself. "Now I know where to come when my sweet tooth acts up."

"My candy drawer is always open to you," Carrie said a bit flirtatiously.

Will grinned. "I'll keep that in mind," he drawled.

Chapter 13

The next witness, Dr. Gerald Peckham, was a neurosurgeon at Jackson Memorial. The doctor cut a rather dashing figure. Peckham was fifty years old, and of average height, but somehow his expensive hand tailored charcoal suit made him appear larger than he actually was. His dark hair was just starting to gray around the temples. With her keen eye for fine jewelry, Carrie noticed a Breguet watch peeking out from under Dr. Peckham's suit jacket. Carrie was impressed. That timepiece had probably set him back at least twenty thou. Dr. Peckham obviously pulled down a very substantial income.

In response to Carrie's preliminary questions, the doctor explained that he had obtained his degree from Stanford and done his residency there. He had spent ten years at an East Coast hospital before moving to Chicago, and he had been associated with Jackson Memorial for six years.

"Are you acquainted with Katherine Buckley?" Carrie asked.

"Yes, I am," Dr. Peckham replied. His voice was low and melodious, and he looked Carrie square in the eye when he answered, as if to show he was cooperative but not intimidated. Carrie immediately liked him and decided that he was quite a charmer. In fact, if she didn't look too closely, he reminded her a bit of Cary Grant.

"Did you have occasion to examine or treat Katherine during the time she was a patient at Jackson Memorial?" Carrie went on.

"Yes. In the first several days after she was brought to

the hospital I performed three surgical procedures to relieve intercranial bleeding."

"Have you performed any surgical procedures on Katherine since that time?"

"No."

Carrie cocked her head. "But you remained one of Katherine's treating physicians and examined her regularly, did you not?"

"Yes. Jackson Memorial employs a team approach," Dr. Peckham explained. "Whenever a new patient is admitted, a team of caregivers will be selected to care for him or her. I was appointed to Ms. Buckley's treatment team. That means I was expected to follow up on how she was doing for however long she remained a patient at the hospital."

"By whom were you appointed?"

"By Dr. Robert Morrow, our chief of staff."

"Does Dr. Morrow make all of the team assignments?"

"Yes."

"Who else, besides yourself, was assigned to Katherine Buckley's team?"

Dr. Peckham referred to a file he had brought with him. "Dr. Dawn Redding was Katherine's internist, Dr. Kenneth Luebke was her neurologist, and Dr. Jan Neumann was her critical care specialist."

"How many times did you examine or otherwise have contact with Katherine Buckley?"

"I reviewed her chart weekly and looked in on her at least every other week."

"Did you ever prescribe any medications for Katherine?" Carrie asked.

Dr. Peckham again consulted his file. "In the first week or two after she was admitted, yes. But after that I believe all of her drug needs were attended to by her other doctors."

"Did you ever make any suggestions about Katherine's treatment following the three surgical procedures?"

"Yes," the doctor replied. "I met with her parents on several occasions and told them that I am a firm believer in trying to keep comatose patients stimulated. I encouraged them to talk to Katherine just as they would if she were communicative, to play music that she enjoyed before the accident, to have the television on. I also encouraged them to touch her, hold her hand or lightly massage her arms and legs. Anything that might stimulate her senses."

"What is the purpose of this stimulation therapy?"

"One hopes that it might bring a patient out of the twilight state."

"Do these types of therapy yield positive results?"

"Sometimes."

"Did the therapy yield such a result in Katherine's case?"

Dr. Peckham shook his head. "No, unfortunately there was no change in Katherine's condition from the time of her admission to Jackson Memorial until her discharge. She never gave any indication of regaining any cognitive function."

"Based on your observation of Katherine and your experience with other patients, can you give us your opinion, to a reasonable medical certainty, as to whether you believe Katherine Buckley has any awareness of events around her?"

Dr. Peckham paused a moment and reflected on the question. "I would say it is possible she does. However, there is no way to know for certain."

"Can you quantify the possibility that she does have some awareness of what is going on around her? Is there a twenty percent possibility? A fifty percent possibility?"

"I am afraid there is no way to know that."

"But it is your learned medical opinion that patients in Katherine's condition are sometimes aware of events even though they are unable to communicate that fact?"

"Definitely," Dr. Peckham replied. "We know that is true because there have been studies detailing the histories of any number of patients who have eventually come out of their comas and reported in great detail hearing things that were said in their presence, feeling people touching them, et cetera."

"So in your opinion it's possible that Katherine could be aware of things that have happened since her accident, including the sexual assault that resulted in her pregnancy?"

"It's possible, yes," the doctor replied.

Carrie looked at Von Slaten. He was frowning so deeply she secretly wished his face would freeze in that position. Then she caught Will's eye. He winked at her.

Carrie continued with her questioning. "Doctor, when did you first learn about Katherine's pregnancy?"

"I believe it was the day Katherine was transferred to Converse Medical Center."

"How did you come to hear the news?"

"Dr. Redding told me that morning when I came to the hospital for rounds."

"What was your reaction?"

"I was stunned," the doctor answered. "Nothing like that has ever happened to a patient in all the years I've been in practice."

"Do you have any idea who could be responsible for Katherine's pregnancy?"

The doctor shook his head. "Absolutely none."

"Did you ever see anyone in Katherine's room who appeared to be acting in an inappropriate manner?"

"No."

"You never saw anyone taking indecent liberties with Katherine?"

"No, I did not."

"Let's turn to a slightly different subject," Carrie said. "How would you rate the security precautions at Jackson Memorial?"

"Objection," Dennis Nolden interrupted. "This witness is a neurosurgeon, not a member of the security staff."

"You may answer the question if you are able," Carrie instructed Dr. Peckham.

"I don't know," the doctor replied. "I suppose I'd have to say that security seems more than adequate. We have never had any type of criminal incident at the hospital."

"Until now," Carrie pointed out.

The doctor merely shrugged. In the background, Carrie could see Von Slaten smiling ever so slightly.

"Who is in charge of security at the hospital?"

"I can't think of the fellow's name offhand," the doctor admitted. "I believe it's Glen something. Fish or Fisher, I think."

Carrie changed directions again. "Doctor Peckham, you've mentioned that you were just one member of a care team brought together to treat Katherine Buckley."

"That's right."

"And Dr. Dawn Redding was the internist on the team."

"Yes."

"What was her responsibility in Katherine's treatment?"

"Dr. Redding had the primary responsibility for handling Katherine's day-to-day health care needs. She oversaw such things as monitoring Katherine's vital signs, watching for infection, making sure that she was receiving adequate food and hydration. If she noticed anything out of the ordinary, she would call in another doctor for a consult, if she felt it was needed."

"I take it you have worked with Dr. Redding not just on Katherine's case but on other patients' cases as well?"

"Yes."

"How would you rate Dr. Redding as a physician?"

"Excellent. I've never known her to provide anything other than top-notch care for her patients."

"And that includes Katherine Buckley?"

"Yes."

Carrie nodded. "I believe another name you mentioned was Dr. Jan Neumann."

"Yes. Dr. Neumann is one of our critical care providers."

"What types of treatment would she handle for a patient such as Katherine?"

"I believe Katherine contracted pneumonia a couple of times, and on at least one occasion she had another serious infection. Dr. Neumann would be the person who would make the decision to transfer a patient like Katherine to ICU and then be responsible for monitoring her during the time she was in the critical care unit."

"Again, I assume you have had the opportunity to work with Dr. Neumann on cases other than Katherine's?"

"Yes."

"And what is your opinion of Dr. Neumann's abilities as a doctor?"

"I believe Dr. Neumann to be an excellent critical care provider."

Carrie consulted her notes. "The final person that you mentioned as being on Katherine's team was Dr. Kenneth Luebke, a neurologist."

"That's right."

"What type of procedures would Dr. Luebke coordinate for a patient such as Katherine?"

Dr. Peckham shifted in his chair. "Dr. Luebke would be responsible for ordering tests such as CT scans. He would also have primary responsibility for prescribing any drug or other therapy that he believed might help a patient in Katherine's condition regain cognitive function."

"Such as?"

"It could run the gamut from shock therapy to bio feedback to experimental procedures."

"Do you know whether any experimental procedures were performed on Katherine?"

Dr. Peckham shrugged. "I'm afraid I don't recall for sure. You would have to ask Dr. Luebke."

"I intend to do that," Carrie said. "Now, as with Drs. Redding and Neumann, I assume you have worked in conjunction with Dr. Luebke on other cases?"

"Yes."

To Carrie's ears, Peckham's response seemed to be awfully short and a bit gruff. "And what is your opinion of Dr. Luebke's abilities as a doctor?" she asked.

There was the briefest of pauses, then Dr. Peckham replied, "Fine."

Carrie frowned. "Correct me if I'm wrong, but I believe you indicated that both Dr. Redding and Dr. Neumann had excellent abilities. Am I to infer from your answer about Dr. Luebke that you are not giving him a similar rousing endorsement?"

Another shrug. "You are free to infer anything you want."

Carrie paused momentarily and looked over at Will. He was frowning. What was going on here?

"Now I am quite intrigued," Carrie commented to Dr. Peckham. "Can you tell us any instances in which you believe Dr. Luebke's care of a patient was not up to par?"

"I wouldn't put it that way," the doctor hedged.

"Well, then, let's try this: Is it fair to say that you might have some philosophical differences with the way Dr. Luebke treats his patients?"

Dr. Peckham pondered the question for a moment, then replied, "I suppose you could say that."

"Could you explain for us what those differences are?" Carrie asked patiently.

Dr. Peckham again shifted in his chair, looking uncomfortable now. "Well, as I alluded to earlier, even though I am a surgeon, my treatment philosophy is grounded in the notion that in order to heal the mind, you must employ a holistic approach. While I realize that doctors in general sometimes get a bad rap for overprescribing drugs for their patients, I prefer to take a rather conservative approach to treatment. I believe in using drug therapy only as a last resort."

"Are you saying that you have seen Dr. Luebke prescribe drugs for patients in cases where you felt they were not warranted?"

"On occasion he and I have had our friendly disagreements on this subject, yes," Dr. Peckham admitted.

"Do you feel that Dr. Luebke prescribed drugs for Katherine Buckley unnecessarily?"

"I didn't say that."

"So you believe that Dr. Luebke's treatment of Katherine Buckley was appropriate?"

"I'm afraid I'm not able to answer that."

"Why not?" Out of the corner of her eye, Carrie could see Will furiously scribbling on a piece of paper.

"Because in order to give an informed answer, I would need to see Dr. Luebke's entire treatment record for Katherine," Dr. Peckham explained. "Without it, I would just be speculating."

Will handed Carrie the note he had been writing. She scanned it, then nodded to him. "Dr. Peckham," she said, "if we were to furnish you with a complete copy of Dr. Luebke's treatment records concerning Katherine Buckley, would you be willing to go over them and then discuss them in more detail in a continuation of your deposition?"

"I suppose I could do that," Dr. Peckham replied a bit reluctantly.

"All right, then. Let's adjourn this deposition—say for two weeks—pending your review of Dr. Luebke's records."

"That's fine with me," Dr. Peckham said amiably.

"Thank you, Doctor," Carrie said. "I think this might be a good time for us to take a ten-minute break."

Carrie and Will retreated to her office.

"What do you suppose that was all about?" Will asked.

"I don't know," Carrie admitted. "There's obviously some bad blood between Peckham and Luebke. I wonder what's behind it." She reached into her drawer and pulled out some Tootsie Rolls. "Want one?" she asked.

"No, thanks," Will replied. "When are we deposing Dr. Luebke?"

"Next week," Carrie replied, chewing on her candy.

"Well, with the red flags Peckham sent up today, we're going to have to take extra care preparing for that one."

"Absolutely," Carrie said. "I've got a feeling Dr. Peckham might've put us onto something. Who knows?" she said optimistically. "This could be the big break we've been waiting for."

"Wouldn't that be great?" Will reached across the desk and gave Carrie's hand a quick squeeze. "Way to go, partner. Things are starting to move along now."

Carrie smiled at him. *Now if only things between the two of us would start moving along,* she thought to herself. *That would really be cause for celebration.*

Chapter 14

"Now I remember why I never want to go to these women lawyers' association meetings," Carrie complained to Ann Muchin as they walked out of a meeting room at a swank Michigan Avenue hotel. "The officers of this group are all nuts!"

"Shhh!" Pat Grove scolded. She, along with Madree Williams, was following Carrie and Ann down the hall. "Keep your voice down. There's no need to offend anyone. Why don't we go to the bar and have a drink?"

"After listening to those idiots, I need one," Carrie said.

Ten minutes later the four colleagues were seated at a quiet table in the bar, sipping wine. "What a wasted evening!" Carrie said. "I knew I should've stayed at the office and prepared for Von Slaten's deposition."

"You've been prepared for that forever," Madree gently reminded her.

"Well, then, I could have gone home and cleaned Muffin's litter box. Honestly! What planet are some of these women from? Can you believe someone actually suggested that the group start a mentoring program where we'd go to women's prisons and encourage the inmates to consider careers in law?" She rolled her eyes. "Convicted felons can't even get a law license, for God's sake."

"I don't think they were suggesting that the inmates become lawyers," Madree said. "I think they just wanted to draw attention to the lack of educational opportunities for women in prison."

Carrie sighed. "Well, whatever they were trying to do, they're too far out of the mainstream for me. So if any of you are thinking of inviting me to another one of these little soirees anytime in the next decade, my answer is no." She took a sip of wine, then smiled at her friends. "Thank you for letting me vent. I feel much better now."

"So, has anything developed between you and Will yet?" Pat asked out of the blue.

Carrie immediately turned to Ann. "What have you been telling them?"

Ann shrugged. "Nothing much. And besides, you never said the subject was off-limits."

Carrie scowled.

"So what's up between you and the divine Mr. R?" Madree asked eagerly.

"Nothing," Carrie replied firmly.

"But you'd like something to happen," Pat prompted.

"This is embarrassing," Carrie protested. "It feels like high school."

"All developing romances feel like high school," Madree said sagely. "So you've got the hots for Will. That's understandable. The man is a hunk. The question is what you're going to do about it."

"Probably nothing," Carrie said.

"That's no fun," Pat said. "I think you should go after him. What have you got to lose?"

"You mean besides my self-respect?" Carrie volleyed back.

Madree waved her hand dismissively. "That's the coward's way out. You know what I always say: no guts, no glory. I agree with Pat. Go after him."

"Why not?" Ann put in.

Carrie started to laugh. "With friends like you, who needs enemies?" She took a deep breath, then let it out. "All right. I appreciate the vote of confidence, and I promise to take the matter under advisement. Now I really do need to go home and get my beauty sleep so I'm ready to give old Von Slaten hell in the morning."

"We'll let you off the hook for now," Madree teased. "But rest assured, we're going to be bugging you regularly for updates on this situation."

*   *   *

Carrie was psyched up for Werner Von Slaten's deposition. She had watched the hospital's administrator sitting through questioning of the other witnesses over the past couple of days. In each instance he had listened intently to the testimony, passed frequent notes to his attorneys, showed obvious irritation when witnesses gave answers that displeased him, and he had frequently given Carrie overtly nasty looks. All in all, he appeared to be enjoying the legal process. Carrie greatly looked forward to putting him on the hot seat and at least trying to make him squirm.

On the day he was to give his testimony, Von Slaten was, as usual, well dressed—double-breasted navy suit, white shirt, and conservative tie. After the court reporter administered the oath and Von Slaten promised to tell the truth, the whole truth, and nothing but the truth, he sat back in his chair, crossed his legs, and gave Carrie a cold little grin. He obviously was ready to do battle.

So am I, you arrogant bastard, Carrie thought to herself as she glared back at him. *You'd better brace yourself because you could be in for a bumpy ride.*

She began by going through Von Slaten's background, schooling, and previous employment. Prior to coming to Jackson Memorial five and a half years ago, Von Slaten had spent eight years at a smaller hospital in Seattle, and before that he'd been in Baltimore. Earlier in his career he had spent several years at a large Wall Street law firm.

"Were there any assaults, sexual or otherwise, on patients at any of the hospitals you were previously associated with?" Carrie asked.

"No," Von Slaten replied, scowling at her.

"Did those other hospitals ever have problems with patients engaging in sexual activity of any sort?"

"It is not unheard of for patients to engage in consensual sexual relations with each other," Von Slaten replied smoothly.

"Consensual activity aside, no patient was ever sexually assaulted at any of the hospitals where you were previously employed?"

"No."

"Was a comatose patient ever mysteriously impregnated at any of those other facilities?" Carrie asked.

"No." The administrator's scowl deepened.

"What are your duties as administrator at Jackson Memorial?"

"My duties run the gamut from making decisions regarding building-and-grounds upkeep to helping establish long-term growth plans to giving advice on legal matters."

"Who hired you, Mr. Von Slaten?"

"The hospital's board of directors."

"Do you have a written employment contract?"

"Yes."

"What is the term of that contract?"

"Two years."

"When does it expire?"

"In about six months."

"What is your salary?"

Von Slaten frowned and glanced over at his attorneys. Dennis Nolden gave a small nod, indicating that this line of questioning was appropriate.

"Two hundred twenty-five thousand dollars a year."

"Do you customarily receive year-end bonuses?"

"I have in the past, yes."

"What was the amount of your last bonus?"

"Thirty thousand dollars."

"Can the board of directors terminate your contract prior to its expiration date?"

"The contract can be terminated only for good cause," Von Slaten said smugly.

Carrie paused and took a sip of water. She hoped that by the time the *Buckley* lawsuit was over, the board would have good cause to unload this turkey.

"Are you involved in hiring any staff for the hospital?" Carrie inquired.

"Only administrative personnel."

"You have no involvement in hiring medical personnel?"

"No."

"Who is responsible for that type of hiring?"

"It depends on what position is being filled." Von Slaten shifted in his chair. "With respect to hiring decisions relating to medical personnel, there is a chain of command starting with the chief of staff."

Carrie referred to her notes again. "That would be Dr. Robert Morrow."

"That's right."

"Does Dr. Morrow himself do any hiring?"

"Yes, he is involved in filling all physicians' positions, with input from a committee that helps screen candidates."

"Who hired Dr. Morrow?"

"The full board of directors made the final decision, but prior to that they had assembled a search committee consisting of several board members, several physicians, and a number of laypeople."

"Were you a member of that committee?"

"No. Dr. Morrow had already been on staff about five years when I arrived at Jackson Memorial. However, he has announced his retirement effective August thirtieth, so plans are currently under way to find his replacement. I will be a member of that search committee."

"Who is responsible for hiring nurses?"

"Ms. Sandow, the hospital's nursing supervisor."

"Does Ms. Sandow also use a committee when she does her hiring?"

"I believe she does, yes."

"Who hires orderlies and receptionists?"

"I believe they are hired by the supervisor of the particular shift involved."

"Does the hospital have a personnel director?"

"Yes."

"What is that person's name?"

"Lee Arthur."

"How long has Mr. Arthur been employed by the hospital?"

"About eighteen months."

"Would Mr. Arthur handle personnel matters relating to physicians or just nurses and other staff?"

"All of the above."

"Mr. Von Slaten, during your tenure at Jackson Memorial, have any medical malpractice suits or other actions raising claims of negligent treatment of patients been filed against either the hospital or any of its doctors?"

"Objection," Dennis Nolden spoke up. "This line of inquiry is irrelevant." Anticipating Carrie's next question, he added, "Mr. Von Slaten may answer the question, but we reserve our right to bring this matter up with Judge Little at a future date."

"Fine," Carrie said congenially. Turning back to the witness, she said, "Do you remember the question, sir, or would you like to have it read back?"

"I remember the question," Von Slaten growled. "And the answer is yes."

"How many such actions have been filed during your tenure?"

"During my tenure, one action was filed. It named the hospital and one of the doctors on staff."

"What was the nature of the plaintiff's claim?"

Von Slaten cleared his throat. "A schizophrenic patient under the care of Dr. Kenneth Luebke committed suicide. His family sued Dr. Luebke and the hospital, alleging that the patient's suicidal tendencies should have been diagnosed."

"What specifically did the plaintiffs claim Dr. Luebke did wrong?"

"They asserted that he prescribed inappropriate and excessive drugs that caused the patient's mental condition to deteriorate and ultimately led to his suicide."

"What was the claim against the hospital?"

"Negligent hiring and inadequate supervision of Dr. Luebke."

"What was the outcome of the case?"

"The matter was tried to a jury, which found no negligence," Von Slaten replied smugly.

"And that was the only case, prior to this one, in which the hospital was named a defendant in a malpractice-type action, at least during your tenure as the hospital's administrator?"

"Yes."

"Are you aware of any such actions that have been filed against individual doctors on staff at Jackson Memorial?"

"I am not aware of any, no."

"You were present earlier this week for Dr. Peckham's deposition, correct?"

"Yes."

"Dr. Peckham seemed to be of the opinion that Dr. Luebke has a tendency to engage in excessive and/or risky treatment practices. Do you concur with that opinion?"

"Objection," Dennis Nolden spoke up. "That line of questioning is outside the scope of this witness's expertise."

Carrie looked at Von Slaten, indicating she was waiting for his answer.

Von Slaten shrugged. "I have no reason whatsoever to doubt Dr. Luebke's abilities as a doctor."

"Do you hold the same opinion of all the other doctors on staff?"

"Yes."

"Do you have much contact with the patients at the hospital?"

"Rarely. I try to leave the medical end of the hospital in Dr. Morrow's capable hands and confine myself to administrative matters."

"I see," Carrie said, as if she found this information particularly interesting. She paused to take a sip of water, then said conversationally, "Let's talk about the hospital's security for a moment. Do you have a security department?"

"Yes."

"Who is the head of that department?"

"Glen Fisher."

"Does Mr. Fisher have any assistants?"

"Yes, five of them."

"Who is responsible for establishing security regulations for the hospital?"

"There was a security plan in place when I arrived," Von Slaten replied. "I do not know who promulgated it, but it remains in force today."

"If someone, whether it be a staff member or a patient's

family, were to express a concern about security at the hospital to Mr. Fisher or his staff, is it likely you would be made aware of this concern?"

"I assume I would, yes."

"During the time you've been at Jackson Memorial, has anyone expressed such a concern?"

"Not to my knowledge."

"Could you please explain the security procedures in effect at Jackson Memorial, as best you understand them?"

"Normal, commonsense things. Visitors are expected to check in at the registration desk."

"*All* visitors?"

"Generally."

"What about families of long-term patients, such as the Buckleys? Surely they aren't expected to check in at the desk every time they come to visit?"

The administrator gave a short cough. "Well, of course, if visitors are known to the hospital staff, they can proceed directly to the patient's room without announcing themselves."

"I see," Carrie said. "Are there any security people posted throughout the building?"

"No."

"Does the security force conduct regular patrols of the buildings or grounds?"

"I don't believe so," Von Slaten replied with more than a hint of irritation.

"Why not?"

"Because we're running a hospital, not a prison," Von Slaten shot back.

"Are the doors at the hospital routinely kept locked?"

Von Slaten shifted in his seat. "Of course."

"How many entrances are there to the hospital?"

Von Slaten paused a moment to think. "I believe there are three in addition to the main entrance."

"Is the main entrance routinely locked?"

"Well, not during the day." Von Slaten backtracked a bit on his earlier answer. "The main door is locked after normal visiting hours."

"During what hours is it locked?"

"Ten p.m. until six a.m."

"What about the other three entrances? Are they locked at all times?"

Von Slaten hesitated a fraction of a second, but then answered boldly, "Of course."

"You're certain of that?"

"Yes."

Carrie took a long drink of water, savoring what was to come. "Mr. Von Slaten, do you recall the meeting you and I had in your office earlier this month?"

"Yes." Von Slaten frowned, indicating he didn't recall it fondly.

"Would it surprise you to learn that after leaving your office that day, I walked out the main entrance, went around the building and walked to a side entrance, where I found the door most assuredly unlocked?"

Von Slaten's mouth gaped open as Carrie continued. "And would it also surprise you to learn that I went through that entrance, walked up the stairs to the third floor, and could have gained access to any patient's room without anyone questioning my presence? Now I'm not an expert on security either, but those conditions don't strike me as particularly secure. What's your opinion?"

"Objection!" Dennis Nolden said belatedly. "Argumentative."

Von Slaten had turned a deep shade of crimson. "I remember your visit to the hospital only too well, Ms. Nelson," he snarled. "And what I recall most vividly was discovering you in the patients' ward and having to threaten to call the authorities to physically eject you before you would leave."

"Really?" Carrie gave a small smile. "I guess that part must have slipped my mind." She pretended to shuffle through her notes. "Let's assume for a moment that there was simply a momentary lapse in security the day I visited the hospital. And let's also assume that the side doors *are* normally kept locked. Who has keys to those doors?"

"I don't know for certain," Von Slaten admitted. "I would imagine most of the staff members have keys."

"Do you have keys to those doors?"

"Yes," Von Slaten admitted somewhat hesitantly.

Carrie moved in for the kill. "So there would be nothing to stop any staff member, including yourself, from entering the building through a side door, taking the stairs to the third floor, sneaking into a room such as the one occupied by Katherine Buckley, and viciously assaulting the patient, now would there?"

"Objection!" Dennis Nolden shouted.

"I withdraw the question," Carrie said quickly, but her diatribe had had its intended effect. The veins in Von Slaten's neck bulged out so prominently that he looked as though he were having a coronary.

"I think this would be an excellent time to take a break," Carrie said smoothly. "Why don't we reconvene in about ten minutes?"

Chapter 15

The hospital turned over its patient lists on Friday afternoon. Having been unsuccessful in resisting Carrie's demand for the information, Von Slaten and his attorneys had apparently decided to flood their opponents with material, no doubt hoping that the more people Carrie had to contact, the less chance she would have of stumbling across someone who might actually have some information that would help to prove that the hospital had been negligent in its treatment of Katherine Buckley.

While Jackson Memorial's patient population on any given date hovered around six hundred, and while the majority of those patients were long-term residents, about one-quarter of the hospital's beds were filled with people whose stays were of short duration. As a result, the total number of patients who had passed through the hospital during Katherine Buckley's eight-month tenure was in excess of twelve hundred.

Contemplating the monumental work that would be involved in attempting to contact the guardians of all those souls had caused Carrie's spirits, which had been pretty high following her success at Von Slaten's deposition, to plummet. "This was a stupid idea," she berated herself as she dropped the hefty patient list on Will's desk.

"I'll admit it's going to be a bigger job than we anticipated," Will agreed, "but I still think the idea is sound. It won't be an impossible task. We'll just need to call in some reinforcements." He then promptly E-mailed all of the firm's lawyers and paralegals, explaining the problem and entreating anyone who had a few hours to spare to come to the office on Saturday morning for a massive phone-a-thon.

A dozen casually dressed altruistic souls answered the call for help and met in the firm's library around ten o'clock on Saturday to receive their assignments. The response reminded Carrie how happy she was to be working at Ramquist and Dowd. There was really no one at the firm who wasn't willing to drop whatever he or she was doing to help a colleague in need. Even Burt Ramquist came to offer his services. Carrie couldn't imagine J. Richard Toussant stooping so low as to make phone calls. Hell, the way senior partners at Henley, Schuman were waited on hand and foot, she seriously doubted J. Richard ever placed his calls himself.

Carrie had split the patient list into sections and she handed each volunteer a group of twenty names. "If by some miracle you manage to reach all the people on your list and aren't completely burned out yet, come see me and I'll give you some more names," she said.

By noon, slow but steady progress had been made. Carrie sent out for pizza and after a quick bite in the firm's lunchroom, she, Ann Muchin, Pat Grove, and Madree Williams retired to Carrie's office for a brief chat before resuming their phone duties.

"I don't think it's going too badly," Madree said optimistically. "I've lined up five guardians who are willing to let you interview their patients."

"I have four so far," Pat Grove put in.

"I have six," Ann said proudly.

Carrie rolled her eyes. "You *would* have the record," she needled her friend. "I suppose you're expecting some sort of prize."

Ann stuck out her tongue.

"I really appreciate the help, guys," Carrie said, "but the more I think about this idea, the more it seems like we're looking for the proverbial needle in a haystack."

"It's a viable idea, and you won't know if it pans out unless you try," Pat said encouragingly.

"I know," Carrie said, "but think about it. Even if a

patient at the hospital did witness something, what are the odds someone who is hospitalized for a mental disorder is going to be able to give a coherent description of what they saw?"

Ann shrugged. "Don't prejudge the result until you've at least interviewed a sampling of the patients. You can always abandon the project if it truly ends up looking like a lost cause, but for now I say go with your first instinct."

"You're right," Carrie nodded. "I guess I'm just starting to get a little paranoid."

"It's too early for that," Pat pointed out cheerfully. "The case has barely gotten off the ground."

"I realize that," Carrie said, "but I'm beginning to see how difficult it's going to be to find out who assaulted Katherine. I'm accustomed to handling civil cases, where there are a lot of witnesses to the alleged wrong. They might disagree on what happened, but at least they're all able to testify and the jury can sort out their stories and weigh their credibility. I've never been involved in a case where the victim couldn't give her version of what happened."

"This must be how the police feel when they're investigating a murder," Madree suggested. "The victim isn't around to tell what happened, so to figure it out, the police have to rely on people the victim knew."

"Yes, but if my suspicions are right and someone at the hospital attacked Katherine, that person is obviously not going to speak up and tell me about it," Carrie replied. "And Von Slaten and the board have apparently decided that their best defense is to keep pointing the finger at Katherine's boyfriend."

"I know you don't want to consider this possibility," Madree said, "but let's assume for a minute that the boyfriend *was* the one who attacked her. Couldn't the hospital still be found negligent for allowing it to happen on their watch?"

Carrie made a face. "I don't think so. The boyfriend is virtually a member of the Buckley family. He was at the hospital all the time, with the family's blessing. I think the hospital would have every right to claim that the family should have been on notice that he might pose a danger to Katherine and as long as the family encouraged his visits, the hospital would be absolved from any responsibility for anything he did while he was there. But," she added, tossing back her hair, "I just don't believe the kid did it. Will had him in a law school class and said he was just wonderful, and I've met him myself, and I agree he just doesn't seem the type."

"From the way you've described the depositions so far, it sounds to me like the neurologist is a suspicious character," Ann commented.

Carrie nodded. "That's the impression I got."

"When are you taking his deposition?" Pat asked.

"Next week."

"Maybe you can squeeze some useful info out of him," Pat said.

"I hope so." Carrie crossed her legs. "I'm curious. Have any of you encountered any guardians who absolutely refuse to allow us to speak to their patients?" she asked her colleagues.

"I had one tell me to go to hell, then hang up on me," Madree replied.

"I had one tell me her family has been through enough dealing with her son's mental illness and I should be ashamed of myself for even thinking of imposing on them," Pat said. "But most people have been very understanding."

"Have you gotten the impression that the hospital might have already contacted any of these people?" Carrie asked.

"It hasn't sounded like it," Ann answered.

Pat and Madree also shook their heads.

"That's a relief," Carrie said. "Our task is going to be difficult enough without Von Slaten and his people poisoning people against us. But frankly, I am a little surprised the hospital hasn't tried to sabotage us."

"If I were you, I'd be happy for small favors," Madree put in.

At that moment, the door to Carrie's office opened and Will burst in. "Hi," he said. "I'm sorry I'm so late. I just got back from dog obedience class."

"How is the big puppy doing?" Madree asked.

"Great," Will replied. "He's a quick study. So, are you having much luck getting the guardians to cooperate?"

"It's going okay," Carrie replied, explaining their progress. "It's just awfully tedious."

"Good. I'd better get to my post," Will said as he headed back out the door. "Catch you all later."

"Now that is one fine-looking hunk of man," Madree commented as soon as the door shut behind Will. Turning to Carrie, she asked, "Any progress in that department?"

Carrie shook her head. "Unfortunately, no. He seems more interested in his dog than me."

"Maybe you should get a dog yourself," Pat suggested helpfully. "Then you and he could go to training class together."

"I don't want a dog," Carrie said in an exasperated tone. "All I want is a date."

Madree grinned mischievously. "If you ask me, I think what you really want is to get laid."

Ann and Pat guffawed.

"Honestly!" Carrie exclaimed, getting up from her desk and walking over to the window. "What is so terrible about me being attracted to someone I work with and wanting to get to know him better?"

"It probably wouldn't work out anyway," Ann said blithely, "so why bother?"

Carrie swung around to face her friend. "That's crap! Just because you don't want to devote time trying to cultivate a relationship with someone because it might interfere with your Type A personality, don't try to condemn me because I am interested in a relationship."

Ann's face fell. "I was only making a joke," she said. "You don't have to get nasty about it."

"I'm sorry," Carrie said quickly. "I'm just starting to get a little frustrated."

"Maybe you need to be more direct," Madree suggested. "I know you've been nice to him and you invited him to come to O'Malley's for drinks, but you'd probably do the same for anybody in the office. I think you need to come right out and let him know you're interested."

"How do I do that?" Carrie asked.

"By asking him for a real date," Madree replied.

"I don't know," Carrie hesitated. "Asking him to join us all at O'Malley's was very casual, so I could pretend it was no big deal when he said he had other plans. But if I ask him out on a real date and he turns me down, I'll be mortified and it'll be hard for me to face him afterward and everyone in the office will know about it—" Her voice trailed off.

"No guts, no glory," Madree replied.

"Say," Ann spoke up, "today is the twenty-eighth of February. Isn't that the day when women are supposed to ask men out?"

"Ann, you are pathetic!" Pat said, rolling her eyes.

"So you've often told me," Ann replied good-naturedly. "What did I say wrong now?"

"Sadie Hawkins Day only comes around in leap year, on February twenty-ninth," Pat patiently explained. "And traditionally that was when women would ask men to marry them."

"I knew that," Ann bluffed. "My point was that I agree with Madree that if Carrie really wants to get to first base with the guy, she should take the initiative and ask him out."

"Come to think of it, I asked my husband out on our first date," Madree said.

"You did?" Carrie said. "How did it turn out?"

"We ended up having a big fight and didn't speak to each other for two weeks afterward."

Carrie's jaw dropped.

"But it turned out fine," Madree hastened to add. "We just needed a little time to find out we were in sync."

"All right, I'll give the idea some serious thought," Carrie said. "Thanks a lot for the advice, guys. Now we'd better get back to our lists."

As Ann and Madree went back to their own offices, Pat lingered behind. "At the risk of raining on your parade," she said, "I have to say that Ann might actually have a point about relationships not always being a surefire route to happiness."

"Oh, come on," Carrie chided. "You don't mean to tell me you're sorry you got married."

"Of course not," Pat replied. "But there's a lot to be said for having a well-rounded life that includes a fulfilling career. For instance, I'll bet that when you were getting ready this morning you didn't have two little girls fighting over who could feed the cat and whether they should watch the *Barney* video or the *Cinderella* video first."

"No," Carrie admitted. "I only had to worry about feeding the cat."

"See?" Pat replied with a smile. "Your life is much simpler than mine. By the time I was ready to leave, Alex and Elayna were screaming at each other so loudly that I literally ran from the house to the garage, thrilled that my husband would have to deal with them for the rest of the day. So when you start complaining about what you're missing, don't forget you should also be thankful for what you've got."

"I'll try to remember that," Carrie said, clearly not convinced.

"Good girl," Pat said, squeezing Carrie's arm. "Now having said that, I do think you and Will would make a great couple, and if I were you, I'd pursue him relentlessly until he gave up and threw himself at my feet."

"I was hoping someone would take that approach," Carrie smiled. "Because I've decided that's exactly what I'm going to do."

Chapter 16

March swept into Chicago like the proverbial lion, dropping more than eight inches of wet, heavy snow on the city. On Tuesday morning, before Dr. Luebke's deposition, Carrie had an emergency hearing in her housing discrimination case. The slumlord, Joe Scalerri, had retaliated against the federal lawsuit by filing an eviction action against Carrie's clients. Carrie requested an immediate hearing in order to ask that the eviction action be stayed pending the outcome of the federal case. Through a combination of sweet talk and begging, Carrie had managed to get Judge Dennis Gottschalk's scheduling clerk to reluctantly squeeze her onto the judge's already overcrowded calendar at 8:15 A.M.

Although Carrie had thought she'd allowed herself ample time to get to court, traffic crawled the entire way and she had to run up the stairs and into Judge Gottschalk's second-floor courtroom to avoid being late. Panting and out of breath, she stomped her feet on the floor to rid her black leather boots of the excess slush as she hurriedly took a seat in the courtroom and shrugged off her coat.

She was thankful that she had told her clients not to bother coming to the hearing. "It'll be a very short proceeding, and it's strictly a discretionary call on the judge's part whether or not to grant the stay," Carrie explained in her phone call to Eureka Washington. "There won't be any live testimony, so there's no need for you to come."

"Thank God," Eureka replied. "I can't afford to take off no more time from work."

Carrie had no sooner pulled her file and a pen out of her briefcase than the proceeding that had been going on when she entered the courtroom concluded and the bailiff called her case. *"Scalerri versus Washington et al.,"* he announced.

As Carrie walked forward and took a seat at one of the counsel tables, she saw a middle-aged brown-haired man dressed in a black suit rise from a chair near the back of the room. He came forward and sat down at the other table. *Must be the slumlord's lawyer,* Carrie mused. She turned to take a quick look around the crowded courtroom. She didn't see Scalerri. That was fine with her. The day would be much brighter for not having to see his ugly mug.

"May I have the appearances, please," Judge Gottschalk, a very tall, stocky man in his fifties, called out in a booming voice.

"Edward Squiers for the plaintiff, Your Honor," the brown-haired man declared.

"Carrie Nelson for the defendants." Carrie was not familiar with Squiers but could only hope he would be easier to deal with than his client.

"Tell me about this big emergency, Ms. Nelson," Judge Gottschalk said. "And make it short and sweet. I've got a busy day ahead of me."

Carrie briefly explained the nature of the federal lawsuit. "Because the federal action was filed first, I am asking the court to hold the eviction matter in abeyance pending the outcome of the federal case."

"Mr. Squiers, what say you to that proposal?" the judge inquired.

"Your Honor, we believe that action would be fundamentally unfair. For all we know, the tenants have no intention of vigorously pursuing the federal case. It could languish for months or even years. In the meantime, my client is being deprived of the right to take possession of his property that is vested in him by virtue of the lease signed by each of the tenants."

"I take it that means you oppose Ms. Nelson's motion to hold this matter in abeyance," the judge said dryly.

"We do, Your Honor," Squiers replied.

As the judge shuffled through some papers in front of

him, Carrie could almost see the wheels turning in his head. Gottschalk had an extremely busy docket. Agreeing to Carrie's request would get one case out of his hair, at least temporarily and perhaps forever, depending on the outcome of the federal suit. The judge scratched some notes on a legal pad, then looked up at Carrie and said brightly, "Your idea sounds like a good one. Having given the matter due consideration, the court orders that the eviction action be held in abeyance for a period of six months."

Turning to Squiers, the judge added, "If, at the end of that time, the federal suit has not been disposed of, you may bring a motion to have this ruling reexamined." The judge banged his gavel down on the bench. "Next case."

As Carrie threw on her coat and prepared to head back to the office, Squiers caught her by the sleeve. "Joe just retained me yesterday," he said. "I guess I'm going to be handling the defense of the federal suit, too. Any chance we can maybe settle this whole thing?"

Carrie shrugged. "That all depends. Get me a written proposal and I'll take it up with my clients."

Squiers nodded. "Sounds good. I'll be in touch."

Carrie raced off to her car, chuckling to herself. Squiers obviously didn't know Joe Scalerri very well. There was no way in hell the slumlord would authorize a settlement, and if he got wind of the fact that his lawyer was proposing such a blasphemous thing, poor Eddie Squiers would almost certainly be fired and from the rumors she'd heard about Scalerri, perhaps even find himself roughed up a little, courtesy of one of Joe's many seedy friends. *Too bad,* Carrie thought blithely as she reached the car. That was the price Squiers would have to pay for taking on such a lowlife as a client.

Dr. Kenneth Luebke was by far the most contentious witness deposed to date in the *Buckley* case. From the moment the court reporter administered the oath, it was readily apparent that the doctor would have preferred performing brain surgery on himself to giving testimony in a lawsuit.

Dr. Luebke was taller than average. In his fifties, he had a thick head of sandy-colored hair. Unlike the other witnesses, who relied on Dennis Nolden and Charlene Bull to represent their interests, Dr. Luebke brought his own lawyer with him to the deposition. Steve O'Connor, a nice looking man in his mid-forties, was a partner at one of the city's many large law firms. Carrie had encountered him briefly on a couple of other cases, and he had seemed like a decent enough fellow. It would be interesting to see how he dealt with this obviously disgruntled client.

Will was handling Dr. Luebke's questioning, which gave Carrie the opportunity to sit back and observe. After having the doctor detail his impressive credentials and explain that he had been associated with Jackson Memorial for nine years, Will moved into his treatment of Katherine Buckley.

"When did you first become involved in Katherine's treatment?" Will asked.

"The day she arrived at the hospital," Dr. Luebke replied in a clipped tone.

"Did you continue to treat her throughout the time she remained a patient?"

"Yes."

"What did your treatment of Katherine entail?"

"I was primarily responsible for assessing and then attempting to restore her neurological function."

"Could you be a little more specific?"

"I worked with the other physicians on Ms. Buckley's care team to develop a plan that would help maintain her physical well-being as well as maximize recovery of her neurological function."

Will referred to notes he had made from Katherine's medical records. "In the course of your treatment, did you prescribe various drugs for Katherine?"

"Yes."

"Soon after her arrival, Dr. Peckham performed several procedures to halt intercranial bleeding, did he not?"

"Yes."

"And Dr. Peckham also prescribed drugs to reduce swelling in Ms. Buckley's brain?"

"That is correct."

"Once that problem was under control, you administered several drugs that you hoped would restore neurological function."

"Yes."

"Were any of this latter category of drugs experimental?"

The doctor frowned and hesitated a moment but then answered, "One of the drugs is considered experimental, yes."

Carrie nodded and scratched a note on her yellow pad. She'd had Jackie Crabb go through the list of Katherine's meds and that research had revealed that Dr. Luebke had prescribed a drug not yet approved by the FDA.

"That would be vicephrin?" Will prompted.

"Yes."

"Had you prescribed that drug for other patients before choosing it for Katherine?"

"Yes."

"Did the drug produce the desired result in those other patients?"

"In two of them it did, yes."

"Did it produce the desired result in Katherine?"

"No."

"In fact, none of the drugs or other therapy tried on Katherine restored any brain function, isn't that correct?"

The doctor shifted irritably in his chair. "Yes, it is. Unfortunately, nothing that we tried brought about any change in her condition."

"Did you ever consider trying any other therapies or consulting other experts in the field in an effort to help Katherine?"

Dr. Luebke looked to his attorney for assistance. O'Connor spoke up immediately and said, "I'm going to object to a continuation of this line of questioning and instruct Dr. Luebke not to answer. Counselor, I've reviewed your complaint against the hospital, and nowhere does it state a claim against Dr. Luebke or, for that matter, against any other medical provider for any deficiencies in Katherine's treatment. Let's stick to the germane inquiry here, which is what, if anything, my client might know about the circumstances under which Katherine Buckley became pregnant."

Don't worry, Carrie thought to herself. *That line of questioning will be coming right up.*

"I intend to take your objection up with Judge Little at a later date," Will replied. Turning back to the doctor, he asked, "How did you come to learn about Katherine's pregnancy?"

"Mr. Von Slaten told me."

"When was that?"

"I believe it was the day after Ms. Buckley was transferred to her new hospital. I had been at a medical conference in Portland the two days prior to that, so I didn't learn what had happened until I returned."

"What was your reaction when you learned about the pregnancy?"

"I was surprised, of course."

"Merely surprised?"

Dr. Luebke frowned. "What do you want me to say? That I went into shock?"

"Ken," Steve O'Connor said in an admonishing tone. In response to his lawyer's rebuke, the doctor clenched his jaw.

"Dr. Luebke, did you ever walk into Katherine's room and find a man alone with her?"

"Yes, I believe at various times I observed Katherine's father, her fiancé, and the family's minister alone with her."

"Were *you* ever alone with Katherine?" Will asked.

"What kind of question is that?" Dr. Luebke snapped. "Of course I was! I was her doctor."

Carrie suppressed a smile as Will moved on. "Did you ever notice any man behaving inappropriately around Katherine?"

"No."

"Do you have any idea who might be responsible for the pregnancy?"

"Objection," O'Connor interjected. "Calls for speculation. You may answer," he instructed Luebke.

"I have no idea whatsoever."

"Do you think it's within the realm of possibility that another patient at the hospital could have assaulted Katherine?"

"Objection," O'Connor said again. "Same grounds."

"I suppose anything is possible," the doctor answered curtly.

"During the eight months Katherine was a patient at the hospital, were there ever any patients there whom you would term violent or dangerous?"

The doctor shrugged. "It's very difficult to answer that. Occasionally we do get patients who exhibit wild or uncontrollable behavior, but in all such cases those persons are segregated in a locked ward and the most stringent security precautions are maintained to see that they do not harm themselves or others."

"Are the individual rooms where those patients are housed locked?"

"Yes."

"Are such patients kept in restraints?"

"If their condition demands it, yes."

"Who has access to the keys that open those locked doors?"

"Appropriate staff people."

"Such as yourself?"

Dr. Luebke glared at Will. "Of course. What are you suggesting?"

We're suggesting that security at your hospital is virtually nil, Carrie thought.

"Nothing at all," Will replied blithely. "I'm merely trying to gather information."

"Then I'd appreciate it if you'd keep your personal sarcasm to yourself," the doctor snarled.

"I move to strike that last response," O'Connor said.

"I join in the motion," Charlene Bull hastened to add.

"Well, I object to your objections," Will shot back. "I think the transcript should accurately reflect Dr. Luebke's state of mind and his obvious belligerent attitude and lack of respect for these proceedings."

My, my, Carrie thought, shifting in her seat. *Things are beginning to get a little tense.*

"Why don't we take this up with Judge Little?" O'Connor said in a raised voice.

"Fine," Will answered curtly. "Dr. Luebke, have you ever been sued for medical malpractice?"

Dr. Luebke's face instantly turned a deep shade of crimson.

"Objection," O'Connor snapped. "That is completely irrelevant to this proceeding."

Will ignored the lawyer. "Isn't it true, Doctor, that you have been sued at least four times and in each case the plaintiffs claimed that you used inappropriate or excessive forms of treatment that caused them substantial harm?"

"Objection!" O'Connor bellowed.

Carrie smiled to herself. The strategy she and Will had devised was working. They had obviously struck a nerve.

Will pressed on, watching Dr. Luebke's face grow even more mottled. "And isn't it true that two of those cases ended in a settlement being paid by your malpractice carrier?"

"Objection!" O'Connor virtually screamed the word. "You are completely out of line here, counselor, and if you persist in this harassment I will ask Judge Little to find you in contempt."

"In that case, I have no further questions at this time," Will said smoothly, "but I reserve the right to recall this witness at a later date."

That was too much for Dr. Luebke. He jumped to his feet. "The hell you will!" he exclaimed, pointing his index finger angrily at Will. "I've endured all the indignities I'm going to from you. I know where all this is coming from. I'll bet dollars to doughnuts that Gerald Peckham is filling your head with this nonsense. Well, I wouldn't put much stock in what he says, if I were you."

"And why is that?" Will asked politely as the court reporter continued to record every word that was uttered.

"Because he dearly covets the chief of staff position that's opening up this summer," Dr. Luebke spat, "and he views me as his chief rival and has made it clear that he will resort to any lengths to get the job, that's why." With that, the doctor stormed angrily out of the room, his lawyer in close pursuit.

Well, well, Carrie thought as she looked at the empty chair where Dr. Luebke had been sitting. Something had obviously tripped the man's trigger. It was going to be an interesting exercise to try to learn what it was that got him so rattled.

Chapter 17

Carrie already had her coat on and was ready to head to Jackson Memorial to begin her first round of patient interviews on Friday morning when her intercom buzzed. "Carrie Nelson," she answered, snatching up the receiver.

"Carrie, it's Karen Hundley," Will's secretary announced herself. "Todd Fleming is calling for Will, but he's in court all day. Do you have time to talk to him?"

"Sure," Carrie replied. "Hello, Todd?"

"Carrie?" a very weary voice said.

"Yes. What can I do for you?"

"Detective Clauff was back to interview me two more times this week. I can't take much more of this."

"I'm so sorry to hear that," Carrie replied. "Would you like me to talk to him? Try to persuade him to back off?"

"It won't do any good," Todd replied bitterly. "He's made that very clear. Listen, the reason I'm calling is I've been giving this whole thing a lot of thought, and I'd like to take a lie detector test to help clear myself. I was wondering if you could set it up."

"Do you really think it would help?" Carrie asked. "After all, the results of lie detector tests aren't admissible in court."

"I know that, but I've heard that sometimes prosecutors can be persuaded not to file charges if a suspect passes a test conclusively. I know it sounds desperate," Todd said, his voice quivering, "but I'm at the end of my rope. I offered to submit to a blood test to disprove paternity, but I talked to one of Katherine's doctors and she said it could be dangerous to Katherine and the baby to try to obtain a fetal tissue sample right now. She said she'd prefer to wait until the baby is born to do any testing, but I can't stand to wait that long. I'm going to go crazy if I don't get this resolved soon. Please help me." The young man sounded near tears.

"I'll try," Carrie promised. "Exactly what is it you want me to do?"

"See if you can find someone reputable to administer the test and then try to sell the detective and his boss on the idea."

"I'll see what I can do," Carrie agreed. "But I can't guarantee that the police will go for it."

"I understand," Todd said, sounding greatly relieved. "But at least I'll feel like I'm doing something constructive instead of just sitting here waiting for the axe to fall."

"Leave it to me. I'll get back to you as soon as I can. In the meantime, try to keep your chin up," Carrie said encouragingly. "You've got finals coming up, and you've got to be psyched for those."

"Thanks, Carrie. I really appreciate it."

"Poor kid," Carrie murmured as she hung up the phone. She wanted to be able to tell him everything would be okay, but if the truth were known, with every day that went by she was a bit less confident that she would ever be able to find out what had really happened to Katherine.

In the past week, Carrie and her colleagues had obtained written authorizations from the guardians of fifty patients agreeing that their loved ones could be interviewed about their knowledge of Katherine's assault. Some of those patients had already returned home or been transferred to other facilities, and Will and Jackie Crabb were going to concentrate on interviewing that group.

The interviews with patients at the hospital were going to be very time-consuming, and Carrie knew she would need help if she was to have any chance of getting through them in time. She had enlisted two of the firm's paralegals, Joan Bedner and Teresa Timkin, to help with her preliminary talks with the patients.

As Carrie drove to the hospital, her two passengers, both

ebullient women in their thirties who were well aware of Carrie's reticence about the assignment, engaged in some good-natured kidding at their superior's expense.

"This will be fun," Teresa said. "Just like *One Flew over the Cuckoo's Nest*."

"I agree," Joan said. "But I think we're going about this wrong. I think Carrie could get more information if she went undercover at the hospital, like that woman reporter in the 1880s who pretended to be a mental patient and then wrote an exposé about the horrid conditions in the hospital. What was her name?"

"Nellie Bly," Teresa replied.

"That's right," Joan said. "Don't you think that would be a challenging assignment, Carrie?"

"What I think is that you two are going to find yourselves in the unemployment line if you keep this up," Carrie grumbled. She pulled into the hospital's parking lot. "Well, here we are. Any last-minute questions?"

"Nope," the two women answered in unison.

"Well, then, let's get out there and strike a blow for truth, justice, and revenge for poor Katherine Buckley."

The three women got out of the car and headed for the building.

Carrie had with her thirty authorizations covering patients still residing at Jackson Memorial. She, Joan, and Teresa had split them up and agreed that they would work until five o'clock, covering as many patients as they could. While Carrie had the utmost faith in her assistants' abilities, she had told them that if it sounded even remotely possible that a patient might have some useful information, Carrie was to be notified and she would reinterview that patient herself.

Although Von Slaten had initially demanded that he be present whenever Carrie interviewed anyone at the hospital, he had apparently realized that following through on this requirement would require an inordinate amount of his time, so Dennis Nolden had sent word that Carrie was merely to give copies of the signed authorizations to the nursing supervisor on duty and then she would be free to talk to the patients.

All of the day's planned interviews were with patients on the third floor, where Katherine had been housed. The first person on Carrie's list was Gary Harwood. "Down the hall on the left," the nursing supervisor directed.

Carrie located the room, then stood outside a moment and took a deep breath. *Well, here goes,* she thought as she gave a brief knock and walked inside. She immediately saw a person sitting in a chair, but then she did a double take. Instead of Gary Harwood, the room's occupant was a young dark-haired woman, dressed in a plaid skirt and a black pullover sweater, ribbed black pantyhose, and black loafers. She was looking at the current issue of *Vogue*. "Can I help you?" the young woman asked pleasantly.

"Ah . . ." Carrie stammered. "I'm sorry. I must have the wrong room. Please excuse me."

"No problem," the woman said, turning her attention back to her magazine.

Carrie walked back to the reception desk. "I must have misunderstood the room number you just gave me," she said to the nurse. "I'm looking for Gary Harwood, but there's a woman in that room."

The nurse laughed. "That's the right room. Didn't anyone tell you?"

"Tell me what?" Carrie asked, perplexed.

"Gary Harwood has a dual personality. What you just saw was *Mary* Harwood."

Carrie's face dropped. "You're kidding me. That couldn't have been a man."

The nurse nodded emphatically. "Oh, yes, it is. He's got quite a touch with hair and makeup, doesn't he? He's got an eye for fashion, too. He's always giving us women tips on accessorizing."

Carrie could feel her stomach churning. This job was going to be even more difficult than she'd anticipated. "So I should call him Mary?" she asked, swallowing hard.

The nurse nodded. "That's right." On seeing Carrie's unease, she added, "There's nothing to be afraid of. He's perfectly charming, whether he's Gary or Mary."

Carrie marched resolutely back down the hall and knocked on the door again. When bidden to enter, she walked in and mustered up a warm smile. "Sorry to bother you again, but it turns out you *are* the person I wanted to see."

"Really?" Mary/Gary replied. "That's wonderful. I love company." She patted the chair next to her. "Come, sit down." As Carrie complied, Mary/Gary said, "I love your red coat."

"Thank you," Carrie replied weakly.

"Red's a great color on you. You should always stick with either bright colors or black. Anything in between will wash you out."

"I'll remember that," Carrie murmured. She took a deep breath. "My name is Carrie Nelson, and I'm a lawyer. Your mother said it would be all right for me to talk to you."

"Of course," Mary/Gary said matter-of-factly, as if being interviewed by a lawyer was an everyday occurrence. "What can I do for you?"

Relieved that Mary/Gary at least *sounded* like a rational human being, Carrie briefly described what had happened to Katherine and outlined her own quest to find the person responsible.

"Pregnant!" Mary/Gary said, aghast. "How awful! How traumatizing! The poor dear. Yes, I remember Katherine very well. I often walk around the halls for something to do. Sitting in here all day makes me stir-crazy," she confided. "And every time I'd walk past Katherine's room, I'd think how tragic her situation was. But did I witness anything happening to her? No, I did not. Of course I would have reported it if I had. We girls need to stick together, you know."

Carrie got up from her chair. "Well, thank you for your time."

"I'm sorry I couldn't be any help," Mary/Gary said ruefully. "But I enjoyed our little chat. Do stop in again if you're in the area. And if I might make a suggestion?"

"Ah . . . sure," Carrie replied.

"Your lipstick is a tad on the light side," Mary/Gary said. "Chanel just came out with a new wine shade that would look fabulous on you."

"I'll look for it," Carrie said weakly as she fled the room.

All right. Carrie gave herself a mental pep talk as she walked back to the nurse's station. *That's one down. It wasn't so bad. It was bizarre, but it wasn't so bad.*

The next three patients, two (actual) women and a man, were not as strange as Mary/Gary, but they were no more illuminating when it came to having any knowledge of what had happened to Katherine. At four-twenty, Carrie gave the nursing supervisor the guardian's authorization for her last interview of the day, Scott Rouleau.

Madree Williams had been the one who had made contact with Scott's sister and guardian, Laurie Rouleau. As Carrie walked down the hall toward Scott's room, she looked over the notes Madree had made during her phone conversation with Laurie. "She saw the blurb in the paper about what happened to Katherine. Thinks it's awful and is happy to have us talk to Scott, although she doubts he will be much help. He's been at the hospital five months. He suffered brain trauma following a car accident. He is also paranoid schizophrenic, and the accident greatly aggravated his condition. He has some good days, but more bad ones. On the bad days he is often delusional and is apt to think he's Julius Caesar or some other illustrious personage. Before his illness got out of control, Scott used to design computer games, and he is very intelligent. Laurie wishes us luck."

Scott's room was across the hall from Katherine's, near the stairway. Carrie rapped on his door and heard a clear voice respond, "Come in." Opening the door and stepping inside, she encountered a good-looking dark-haired man in his late twenties sitting at a desk, a laptop computer in front of him.

"Scott?" Carrie asked.

The young man turned toward her, stuck out his chin, and announced imperially, "I am Ra, the Sun God."

Okay, Carrie thought. *At least he's sticking with the correct gender instead of proclaiming himself Marie Antoinette.* Deciding that the best tactic might be to ignore the identity issue, she said conversationally, "Your sister, Laurie, said it'd be all right if I talked to you. Is that okay with you?"

"Certainly," Scott replied, looking down his nose at her. "What is your name?"

"I'm Carrie Nelson, and I'm a lawyer. Do you understand what that means?"

"Of course. Abraham Lincoln was a lawyer. So were Thomas Jefferson and John Marshall." He cocked his head and pointed to the chair next to him. "Would you like to sit down?"

"Yes, I would," Carrie replied. After taking her seat, she said, "Do you remember Katherine Buckley? She was a young woman who used to be in a room across the hall."

"What happened to her?" Scott asked. "She's not there anymore. Is she dead?"

"No, she's not dead. She was moved to a different hospital. Do you remember Katherine?"

There was no reply.

"Katherine and her family are my clients. The reason I wanted to talk to you is I was wondering if you ever saw anyone hurt Katherine or do something bad to her."

"Is she dead?" Scott asked again, this time in a louder voice.

Carrie shook her head. "No. She's alive, but she's not here anymore." She suddenly realized what might have prompted Scott's question, and she went on, "Katherine is in a coma. Do you understand what that means? It's like she's asleep permanently. She can't wake up. Is that why you thought she was dead?"

No response.

Carrie tried again. "Scott, did you see something happen to Katherine?"

More silence.

"Did you ever look into Katherine's room?"

"My doctor says I shouldn't talk to the other patients."

"Why is that?" Carrie asked.

"He says I scare them." He looked at Carrie intently. "Are you scared of me?"

"No," Carrie replied, "I'm not scared of you. Who is your doctor?"

"Dr. Luebke," Scott answered.

Carrie suppressed a groan. That man again. She was starting to see a pattern.

"Scott, can you tell me anything at all about Katherine?"

"I am King Tut, Ruler of All Egypt." Scott crossed his arms in front of his chest.

Carrie suddenly felt weary and dejected. This whole day had been a waste of time. She got up from her chair. "Thank you for your time, Scott. It was nice talking to you."

"Give me liberty or give me death!" Scott shouted as Carrie left the room.

She met up with Joan and Teresa at the nurses' station. "Let's get out of here," Carrie urged. "I'm starting to feel like the walls are closing in."

Once they had left the building, Carrie asked, "So, did either of you come up with any leads?"

"Nothing," Joan replied. "But I did learn that a man's libido is evidently the last thing to go. One old guy I interviewed, who was clearly in the advanced stages of Alzheimer's, kept asking me if he should show me why they used to call him 'Big Dick.' There's definitely no pervert like an old pervert."

"Speaking of perverts," Teresa laughed, "thanks a lot, Carrie, for making me interview Bob Brakefield."

"Why?" Carrie asked. "What did he do?"

"He pinched me in the ass!" Teresa exclaimed.

Carrie laughed. "You're kidding! What did you do?"

"I slapped him across his wrinkly old face," Teresa replied.

"Oh, great." Carrie rolled her eyes. "I hope no one saw you or we'll get hit with a lawsuit for abusing patients."

"No one saw it," Teresa assured her. "And I don't think

it fazed him much. He looked very hurt for a minute, but when I left the room he told me I was a nice person."

"Swell," Carrie said. They had reached the car. As Carrie was unlocking the doors, a late-model, obviously very expensive sports car pulled up next to them. The driver rolled down the window. It was Dr. Peckham.

"Ms. Nelson. How are you today?" the doctor asked pleasantly.

"Fine," Carrie replied. "And you?"

"Very well. I thought you might be interested to know that I have completed my review of those medical records we spoke about at my deposition, and I am prepared to reconvene the proceeding at your convenience."

Carrie brightened. At least someone connected with the hospital was willing to cooperate with her investigation. "That's great. I'll talk to the hospital's lawyers and have them schedule a mutually convenient date."

"Good," Dr. Peckham replied. "Have a nice evening." He rolled up the window and headed toward the staff parking lot.

"That's some car he's driving," Teresa said, as the three women got into Carrie's vehicle. "What kind is it?"

"It's an Aston Martin DB7," Joan replied without hesitation. "They go for about a hundred and thirty thou."

"How did you know that?" Carrie asked, impressed. "At that price there can't be more than a handful of them in the whole state."

"A few years back my brother worked at a place that detailed expensive cars," Joan replied. "I still keep up on high-end autos. It's sort of a hobby."

"A hundred and thirty thousand for a car," Teresa said incredulously. "Talk about conspicuous consumption!"

"Yeah," Carrie agreed, as she pulled out of the parking lot. "And people think lawyers make too much money."

Chapter 18

On Monday morning Carrie and Will met in his office and compared notes on their patient interviews.

Will and Jackie Crabb had worked all day Saturday tracking down former Jackson Memorial patients who were now scattered all over the greater Chicago area. Unfortunately, their efforts had turned up as little information as Carrie's team had unearthed at the hospital.

"We came up with a big goose egg," Will said ruefully, leaning back in his chair.

"Us, too," Carrie said, adjusting the belt on her maroon wool dress. "It's depressing, isn't it?"

Will nodded. "What's even more depressing is seeing firsthand how much misery there is in the world. God, some of the people we talked to were in pretty rough shape. I spoke to one guy who'd tried to commit suicide by cutting his head off with a chain saw."

"That's gross!" Carrie exclaimed, making a face. "With all the possible ways to kill yourself, who would think of that method?"

"I don't know," Will said. "It must've just been a cry for help. All the poor guy succeeded in doing was giving himself a scar that makes him look like Frankenstein's monster. Anyway, seeing people in such bad shape sure makes you thankful for what you've got."

"That's true," Carrie agreed. "I just wish we'd found one person who could report seeing something odd going on in Katherine's room. Even if the report didn't pan out, at least I'd feel like we were on the right track."

"I guess it was naive of us to think this was going to be easy," Will commented.

"So you don't think we should forget about the patient angle and just concentrate on interviewing everyone on staff?" Carrie asked earnestly.

"Forget about interviewing the patients? No way!" Will replied at once. "It's much too early even to consider that."

"What if it turns out that one of the patients whose guardian refused to give us authorization is the one person who saw Katherine being assaulted?" Carrie pressed.

"If we aren't allowed to talk to that patient, we'll never find that out, will we?" Will countered. "Look, we don't know what we might come up with. We just have to keep pecking away at our list."

"You're probably right," Carrie agreed, "but you have to admit it's disheartening to work this hard and have nothing to show for it."

"I'm sure you'll agree that Katherine and her family are worth working hard for," Will said, giving her a gentle prod.

"Of course they are," Carrie said, rising to the bait. "I'm just tired and grumpy today. Pay no attention to me when I'm like this."

Will smiled. "It's pretty hard not to pay attention to you."

Carrie could feel her pulse quicken. She was just as attracted to Will as ever, and she wanted to take her friends' advice and do something about it, but so far the timing just hadn't been right. Dared she hope that he was starting to have similar feelings?

"What do you mean, it's hard not to pay attention to me?" she asked evenly.

"I just meant that whenever you're around you're always so intent on what you're doing and so self-assured that it's hard to ignore you."

"Oh." Carrie's heart dropped to her feet. So much for thinking that Will was sharing her romantic feelings. She pretended to rub her eyes to keep him from seeing her disappointment. "Well, anyway, speaking of Katherine and her family, I got a call from Todd Fleming on Friday. Actually, he'd called for you, but when he found out you were out of the office, he asked to talk to me."

"How's he doing?" Will asked with obvious concern.

"He's hanging on," Carrie replied, "but that damn detective is still on his case and Todd is desperate to do whatever it takes to get out from under it."

"Such as?" Will asked.

"He wants us to set up a polygraph test. He thinks if he passes it, the detective will have to start looking for a new suspect."

Will rubbed his hand over his chin. "What do you think of the idea?"

"I'm not sure," Carrie replied. "I told Todd I'd look into it."

"Do you really think it's wise?" Will asked. "What if he fails the test?"

"How can he fail it if he didn't assault her?" Carrie countered. "It seems to me it's a no-lose situation for Todd. If he passes conclusively, we can put pressure on the detective to ease up on him. And if the result is inconclusive, he won't be any worse off than he is now. Right?"

"Well, when you put it that way—" Will agreed.

"Do you know any polygraph operators?"

"No, I don't," Will replied. "But didn't Burt handle some criminal cases years ago? He might still have some contacts in that field."

"That's a good idea," Carrie said. "I'll go talk to him right away." She got up from her chair.

"Are you doing any more patient interviews this week?"

"Yeah. I'm planning to go back to the hospital on Wednesday. And Joan and Teresa will probably go up there on their own tomorrow."

"Jackie and I are going to do some more over the next few days, too."

"Well, then, good luck to us all."

"Right," Will agreed. "And let's get together sometime

on Thursday to go over our strategy for Friday's depositions."

"Sounds good." Carrie gave a small wave as she headed out the door. Once out in the hall, she closed her eyes for an instant and heaved a big sigh. It was probably a good thing the *Buckley* case was going to be consuming most of her free time for the foreseeable future because it was obvious that Will Rollston had more romantic inclinations toward his dog than he did toward her.

From Will's office, Carrie headed right over to speak to Burt Ramquist. Stopping for a moment at Dona Winkler's desk, she picked up an eight-by-ten photo of a smiling boy in a black robe. "Is this your son?" she asked. "He's sure growing up."

"Isn't he?" Dona agreed proudly. "Ryan started singing in a boys' choir about six months ago and just loves it. They're going to a competition in New Haven this summer. He's already counting the days."

"Good for him," Carrie said. "More kids should cultivate wholesome interests like that." She motioned toward Burt's office. "Is he busy? I could use some advice about the *Buckley* case."

"Go right on in," Dona replied. "He's working on a brief, but interruptions never seem to bother him."

Carrie knocked lightly on the senior partner's door, then opened it and walked into his office.

Burt Ramquist was sitting at his desk, which was stacked two feet high with books and papers. Elvis's "If I Can Dream" was playing softly in the background.

"Carrie," Burt greeted her warmly. "Have a seat. How goes the battle?"

Carrie plopped down in one of the chairs in front of the desk. "I think it's going to get ugly before it's over."

"You're probably right," Burt agreed. "As a matter of fact, I got a call a little while ago from Steve O'Connor." Seeing Carrie's surprise, Burt said facetiously, "You remember him? Dr. Luebke's lawyer."

"I remember him," Carrie replied. "Why was he calling you?"

"To complain about what he termed Will's and your inappropriate, disrespectful treatment of his client."

"That little weasel!" Carrie exploded, her depression and lethargy of moments before now forgotten. "Why did he call you? Why didn't he come to Will and me directly if he has a problem with our tactics?"

"Don't get excited," Burt chuckled. "Mr. O'Connor was obviously under the misimpression that as a name partner at this firm I somehow have control over your behavior and/or demeanor. I believe I disabused him of that notion."

"How did he take that news?" Carrie asked.

"I don't think he was pleased, but he was a gentleman and hid his disappointment fairly well." He looked at her expectantly. "What can I do for you?"

Carrie explained her conversation with Todd Fleming. "Do you know any reputable polygraph operators?"

"As a matter of fact, I do," Burt replied. "Call John Ruppert. He has an office on Halstad. And if he can't help you, then I'd suggest Charlie Bohachek. Both of them have been in business a long time and are highly respected in their field."

"Great. I'll get in touch with them right away. Do you think having Todd pursue a polygraph exam is a dumb idea?"

"Nothing is ever a dumb idea if it works," Burt replied with a smile. "Seriously, I don't know what to tell you. It's an area that generates a lot of controversy. I guess my feeling is that if Todd truly wants to pursue it, then you have an obligation to help him."

Carrie nodded. "That's exactly how I felt."

Burt leaned back in his chair. "So, how are things going with the case?"

"I'd like to say slow but sure, but up until now it's been more like slow and futile." She filled him in on the patient interviews. "They're going to be very time-consuming, and we may have to abandon the idea at some point, but for now we're going to give it our best shot."

"Has any useful information come out of the depositions?" Burt asked.

Carrie shook her head. "Not much. The most interesting thing to me is that for some reason Dr. Luebke is obviously very unhappy to be involved in this case. He basically got up and walked out of his deposition and said he had no intention of coming back at a later date. And now with O'Connor's call to you, I can't help but wonder if the good doctor doesn't have something to hide."

"Maybe he just dislikes lawyers. A lot of doctors do, you know. One nasty malpractice case can ruin them for life, even if they're exonerated."

"Maybe," Carrie said skeptically. "But I just have a feeling there's something more to it than that."

"Didn't I hear Will mention that this Dr. Luebke is vying for the hospital's chief of staff position?"

"That's right. He and Gerald Peckham, the neurosurgeon who treated Katherine, are both angling for the job."

"What kind of a fellow is Dr. Peckham?"

"I think he's very nice," Carrie replied. "He's one of the few people connected with the hospital who haven't treated me like I'm some sort of pariah. In fact, he's the one who first put me onto the notion that Dr. Luebke might be hiding something."

"How did that come about?"

Carrie explained about Dr. Peckham's comments at his deposition that Dr. Luebke sometimes engaged in unnecessary treatment. "I'm doing a follow-up deposition of Dr. Peckham on Friday to pin him down on his opinion about Dr. Luebke's care."

Burt frowned. "Be careful not to let him bamboozle you."

"What do you mean?" Carrie asked, obviously surprised at the comment.

"From what you've told me, it sounds like each doctor has an axe to grind. They both want the chief of staff position, and being the hard-driving people they are, they're probably willing to do almost anything to get it, including engaging in character assassination of their rivals."

"I don't know about that," Carrie said. "I'm usually a pretty good judge of character, and right now my gut is telling me that Peckham is one of the good guys and Luebke is something else. Just exactly what else he is, I don't know, but I intend to find out."

"Do you have any other possible suspects?" Burt asked.

Carrie shook her head. "Not really. So far it looks like the only men who were ever seen alone with Katherine, besides her doctors, were her father, Todd Fleming, and an Episcopal bishop who's an old friend of the family."

"Could the bishop have done it?" Burt prompted.

Carrie made a face. "I don't think so. I met him, and he seemed very nice."

"Well, if I were you I wouldn't rule him—or anyone else—out just yet."

Carrie sighed. "I know it's totally irrational, but I keep hoping Katherine will miraculously come out of the coma and tell us just exactly what happened to her. Not only would that be wonderful for her family, it'd sure make the case a lot easier."

Burt smiled. "I think she's counting on you to make the case for her."

Carrie nodded. "I know that. It's what keeps me going day to day. But I have to admit it's a little scary being one full month into discovery and still having absolutely no leads."

"You can do it," Burt said encouragingly. "You just have to keep the faith. Or—" he fingered his tie tack—"as someone once eloquently put it, you gotta take care of business, baby."

Carrie smiled. "That's good advice, as always." She got up from her chair. "Thanks a lot for the leads on a polygraph examiner. I'll keep you posted."

"My door's always open," Burt called after her.

Chapter 19

Friday, March 13, was filled with depositions in the *Buckley* case. Carrie was not superstitious, but when she arrived at the office, she did catch herself hoping that the day would not bring any sort of bad luck.

The morning started out with Will taking testimony from Dr. Robert Morrow, Jackson Memorial's outgoing chief of staff. Dr. Morrow, a courtly gray-haired gentleman in his early sixties, was a neurologist who had held the chief of staff position for eleven years.

Dr. Morrow confirmed what other staff members had already explained about the appointment of a team of medical personnel to handle the various needs of each incoming patient.

"Do you hand-select the doctors who will serve on these teams?" Will asked.

"You could say that, yes," the doctor replied.

"Is anyone else involved in that process?"

"My nurse, Bonnie Herner," the doctor replied.

"What role does Ms. Herner play in assembling the teams?" Will inquired.

"Generally she will suggest a team and submit the names to me for my approval." The doctor shifted a bit in his chair. "Jackson Memorial is not a huge facility. We have a finite number of doctors with staff privileges, so there won't be a large list of people to choose from to fill the slots on a team, particularly in some of the specialties, such as neurosurgery. So when a team needs to be assembled quickly, Ms. Herner will pull together three or four doctors who happen to be available, and I will almost always okay her choices."

"Under what circumstances would you override a choice made by Ms. Herner?"

"Normally I would do that only to even out workload."

"Do you take the personalities of the doctors into account when assembling teams?"

Dr. Morrow frowned. "I'm not sure I understand your question."

"Are there certain doctors who work more compatibly together than others? If so, do you try to put those people on the same team?"

"The practice of medicine isn't a personality contest," Dr. Morrow replied a bit tartly. "All of our doctors are expected to comport themselves like professionals, so we rarely run into any conflicts. Besides that, each person on a team represents a different medical specialty, so conflicts tend to be minimal."

"If there were a conflict between two doctors as to a patient's treatment, how would that be resolved?" Will asked.

Dr. Morrow thought for a moment, then responded, "Hopefully the two doctors would be able to work it out between themselves. If they couldn't, I suppose they would come to me to referee."

"Has that situation ever arisen since you have been chief of staff?"

"Thankfully not," the doctor replied, with obvious relief.

"Dr. Morrow, as you know, two of the doctors who were assigned to Katherine Buckley's team were Dr. Gerald Peckham and Dr. Kenneth Luebke. Were you responsible for selecting them to treat Katherine?"

"Yes."

"In your opinion, is Dr. Peckham a good doctor?"

"Unquestionably." Dr. Morrow nodded decisively.

"What about Dr. Luebke?"

"Same answer."

"Do you know if Drs. Luebke and Peckham ever disagreed on a course of treatment for Katherine Buckley?"

"Not that I am aware of."

"Are you aware of any animosity of any sort between the two doctors?"

"No, I am not."

"Dr. Morrow, I understand you plan to retire this summer."

"That is correct."

"Are you aware that both Drs. Luebke and Peckham have expressed interest in succeeding you as chief of staff?"

"I have heard talk to that effect, yes."

"Is there anything about the two men that would lead you to recommend one over the other?"

"No, there is not," the doctor said with a little smile. "Both are very capable. And I might add that I consider myself fortunate that a committee will be making that decision, rather than me."

"But you know of no reason why either man would not be qualified to be chief of staff at Jackson Memorial?" Will pressed.

Dr. Morrow shook his head firmly. "No, I do not."

"Thank you, Doctor. I have no further questions."

After a short break, Carrie conducted the continued deposition of Dr. Peckham. For this round of testimony, Dr. Peckham, too, had retained his own attorney. Diane Knipfer was a partner at a firm specializing in medical malpractice defense. Carrie had dealt with Diane on a number of other cases and thought she was both a good lawyer and highly scrupulous.

"Before we get started, I'd like to make a brief statement on the record," Diane, a tall blond woman in her late thirties, said.

"Fine," Carrie nodded.

"I want to make clear that Dr. Peckham is appearing here voluntarily today and that he will answer questions only about treatment furnished to Katherine Buckley while she was a patient at Jackson Memorial. The scope of his testimony will cover treatment he furnished as well as his opinion of the treatment furnished to Katherine by other medical personnel at the hospital. Dr. Peckham will not answer questions about treatment of any other patients or about any other matters." Diane turned to Carrie. "With that understanding, you may proceed."

"Dr. Peckham, thank you for working us into your busy schedule," Carrie said pleasantly. Although it galled her to have to kiss anybody's ass, she had learned that sometimes a well-placed compliment could do wonders in smoothing the way with a witness. Besides, she felt that she had a good rapport with this witness and wanted to do whatever she could to foster it.

The doctor smiled and nodded in response.

"Doctor, at the time of your earlier deposition you indicated you had not had an opportunity to review Katherine Buckley's entire medical record. Am I to understand that you have now had a chance to conduct such a review?"

"That is correct," Dr. Peckham replied.

"Have you had a chance to review the medical treatment provided to Katherine Buckley by Dr. Dawn Redding?"

"Yes, I have."

"Do you have any criticisms of Dr. Redding's treatment of Katherine?"

"I would like to interpose a continuing objection to this entire line of questioning," Charlene Bull spoke up. "As was pointed out in one of the earlier depositions, the Buckleys' lawsuit does not contain a cause of action for medical malpractice. Consequently, questions about treatment are not relevant." Turning to Dr. Peckham, she added, "You may answer the questions today, Doctor, to the extent you are able to do so. Sometime in the future, we lawyers will ask the judge to decide whether or not this information is germane to the case."

"Do you remember my question, or would you like to have it read back?" Carrie asked.

"I remember it," Dr. Peckham replied. "You wanted to

know if I have any criticisms of Dr. Redding's treatment of Katherine Buckley. The answer is no, I do not. In fact, reading through Katherine's entire record has refreshed my recollection of how very fragile her physical health was during much of the time she was a patient at Jackson Memorial. It appears to me that Dr. Redding did an outstanding job of monitoring Katherine's condition and treating her when emergencies arose, such as the several bouts with pneumonia."

"Have you also had a chance to review the medical treatment provided to Katherine by Dr. Kenneth Luebke?"

"Yes."

"And do you have any criticisms of Dr. Luebke's treatment of Katherine?"

"I don't know if 'criticism' is exactly the right word," Dr. Peckham said, hedging a bit.

"Did you and Dr. Luebke ever disagree about Katherine's treatment?"

"Yes, we did, on at least two occasions."

"What was the nature of the disagreements?"

"The first was with respect to the administration of an experimental drug, vicephrin."

"What is the purpose of the drug?" Carrie asked.

"It is meant to be an aid to restoring cognitive function in comatose patients. It has been used for a number of years in Sweden."

"What was your objection to Dr. Luebke's trying the drug on Katherine?"

"My opinion after I reviewed the literature was that the potential side effects far outweighed any likely benefits."

"What type of side effects are you talking about?"

"Some patients experienced seizures and a handful suffered heart failure."

"Did you express those concerns to Dr. Luebke?"

"Yes, I did, as soon as I learned that he had begun administering vicephrin to Katherine."

"What was Dr. Luebke's response?"

Dr. Peckham gave a small smile. "Basically he told me it was his call and I should butt out."

"So he ignored your concerns?"

"He discounted them, yes."

"For how long a period of time did Katherine receive vicephrin?"

"I believe for about two weeks."

"Did it have the desired effect of restoring any cognitive function?"

"No, it did not."

"You mentioned that you and Dr. Luebke had a couple of disagreements about Katherine's treatment. What was the other one?"

"Dr. Luebke proposed utilizing shock therapy."

"When did he propose that?"

"I believe it was shortly after the vicephrin failed to have any effect."

"Did you oppose the shock therapy option?"

"Yes, I did, strenuously. And so did Dr. Redding."

"Why did you and Dr. Redding oppose it?"

"We both firmly believed that in Katherine's already weakened physical condition, it could prove fatal."

"Did Dr. Luebke accede to your views?"

"He did, somewhat grudgingly."

"Did you have any other disagreements with Dr. Luebke about Katherine's treatment?"

Dr. Peckham hesitated a moment, then answered, "No."

"From your review of the record, do you have any other criticisms of Dr. Luebke's treatment of Katherine?"

Another slight pause. "No."

Carrie was disappointed that Dr. Peckham had been this reserved in his criticism of Dr. Luebke. She sensed that he had more to say on the subject, but obviously she wasn't asking precisely the right questions. Knowing full well that she was treading on thin ice, she followed her instincts and asked, "Have you and Dr. Luebke ever disagreed on a course of treatment for any patient other than Katherine Buckley?"

"Objection!" Charlene Bull and Diane Knipfer sang out in unison.

"This line of questioning is directly contrary to the permitted scope of inquiry I outlined at the start of Dr. Peckham's testimony," Knipfer went on. "I will instruct the doctor not to answer this question or any others in that vein."

Dr. Peckham gave Carrie a look that said, *Sorry. I'd like to help you, but my hands are tied.*

"I have no further questions," Carrie said graciously.

"I have just a few," Charlene Bull said. "Doctor, you indicated that the vicephrin did not bring about a change in Katherine Buckley's condition. Is there any indication that the administration of vicephrin harmed Katherine in any way?"

"No."

"In your opinion, did any treatment provided by Dr. Luebke harm Katherine Buckley in any way?"

A pause. "No."

"In your opinion, Dr. Peckham, was there any medical treatment that could have been provided to Katherine Buckley that might have improved her condition?"

With obvious sadness, Dr. Peckham shook his head. "I don't believe so, no."

Charlene Bull nodded. "Thank you, Doctor. No further questions."

As Dr. Peckham and his lawyer got up to leave, Carrie felt frustrated that she hadn't been able to dig up more dirt on Dr. Luebke. She wasn't so sure that Luebke's treatment of Katherine wasn't connected in some way to her assault. Maybe there was another way to get at that information. She'd have to give it some more thought.

The day's final witness was Alessandro Delgado, the night-shift nursing supervisor in charge of Katherine's ward. Delgado was tall, black-haired, and very good-looking. In her preliminary questioning, Carrie learned that he was thirty-four years old and the son of Cuban immigrants. He had been at Jackson Memorial two and a half years, having previously worked in hospitals in Vancouver and Atlanta.

"Was Katherine Buckley one of the patients under your care?" Carrie asked.

"Yes, she was," Delgado replied in a deep, melodious voice. "I think Katherine was everyone's favorite patient. So young. Such a tragic thing, her accident."

As Delgado spoke, he looked deep into Carrie's eyes. She felt herself start to flush a bit. This witness was quite obviously flirting with her.

"Your shift runs from eleven p.m. until seven a.m.," Carrie said, clearing her throat. "I assume there are not very many visitors in the hospital during those hours."

"Not unless a patient is in the ICU or is in critical condition. Under those circumstances, family members may be in the hospital around the clock."

"Do you recall if Katherine Buckley ever had visitors during your shift?"

"I believe she did on a number of occasions," Delgado said pleasantly. "When she first arrived and when she was suffering from pneumonia."

"Who were the visitors, if you recall?"

Delgado thought for a moment. "Her parents. Brother and sister."

"Anyone else?"

Delgado leaned back slightly and pursed his lips. "I think her boyfriend might have been there once or twice. Oh, and I think I remember seeing a man who looked like a priest."

"Did you ever observe any person engaging in inappropriate behavior with Katherine?"

"No." Delgado shook his head decisively.

"Have you ever observed any unauthorized persons on your ward during your shift?"

"No."

"Are the doors to the hospital typically locked during the hours you work?"

Delgado leaned forward again and concentrated his gaze on Carrie. "I believe the side doors are locked. The main door remains open, but there is a receptionist on duty round the clock."

"To your knowledge, have there ever been any security problems at the hospital?"

"No."

"No break-ins, no burglaries?"

"Not that I'm aware of."

"In the course of your employment at Jackson Memorial, have you had the occasion to work with Dr. Gerald Peckham?"

"Yes, I have."

"As a medical professional, what is your opinion of Dr. Peckham's treatment of Katherine Buckley?"

"I object," Charlene Bull said. "This witness is not competent to make that judgment. You may answer the question, Mr. Delgado, subject to my objection."

Delgado gave Charlene a bemused look, clearly conveying that he thought lawyers' machinations were silly.

"From what I saw, it appeared that Dr. Peckham's treatment of Katherine was above reproach."

"Let me ask you the same question with respect to Dr. Dawn Redding."

"My answer would be the same."

"What about Dr. Kenneth Luebke's treatment of Katherine Buckley?"

Delgado shrugged. "I'm not aware of any deficiencies in Katherine's treatment by anyone on staff at Jackson Memorial."

"Do you have a good working relationship with Dr. Peckham?"

"Given the hours I normally work, I don't have a great deal of contact with him, but yes, I do."

"With Dr. Redding?"

"Yes."

"With Dr. Luebke?"

Delgado shrugged again. "I guess so," he said, casually crossing one leg over the other.

Carrie pounced on the witness's slight hesitation. "Have you ever had a problem with Dr. Luebke?"

Another slight pause. "Not really, no."

"None at all?"

"Well—" Delgado looked Carrie straight in the eye again. "I did have a slight misunderstanding with Dr. Luebke early in my career at Jackson Memorial."

"What type of misunderstanding?"

"I was working on the day shift and was involved in a car accident on the way to work. As a result, I was two hours late. When I finally arrived, Dr. Luebke strongly reprimanded me in front of other staff members."

"And you took umbrage at that?"

"Yes. I thought his reaction was inappropriate, both because he was not my direct supervisor—Nurse Shirley Sandow was—and because there was no reason to rebuke me in public."

"Did you raise these concerns with Dr. Luebke?"

Delgado flashed a brilliant smile. "I did better than that. I raised them with the nurses' union."

"And did you ultimately achieve satisfaction for your complaint?"

"Yes, I did. The union rep informed Dr. Luebke in writing that what he did was inappropriate."

"Do you harbor any ill will toward Dr. Luebke as a result of that incident?"

Delgado shrugged. "No. Life is too short to hold grudges."

"One more question, Mr. Delgado. Do you have any idea who might be responsible for impregnating Katherine Buckley?"

Delgado shook his head. "None whatsoever."

"I think that wraps it up. Thank you for your time, Mr. Delgado."

The witness gave her a slow, seductive smile and looked her up and down before replying. "The pleasure was all mine, Ms. Nelson."

As Carrie prepared to head back to her office, she couldn't help but feel a bit dejected. Another day of hard work had yielded no information connecting Jackson Memorial with Katherine's pregnancy. The clock was ticking and she had nothing to go on other than the vague feeling that Dr. Luebke was not a nice person. And vague feelings were not going to be enough to help the *Buckley* case survive the hospital's motion to dismiss her lawsuit for lack of proof.

Chapter 20

On Saint Patrick's Day everyone in Chicago became a little bit Irish. The city even went so far as to dump gallons of green dye into the Chicago River. In Carrie's opinion, the river didn't look too inviting at the best of times, and the dye made it look more like a cesspool than something out of the Land of Erin. But then, who was she to quibble?

O'Malley's Bar and Grill rolled out the green carpet to celebrate this particular holiday. Carrie and many of her colleagues joined in the fun, partaking of a dinner of corned beef and cabbage, washed down with too many pints of ale.

"This is great!" Will said to Carrie as the waitress brought another round of drinks to the table. "The people at my old firm hardly ever socialized with each other."

"We never did at Henley, Schuman, either," Carrie said, raising her voice in order to be heard above the din of the boisterous crowd. "We were too busy chalking up billable hours."

"Would you like to dance?" Will asked.

"Sure," Carrie replied at once.

"Save our seats," Will instructed Tammy and Dona as he and Carrie got up.

The dance floor was jammed, and the music was the loud and raucous variety that did not lend itself to dance partners' having any physical contact with each other. Still, Carrie was pleased that Will had at least asked her. Of course, as soon as they returned to the table, he danced with Ann, Madree, and various secretaries in quick succession, so Carrie realized it would probably be overoptimistic to view his friendliness as an awakening of any sort of romantic interest in her.

The following day brought another round of patient interviews. Carrie pulled into the hospital's parking lot at nine in the morning. Before getting out of the car, she flipped down the visor and looked at herself in the mirror. Her eyes were a little bloodshot. Since she hadn't gotten to bed until one in the morning, that was hardly surprising.

As she touched up her lipstick, her thoughts again turned to Will. In spite of the fact that the previous evening had been very pleasant, she couldn't help feeling a little down. *Just forget about him,* Carrie chided herself. There were any number of good reasons why it made no sense to pine for her handsome partner. She knew it was never a good idea to become romantically involved with people at work because if the personal relationship went sour, the parties' continuing professional relationship would invariably be strained.

Besides that, Carrie realized that she really didn't have sufficient time or energy to nurture a relationship. While she wasn't a workaholic like her friend Ann, the job did frequently require long hours and weekend work. And there were many nights when she arrived home after a day of heated depositions or tense settlement negotiations greatly relieved that she could spend her remaining waking hours in the quiet company of her cat.

"The hell with it," she muttered out loud as she snapped the visor back up. All this romantic drivel was getting her nowhere. She had work to do. Maybe Tammy was right. She should forget about Will and take in another pet.

The morning's interviews yielded nothing. Carrie talked to two patients, one elderly and one in his twenties, both suffering from bipolar disorder. Both had a vague recollection of who Katherine was but could shed no light on who might have assaulted her.

At noon, feeling a headache coming on, Carrie decided to go down to the cafeteria in the building's lower level, for a cup of coffee and a snack. As she stood waiting for the elevator, a well-dressed, slightly built young man walked past her. "Hello, Ms. Nelson," he said brightly.

"Hi," Carrie replied, looking at the man. Did she know him? He didn't look at all familiar.

The young man leaned closer and whispered, "I'm glad to see you took my advice. That darker lipstick is *so* much more flattering on you."

As the young man continued briskly down the hall, Carrie's mouth dropped open. It was Gary/Mary Harwood! She never would have recognized him/her. The elevator door opened. "I don't suppose the cafeteria serves alcohol," Carrie muttered to herself as she pushed the Down button.

Fortified by several cups of strong coffee and a reasonably tasty chicken salad sandwich, Carrie went back to her interviews. In midafternoon she had her most interesting patient conversation to date. The patient was a young man in his late twenties named Brian Mabbs, who was suffering from paranoid schizophrenia. He had been in and out of the hospital over the past four months and remembered Katherine well.

"She never woke up," Brian said. His speech came slowly, and he seemed somewhat lethargic.

"That's right," Carrie said encouragingly. "Katherine never woke up the whole time she was here. Brian, do you ever remember seeing anybody going into Katherine's room at night?"

"We're supposed to stay in our rooms at night," Brian replied.

"I understand." Carrie nodded.

"But I don't always do it," Brian said conspiratorially. "I have insomnia and the pills they give me make me sick, so I don't always take them."

"So you're saying you *did* see someone going into Katherine's room at night?" Carrie prompted, trying to move the young man's narrative along.

"Sometimes when I can't sleep, I get claustrophobic and I have to get out of here and walk around. I'm real quiet because I know I'll get in trouble if anyone sees me."

"Did you see something going on in Katherine's room when you were in the hall one night?" Carrie asked eagerly.

Brian sat silently for more than thirty seconds, then nodded slowly. "One time in the middle of the night I remember seeing somebody open her door and go inside."

Carrie's eyes widened. "Where were you at the time?"

"A few doors down the hall."

"Do you remember how long ago this happened?"

"I think it was around the time they first brought me here," Brian answered.

"In November?" Carrie prompted. That was when Katherine became pregnant.

"I guess so," Brian said hesitantly. "I kind of lose track of time."

"What time of night was it?"

"I'm not sure. I think it was late, maybe the middle of the night."

"Two o'clock? Three?"

Brian nodded. "Something like that."

"What did the person you saw look like?"

"It was a man," Brian answered.

"How old was he?" Carrie asked patiently.

"I don't know. He couldn't have been real old because he seemed to move pretty fast."

"Was he tall or short?"

"I think he was taller than average."

"What color was his hair?"

"It was pretty dark in the hall, but I'd say it was a medium color."

"Could you see his face?"

Brian shook his head.

"What type of clothes was he wearing?"

"I don't know."

"Well, did it look like he was wearing a doctor's coat or scrubs or civilian clothes?" Carrie asked impatiently.

Brian shrugged. "I don't know. Like I said, it was dark."

"Do you know how long this person stayed in Katherine's room?"

Brian shook his head again. "I was afraid I'd get caught in the hall, so when I saw him, I went back to my room right away."

Carrie leaned forward. "Brian, this is very important. Did you ever tell anyone else about what you saw that night?"

Brian shook his head nervously. "No."

Carrie was excited. This wasn't much to go on, but at least she'd finally found someone who said a man had gone into Katherine's room late one night around the time the baby had been conceived. She was jotting down some notes from the conversation when the door opened and a fashionably dressed woman in her fifties walked in.

Carrie introduced herself to the new arrival.

"Oh, yes," the woman said. "I spoke to you on the phone last week. I'm Marian Mabbs, Brian's mother." Turning to Brian, she asked, "Have you had a nice talk with Ms. Nelson?"

"Yes, Mother," Brian answered politely.

"Brian has given me some information that might prove to be quite helpful," Carrie put in. She briefly explained their conversation to Mrs. Mabbs.

"That's nice," Mrs. Mabbs said evenly, but her face looked strained. Then she asked Carrie, "Could I have a private word with you?"

"Certainly." Carrie stepped out into the hall. Mrs. Mabbs followed.

"I may not have thought this through very well when I said you could talk to my son," the older woman said. "Just what exactly is his involvement in your case going to be?"

"I'm not sure," Carrie admitted. "I hope that someone else will be able to corroborate what Brian saw, and the person who went into Katherine's room can be identified."

"You aren't expecting Brian to testify in court, are you?" Mrs. Mabbs asked with obvious concern.

"I honestly can't answer that right now," Carrie admitted.

"It simply cannot come to that," Mrs. Mabbs said emphatically. "Brian's mental state is very fragile. He's been in and out of here seven times since November first. He'll seem to be doing better, but as soon as he's sent home, he relapses. If you ask me, that doctor has him so pumped full of drugs that his recovery is being hindered."

"Which doctor is that?" Carrie asked, already fairly sure she knew the answer.

"Luebke," was the prompt response.

"Have you ever told Dr. Luebke your concerns about Brian's medication?" Carrie asked.

"Yes, I have, and he has basically told me that he is the doctor and I should keep my opinions to myself."

"Surely Brian has other doctors treating him besides Luebke. Have you expressed your concerns to them?"

"Yes." Mrs. Mabbs sighed. "They all assure me that Dr. Luebke is a very good doctor and I just need to give Brian's treatment plan more time. They're probably right. I have to admit that he seems to be doing better recently, even though he acts like he's drugged to the gills. But at least he has stopped acting out and laughing uncontrollably for hours on end, so there has been progress."

An idea suddenly popped into Carrie's head, and she said with some urgency, "I understand your concerns, and I promise I'll do whatever I can to make sure no harm comes to Brian as a result of what he saw. But right now, would you mind if I asked him a couple more questions?"

"I suppose not," Mrs. Mabbs replied with little enthusiasm.

Carrie and Brian's mother went back into the room. "Brian, do you have any idea who the person you saw going into Katherine's room might have been?"

"I figured it was probably a doctor," Brian answered.

Carrie's heart beat faster. This was the response she'd been hoping for. "What makes you think it was a doctor?" she asked evenly. "I thought you said you couldn't see how he was dressed."

"I couldn't, but who else would be around that late at night?"

Carrie took a deep breath. "Brian, is there any possibility the person you saw was Dr. Luebke?"

"That's preposterous!" Mrs. Mabbs said sharply. "Of course it wasn't Dr. Luebke! Was it, Brian?"

Brian merely shrugged and said, "I keep telling you I don't know who it was."

"You see," Mrs. Mabbs said to Carrie triumphantly. "Why don't you watch TV now, dear?" she said soothingly to her son. "I'll see Ms. Nelson out."

"Good-bye, Brian," Carrie said as Mrs. Mabbs took hold of her elbow and attempted to hurry her out into the hall. "It was nice talking to you."

Brian didn't even look up. He was already engrossed in a television program.

"What do you mean by putting such absurd ideas into my son's head?" Mrs. Mabbs demanded when they got outside. "He's already delusional. I don't appreciate your filling him full of wild stories about how his doctor attacked another patient."

"I'm only trying to get at the truth," Carrie protested. "And you did give me permission to speak to Brian."

"Well, then, I rescind that permission," Mrs. Mabbs fairly shouted. "Do you understand? If you ever go near my son again, I'll sue you! Why, you've probably set his recovery back two months!"

"Fine," Carrie said coldly. She headed down the hall, muttering to herself, "I hope someday when you're in need of help, someone refuses to come to your aid." As she stomped off toward the elevator, she could sense someone watching her. Turning her head, she saw Scott Rouleau standing just inside the door to his room.

"I am a Knight of the Round Table," Scott announced proudly. "Would you like to join me on a Crusade?"

Oh, no, Carrie groaned. She wasn't in the mood for another encounter with him.

"Hello, Scott," she said pleasantly. "You want me to look at something in your room?"

Scott nodded.

Carrie hesitated. She was eager to get back to the office to pursue her theory of Dr. Luebke's involvement in the case, which had only been strengthened by her unpleasant conversation with Mrs. Mabbs. However, there was something rather pitiful about Scott, and she hated to hurt his feelings by refusing his offer to socialize.

"Okay," she said. "But I only have a minute."

Carrie followed Scott into his room. The young man was more subdued today than during her last visit with him. He walked over to the desk that held his laptop computer. He rapid hitting various keys, then stepped back and said, "Here it is."

Carrie stepped forward and looked at the screen. It said in bold print, "Welcome to the Crusades. Press Enter to begin your quest for the Holy Grail." Carrie hit the Enter key, and the screen changed to reveal an elaborate scene complete with knights on horseback and maidens in diaphanous gowns.

Remembering from Madree's notes that Scott was a computer whiz, Carrie asked, "Did you design this game yourself?"

Scott nodded proudly. "Would you like to play?"

"I'd love to, but I'm afraid I really don't have time right now." Seeing Scott's face fall, she added quickly, "I'll be back again soon and you can show me how the game works. I promise."

As she walked toward the door, Scott said softly, "Poor Katherine. I feel sorry for her."

Although she thought the comment was just a bit odd, Carrie merely nodded and said, "Good-bye, Scott. I'll see you soon."

When Carrie arrived back at the office in the late afternoon, she ran into Michelle Brud, the firm's head of computer services. A hard-charging blonde in her early thirties who had a standing offer to work at Microsoft's headquarters but didn't want to uproot her young family from Chicago, Michelle said, "Carrie, I've been meaning to talk to you. I have all of the *Buckley* deposition transcripts and exhibits that have been produced so far up and running in an application. You're welcome to test it out if you'd like, to see if you want me to make any changes.''

"There's no need for that," Carrie replied. "If you say it works, then it works.''

"Well, just keep funneling me everything you might want to use at trial and I'll have it all ready to go when the time comes," Michelle said brightly.

"Thanks," Carrie said, patting Michelle on the arm. "Now all I have to do is uncover enough evidence to keep the judge from dismissing the case before trial.''

"You can do it," Michelle said encouragingly, as she hurried off.

"I hope you're right," Carrie murmured.

Back at her desk, Carrie dialed Jackie Crabb's number. When the paralegal answered, Carrie briefly explained her conversation with Brian Mabbs. "I want you to try to dig up any information you can on Dr. Kenneth Luebke," she said. "Call the licensing board. Check the plaintiff-defendant table in all the local courts. Use any other sources you can think of, even if they're devious. I just have the feeling that man is hiding something, and I want to know what it is.''

"Do you really think Dr. Luebke might have assaulted Katherine?" Jackie asked incredulously.

"I don't know," Carrie admitted, recognizing how serious that charge was. "But for the first time in six weeks I feel like I've finally gotten a tiny break in the case. And how interesting that the person who may be implicated is the only one who's been uncooperative and belligerent in responding to our discovery requests.''

"But even if it was Luebke who went into Katherine's room that night, you still don't know that anything untoward happened," Jackie said. "Maybe he was there to check on her. After all, Katherine was his patient.''

"Believe me, I realize the implications this could have,"

Carrie said soberly. "I have no intention of going public with this idea. But my gut tells me I made some progress today, and I don't want to leave any stone unturned in following up on it."

Chapter 21

The following Sunday afternoon Carrie walked several blocks to the Blockbuster Video store near her home. Ann was coming over with Chinese takeout, and Carrie had offered to pick up a film. As Carrie surveyed the Classics section, vacillating between Alfred Hitchcock and the Marx Brothers, she heard a familiar voice behind her.

"Do you mean to tell me you're not working today?"

Carrie swung around. "I'm afraid you caught me redhanded," she said to Will. Like Carrie, Will was dressed in jeans and a sweater. "What are you doing way down here? Don't you have any video stores in Skokie?"

"We do, but unfortunately none of them have what I need," he replied.

"Which is?"

"Conan the Barbarian."

Carrie gave him a strange look.

"Don't get the wrong idea," Will laughed. "My ten-year-old cousin is coming to visit tonight. He's in a Schwarzenegger phase, and I foolishly promised him that he could watch any Arnold movie he wanted. I didn't realize that *Conan* has become a collector's item. I called nine stores, and this is the only one that has it."

"It's nice of you to go to all that trouble," Carrie said.

"Zach is a good kid, and I don't want to go back on my word. What are you viewing today, if I might ask?" He peered at the two videos she was holding. "Ah. *North by Northwest* and *A Night at the Opera.* That's quite a study in contrasts."

"I've decided it's definitely a Marx Brothers kind of

night," Carrie said, putting the Hitchcock film back on the shelf.

"Have a good evening," Will said, giving her a friendly pat on the arm.

"Yeah. Nice seeing you," Carrie replied. *Very* nice, she added silently as she appreciatively watched his athletic figure depart. That ten-year-old cousin was one lucky kid.

Spring arrived in Chicago with a vengeance, with temperatures jumping twenty-five degrees overnight. The last vestiges of snow disappeared, and tulips and crocuses began to show their heads. Lawns that a week earlier had been brown and barren suddenly looked as though they had been treated to a thick coat of green paint. Carrie always felt as if spring in the Midwest was a magical time, and she resented having so little time to be outside and enjoy it.

Early on Monday morning, Carrie was in her office preparing for another day of depositions in the *Buckley* case when Madree Williams knocked lightly on the open office door and stepped inside. "How's it going?" Madree asked.

"I'm exhausted already, and it's barely eight o'clock," Carrie replied ruefully, rubbing her eyes. "It's so nice outside that I resent being cooped up in here. I wish there were some way I could play hookey."

"It's supposed to be nice all week," Madree said. "Maybe you can sneak out early one day."

"I'm afraid that's wishful thinking," Carrie said, motioning to the stack of papers piled all over her office. "Speaking of which, thanks a bunch for agreeing to defend the initial depositions in the housing discrimination case. I'm sorry I won't be able to help out, but between the *Buckley* case and the back-and-forth settlement negotiations in my medical malpractice action, I've just been snowed under."

"No problem," Madree said, with a dismissive wave. "I was lucky enough to have a couple of things settle recently, so I've got a bit of extra time."

"Well, I really appreciate it," Carrie said sincerely. "I hope I'm able to repay the favor sometime."

"It's no big deal," Madree said. She turned to go, then abruptly reversed course. Carrie gave her a quizzical look. "I've been debating whether I should tell you this or not," Madree said in a low voice, "but I decided you ought to hear it. Gerald and I were at Luigi's, that new Italian restaurant on the north side, on Saturday night, and Will came in with a woman."

"Oh," Carrie said, trying to keep her voice even.

"I didn't know if you'd made any progress with him, but I thought you might be interested in hearing that."

"I am interested," Carrie said. "I ran into Will yesterday at Blockbuster. He was picking up a movie for his ten-year-old cousin. Apparently his social calendar was quite full this weekend. So give me the gory details. What did she look like?"

Madree shrugged. "Reasonably attractive. Short dark hair. She was wearing a black suit."

"Did they seem to be having a good time?"

Madree hesitated a moment. "I don't know. I guess so."

Carrie pursed her lips, then said, "They weren't cuddling or anything disgusting like that, were they? If they were, don't tell me. It would just make me sick."

Madree laughed. "No cuddling, no pawing, no billing and cooing. For that matter, maybe we're jumping to conclusions. Maybe she was a prospective client."

Carrie guffawed. "Right. And I'm going to play center for the Bulls next season." She sighed. "I'm glad you told me. You're a good friend. This should disabuse me once and for all of the stupid notion of trying to pursue a relationship with someone I work with."

"It's not a stupid notion," Madree protested. "I really like Will, and I think the two of you could be good together. I've just always thought it's best to know what you're up against. That way you're better able to combat it."

"So how do you suggest I combat this treacherous foe?" Carrie asked, her mood lifting a bit. "Cut and dye my hair? I do already own several black suits."

"Just stop procrastinating and ask him out," Madree advised. "That's the only way to find out if he's interested. I know it's easy to make excuses why you haven't done it— you're busy, the timing's not right, whatever. You and I both know those are just cop-outs. If the man truly sparks your interest, can the excuses, get off your butt, and do something about it."

As Carrie opened her mouth to protest, Madree said firmly, "Just do it. You'll regret it if you don't. Now give 'em hell today. We'll talk again soon." She turned quickly and took her leave.

Carrie gave a brief smile, grateful that she had some good female friends at the firm that she could confide in. She knew Madree was right. She either had to try to foster a relationship with Will or chalk the idea up as a lost cause. She hated to admit it, even to herself, but she had been spending far too much time daydreaming about him. That really wasn't like her. She was generally a doer, not a dreamer. Speaking of which, she thought as she looked at the clock, she'd better hightail it down to Mr. R's office so they could work on their last-minute strategy for the day's depositions.

Glen Fisher was Jackson Memorial's chief of security. As Will began his questioning of the burly, dark-haired man, Carrie leaned back in her chair and glanced across the table at Werner Von Slaten. The hospital's administrator apparently hadn't lost his zeal for the case—so far, he had sat through every moment of every witness's testimony. Carrie wondered where he found the time to carry out his administrative duties. He probably had a top-notch assistant. Hell, Carrie wouldn't be surprised if the place actually ran better when he wasn't there.

Fisher had been employed at the hospital for seven years. He had a staff of five full-time guards. During his tenure there had been some minor vandalism to the outside of the building and the occasional petty theft inside, but nothing serious and certainly nothing violent.

"Did anyone on staff ever report seeing any suspicious activity in the building?" Will asked.

"No," Fisher replied in a booming bass voice.

"Did the family member of a patient ever make such a report?"

"Never."

"When did you learn about the assault on Katherine Buckley?"

"I believe it was the day after her pregnancy was discovered," Fisher answered.

"How did you come to learn about it?"

"Mr. Von Slaten told me about it."

"Did you know who Ms. Buckley was?"

Fisher shook his head. "No. I have very little contact with patients."

"When you heard about Ms. Buckley's pregnancy, were you surprised?"

"Of course. I think everyone was surprised."

"Do you have any idea who might have been responsible for impregnating Ms. Buckley?"

"No, sir, I most certainly do not."

As Will continued his inquiries, Carrie found her mind wandering. Her conversation with Madree had bothered her more than she cared to admit. While it was disappointing to think that Will might not be interested in her, it was devastating to hear that he was apparently interested in someone else. Carrie knew this logic made no sense, but she couldn't help it. That was how she felt.

She began doodling on her legal pad, drawing smiley faces and bow ties. Her fixation with Will was beginning to affect her mood. She was already under enough stress from the *Buckley* case. She didn't need any other annoyances in her life. Besides, she was too old for this kind of thing. She was thirty-three. She should have outgrown schoolgirl crushes fifteen years ago.

Her doodles turned darker, the smiley faces morphing into terrifying creatures with horns and protruding tongues. She had to put an end to this. Maybe Madree was right. She needed to be more direct. She would just have to ask Will out and let his answer dictate the future. If he said yes, Carrie would move forward and see where the relationship might lead, if anywhere. If he said no, she would accept it and move on with her life.

Carrie nodded her head decisively, pleased to have at last decided what to do. She was not going to let this drag on anymore. She would ask Will out by the end of the week and put an end to this nonsense. Feeling like a great weight had been lifted off her shoulders, she found her mind wandering farther afield. She pondered where she might like to go on vacation. The summer was going to be occupied with the *Buckley* case, but fall was a nice time to travel. She had an old high school friend who'd recently relocated to Boston and had been pestering Carrie to come out and visit. Autumn in New England was always pleasant.

Carrie was so wrapped up in her private reverie that she completely lost touch with what was happening around her. The last she'd noticed Will was still deeply engrossed in uncovering all the minute details of Jackson Memorial's security. Suddenly, just as she was picturing herself walking across Boston Common on a brisk fall day, she felt someone touch her arm. She gasped and started so abruptly that she nearly jumped out of her chair. It was Will. Fisher's deposition had ended and everyone else had left the room.

"Are you all right?" Will asked a bit anxiously. "You looked like you were in your own little world."

Carrie's face reddened. Thank God he couldn't read her mind. "Since you had the deposition well in hand, I took the opportunity to do a little daydreaming," she said flippy, "and before I knew it, I had drifted off to such a scintillating place that I couldn't tear myself away."

"Okay," Will said, not sounding entirely convinced that his co-counsel was in complete charge of her faculties. "Would you like me to handle the next witness?"

"Oh, no," Carrie said quickly, shuffling through her file to find her notes for the upcoming witness. "I'm fine. In fact, I feel as refreshed as if I'd taken a nap. I'll handle the next witness, no sweat."

The witness in question was Kim Van Rear, a nurse on the hospital's night shift. A petite woman in her late twenties, Van Rear had been employed at Jackson Memorial about a year.

Carrie led the nurse through a description of her contacts with Katherine Buckley, the type of treatment Katherine received, and the ups and downs in Katherine's physical condition.

"Comatose patients are always very susceptible to infections and to pneumonia," Nurse Van Rear explained. "And Katherine had her share of those ailments. Fortunately, she always responded to aggressive treatment."

"What about Katherine's mental condition?" Carrie asked. "Was there any change in that from the time she arrived at the hospital until she left?"

"No," the nurse shook her head. "There was apparently never any improvement in her neurological function."

"What hours do you work?"

"Generally eleven to seven."

"Is Mr. Delgado your supervisor?"

"Yes."

"My understanding is that there are not very many visitors in the building at night. Is that correct?"

"That's right," Nurse Van Rear replied. "Overnight visitors are generally allowed only if a patient is in the ICU."

"Do you ever remember Katherine Buckley having visitors during your shift?"

The nurse thought a moment. "I believe when she was battling pneumonia, her family stayed with her round the clock."

"Her parents?"

"Yes. And I think one night her boyfriend was there and another night a minister was in her room for an hour or two."

Out of the corner of her eye, Carrie could see Von Slaten smile at this volunteered information. She suspected the hospital's administrator had coached everyone on his staff to try to implicate Todd whenever possible.

"On the evening you are describing, was Katherine's boyfriend alone with her in the room?" Carrie asked.

The nurse thought a moment, then said, "No, I believe he was there along with Katherine's parents."

Carrie merely nodded but silently directed a jab toward Von Slaten. *Go ahead and throw all the crap you want at Todd Fleming. It's not going to stick because he's not the culprit.*

"Ms. Van Rear, during the time Katherine was at the hospital, did you ever notice anyone go into her room who didn't belong there?"

"No."

"Did you ever observe anyone in Katherine's room acting in an inappropriate manner or taking indecent liberties with her?"

"No."

"Did you ever observe any sort of suspicious activity in the hospital?"

"No."

"Did you ever observe any type of suspicious activity on the grounds of the hospital?"

The nurse paused a moment before answering. "Well—" she began haltingly. "I'm not sure if it was suspicious activity or not, but one time I did think I saw something . . ." Her voice trailed off.

"What did you think you saw?" Carrie asked eagerly.

"All of the night-shift workers get free parking in the parking garage. It's a security precaution so we don't have to walk outside in the dark. One night when I got out of my car and was walking toward the stairway leading into the hospital, I thought I might have seen someone duck behind a post."

"When was this?" Carrie asked.

"It was shortly before Thanksgiving," Nurse Van Rear replied.

"What happened then?"

"Nothing. I went into the building and worked my shift."

"Did you report this incident to Security?"

"No."

"Why not?" Carrie asked incredulously.

The nurse looked sheepish. "Because once I got inside

the building I felt foolish and figured I must have been imagining things. As soon as I came inside, I saw one of the aides who works on my shift. She had just come from the parking ramp, and I asked her if she'd seen or heard anything. She said she hadn't, so I decided my imagination must just have been working overtime."

"Did you discuss this incident with anyone else at the hospital?"

"No."

"Did anything suspicious or unusual occur during your shift that night?"

"No."

"Is there any way you could pinpoint the exact date this incident might have occurred?"

The nurse thought a moment, then said sadly, "No, I'm sorry. I know it was before Thanksgiving because I remember the turkey decorations were up on the walls. But there's no way I could reconstruct the exact date."

"Was the person you saw in the parking ramp a man or a woman?"

"I'm not actually sure I did see anyone," the nurse said. "It was more that I sensed someone's presence."

"Thank you, Ms. Van Rear. I have no further questions."

As Charlene Bull began to ask a few questions of the witness, Carrie sat back in her chair, her jaw clenched in frustration. The information provided by Nurse Van Rear was a real teaser. Had there been someone lurking in the parking ramp on a night around the time Katherine got pregnant? And most important, if there was someone in the parking ramp that night, was it possible that that person had something to do with the assault? Once again, Carrie had too many questions and too few answers.

Chapter 22

Carrie woke up on Friday wondering where the week had gone. With every day that passed, she could feel her frustration mounting. Two more days of depositions and another day of patient interviews had brought her no closer to finding out who had assaulted Katherine Buckley.

She arrived at the office that morning looking forward to a brief respite in the *Buckley* case. The deposition of a rehabilitation expert in one of her medical malpractice cases would take up most of the day. Although her mind was never completely free from thoughts of Katherine's plight, it would be nice to spend a few hours on something else.

After shedding her coat, smoothing out her navy silk dress, and changing from tennis shoes into navy-and-cream heels, Carrie walked down to one of the break rooms to get a cup of coffee. Will was there, helping himself to a refill.

"Todd should be ready to start his polygraph examination about now," Will said, looking at his watch.

Carrie nodded, silently thanking herself for having changed her shoes and washed her hair that morning. She had followed through on her promise to Katherine's boyfriend to arrange for him to take a lie detector test. After scheduling the exam with one of the operators recommended by Burt Ramquist, she had called Detective Clauff to feel him out on the possibility of formally eliminating Todd as a suspect provided the test results were clean.

The suggestion seemed to amuse the detective. "You know I can't make any promises until I see the results of the test," he'd said, sounding as if he were on the verge of laughter. "Who knows, maybe he'll fail so miserably that he'll be forced to confess."

With great restraint, Carrie ignored the comment. "I realize you can't make any promises. I'm just asking you to be receptive to the idea *if* Todd passes."

"I'm always receptive to anything reasonable," the detective replied, implying that Carrie's idea was not in that category.

"So *if* the results are positive, you will at least consider the possibility of dropping Todd Fleming as a suspect," Carrie pressed.

"Time will tell," the detective volleyed back. "If Mr. Fleming feels that taking a polygraph is in his best interest, then I guess he should go ahead and do it. I'll look forward to hearing the results—good or bad."

"Thank you *so* much for your consideration," Carrie said caustically as she hung up the phone.

"Maybe it would've been better to wait until after Todd had actually taken the test and we'd seen the results before talking to the detective," Will suggested as he took a sip of his coffee. "This way we've tipped our hand."

"I probably would have been in favor of that, too," Carrie replied, pouring herself a cup of java, "but Todd insisted that the police be notified in advance. He said that would show he was confident about passing the test, which in turn means he was being truthful when he told them he didn't do it." She set the coffeepot back on its hot plate. "When all is said and done, it's really Todd's call to make."

"You're right," Will agreed. "I just hope he passes with flying colors and that the police will then cross him off their list and move on to trying to find out who really did assault Katherine."

"That would be nice," Carrie agreed. "I remember when I first talked to the detective, I foolishly thought the police would be able to help us make our case. Obviously that was wishful thinking."

"Don't be discouraged," Will said. "We're going to get to the bottom of this thing yet."

"Some days I wonder."

"Are Joan and Teresa going back to the hospital for more interviews today?"

Carrie nodded. "Yes." She took a sip of her coffee. "Pretty soon we're going to have to consider pulling the plug on that aspect of the investigation. I'm afraid it's turning into a bottomless pit that's yielding nothing."

Will smiled. "You're bound and determined to say you made a mistake thinking a patient might be the key to solving the puzzle, aren't you? Well, I still think the idea is a good one and if my vote counts for anything, I say it's still too early to discontinue the interviews."

"At some point we're going to have to face the fact that we can't spare the resources," Carrie said.

"At some point," Will agreed. "But we're not there yet. After all, you got some useful information out of Brian Mabbs."

Carrie raised one eyebrow. "I think calling what I learned from Brian Mabbs 'useful' is gross hyperbole."

"Well, he says he saw a taller-than-average-man go into Katherine's room in the middle of the night around the time she got pregnant. I'd say that's useful."

"Maybe it was a staff member making a legitimate check on a patient. After all, there are several male nurses and aides on the night shift. Or maybe Brian was so drugged up that he imagined the whole thing."

"Don't start getting pessimistic on me," Will counseled. "This is a good case and we're going to win it. That's a promise."

"Can you guarantee I'll win tomorrow night's Lotto drawing, too?" Carrie countered.

Will laughed and topped off his coffee. "That I can't do. Just hang in there. We're going to crack this thing."

Carrie stood there a moment after he left, all too conscious of the fact that today was her self-imposed deadline for asking him out and that she had just missed a golden opportunity. The situation had been perfect. They were being chatty and companionable. Why hadn't she said something?

Because I'm a wimp and I'm afraid of rejection, that's

why, she scolded herself. She added a shot of hot coffee to her cup and headed back to her office. She glanced at her watch. It was only eight-thirty. Her deposition should be over by midafternoon. She'd have plenty of time after that to reconnect with Will and make her move. And if she chickened out again—well, as any good lawyer knows, deadlines can always be extended.

The rehabilitation expert's deposition dragged on longer than Carrie had expected. At three o'clock, the attorney representing the opposing side was still deeply entrenched in his questioning. The conference room was a bit stuffy, and Carrie was starting to get sleepy and bored. She was just contemplating calling for a short recess when her secretary walked briskly into the room, came around the table, and handed Carrie a note. "Urgent phone call in *Buckley* case," the message said.

"What's this about?" Carrie whispered. "Did something happen to Katherine?"

Tammy shook her head. "A man is on the phone," she whispered back. "He refuses to identify himself, but he says it's imperative that he speak with you right away because he has some important information about the *Buckley* case. I told him you were in depositions, but he insisted on holding while I gave you the message."

Carrie frowned. What the hell could this be about? Oh, well. She'd been hankering to take a break anyway. "Excuse me," she interrupted the other lawyer's most recent tedious question. "I have an important phone call I've got to take. Could we take a short recess?"

As she and Tammy hotfooted it back to her office, Carrie asked, "Why won't the guy give his name?"

"I don't know," Tammy replied. "I asked him three times, and he said his name wasn't important but he *had* to talk to you right away."

"Does he sound like a nut?"

"Actually, it sounds like he's trying to disguise his voice, like he's talking through a scarf or something. His voice sounded rather unnatural."

"Great," Carrie mumbled as she entered her office and rounded the desk. A wacko caller was just what she needed on a Friday afternoon. It suddenly occurred to her that perhaps the caller was one of the patients at the hospital. She hoped that wasn't the case. She was in no mood to hear Scott Rouleau announce that today he was Louis XVI.

"This is Carrie Nelson. Can I help you?" she said briskly when she picked up the phone.

"Ms. Nelson, I have some information for you." The voice on the other end of the line was raspy and low. Either the person was very sick or he was trying extremely hard to disguise his voice.

"Who is this?" Carrie asked sharply.

"That doesn't matter," the man replied.

"It matters to me," Carrie retorted. "I'm not in the habit of talking to people who won't identify themselves."

"I understand you've been looking for some information about Dr. Luebke," the man went on, ignoring Carrie's comment. "I think I can help you out."

Carrie's interest was immediately piqued. "How can you help me?" she asked.

"Take down this name and address: Delores Starling, 3209 Laura Lane, Vernon Hills. Have you got that?"

"Yes, I've got it," Carrie said, scribbling the information on a scrap of paper. "What does this person have to do with Dr. Luebke?"

"You talk to her. She'll fill in the blanks for you. Good luck."

"Wait! What blanks will she fill in?" Carrie demanded. "How do you know about her? Who are you?" But the line was dead. The mysterious caller had hung up.

Carrie hung up the phone and sat there a moment in surprise. This was probably some sort of prank. Delores Starling probably didn't exist. And if she did, it was doubtful she had any connection to Dr. Luebke that would benefit Katherine Buckley's case. Cognizant of the fact that she was holding up the resumption of the rehabilitative expert's deposition, Carrie picked up the phone and dialed Information. Her curiosity was piqued, and it would take only another minute or two to find out if her enigmatic caller's tip held water.

Information verified that there was a D. Starling living in Vernon Hills, a suburb on the city's far north side. Carrie dialed the number she'd been given. After five rings, an answering machine kicked in. She left a brief message identifying herself, leaving her number, and explaining that she would like to talk to Delores Starling about Dr. Luebke. Then she went back to her deposition, thinking that this whole exercise had probably been nothing but a big waste of time.

The deposition finally ended around four-thirty. When she got back to her office and checked her voice mail messages, Carrie discovered, to her surprise, that D. Starling had called back. She dialed the number again, and the phone was answered by a husky-voiced woman of indeterminate age.

"Ms. Starling?" Carrie asked.

"Yes."

"This is Carrie Nelson. Thanks for getting back to me." Now that she had the woman on the phone, she wasn't sure what to say. She cleared her throat and plunged ahead. "I have a case pending against Jackson Memorial Hospital on behalf of a patient who was under Dr. Luebke's care. I was told you might have some information about Dr. Luebke." She held her breath and hoped Ms. Starling wouldn't demand to know who had given Carrie her name or say she had never heard of Dr. Luebke. However, Carrie wasn't prepared for the response that Delores Starling did give.

"Did that son of a bitch rape your client, too?"

Part II

Chapter 23

After a long moment in which Carrie tried to catch her breath, she asked, "What did you say?"

"I'll go to my grave believing he raped my daughter," Ms. Starling replied. "I was just wondering if he did the same to your client."

"As a matter of fact, my client was raped," Carrie replied.

"He probably did it," Ms. Starling said firmly. "It's in his nature."

"May I ask when this incident involving your daughter occurred?" Carrie asked carefully.

"Eight years ago. Gwen was twenty."

"Was your daughter a patient at Jackson Memorial?"

"She was never hospitalized. Luebke treated her on an outpatient basis."

"And during the time he was treating her, he sexually assaulted her?"

"I'd stake my life on it."

"Ms. Starling, did your family ever file a lawsuit against Dr. Luebke or report him to the licensing board?"

"I reported him to the board, but that's as far as it went," the woman answered bitterly.

"Why is that?"

"Because my daughter swore up and down that nothing happened and as an adult she was the only one who had the right to bring a claim. So the bastard got off scot-free."

Carrie could feel her frustration mounting. Just when she felt she was on the verge of a breakthrough in the case, another obstacle was thrown in her path. "Has your daugh-

ter ever deviated from her claim that Dr. Luebke did not
assault her?"

"No, she hasn't, but I know better. I've got proof he
did it."

"What kind of proof?"

"Copies of letters he wrote her, gifts he gave her. I know
he did it. I just couldn't prove it without Gwen's help."

"Ms. Starling, I'd really like to sit down and talk to you
at greater length about this. Would that be all right with
you?"

"Sure."

"Would you be free tomorrow morning?"

"I've got to take my elderly mother to the beauty shop
at eight-thirty, but I should be home by ten or so. You
could come by after that."

"That'd be great. Give me the directions and I'll be
there."

After concluding her phone call with Ms. Starling, Carrie
flew down the hall into Will's office. He was dictating a
brief.

"Stop the presses!" Carrie shouted. "I've got some dynamite news!"

"What is it?" Will asked. "You look like you just won
that Lotto jackpot."

"I did better than that." She quickly filled him in on her
mysterious phone call and her conversation with Delores
Starling.

"This all sounds like something out of a movie script,"
Will said skeptically. "Who was the guy on the phone and
how did he know about this Starling woman?"

"I don't know, and for the moment I don't particularly
care," Carrie replied blithely. "All that matters is that I've
finally got some dirt on Dr. Luebke. I knew something was
out there. I could feel it."

"I don't want to be a wet blanket here," Will said cau-
tiously, "but don't get your hopes up too much. This all
sounds far too contrived to be true."

Carrie frowned. "Delores Starling certainly sounded real.
And when I see her in person tomorrow, I should be able

to tell if she's legit or not." She leaned forward and put her palms on Will's desk. "Don't you see what this means? This could be the key we needed to unlocking the whole case. I know it maybe won't pan out, but for now—for the first time—I feel there's real hope that we're going to be able to pull this thing off. You're the one who's usually the optimist. Well, then, join me in being optimistic about this."

Will looked at her for a long moment, then smiled. "Okay. You got yourself a deal. I agree that Delores Starling could be the salvation we've been looking for. Even if things don't pan out tomorrow, there's no reason why we shouldn't have cause to celebrate today."

In Carrie's exuberant mood, that comment sounded like the perfect opening. "Speaking of celebration," she segued. "I'm going to stop by O'Malley's tonight for a drink or two. Would you care to join me?"

Will paused only half a second before answering, "I'd love to."

"Great. I'll let you get back to whatever you were doing. Why don't you swing by my office when you're ready to leave? There's no hurry. I've got plenty to do."

"Sounds like a plan."

Carrie floated back to her office, high on adrenaline and lust. The hell with winning the Lotto jackpot. What she had in mind was something with far higher stakes.

Chapter 24

Over drinks and shared appetizers, there was much buzz among the assembled Ramquist and Dowd employees at the Friday night after-work get-together at O'Malley's about Carrie's mysterious gentleman caller.

"You've got your very own Deep Throat," Madree Williams joked. "I hadn't realized the *Buckley* case had turned into a covert operation."

"Do you have any idea who it could have been?" Dona Winkler asked.

Carrie shook her head. "It could be anybody. We've been beating the bushes pretty hard for any dirt on Dr. Luebke. My guess is that word of our inquiry spread and some Good Samaritan decided to call and help us out."

"But why all the cloak-and-dagger stuff?" Tammy asked. "Why wouldn't the guy identify himself?"

"A lot of people are afraid of getting involved," Will offered. "They want to see justice done, but they don't want to get sucked into the legal process themselves, so they offer information but insist on retaining their anonymity. I've heard it happens all the time in police investigations. Somebody will call and report drug dealing going on in his neighborhood but will refuse to give his name. There's a lot of paranoia and whether it's warranted or not, folks genuinely fear retaliation if they rat somebody out."

"The important thing is that you finally have something to go on," Terry Payne said. "Does this Ms. Starling sound legitimate?"

"Oh, she sounds legitimate, all right," Carrie replied. "It's just a question of whether she can offer anything that we can use in our case." Glancing toward the front of the bar, Carrie said, "Oh, look. Here come Joan and Teresa. I wonder how they made out with their hospital interviews."

Teresa Timkin and Joan Bedner made their way through the crowded bar to join their colleagues. Terry borrowed two chairs from another table and everyone moved a little closer to the person next to them to make room. In the process of shifting his chair, Will's arm brushed against Carrie's knee. "Sorry," he said.

"No problem," Carrie replied sweetly. Out of the corner of her eye, she could see Madree wink at her. Although Will didn't display any particular amorous tendencies, he was friendly and attentive to her. Carrie reminded herself that neither Rome nor hot romances were built in a day.

"I need a drink," Teresa announced as she took her seat. "A great big one."

"Me, too," Joan echoed.

After the waitress had taken their orders, Will said, "I take it your enormous thirst means you didn't stumble upon any smoking guns today."

"No," Teresa replied. "But I did stumble upon Carrie's old buddy Bob Brakefield." She made a face.

"I'm almost afraid to ask," Carrie said wryly. "What did he do now?"

"He made another pass at me," Teresa said.

"I think he has a crush on her," Joan chuckled.

"Go ahead and laugh," Teresa shot back. "Next time I'm going to pay him ten bucks to grope you."

"He actually groped you?" Will asked.

"The old fart snuck up behind me and grabbed my breasts!" Teresa exclaimed. "Can you believe it?"

"What did you do?" Carrie asked, trying hard not to laugh.

"I turned around and barked at him like a mad dog," Teresa replied. "Let me tell you, he turned tail and ran right back to his room."

The story brought loud guffaws from all present.

"I'm going to remember this next time any of you need a favor," Teresa sputtered.

"I'm sorry," Carrie apologized for the group. "But like I told you the last time you had a run-in with him, better you than me."

"I think you have your own admirer at the hospital," Joan put in.

"Really?" Carrie asked. "Who?"

"Scott Rouleau."

"What makes you say that?"

"He seemed to be watching me walk around today, and when Teresa and I were getting ready to leave, he came up to me and asked if you were with us. He wanted to talk to you. He got quite upset when I said you weren't there."

"Oh, great," Carrie said. "Did he say what he wanted to talk to me about?"

Joan shook her head.

"Do you think he has anything worthwhile to say?" Will asked Carrie. "Maybe you should talk to him."

Carrie shrugged. "I doubt it. I think he's probably just lonely. The last time I was there he wanted to show me some computer game he designed. I told him I didn't have time right then but that I'd look at it the next time I stopped by."

The waitress brought a new round of drinks, and the others filled Joan and Teresa in on Carrie's introduction to Delores Starling.

As conversation about the *Buckley* case wound down, Will said, "Is anyone interested in participating in a walk or run to raise funds for AIDS research? My secretary, Karen, is one of the coordinators, and she's trying to line up as many people as she can."

"When is it?" Tammy asked.

"The third Saturday in April," Will replied.

"How far do we have to go?" Dona inquired. "I get blisters on my feet pretty easy."

"There are a variety of distances," Will explained. "There are five- and ten-kilometer walks as well as a ten-kilometer run and a half-marathon."

"Forget the last two," Teresa said. "It might be a good

cause, but somebody would have to pay me a bundle to run more than a block."

"I'll bet if Bob Brakefield were chasing you, you'd run," Joan teased.

"If that old codger were chasing me, I'd turn around and knock him down," Teresa retorted.

"Sign me up for the ten-K walk," Tammy said. "It sounds like fun. Do you have pledge sheets for us to fill out?"

"Karen's got those," Will answered. "I'll see that she gets you one on Monday. Any other takers?"

"I'll talk to my son," Dona said. "If he's interested, I'll do it, too."

"I could probably do the short walk," Madree said.

"I'll have to think about it," Teresa said.

"Anyone else?" Will asked. He turned and looked at Carrie.

"I guess I could do the ten-K walk," she said.

"You're not a runner?" he asked.

"I'm afraid not," Carrie answered. "What are you signing up for?"

"I'm thinking of trying the half-marathon. I'm a little out of shape, but I've got a whole month to do a bit of training."

"I'm game for that if you are," Terry Payne said. "Maybe we could train together."

"Great!" Will said enthusiastically.

"Why don't you join them, Carrie?" Madree chided.

Carrie scowled at Madree and said, "I can't even run one mile, let alone thirteen. I think I'd better stick with walking."

"Well, if you change your mind, let us know," Terry said. "I'll bet Will and I could whip you into shape."

"I'll keep that in mind," Carrie said. As she took another sip of her drink, she looked at Will and thought of some more intimate physical activities she'd like to try with him. She smiled to herself. It wasn't going to happen today or tomorrow, but maybe there was still hope.

* * *

Carrie pulled into the driveway of Delores Starling's ranch-style home around ten-fifteen on Saturday morning. The house was probably about twenty years old and was located on a quiet street lined with similar modest dwellings.

Delores was an angular woman in her mid-fifties with short, curly brown hair. She greeted Carrie at the door wearing tight black jeans and an oversized black and white shirt. She ushered Carrie into the living room and indicated that she should take a seat on a black-and-white sofa.

"Would you like some coffee?" Delores asked politely.

"That would be nice," Carrie replied.

Delores went to the kitchen and returned in a few moments with two mugs of steaming java. After handing one to Carrie, she sat down in a black recliner, set her own cup down on a lamp table next to her, and immediately lit a cigarette.

"I know it's a filthy habit," she apologized, blowing smoke in the air. "And I've tried everything to quit, but I just can't seem to give them up. I hope you're not deathly allergic to smoke."

"Don't worry about it," Carrie said, taking a sip of her coffee. She leaned forward and said conversationally, "Why don't you tell me a little bit about Gwen?"

Delores nodded. "I've been divorced fifteen years. My ex is an accountant and he took up with one of his young assistants. Gwen is an only child. She was thirteen at the time. She coped with the divorce pretty well. I think she realized that her father and I hadn't been getting along for quite some time." Delores took another drag on her cigarette.

"How did Gwen become a patient of Dr. Luebke?" Carrie asked gently.

"The summer after her sophomore year of college, she was rock climbing with some friends when she fell and landed on her head. She was unconscious for two days. She suffered a severe concussion and there was some swelling of her brain. She was in the hospital about ten days, but she just wasn't herself afterward. She had periods of memory loss and poor coordination, and she experienced terrible mood swings. Our family doctor referred her to Dr. Luebke, and Gwen began seeing him on an outpatient basis.''

"What type of treatment did Dr. Luebke prescribe?"

"A lot of different things," Delores replied, snuffing out her cigarette and immediately reaching for another one. "Prescription drugs for the mood swings and the memory loss. Group therapy sessions for a while. Hypnosis." She puffed on her cigarette and gave an involuntary shudder. "All sorts of stuff, and it seemed to get weirder as time went on."

"Did Gwen respond to the treatment?"

"She did," Delores admitted. "By the time she went back to school in the fall, she was doing much better, but she continued to see him twice a month." She took another deep drag on the cigarette and then blew the smoke out. "That's when I think her relationship with Dr. Luebke began to be something more than just doctor-patient."

"What caused you to become suspicious about their relationship?" Carrie asked.

"Lots of little things," Delores replied, sipping her coffee. "Whenever I'd talk to Gwen, it seemed that Dr. Luebke was her favorite topic of conversation. She was a business major, but she started talking about switching to medicine. She showed an almost obsessive interest in learning everything she could about neurology. I suspect she was trying to educate herself so she could talk to him on his level. She began turning down dates and refusing to go out with her friends so she could read medical textbooks."

"Did Gwen have an active social life before the accident?"

"Absolutely," Delores nodded emphatically. "She was a very attractive girl, very outgoing. She had lots of friends. At first I thought the change in her behavior was still attributable to the accident, but then around Thanksgiving I found some letters that Luebke had written her, and that's when I knew something was going on."

"How did you happen to find the letters?"

Delores took a deep breath, then exhaled. "She was home for the weekend and had gone out with some friends and I snooped through her suitcase. I know it was an invasion of her privacy, but I was desperate to find out what was wrong with her."

"What did the letters say?"

"I have a couple of them. I'll show you." Delores got up and walked to the back of the house. She returned in a few moments carrying a small stack of envelopes held together by a rubber band. She handed the bundle to Carrie.

Carrie removed the rubber band and looked at the first envelope. It was addressed to Gwen Starling at her sorority house address. Carrie opened the envelope and pulled out a small greeting card with a brightly colored bird on the front. Opening the card, she read the hand written message, "Gwen, Your spirit reminds me of a bird in flight, far-ranging and limitless in its possibilities. You are truly a special person. K. Luebke."

Carrie replaced that card in its envelope and opened the next one. The front of the card had a photo of a rushing mountain stream. The inside read, "May your life and joys be as endless as this current. Affectionately, Ken."

The third card depicted a starry sky and a sliver moon. Inside was the handwritten message, "She walks in beauty like the night of cloudless climes and starry skies; and all that's best of dark and bright meet in her aspect and her eyes. K."

Carrie replaced that card in its envelope and turned to Delores Starling.

"Well, what would you think if you discovered a middle-aged doctor had written those to his young patient?" Delores demanded.

"I'd think the doctor had something more on his mind than just medicine," Carrie admitted.

"That's what I thought," Delores agreed. "Especially since I also found a packet of birth control pills in her suitcase."

Carrie frowned. "Gwen wasn't sexually active before her accident?"

"Well—" Delores hesitated. "I guess I'm not entirely sure about that."

"I can understand your concern about Gwen," Carrie said carefully, "but at most what you've described sounds like consensual sex. I thought you told me Gwen had been raped."

"He was her doctor and he was more than twice her age," Delores retorted. "She was in a fragile emotional state. Whatever happened between them, I'm sure he pressured her."

"All right," Carrie said. "I take it you confronted Gwen about your suspicions?"

Delores nodded. "I must admit I didn't handle the situation very well. Gwen didn't get home until after midnight the night I found that stuff and by that time I had worked myself up into a frenzy. The moment she walked through the door I began screaming at her and demanding to know what was going on."

"What was Gwen's reaction?"

"She didn't take it too well. She called me a meddlesome bitch, among other things. There was a lot of screaming back and forth before she finally broke down sobbing."

"But she denied any improper relationship with Dr. Luebke?"

"Yes. No matter how much I badgered her, she denied it. She called a friend to come pick her up, packed her things, and left."

"Did you talk to Dr. Luebke about it?"

"You're damn right I did. First thing Monday morning I was on the phone to him. I had to call about six times before he bothered to get back to me. By that time he had already talked to Gwen. He told me nothing had happened, that I should get my mind out of the gutter."

"What happened then?"

"As I told you on the phone yesterday, I filed a complaint about Luebke with the licensing board. He and Gwen both wrote responses denying the whole thing, and that's where it ended. I talked to a lawyer about suing, but he told me that Gwen was of age and I couldn't force her to bring a claim if she didn't want to, so that was the end of it."

"Did Gwen continue seeing Luebke professionally after that?"

Delores sighed. "I really don't know. Unfortunately, as a result of this situation I became estranged from my daughter and remain so until this day."

"You don't communicate with her at all?"

Delores shook her head sadly. "She's an accountant, living in Denver. I have her address—I had to con that out of a casual acquaintance—and I send cards with some money on her birthday and at Christmas, but she never responds. She has made it very clear that she wants nothing to do with me. She's turned all of her friends against me. I can't even find out her phone number. It's been almost eight years since I've talked to her." The woman stubbed out her cigarette and tried hard to fight back the tears.

"I'm sorry," Carrie said, reaching over and patting the woman's hand.

Delores regained control of herself and said, "I have no firm proof, but I will go to my grave thinking that bastard violated my daughter. There was nothing I could do to make him pay for what he did to Gwen. So when you called out of the blue yesterday I saw a chance to help some other poor girl."

"Delores, someone called me yesterday saying they knew I was looking for information about Dr. Luebke and giving me your name and address. Do you have any idea who the caller might have been?"

Delores shook her head. "No, but if I did, I'd thank them. I've been waiting for years to get a chance to pay Dr. Luebke back for what he did to us. Do you think what I've told you will be of any use in your case?" She looked at Carrie hopefully.

"I don't know," Carrie said truthfully. "It certainly sounds like Dr. Luebke has a pattern of questionable behavior in dealing with young female patients, but since it was never proven that he actually assaulted Gwen or even coerced her into some sort of consensual sexual activity,

I'm not sure if I'll be able to make use of the information in my case."

"Would those letters help you in any way?" Delores asked. "If you think they would, take them with you. I've spent enough miserable hours reading them over and over and cursing the day the man was born."

"I appreciate that," Carrie said, picking up the packet of envelopes and putting it in her purse. "And I appreciate your taking the time to talk to me. I know how difficult this must be for you."

Delores nodded. "I miss her so much," she said, staring off into space. "I'd give anything to turn back time to before this all happened." She reached over and gripped Carrie's wrist tightly. "I couldn't help Gwen, but now you have a chance to make up for my failure. You can make him pay for what he did. It's all up to you now."

"I'll do the best I can," Carrie promised.

Chapter 25

April Fools' Day was one of Burt Ramquist's favorite holidays. There was something about this homage to pranksters that brought out the head of the firm's most creative and childlike qualities. Each April 1 he would arrive at the office at daybreak in order to have several practical jokes in place by the time the rest of the staff arrived.

By midmorning, while the secretaries were still guffawing over how Burt had switched the signs on the men's and women's rest rooms and the lawyers were praising his clever E-mail purportedly setting forth a new dress code for the firm—plaid jackets and green fishnet stockings on Tuesdays, black leather and ballet slippers on alternate Fridays—Carrie and Will were in Will's office discussing Delores Starling.

They had been having the same conversation, in various forms, for four days—ever since Carrie had gotten back from her visit with Delores. To date they had not reached an agreement as to whether there was anything they could or should do with the information Delores had provided.

"We could ask Judge Little for a ruling on its admissibility," Carrie suggested optimistically.

"We'd get laughed out of court," Will replied. "The law greatly disfavors evidence of other bad acts, and this doesn't even meet that pathetically low standard, since there was never any proof that Dr. Luebke actually did anything improper to or with Gwen."

"Why would a middle-aged doctor send a twenty-year-old female patient mushy cards like that unless there was something going on?"

"Maybe the doctor is just generally sort of sappy and sends cards like that to all his patients."

"Right," Carrie made a face. "Luebke certainly comes across as the sentimental type. It's so damn frustrating," she grumbled. "I can just feel there's something there, if only I knew how to break through to it."

"Did you have any luck trying to reach Gwen Starling in Denver?" Will asked.

Carrie shook her head. "Her home phone number is unlisted. I called her office a couple of times, but they wouldn't put me through. I left my number, but I know she won't call back."

"It probably doesn't matter," Will said pragmatically. "If she's been denying a relationship with Luebke for the past eight years, I doubt she's suddenly going to break down and admit one to you—even if you are a hell of a good inquisitor."

"So where does that leave us?" Carrie wondered aloud.

"Back at square one, I'm afraid," Will said. "The same place we seem to have been stuck for the past two months."

Before Carrie could respond to that gloomy comment, the door to Will's office opened and his secretary stuck her head in. "Excuse me," Karen said apologetically. "I know you said you didn't want to be disturbed, but Todd Fleming is on the phone, and he sounds very upset. I thought you might want to talk to him."

"Thanks, Karen," Will said, immediately reaching for the phone. "Hello. Todd? It's Will Rollston. What can I do for you? . . . Slow down. I didn't catch that. What did you say?"

Carrie and Will had thought it a bit odd that Todd hadn't called to report how the polygraph exam he had taken five days earlier had gone. Carrie had tried to call the young man several times over the past couple of days but hadn't been able to reach him. Now, watching Will's face, she had a sudden sinking feeling that the exam had not turned out as planned.

"Slow down, Todd," Will said again. "Repeat that last part once more."

As Will looked up at Carrie, he pursed his lips and shook his head. Carrie's stomach began to feel a bit queasy. Todd was clearly not relaying good news.

"You're sure about that?" Will asked. "There couldn't be some sort of mistake? . . . Okay," Will said, picking up a pen and jotting some notes down on a piece of paper. "I'll call him right away. I know how you must feel, but try to keep your spirits up. We'll check it out and get back to you. . . . Okay, buddy. Talk to you soon. Good luck. 'Bye."

As Will hung up, he slammed his fist down hard on the desk. "Son of a bitch! I never would have expected this."

"Let me guess," Carrie said. "Todd flunked the polygraph."

"He didn't exactly flunk," Will corrected her. "It's just that he didn't exactly pass either."

"What does that mean?"

"It means the results were inconclusive."

"How can that be?" Carrie exclaimed. "We all know Todd didn't do it."

"I don't know," Will said. "I feel so sorry for the kid. He sounded like he was on the verge of hysteria."

"Can you blame him?" Carrie asked.

"Not at all," Will said, picking up the phone and punching some numbers. "Apparently the reason we didn't hear from Todd on Friday is that the examiner thought Todd had seemed awfully distraught and that his mental state might have skewed the results. So he scheduled Todd for a second test this morning. Unfortunately, that one didn't turn out any better." He held up a finger as someone answered his phone call.

"Could I speak to Charles Bohachek, please? This is Attorney Will Rollston calling. Thank you." Turning back to Carrie, he said, "Let's see what the examiner has to say and then decide where to go from there.

"Mr. Bohachek?" Will said into the phone. "Will Rollston. I'm calling about Todd Fleming. . . . Yes, I just spoke to him. Mr. Bohachek, Carrie Nelson, who set up Todd's appointment with you, is here in the office with me. Would you mind if I put you on speakerphone so we could both talk with you? Great." Will punched a button on the phone. "Can you hear me, Mr. Bohachek?"

"Loud and clear," a bass voice boomed out.

"Good morning, Mr. Bohachek. It's Carrie Nelson."

"Good morning," Bohachek replied.

"So," Will said, "according to Todd, you termed the results of both his tests inconclusive."

"Yes, unfortunately, that's right," Bohachek replied.

"Does that happen with much frequency?" Carrie asked.

"No, it doesn't," Bohachek answered. "The technology in use these days is quite sophisticated. It's all computerized, which leaves far less room for error and makes it pretty difficult for someone to beat the test. But unfortunately, nothing is foolproof, and some people just aren't good subjects. I would rank Mr. Fleming in that category. "

"Todd mentioned that after the first test on Friday, you thought he was maybe so stressed that it skewed the result," Will said.

"That's right."

"Do you think the same thing could have happened today?" Will asked.

"It's possible," Bohachek said. "It's clear the young man is struggling to keep his life together."

"Is it likely that a third test would come out any different?" Carrie asked.

Bohachek sighed. "It's extremely doubtful. To be honest with you, I've never had a subject yield such ambivalent results two times in a row. Usually whatever the problem was the first time around resolves itself by the second go-round."

"Let me make sure I understand you clearly," Carrie said. "The fact that the results are inconclusive does not necessarily mean that Todd is lying."

"Not at all," Bohachek said confidently. "It just means that for some reason we're not able to tell what's truthful and what's not."

"So Todd could be telling the truth when he says he didn't assault Katherine Buckley," Carrie followed up.

"Absolutely."

"Well, we appreciate your efforts," Will said.

"No problem. I appreciate the referral. I'm sorry I wasn't able to give you the result you wanted. I'll put a copy of my report in the mail for you today, unless you'd rather have me fax it."

"Oh, I don't think there's any particular hurry," Will said wryly. "Thank you."

"Yes, thanks," Carrie echoed.

"My pleasure. I hope you'll keep me in mind in the future. As I said, this is really an anomaly. I am normally able to produce pretty clear-cut results."

After Todd hung up the phone, he and Carrie sat there in silence for a time. Carrie spoke first. "Now what do we do?"

"About what?"

"About notifying Detective Clauff about the results of Todd's polygraph," she answered. "The last time I spoke to him, I really rubbed it in about how I'd let him know as soon as I had the favorable report in hand. God, that was a brilliant ploy," she said, smacking herself on the forehead. "Somebody should protect me from my own stupidity." She got up and began to pace back and forth in front of Will's desk.

"Don't blame yourself," Will said. "I would've done the same thing. Anyone would have."

"Stupid, stupid, stupid," Carrie repeated. "I thought the test was a surefire way to clear Todd's name. Instead I've made things worse for him."

"No, you haven't," Will replied.

"Yes, I have," Carrie insisted. "I never should have agreed to set the test up for him. I had qualms about it from the beginning. So did you, so did Burt. I should have somehow talked Todd out of it."

"You couldn't do that. He's an adult. He's entitled to call his own shots, and he was insisting on going ahead with it."

"I've done some dumb things in my career, but this ranks right up there," Carrie said, continuing to chastise herself.

Will got up, came around his desk to where Carrie was standing, and put his hands on Carrie's shoulders. She involuntarily shivered. "It's not your fault," he said. "Granted, this isn't the result any of us anticipated, but it's not the end of the world. Todd is in the same position today he's been in all along—no better, no worse."

"You're wrong. He is in a worse position because he looks foolish. And so do I. I screwed it up."

"Stop that," Will said, giving her a gentle shake. "You haven't screwed anything up. You're a hell of a lawyer, and you're doing a terrific job on the case, and one way or another we are going to solve this thing."

"I have screwed it up," Carrie said morosely. "I screwed things up for Todd, and for all I know, I've screwed up the whole case. I never should have agreed to take it. I might as well face it: I'm in way over my head." She abruptly pulled away from Will and rushed back to her own office.

Carrie spent the rest of the day working on other matters, trying her best to put Todd Fleming and Katherine Buckley out of her mind. She didn't like to admit it, but she hadn't felt this depressed about a case in a long time. Usually, no matter how badly things were going, she was able to keep her perspective. This would serve as a lesson in why it was a bad idea to take friends on as clients or become personally involved in cases. It was just too hard on her psyche.

She was dictating a report to a client around four that afternoon when her direct phone line rang. She really wasn't in the mood to talk to anyone, but since only friends and clients had that number, she decided she'd better answer. It might be something important. As it turned out, she was unprepared for the magnitude of the call.

"Carrie Nelson," she announced in a lethargic voice as she picked up the phone.

"Ms. Nelson?" A female voice came on the line. "This

is Dr. Kaylee Flanagan at Converse Medical Center. I'm one of Katherine Buckley's doctors."

Carrie felt a sudden chill go through her. "Yes. Has something happened?"

"I'm afraid it has," Dr. Flanagan replied. "Katherine had a seizure early this morning. We got that under control, but then within an hour her whole system suddenly started to shut down." The doctor sighed. "We tried everything, but she just wouldn't respond."

Carrie felt as if she were choking. "Is she—?" She couldn't bring herself to say the word.

"She's on life support," Dr. Flanagan replied. "Her parents asked me to call you. They'd like you to come."

"I'm on my way," Carrie replied. She hung up the phone. Moving around the office as if in a daze, she threw on her raincoat and stuffed some files and legal pads into her briefcase. As she opened a drawer and pulled out her purse, she caught sight of the calendar on top of the desk.

April Fools' Day. Carrie instinctively knew that the delightful innocence of this day had been forever shattered.

Chapter 26

Carrie was in such a state of nervous agitation during the twenty-minute drive to Converse Medical Center that she later marveled that she had arrived in one piece. Before flying out of the office after her phone call from Dr. Flanagan, she had stopped to give Will this tragic update on the case. He had wanted to accompany her, but Carrie had turned him down. No matter how difficult this visit was going to be, she felt it was something she had to do alone.

As Carrie pulled into the parking garage of the large medical complex, she noticed for the first time that day that the sun was shining brightly and the grass was unusually green and lush for so early in the season. It was a beautiful spring day in Chicago. Many more days like this would no doubt follow. But Katherine Buckley would never be able to enjoy them because, although machines were keeping her technically alive, she was for all intents and purposes quite dead.

A pleasant middle-aged woman at the reception desk directed Carrie to Katherine's room on the fourth floor of the complex. As Carrie approached the designated room, the door opened and an attractive brown-haired woman around her own age dressed in a white coat stepped out into the hall. "Ms. Nelson?" the woman asked.

Carrie nodded.

"Kaylee Flanagan," the woman said, extending her hand. "Thank you for coming so quickly."

Carrie shook hands with the doctor. "Are the Buckleys inside?" she asked, motioning toward the room.

"Yes. Katherine's friend Todd is here, too."

Inwardly Carrie groaned. Oddly enough, the news about Katherine's sudden deterioration had put Todd's problem clean out of her mind. Now the mention of his name brought the day's earlier upset rushing back all too clearly. *Poor Todd,* Carrie thought, her throat tightening. He must be on the verge of a breakdown by now. How much anguish could one person stand in such a short span of time?

"Exactly what happened to Katherine?" Carrie asked, stalling in hopes of putting off facing her clients just a bit longer.

"We don't really know what caused it," Dr. Flanagan said ruefully. "But she had a seizure and then everything just stopped functioning."

"Was it the added strain of the pregnancy?" Carrie asked pointedly.

"It could well have been," Dr. Flanagan agreed. "But then again, maybe it wasn't. Katherine was in a very vulnerable state even before the pregnancy. Sometimes things like this just happen."

Carrie sighed. "Maybe in the end it will be for the best," she said quietly. "Immediately after Katherine's accident, when things were touch and go, the Buckleys said they were interested in donating her organs. Have they mentioned anything to you about that?"

Dr. Flanagan looked puzzled. "No, but at this point there's no reason why they would."

Carrie furrowed her brows. "What do you mean? Don't organ recipients have to be found before the life-support system is disconnected?"

Dr. Flanagan's mouth gaped open. "There must be some misunderstanding. The Buckleys aren't going to be disconnecting the life support."

"They're not?" Carrie asked, her stomach churning even more violently than before.

"No, they're adamant about maintaining Katherine's status until the fetus is viable and can be successfully delivered."

For a long moment Carrie thought she was going to

vomit. She took a couple of deep breaths and swallowed hard. Then she had to clear her throat several times before she managed to say, "Doctor, could we possibly take a little walk down the hall? I'd like to discuss this further, but I think it might be best if we had a little privacy."

"Certainly," the doctor replied.

They had walked nearly the entire length of the long hall before Carrie was able to think of something to say that wouldn't sound completely insensitive. "Have the Buckleys really considered all the ramifications of their decision?" she asked carefully.

"I believe so," Dr. Flanagan answered.

Carrie stopped and swung around to face the doctor. "This is insane!" she exclaimed, all semblance of sensitivity thrown out the window. "It's perverse and it's unnatural! What on earth can they be thinking?"

"They want to have their grandchild," the doctor answered simply. "A part of Katherine. The only part of her they'll ever have. Is that really so unnatural?"

"Yes, it is," Carrie replied passionately. "I couldn't understand why they didn't want to terminate the pregnancy as soon as they discovered it, given Katherine's condition and the fact that they don't know who the child's father is. But at least at that point Katherine was still breathing on her own and her heart was pumping under its own power. Now you tell me everything has shut down and a machine is doing all that for her."

Carrie stopped and looked at the doctor imploringly. "The part that was Katherine is gone. All that's left is a shell. I understand that modern medical technology can enable the Buckleys to have their grandchild, but in the process they'll be demeaning Katherine by turning her into nothing more than a human incubator. Is that really what they want?"

Dr. Flanagan ran her tongue around her lips. "I hear what you're saying, and I don't disagree with you. Frankly, this isn't the choice I'd make for a loved one, nor is it something I'd want if I were in Katherine's position. But the Buckleys are Katherine's guardians, and it *is* their choice. No one else can make it for them. Not me—and not you."

"But did you even try to talk them out of it?" Carrie persisted. "Surely they'd listen—"

"We talked at quite some length," Dr. Flanagan cut her off in a stern voice. "And it's apparent that this *is* what they want. Others may not agree with the decision, but we're bound to accept it."

Carrie's eyes welled up with tears. She unzipped her bag, dug out a tissue, and wiped her wet cheeks.

Dr. Flanagan took a step forward and put an arm around Carrie's shoulders. "Are you okay?" she asked gently.

Carrie sniffed loudly and nodded.

"Come on," the doctor said. "The ladies' room is right over here. Why don't you freshen up a bit and then we'll go see the Buckleys? I'll wait for you."

Carrie mutely nodded her thanks and hurried into the rest room. She emerged a few minutes later with clear eyes and freshened lipstick. "I'm ready," she announced to Dr. Flanagan in a strong voice. "And I'm sorry for what I said. Even before you called me, I'd been having a really lousy day and—" Her voice trailed off. "I guess what I'm trying to say is I didn't intend to demean the Buckleys' choice. It's obviously their call."

"Don't worry about it," Dr. Flanagan said. "I understand completely. Now let's go. The Buckleys are waiting for you."

When Carrie walked into the room, the first thing she noticed was how much noise the machinery sustaining Katherine's vital organs made. The rhythmic *whoosh* seemed to reverberate in the close confines of the room. The Buckleys and Todd were sitting close to Katherine's bed. With no hesitation, Carrie immediately walked over to the bed and squeezed Katherine's lifeless hand. Then she turned to the young woman's parents and fiancé. "How are you guys doing?" she asked quietly.

"Okay," Melody Buckley answered. The woman's face was flushed, but her eyes were dry. "We'll get through this

together." She reached over and patted Todd's hand.
"Won't we, Todd?"

Todd nodded. Although the young man looked wan and
tired, he was bearing up far better than Carrie had
expected.

"Thank you for coming, Carrie," Ed Buckley said. "It
means a lot to us."

"No problem," Carrie murmured.

"So," Ed continued, "this change in Katherine's condition isn't going to affect the case's going forward, is it?"

"No, the case will still go on."

"Good," Ed said with satisfaction. "That's what we
want."

"You haven't uncovered any more leads, have you?"
Melody asked.

Carrie shook her head. "Not yet, I'm afraid. But we're
far from done with our investigation."

"If only the police were more cooperative," Ed said. "I
can't for the life of me understand why they keep bothering
Todd. They must just be a bunch of lazy galoots. It will
give me great satisfaction to prove them wrong and see
Todd vindicated."

I hope to God we can do that, Carrie thought to herself.
The way things were going, that was merely a pipe dream.

"Have you talked to Dr. Flanagan?" Melody asked.

"Yes. I ran into her in the hall when I arrived," Carrie
replied.

"She's been just wonderful," Melody said. "Everyone
here at Converse Medical has been. If only we'd arranged
to have Katherine brought here right after the accident—"
Her voice trailed off, then she recovered. "But then we
wouldn't have our grandchild," she added, managing a
small smile.

Ed Buckley nodded as though this were all perfectly routine. Todd seemed to be in his own little world, sitting there
quietly, staring off into space. Carrie suspected the poor
kid was probably in shock. She wished he were more in
control of the situation. Perhaps he could have talked some
sense into Katherine's parents.

After a few more minutes of idle conversation, during which Carrie began to feel more and more claustrophobic, there was a short knock on the door.

"Come in," Ed Buckley called out.

The door opened and Bishop Wilson walked in. In contrast to Carrie's previous meeting with him, today the cleric wore jeans and a plaid shirt. He swiftly crossed the room, embraced Ed and Melody, shook hands with Todd and Carrie, and laid his hand gently on Katherine's forehead. Then he stepped back and said ruefully, "I apologize for my appearance. I came as soon as I got your message. I've been helping my younger son build a fence. By this time next week I may very well have a new grandchild, and my son is insistent that all these household projects be completed before she arrives."

"So you know it's going to be a girl?" Melody asked.

The bishop nodded. "Yes, little Ashley is scheduled to make her debut around the ninth."

"How wonderful," Melody said. "I wouldn't mind having a little granddaughter."

"A grandson would be nice, too," Ed put in.

"As the proud grandfather of two little boys, I heartily agree that either gender is equally welcome," Bishop Wilson said.

For the next fifteen minutes Carrie sat by passively as the bishop and the Buckleys chatted about babies and mundane matters as though Katherine and her noisy life-support systems were not even there. Occasionally even Todd would rouse himself from his lethargy and chime in with some comment. Carrie found herself growing more and more uneasy. The day's events had left her feeling professionally inadequate and emotionally drained. She had to get out of there before she snapped.

Making a show of looking at her watch, she said, "I'm afraid I'm going to have to be heading out. I have an appointment in half an hour."

"Thank you so much for coming," Melody said. "It means a lot to us, and I know it would to Katherine, too."

"Yes, thank you, Carrie," Ed added. "We appreciate all your efforts more than we can express."

"I'll be in touch," Carrie said as she headed for the door.

"I'll walk you down the hall," Bishop Wilson said, following her. "I believe I spied a rest room on my way in, and I see that I didn't do a very thorough job of getting the grime off my hands."

Once out in the hall, the bishop said to Carrie conversationally, "It was very nice of you to come. It really does mean a lot to the Buckleys, and I know this is a place you'd rather not be."

Carrie managed a weak smile. "Is it that obvious?"

The bishop shook his head. "Not at all. You're very adept at hiding your true feelings."

"What's your opinion of the Buckleys' keeping Katherine on life support just so the baby can be delivered?" Carrie ventured to ask boldly.

"You find that decision rather inexplicable, don't you?"

Carrie frowned. "You always seem to know what I'm thinking. Are you a mind reader?" she demanded.

The bishop smiled. "No, of course not. I'm just more attuned to people's feelings than most. What is it that bothers you about the Buckleys' decision?"

Carrie took a deep breath, then exhaled. "It seems unnatural. It seems selfish. It seems humiliating to Katherine." She paused for a moment to collect her thoughts, then added, "I'm not a religious person, but I guess it also seems like the Buckleys are playing God. If this is Katherine's time to go, shouldn't she be allowed to pass away with dignity? That probably sounds crass, but that's how I feel."

"I don't think it's crass," the bishop replied. "You obviously care deeply about Katherine. Ed and Melody do, too. They just see what they should do in a different light than you do."

Carrie nodded slowly. "I'm having a hard time accepting their decision."

"That merely shows you're an ethical and caring person. The world could use more people like you."

As Carrie looked up at the bishop, a sudden thought ran

through her head and before she knew it she blurted out, "Several people have mentioned that you were alone with Katherine on occasion. Would you care to comment on that?"

The cleric's friendly demeanor immediately changed. "Have I ever been alone with Katherine?" he fairly shouted. "Yes, I have. Are you suggesting there is something untoward about that?"

Carrie flushed. *The strain of this case is obviously getting to me,* she thought. *Now I'm accusing a man of the cloth of being a rapist.* "I'm sorry," she said contritely. "I don't know why I said that. Please forgive me."

Bishop Wilson took a deep breath, then exhaled. "That's quite all right. This is a trying time for all of us, isn't it?"

Carrie ran her tongue over her lips and nodded. "I'm worried I might lose the case for lack of evidence," she admitted.

"The case is a long way from over," the bishop counseled, his tone congenial again. "A lot can happen in the next couple of months."

Carrie looked up at him skeptically. "So you can predict the future in addition to reading minds?" she asked dryly.

The bishop smiled. "You make me sound like I should go out and get a job reading tea leaves." He took a step forward and put an arm around Carrie's shoulder. "I can't predict the future, and I can't read minds. But I know you're going to put your whole heart and mind into the case, and if you do that, I don't see how you can possibly fail."

Carrie could feel her eyes tearing up again. "Thank you," she said. "I'll try not to let the Buckleys down."

"You won't. And you won't let yourself down either." As he turned to go, he said lightly, "I'd stake my job on it."

Chapter 27

Early the following morning Will came into Carrie's office. "Are you okay?" he asked quietly.

"Yeah," Carrie replied.

Will sat down in one of the chairs in front of her desk. "I was worried about you. I tried to call you last night."

"I got your message," Carrie said. "I'm sorry I didn't call back, but I just didn't feel like talking to anyone."

"I understand," Will said.

Carrie picked up a pen and began twirling it between her fingers. "The scene at the hospital was rather emotional," she said. She briefly explained her conversations with Dr. Flanagan, the Buckleys, and Bishop Wilson.

"You don't think the bishop could have assaulted Katherine, do you?" Will asked with obvious concern.

"I don't think so," Carrie said, running her hands through her hair. "He's one of the Buckleys' oldest friends. I'm embarrassed to admit that I even thought of such a thing. I guess that shows how desperate I'm getting to solve the case."

"I hate to state the obvious, but at the moment our list of possible suspects is a little light. If you think there's any possibility—no matter how remote—that the bishop could be involved, maybe we should take his deposition."

Carrie held up her hands. "Let's not rush into that. Some other leads might still turn up."

"All right," Will said, seeing that she was upset. "We'll table that idea for now. So what did you do after you left Converse Medical?"

"Well, I was feeling really drained, so I decided to go to a movie."

"Alone?" Will asked.

Carrie nodded. "I don't think I would've been very good company. I ended up going to an animation festival. It was pretty mindless, but it did the trick of taking my mind off Katherine, at least temporarily. Then when I got home around eight, I discovered my house had been vandalized."

"What?" Will asked with astonishment.

"Somebody carved the words 'STOP IT' in the center of my oak front door."

"Did you call the police?"

"Yes, but it's such a minor crime, they made it clear that they probably aren't even going to bother investigating. I called the landlord, too. He came over and said he'd talk to some of the neighbors to see if they saw anything. I'd be surprised if they did. Most people on my block work during the day, and there aren't any retail establishments on the street, so it wouldn't be hard for someone to do minor damage like that without being seen. The landlord said he should be able to get the door sanded down. I hope he's right. It's a wonderful old door, and it made me sick to see it defaced."

"You don't think the message was directed toward you?" Will asked with obvious concern.

"Of course not," Carrie answered immediately. "It was probably just a kid pulling an April Fools' prank." She sighed. "It's really not a big deal. It's just that on top of everything else that happened yesterday—" Her voice trailed off.

"I wish you had called me," Will said. "I could've come over to keep you company."

"That's very nice of you, but I didn't want to ruin anybody else's day."

"Well, if you ever have any other problems like this, you let me know. I'd be happy to help."

"Thanks," Carrie said, her mood starting to brighten.

"And you be careful when you're out alone at night," Will cautioned. "There are a lot of weirdos around, even in the best neighborhoods. I wouldn't want anything to happen to you."

"I'll be fine," Carrie said, smiling at him for the first time. "But I appreciate your concern more than you realize."

Ten days later, Carrie and Madree Williams appeared in federal court to defend a motion for summary judgment filed in the housing discrimination case. Depositions of the key witnesses had now been completed, and Joe Scalerri's attorney was asking the court to dismiss the case before trial. He claimed the evidence showed as a matter of law that Carrie's clients were entitled to no compensation.

While Scalerri's attorney, Ed Squiers, had been very friendly to Carrie at their last meeting, today he looked grim and downcast, failing even to greet Carrie and Madree when they walked into the courtroom. Scalerri, on the other hand, looked positively jovial, purposely catching the women's eyes and giving them a big fake grin.

"He looks like the cat that ate the canary," Madree commented as they took their place at counsel table.

"I'd like to stuff a canary down his throat," Carrie said under her breath.

Although Carrie had told her clients that it would not be necessary for them to come to the hearing, Eureka Washington had insisted on leaving work early so she could attend. "I want the court to know that old Scalerri's badass notions affect real live people," Eureka had said firmly when she met with Carrie and Madree a couple of days before the hearing.

"Besides that," Eureka had confided in a lower voice, "I've got a cousin down New Orleans way that has the power. She filled me in on a couple of techniques and I've been tryin' 'em out, but they work best if you're in the same room with the subject."

"The power?" Carrie asked, perplexed. "What's that?"

"You know," Eureka said, looking at her meaningfully.

"I'm afraid I don't," Carrie insisted.

"She means voodoo," Madree put in.

"Shhhh!" Eureka said. "Don't you go usin' that word. It gets white folks all riled up."

Carrie smiled to herself as she recalled that conversation and turned around to look at Eureka, who was seated in the first row of the spectator section, directly across from Scalerri. Sure enough, Eureka was staring at the slumlord so intently that Carrie wouldn't have been at all surprised to see the man's head suddenly burst into flames.

Judge Beddingfield's clerk called the case. After the attorneys had announced their names for the record, the judge turned to Ed Squiers. "I've read your written submissions, counselor," the portly gray-haired judge said in a booming voice. "Give me a brief summary of why you think I should dismiss this case, with the emphasis on the word 'brief.' "

"Certainly, Your Honor," Squiers said, getting to his feet. "The undisputed evidence shows that the lease terminations are entirely consistent with the express written terms of the leases. Each lease contains a provision allowing termination for inappropriate behavior by tenants. One member of each of the plaintiffs' families was arrested for criminal behavior. There is no requirement that the criminal behavior occur on the premises. Thus, we contend that the lease terminations were lawful and the plaintiffs' civil rights suit is merely a smoke screen to thwart Mr. Scalerri from exercising his rights as a landlord. And that is why you should grant our motion for summary judgment." Squiers sat down.

"Thank you, counselor," the judge said. "Ms. Nelson, your turn."

Carrie nodded and stood up. Taking a quick look behind her, she saw that Scalerri was grinning broadly, while Eureka Washington's glare had intensified.

"The defendant appears to be confused about exactly what is at issue in this case," Carrie said. "His arguments about the language of the lease might be germane in the eviction action—which, as he is well aware, has been stayed pending resolution of this case—but those arguments are immaterial here. The salient issue before us is whether the defendant deprived my clients of any fundamental right or discriminated against them on the basis of race, gender, or any other protected classification." Carrie paused and took a sip of water.

"Each of my clients is a member of a racial minority," Carrie continued, "and each is a single female head of household. The defendant's attempt to evict the plaintiffs from their homes is nothing more than thinly veiled discrimination." She took another sip of water. "In order to prevail on a motion for summary judgment, the moving party must establish that there are no material factual issues in dispute and that, as a matter of law, the moving party is entitled to judgment. The defendant has not met that burden here, since it is obvious that there are numerous disputed factual issues. Thus, their motion must be denied." She sat down.

"Thank you, Ms. Nelson," Judge Beddingfield said. "While I frequently take these types of motions under advisement, in this case I am prepared to issue my ruling now." He referred to the legal pad in front of him. "I find that the existence of disputed factual issues precludes the entry of summary judgment. The defendant's motion is denied. The plaintiffs shall draft an order for my signature. Thank you, ladies and gentlemen." Then, addressing his bailiff, he directed, "Call the next case."

As Carrie and Madree packed up their briefcases and began to walk from the counsel table toward Eureka, Carrie saw Scalerri and his attorney making their way toward the door of the courtroom. Lawyer and client both looked downright grim. As Carrie watched, she saw Eureka continue to stare at Scalerri, a look of pure concentration on her face. Just before Scalerri reached the door, his legs suddenly seemed to buckle and if his lawyer hadn't caught him, he would have fallen to the floor. Squiers put his arm around his client's waist and half dragged him out of the courtroom.

When Carrie, Madree, and Eureka left the courtroom a moment later, they saw Scalerri and his lawyer sitting on a nearby bench. Eureka gave her head a proud toss and emit-

ted a small grunt of satisfaction as she walked past. When
the three women were safely in the elevator, Madree said
to Eureka teasingly, "Poor Mr. Scalerri didn't look well.
What do you suppose could have happened to him?"

"I told you my cousin was teaching me the power," Eureka said proudly.

Carrie furrowed her brows. "You don't mean to tell me
you actually think you had something to do with making
him trip?"

"He didn't trip," Eureka replied. "He done lost all the
strength in his puny little legs."

"And you were the cause of that?" Carrie asked
skeptically.

"Damn straight," Eureka replied, nodding her head
vigorously.

"Is that so?" Carrie asked, musing on the situation.
While she considered voodoo to be so much bunk, she had
to admit that there were times when having the power
could come in handy. "Say," she said casually when the
elevator reached the ground floor. "I don't suppose you'd
consider giving me a few lessons? You see, I've got this
case where I'm up against some really repulsive people who
run a mental hospital—"

"Stop it right there!" Madree ordered as they headed
out of the building. "I refuse to let you get mixed up in
black magic."

"Sister, you're no fun," Eureka scolded. "Tell you what
I'll do. To thank you for winning this big motion, I'd like
to buy you both a cup of coffee and a piece of pie. I know
a nice little place a coupla blocks over that serves fruit pies
so good they'll make you cry. And while we're eatin,' I'll
fill you in on the basics of the power, just for fun."

"Oh, all right," Madree agreed. "Just for fun."

"Sounds good to me," Carrie said. Putting an arm
around Eureka's shoulders, she said confidentially, "How
about if I describe the two really bad guys at the hospital?"

Carrie had to jump swiftly to the left to avoid being hit
by Madree's strong right jab.

Chapter 28

The weather forecast for the day of the AIDS walk had been partly sunny and sixty-five degrees. Unfortunately, from the moment Carrie rolled reluctantly out of bed at seven that morning and looked out the window, she could tell that all the fancy radar and Doppler systems had gone seriously awry. There was a heavy layer of frost on the cars parked on the street below her, and the lawns wore a glistening white coating. Clearly an Alberta Clipper must have descended upon the Windy City while it slept.

As Carrie hurriedly gulped down a bowl of cereal and a cup of coffee, she seriously considered bowing out of the walk, but her pride wouldn't allow her to do so. The event was for a good cause, and she had raised more than eight hundred dollars in pledges. She wouldn't feel right about collecting any of it unless she actually walked the 6.2 miles. In addition, several other people from the firm had already dropped out for reasons beyond their control.

Ann had fallen down some stairs two days earlier and badly twisted her ankle, putting her out of commission. Tammy had come down with bronchitis and was going to spend the weekend at home babying herself. Various other potential walkers had found other things to do instead. Carrie had never been one to let people down, and she felt she owed it to Will and his secretary to do what she'd promised. So dressed in what she hoped were sufficient layers of clothing to keep her comfortable, she set out to do her good deed for the week.

Will had arranged for two large vans to shuttle Ramquist and Dowd participants from the office to Grant Park, which was the starting point for all events. He greeted Carrie warmly when she walked into the firm's reception area.

"Good morning! I'm glad to see you made it. Unfortunately, the weather has caused a number of the less hardy souls in our group to defect."

"I don't blame them," Carrie said, helping herself to a cup of coffee from one of the pots on the reception desk. "You can see your breath outside. I just hope it doesn't snow before it's over."

"It'll be fine," Will assured her. "Once you get moving you'll warm up." He consulted a list of the event's participants. "It looks like you're the only person from our group doing the ten-K walk," he reported.

Carrie frowned. "You mean everyone else dropped out?" she asked, dismayed.

"They didn't all drop out," Will replied. "Some of them switched to the five-K walk because of the cold. You can do that too, if you'd like."

What she would have liked was to go home and go back to bed, but she wasn't about to admit she was a quitter. "No, I'll stick with my original category," she said unenthusiastically.

"That's the spirit!" Will said. Leaning closer, he said, "If you play your cards right, maybe I'll buy you lunch when we're finished."

Carrie immediately brightened. That was certainly something to look forward to. "You're on," she said, smiling at him.

The short van ride to Grant Park was followed by what seemed like an interminably long wait for Carrie's event to get under way. The runners took off first. "See you at the finish line," Will called cheerfully as he and Terry Payne bounded out of the van to await the start of the half-marathon.

Carrie waited in the warmth of the van as long as she could before finally climbing out into the cold. As she stood silently among the throng of other walkers, she looked down at the plastic number pinned to her jacket. It read "1858." Did that mean there were around two thousand other crazy souls like herself out here braving these frigid conditions? The whole city must be nuts.

As she was standing there, moving her feet up and down to keep them warm and trying not to think about the miserable weather, she heard a familiar voice call, "Hello, Carrie." Looking around, she saw Dr. Peckham. The always stylish doctor was dressed in black jeans and a black-and-red down jacket.

"Hello," Carrie replied. "Are you walking, too?" she asked, hoping that she might have someone friendly to talk to en route after all.

"No, we're just volunteers this year," the doctor replied. "We're going to be working in the first-aid tent." For the first time Carrie noticed the woman at the doctor's side. "This is my wife, Justine," he said, putting his hand on the woman's arm. "Juss, this is Attorney Carrie Nelson."

As the women murmured polite hellos, Carrie took a closer look at Mrs. Peckham. "Trophy Wife" was the descriptive term that sprang immediately to mind. Justine Peckham appeared to be in her early thirties, tall, tan, and toned. Her ring finger sported a diamond the size of the Sears Tower, and she wore her blond hair long and straight. She was dressed in black Spandex tights with a form-fitting aqua-and-black top that showed off oversized—and probably surgically enhanced—breasts.

Seeing Justine Peckham in the flesh, Carrie better understood the doctor's choice of a super-expensive sports car. He was obviously trying to show that he still had his virility. Well, there was nothing wrong with that. After all, the man worked hard and could apparently afford all his toys. He might as well enjoy himself while he could. Carrie assumed there had been a predecessor Mrs. Peckham, and she couldn't help but wonder what that woman had looked like and how she had fared in the divorce settlement.

"Walkers, take your places!" A booming command came over the loudspeaker.

"That's my cue," Carrie said. "It was nice to see you," she said to the doctor. "Nice meeting you," she added to his wife.

"Good luck," Dr. Peckham called encouragingly. "Try to stay warm."

"I'll try," Carrie shouted back as the starter pistol went off and two thousand icy bodies lumbered across the starting line.

Carrie's hope that she would warm up once she actually started walking faded rather quickly. After the first mile her feet began to feel like clumps of ice. She heard someone near her say that the temperature was thirty-six and the wind chill fifteen. Hearing those figures made her teeth chatter, and she pulled her stocking cap down more firmly on her head.

This too shall pass, Carrie told herself as she grimly kept marching forward. She had figured that by maintaining a fairly brisk pace she should be able to finish the course in around an hour and forty-five minutes. She had hoped to have a walking companion with whom she would be able to carry on a lively conversation that would cause the time to fly. Absent that, she decided she would just have to think about something other than how she was turning into a human icicle. Not surprisingly, the *Buckley* case was the first thing that sprang to mind.

The complete lack of progress in the case was starting to become a serious worry for her. On half a dozen occasions over the past several weeks she had suddenly awakened in the middle of the night and sat bolt upright in bed, short of breath and trembling, having dreamt that she had lost the case. The trial was now less than three months away—assuming that in the interim she found some scintilla of evidence linking the hospital to Katherine's pregnancy. If she didn't, there wouldn't be any trial. The case would merely be unceremoniously dismissed.

What am I overlooking? Carrie asked herself. The depositions of hospital staff members were winding down. The interviews with patients were continuing, largely at Will's insistence. At the end of every week that went by with no breakthroughs, Carrie would urge calling a halt to the interviews. "We have limited resources," she pointed out. "They could be put to better use."

"Doing what?" Will always countered. "We don't have any other leads—unless you've thought of a way to get Dr. Luebke to come in and sign a written confession," he said teasingly.

It was true that Luebke remained Carrie's primary suspect, even though she had not one crumb of evidence to back up her hunch. The man just acted like he was hiding something. And the episode with Gwen Starling smacked of something illicit, but there was no proof of that either. Even though Luebke had made it clear that he would refuse to cooperate further in the lawsuit, Carrie had already decided to subpoena him for a second deposition. She wasn't sure what more she could get out of him, but maybe just getting him royally pissed off would shake something loose.

Carrie passed a sign that designated Mile 3 and felt relieved that she was almost halfway through the course. Her feet felt a little warmer, and if she kept her head down the wind didn't bite her face quite so badly. No matter what happened—and she was still hoping for a positive outcome—the Buckley case had taught her a valuable lesson: it was not a good idea to handle legal matters for friends.

At Mile 4, Carrie suddenly felt something sting her face. "Ow!" she said aloud, looking around. Had a tiny rock hit her? Then another little missile struck and she knew. "Shit!" she mumbled under her breath. It was starting to sleet. It was time to pick up the pace. She covered the next mile walking as fast as she possibly could. Many people around her had either moved into a slow run or left the course in search of shelter.

At Mile 5, Carrie's breath was coming hard and the sleet was coming down harder. It felt like tiny shards of glass pricking her face. She wished she had brought a wool scarf. What kind of weather was this for the third week in April? This was only Chicago, for God's sake, not the North Pole. She tried to pull her jacket up to cover part of her face.

Over the next quarter mile the temperature went up a bit and the sleet turned into a cold, hard rain. *Dammit!* Carrie screamed to herself as she tried to move faster still.

Damn Will for talking her into this stupid event. Damn her friends who backed out on her. Damn AIDS for coming into existence so that this fund-raiser was needed in the first place. Halfway between Mile 5 and Mile 6, the sky opened up and the rain turned into a downpour. The remaining bedraggled walkers quickened the pace as best they could, their soggy feet splashing cold puddles of water as they went.

Carrie was already wheezing from the unaccustomed exertion. *I've got to get out of this weather before I catch pneumonia,* she said to herself. She didn't know where she was going to find the energy, but she had to try to run the rest of the way. Her clothes were weighted down with rain, and she felt as though she were running across the bottom of a swimming pool. Her legs felt like they had weights attached, and her side was starting to ache.

How can people actually claim to enjoy running? she wondered as she sprinted along. Anyone who does this regularly ought to have their head examined. Just when she thought her lungs were going to burst, she glimpsed the finish line off in the distance. She only had to last another six blocks.

I can do this, she chanted over and over as she kept slogging onward. *I got through law school with flying colors. I've tried multimillion-dollar cases and won them. I can goddam well run six more blocks.* Taking a big gulp of air, she gave one final push and ran the rest of the way at full speed.

Stumbling over the finish line, she began to cough uncontrollably. She looked around, completely disoriented. She felt like she was going to die. She needed something hot to drink. She needed a cough drop. She needed—

"Carrie, you made it!" Suddenly Will's arms were around her, and she discovered that was what she needed most of all. "A lot of people dropped out when it started to rain, but I might have known you'd see it through. I saw you cover that last block. That was a great effort. Are you all right?"

"I'm fine," Carrie wheezed, now oblivious to the fact that her entire body was racked with chills. "Piece of cake."

Will rubbed her arms to get the circulation going. "Come on. The vans are right over here and there's hot coffee aboard."

As she leaned against Will and allowed herself to be guided along, she looked up at him and asked weakly, "Are we still on for lunch?"

"We sure are," Will replied, giving her a hug.

"Good," Carrie replied smugly. She was feeling warmer already.

On the short ride back to the office, Will mentioned a number of possible places they might go for lunch and then in passing commented, "Or, if you'd prefer something really casual, you could come to my house. I made a pot of chili last night."

Carrie jumped at the invitation. "That sounds great," she said, trying not to sound too eager. "I'd like to go home first and shower and change clothes, but I could probably be there around twelve-thirty."

"Perfect," Will said. "That'll give me time to vacuum. You're not allergic to dogs, are you?" he asked anxiously.

"No, I love dogs. And don't bother to vacuum on my account. My motto is that no outfit is complete without cat hair."

Will laughed. "Good philosophy," he said. He gave her directions to his house. "See you in a bit."

Carrie rushed home, took a long, hot shower, dried her hair, and padded around her bedroom in her blue terry-cloth robe trying to decide what to wear. After rejecting a couple of potential outfits as too dressy, she finally settled on a pair of jeans and an oversized fisherman's knit sweater. Throwing on a khaki-colored leather jacket, she gave her cat, which was perched atop the sofa, a couple of pats on the head as she headed out the door. "Wish me luck, Muffin," she said. "This could be my lucky break." In response, the animal yawned and went back to sleep.

Butterflies were twirling about in Carrie's stomach as she pulled up in front of Will's rather modest two-story home in Skokie, half a dozen miles north of the city. *Calm down,* she told herself as she got out of the car. *This isn't really a date. It's just Will's way of thanking me for being a good sport. It's just a friendly gesture,* she thought as she rang the bell. Two colleagues having lunch. No big deal. Then why did she feel as if her legs had turned to Jell-O?

The door opened and Carrie found herself warmly greeted by Will and an enormous gray dog. "Come on in. Well, this is Floyd," Will said proudly. "I'm still working on curtailing his natural exuberance around guests, so don't be alarmed if he tries to jump on you."

Carrie leaned down and patted the beast on the head. The dog sniffed her hand. "He probably smells my cat," Carrie said. She gave the animal another pat. "He's a good boy. I think we'll get along fine."

Lunch was simple but hearty, consisting of a salad of mixed greens, chili, and crusty bread, all washed down with an excellent Merlot. "This was great," Carrie said when they'd finished. "Do you cook often?"

Will laughed. "Making chili is hardly cooking, but yeah, I do cook occasionally, when the mood strikes me. How about you?"

Carrie shrugged. "I'm afraid microwave meals are far too convenient."

"I know what you mean, although I favor takeout myself."

"So you and Terry finished the half-marathon in the top twenty," Carrie said. "I'm impressed."

"Don't be," Will replied. "There weren't very many good runners entered. My secretary's boyfriend, Gene Turnipseed, finished third. He's got some age on him now, but in his prime he was a really good runner. He finished in the top ten in the Chicago marathon several times. So I gather you're not ready to take up competitive racing," he teased.

Carrie groaned. "Hardly. I probably won't be able to move tomorrow. I must be more out of shape than I thought."

"You're not out of shape. You're just taxing muscles you

don't normally use. Take a hot bath before you go to bed and a couple of Advil if you're aching and you'll be good as new tomorrow." He motioned at her empty wineglass. "Would you care for a refill? We could go into the living room."

"Why not? After this morning, I think we both deserve a treat."

Carrie settled in on a navy leather sofa and looked around the room. "You have a nice house," she commented.

"Thanks," Will said, taking a seat beside her. "I can't say it's my dream home, but it's kind of a good feeling to have something that's mine, and it's also good practice for the time I might have something larger. It's a good outlet for pent-up energy, too. I find I actually enjoy puttering around the yard."

Carrie looked around the room. One wall was dominated by a large poster depicting John Steed and Emma Peel, the characters in the 1960s British spy spoof *The Avengers*. "So you're an *Avengers* fan?" Carrie asked.

"You bet. I watch it whenever I can find it on cable. They don't create characters like that anymore. They were witty, urbane, fearless—"

"Admit it," Carrie interrupted. "You just like to look at Mrs. Peel in those black-leather cat suits."

"That, too," Will agreed, taking a sip of his wine. "I had a tremendous crush on her when I first saw the show as a kid. I was devastated when they found her husband in the jungle and wrote her out of the show."

Carrie laughed. Her nervousness had evaporated during lunch. She felt relaxed and unpressured, just kicking back and enjoying a quiet afternoon with a friend. "It feels nice just to sit here and not do anything," she commented. "That doesn't happen too often."

"I think you push yourself too hard," Will said.

"I probably do take on more projects than I should," Carrie admitted, "and once I've got them I feel like I have to give them my best. Speaking of which, while I was freezing and drowning this morning, I decided we should definitely subpoena Dr. Luebke for another deposition. I know we got squat out of him last time, but I'd like to give it one more shot. What do you think?" She looked at him expectantly.

"What I think is that I don't want to talk about work today," Will said, moving closer to her.

"You don't?" Carrie asked, suddenly feeling nervous again.

Will shook his head. "We live and breathe work most of our waking hours. I think we should call a moratorium for today."

"Okay," Carrie said weakly. "Then what would you like to talk about?"

Will slid closer and put his arm around her. "Well," he said softly, "I was thinking maybe we could talk about you." He paused a moment and looked into her eyes. "Or then again, maybe we don't have to talk about anything for a while." With that he leaned over and kissed her gently on the lips.

Oh, my God! Carrie's brain screamed in reaction to this delightfully unexpected pleasure. Not talking at all definitely seemed to be a wonderful idea.

Chapter 29

On Monday, as Carrie slyly told a few friends at the office about her afternoon idyll with Will, her pals begged for details.

"Tell me everything!" Madree shrieked after Carrie whispered the news in her chum's ear when the two women met at the coffeemaker early that morning.

"Shhh!" Carrie exhorted, looking around frantically. "I'd rather not broadcast this to the world just yet. Come into my office and I'll fill you in."

Moments later, behind closed doors, Madree sat in front of Carrie's desk, bouncing her knees up and down. "So, give," she said, leaning forward eagerly. "Is he good in bed?"

"We didn't get that far," Carrie answered rather crossly.

"You didn't?" Madree asked incredulously. "Why not? I would have—assuming I weren't already married, of course."

"I know *you* would have," Carrie said, raising her eyebrows, "but there are times to hurry things and times not to, and this was a time not to." She paused and then asked, "Does that make any sense at all?"

Madree shrugged. "Not to me it doesn't. I would've nailed him while I had the chance, but go on. If you didn't have sex, what exactly did you do?"

"Well, we kissed—a lot."

"Is he a good kisser?"

Carrie smiled, remembering. "Oh, yeah. He's definitely a good kisser."

"Okay, we've got great kissing," Madree said enthusiastically. "That's a good start. Anything else happen? Any groping, any removal of clothing?"

Carrie shook her head. "No, not really. We just kissed."

Madree's jaw dropped. "You spent the whole afternoon on a couch with that gorgeous man and you just kissed? What on earth is the matter with you?"

"It wasn't all afternoon," Carrie protested. "It was probably an hour or so."

"What did you do after that?"

"I went home."

Madree made a face. "You are hopeless! You went home? Why?"

"Because I was exhausted and I felt like I was coming down with something and the afternoon had been wonderful so why stick around and spoil it?" Carrie answered, the words spilling out in a rush. "What kind of a friend are you, anyway? I told you what happened because I thought you'd be happy that I'm finally making some progress after salivating after the man for months. Why are you making me feel like I'm an idiot?"

"I'm sorry!" Madree said at once. "I didn't mean it that way. You know me. I tend to be more assertive in these matters than a lot of women. Of course I'm happy for you. I'm thrilled. It sounds like you're absolutely on the right track. Just don't let things cool down. Do you have a date scheduled with him?"

"Nothing definite," Carrie admitted. "But we did agree to get together one night this week."

"Get something firmed up right away," Madree counseled. "You've got him hooked. Now you need to start reeling him in before he snaps the line."

"Don't you think that sounds just a little bit mercenary?"

"Honey, relationships with men, by their very nature, *are* mercenary. You may as well admit that up front and use it to your advantage." Madree got up, came around the desk, and hugged Carrie. "Congratulations. You're far too nice a person to be alone. I hope this works out for you."

"Thanks," Carrie said smiling. "I must admit it certainly

has boosted my morale. I've been sort of floating for the past thirty-six hours."

As she left the office, Madree gave a thumbs-up. Ann Muchin and Pat Grove were similarly delighted for their friend when they heard the news.

Around ten o'clock, Will stuck his head in Carrie's office. "Hi," he said. "I just got in. I had an emergency hearing this morning to try to get a temporary restraining order to stop a client's key employee from leaving and spiriting away trade secrets."

"What happened?" Carrie asked.

"I won," Will said, grinning. He walked over to Carrie's desk. "So, how are you this morning?"

"Fine," she said, trying to ignore the fluttering in her stomach.

"Glad to hear it," Will said. "Well, I'd better get to work. I've got a lot to do today."

"So do I," Carrie replied. As Will turned to go, she said, "Say, how would you like to do something on Thursday? Maybe dinner and a movie?" She tried not to look over-eager as she waited for his reply. Fortunately it wasn't long in coming.

"Thursday sounds good," Will replied, nodding. "I'll be looking forward to it."

"Me, too," Carrie said.

As soon as he had left, Tammy came into Carrie's office carrying a stack of mail. "Is something going on between you and Will?" she asked innocently.

"No. What makes you ask that?" Carrie answered too quickly.

"Well, you both seem awfully happy for a Monday morning," Tammy replied. "So I was just wondering."

"No, nothing's going on," Carrie lied. "How are you feeling?"

"Much better, thanks," Tammy replied. "I slept most of the weekend." She set the mail down on Carrie's desk. "A while back you told me you were in the market for a nice straight single guy. If you want my opinion, Will seems like he'd qualify in spades. You might want to give him some thought."

"I'll keep that in mind," Carrie said noncommittally. When Tammy had left, Carrie felt a bit chagrined that she hadn't been honest with her secretary. The two women were close, and there was no doubt Tammy would keep a secret if Carrie asked her to. There was no reason why Carrie couldn't have 'fessed up to Saturday's activities, except she had the feeling that if she talked too freely she would jinx any chance the relationship might have. And after all, there really wasn't much of a relationship yet. There would be plenty of time to spread the good word later, assuming there was something to report.

Two days later, Wednesday, April 22, brought a series of aggravating developments in the *Buckley* case.

Carrie was still trying to settle the medical malpractice suit that was scheduled for trial in early June. If the case didn't settle soon, she was going to have to start preparing for trial, an exercise that would take far more time and energy than she currently had available. She badly wanted the case wrapped up and had decided to devote the entire day on Wednesday to bringing it to a conclusion. In the midst of back-and-forth phone conversations with the defendants' lawyers, she received an unwelcome call from Detective David Clauff.

"Ms. Nelson, long time no hear," the detective said jovially. "What's new?"

Carrie felt her stomach churn. "Not much," she replied blithely. "What's new with you?"

"As I recall, you were going to get back to me with the absolute, incontrovertible proof that young Mr. Fleming had passed a polygraph exam with flying colors. Do you remember that conversation?"

"I don't think that's quite what I said," she hedged.

"Well, it's close enough. So, I hear your boy didn't exactly pass the test in the manner you so cavalierly predicted."

"Who told you that?" Carrie demanded.

"A little bird," the detective shot back.

Carrie momentarily considered denying it but quickly figured it was hopeless. "So is there a purpose for your call other than to irritate me?" she asked, taking the offensive.

"In case there was any doubt, I just wanted to let you know that the pressure is still on the hapless Mr. Fleming," Clauff answered breezily. "He'd better continue watching his back—because we're watching it."

Carrie's long-pent-up anger over Todd Fleming's treatment finally exploded. "I'm getting tired of this cat-and-mouse game," she said heatedly. "Why don't you just put up or shut up? If you think you have enough evidence to charge Todd Fleming with assault, then go ahead and do it. But you'd better be damn sure that you've got enough to make the charges stick before you take any action that could ruin the life of a kid who's three weeks away from graduating from law school with honors."

"I don't appreciate your tone, Ms. Nelson," the detective said in an icy voice.

"And I don't appreciate yours, Detective," Carrie replied in the same manner. "Now, if you'll excuse me, I have work to do. Good day." She slammed down the phone.

An hour later Carrie received an irate call from Dr. Luebke's lawyer. "We received your subpoena purportedly scheduling a continuation of Dr. Luebke's deposition for next week," Steve O'Connor said in an acrimonious tone. "Even though it's so laughable as to barely deserve the dignity of a response, I thought I would do you the courtesy of letting you know that I intend to schedule a hearing before Judge Little to quash the subpoena. As we made clear at the conclusion of Dr. Luebke's first deposition, he has nothing further to add with respect to Ms. Buckley's treatment, and it is clear that your attempt to continue the deposition is nothing more than a fishing expedition. For that reason I intend to ask Judge Little to rule—"

"Fine," Carrie cut him off. "Schedule a hearing. Ask the judge to rule on whatever you want. Tell Dr. Luebke he can go fly a kite. I really don't care what you do. Just quit bothering me."

"You don't need to be sarcastic," O'Connor said indignantly.

"Yes, I do," Carrie replied. "It's been that kind of day. For once I'm trying to do something unrelated to the *Buckley* case and I find myself thwarted at every turn. So schedule the damn hearing, let me know when it is, and don't bother me anymore." She slammed down the phone again.

God, I'm turning into a total bitch, she thought crossly. She'd better get a break in the case soon or she was likely to start physically assaulting people who crossed her. She continued her negotiations in the medical malpractice case over the lunch hour and by early afternoon was on the verge of having the matter settled. She was taking a short break and eating a cup of mushroom soup at her desk when Joan Bedner stopped by.

"Teresa and I are back from another enlightening morning at Jackson Memorial," Joan announced, plopping into a chair in front of Carrie's desk. "And I'm pleased to announce that our record of finding out absolutely nothing still stands."

Carrie wiped her mouth with a paper napkin. "Why doesn't that surprise me?" she asked wryly.

"But I didn't stop by just to give you that depressing bit of news," Joan went on. "Your buddy Scott Rouleau was really agitated today."

"Over what?" Carrie asked.

"Apparently over the fact that you've never come back to talk to him," Joan replied. "As soon as he saw me, he ran out into the hall and shouted, 'King Arthur demands to speak to Queen Guinevere at once! It is of vital importance to the Kingdom of Camelot.' It was really rather embarrassing. I managed to get away from him and go to a different floor, but later on I was back on the third floor and he started in on me again. I finally got a nurse to take him back to his room and try to calm him down."

Carrie grimaced. "So you're saying I should go talk to him."

"It would make life a lot easier for Teresa and me," Joan replied. "His outbursts today were clearly riling up some of the other patients, which is not going to be conducive to getting them to open up to us."

"We're not going to get any useful information out of the patients anyway," Carrie grumbled. "I told Will long ago that I made a big mistake pushing for these patient interviews." She threw her Styrofoam soup container into the wastebasket and got up from her chair.

"You know how they say bad things come in threes?" Carrie asked as she put on her raincoat. "Well, I've already had two highly irritating conversations relating to the *Buckley* case today. I might as well make it three by talking to Scott Rouleau."

"I didn't mean to suggest that you should drop everything and go see him right now," Joan protested.

"I'd just as soon get it over with," Carrie said. "Otherwise it'll just continue to be one of those unpleasant tasks that keeps hanging over my head—like when you know you should schedule an appointment to have your teeth cleaned but keep putting it off because it's distasteful. Although, come to think of it, I'd sooner have a root canal than go to Jackson Memorial today. Oh, well. Such is life." She gave Joan a little wave as she headed for the door. "Wish me luck. I'm definitely going to need it."

Carrie spent the short drive to the hospital trying to clear her mind of the day's frustrations. While she wasn't entirely successful, she was feeling slightly calmer by the time she pulled into the parking lot. She quickly made her way to the third floor, where she found Scott Rouleau in his room playing a computer game. "Hi, Scott," Carrie said. "How are you doing?"

The young man grinned happily when he saw her. "Guinevere! You have returned."

"I have indeed," Carrie said with resignation as she took off her raincoat and pulled up a chair. "My assistant, Lady Joan, said you wanted to see me."

"You promised you'd come back and play the game I developed," Scott said, seeming to slip back into reality. "I've been making a few format changes. Here, let me reset it for you so you can start the quest for the Holy Grail at the beginning."

"I can't wait," Carrie said with forced enthusiasm.

She spent the next ninety minutes trying to negotiate the twists and turns of Scott's elaborate computer game. Scott sat at her elbow, watching her every move and countless times saving her from imminent destruction by the forces of evil. It was largely through his efforts that Carrie managed to make her way to Level Three of the journey toward the Holy Grail.

"Very good!" Scott praised her. "Only seven levels to go."

Carrie groaned. Her eyes were stinging and she was starting to get a headache. She looked at her watch. "Gee, Scott, I'd love to stay here all day and finish the journey, but unfortunately I have an appointment downtown. Can we maybe save my position so I can pick up where I left off another time?"

"Yes," Scott said, clearly sad that she had to leave.

As Scott frantically punched various keys on the computer, Carrie got up and put on her raincoat. "I appreciate your spending this much time with me today, Scott," she said, eager to beat a quick retreat. "I really enjoyed it, and I hope we can do it again soon." She began to edge toward the door.

"Wait!" Scott bellowed. "Guinevere may not leave yet."

"And why is that?" Carrie asked warily.

"Because King Arthur wishes to bestow upon you a token of his admiration." The young man got up, walked over to a dresser, opened the bottom drawer, and began digging frantically through what appeared to be a pile of mismatched socks. "Aha!" he exclaimed triumphantly, pulling something out from underneath. "Here it is." He held out a small object to Carrie.

It was a computer disk. She took it. "Thank you, Scott," she said, slipping it into her purse. She assumed it was a copy of the Holy Grail game. "This is very nice of you. Maybe if I practice at home I'll be able to do a better job next time I visit you."

As she turned to go, Scott squeezed her arm. "King Arthur is the protector of damsels in distress," he said.

"That's good to know," Carrie said, forcing a smile. "Well, I've really got to run now. See ya." She hurried off before he could call her back or make a scene over her departure.

On the drive back to the office, she chastised herself for going to the hospital. It wasn't like she had a lot of spare time. With the commute, she'd just wasted more than two hours. She was going to have to learn to be more disciplined about her time.

Back in the office, she saw a note on her desk and let out a whoop of joy. The defendants in the medical malpractice case had raised their offer. The case was settled. "Yes!!" she exclaimed. At least one thing had gone right today.

After phoning her clients and telling them the good news, she looked at the clock. It was nearly four. She wasn't in the mood to start any new projects. On impulse, she retrieved Scott Rouleau's computer disk from her purse and slipped it into the A drive of her computer. Spending half an hour or so playing a game sounded like just the ticket.

Twenty minutes later she pulled the disk out of her computer, cursing. Try as she might, she had been unable to get the game to load. Every time she tried to access the disk, she got a strange error message. The disk must be faulty. So much for having a bit of end-of-the-day relaxation. To hell with it. She was going home.

She nearly threw the computer disk into the waste basket, but on impulse took it with her and on her way out of the office swung by to see Michelle Brud. As usual, the firm's technology guru was running three different computers at once, her fingers flying nimbly from one keyboard to the next.

"I've got a challenge for you," Carrie said, tossing Scott's disk down on Michelle's desk. "If you have a few minutes, see if you can access the file that's on this disk."

"What's on it?" Michelle asked, her fingers still tapping away on the keyboards.

"I think it's a game about searching for the Holy Grail. A guy who's a patient at Jackson Memorial but used to be an up-and-comer in the computer industry developed it and gave me this disk. But I can't get the game to load, so either I'm just too dumb to make it work or the disk is bad, or both."

"I'll take a look at it," Michelle said, barely looking up from her typing.

"Thanks," Carrie said. "There's no hurry. It's not important, and besides, I'm leaving for the day."

"Gotcha," Michelle replied.

The loud and persistent ringing of the phone next to her bed woke Carrie from a deep sleep. Groaning, she rolled over and peered at the clock. It was twelve-thirty. Who would be calling at this hour? It must be an emergency. *Oh, God,* she thought, breaking out in a cold sweat. She hoped nothing had happened to her parents or her brother.

"Hello?" she said, grabbing up the phone.

"Carrie?" a feminine voice asked. "This is Michelle."

"Michelle." Carrie sleepily rubbed her eyes as her cat stirred at the foot of the bed. "What's wrong?"

"I'm really sorry to bother you at this hour, but I've been working on that damn computer disk all night and I just broke the code."

"The code?" Carrie repeated dumbly.

"The contents of the disk were encrypted," Michelle explained. "It was a first-rate job. I can usually break those things in a matter of minutes, but this one took me five hours. My husband was ready to shoot me. Anyway, I think maybe we should meet at the office right away so you can see what's on it."

By now Carrie was thoroughly muddled. "I appreciate your hard work, but I already know what's on it. I played the game this afternoon."

"No, you don't understand," Michelle said urgently. "It's not a game. It's pages and pages of text. And unless I'm badly mistaken, they represent the key to cracking the case."

"What case?" Carrie asked, feeling as though her head were filled with cobwebs.

"The *Buckley* case," Michelle fairly shouted.

Carrie sat bolt upright. "I'll meet you at the office in twenty minutes," she said.

Chapter 30

Carrie arrived at the office around one o'clock in the morning. She had never been in the building at that hour, and the place had an eerie stillness about it. Michelle was already waiting in the lobby and had turned on a couple of lights. "It's spooky in here," Michelle said, shivering. "It's also freezing. The temperature must automatically be turned down about fifteen degrees at night."

Carrie nodded in agreement and pulled her leather jacket tighter around her. She had phoned Will immediately after getting Michelle's call, wanting him to be privy to whatever revelation might be contained on Scott Rouleau's computer disk. Within moments of Carrie's arrival, the front door opened and Will strode in. Like Carrie and Michelle, he was wearing jeans and a sweatshirt and his hair looked disheveled.

"At least traffic is light at this hour," he said in a small attempt at levity.

Carrie smiled at him in response. She was glad he was there. Whatever Michelle had discovered, she didn't want to face it alone.

"Are we all set?" Michelle asked briskly. "Let's go into my office and I'll set this up." Carrie and Will silently followed Michelle down the hall. When they reached her office, Michelle sat down at her desk, booted up one of her computers, and then inserted the disk into the A drive.

"The guy who did this must be an absolute genius," Michelle said as her fingers flew across the keyboard. "I won't bore you with the technical specifics of what he did, but I've never seen such a sophisticated encryption before. He could make a fortune capitalizing on his knowledge. I'd love to pick his brain about how he came up with this. I just can't believe someone with this talent is in a mental hospital. What a shame."

As Michelle continued punching keys, the screen filled with text. "Here we go," she said. "It's a journal of his experiences at the hospital," she explained. She got up from her chair and motioned to Carrie. "Why don't you sit here? And Will, you can take the files off that chair and sit next to her. It'll be easier for you both to read that way."

Carrie sat down at the desk, and Will pulled a chair up next to her. They both stared at the screen. Carrie, her heart pounding, was wondering what Scott Rouleau's diary could possibly reveal about the assault on Katherine Buckley. With no little trepidation, she began to read.

The first entry was dated October 7.

I've been here four days and I hate it. I was in a strait-jacket the first twenty-four hours. I guess they thought I was going to hurt myself. I wouldn't do that, but I sure would've liked to give the two orderlies who brought me to my room a good working-over. The SOBs twisted my arms until it felt like they were going to break. They seemed to be enjoying themselves. They must be sadists. I'd like to give them a taste of their own medicine.

October 10. They moved me to the third floor and stopped the round-the-clock surveillance. I guess they decided I'm making progress and am not likely to off myself. Laurie came to visit after work. The demons were really strong today and I'm afraid I wasn't very nice to her. I kept screaming that I was the Sun King and demanded to be released immediately or I was going to have someone beheaded. I don't know what comes over me to make me act like that. It's as if another person takes over my body. I try to fight it but I'm not strong enough. I could tell I hurt Laurie's feelings and I felt bad but I couldn't make myself apologize. Then after she left I felt shitty.

"Can I scroll down?" Carrie asked Will.

"Yeah," he replied. "Isn't it amazing that the guy is able to be so dispassionate about recording his problems?"

"I thought the same thing," Carrie said. "If you'd talked to Scott, you would never believe he could be this coherent in his thoughts." She advanced the text on the screen, and she and Will continued their journey into Scott Rouleau's private hell.

October 13. I'm taking six different medications. I don't know what each one is supposed to do but in combination they have fucked up my whole system. My sense of taste is shot. I get hot flashes followed by cold sweats. I have terrible insomnia. Dr. Luebke was in to see me this morning and I complained about it to him. He said I have to be patient and give my body time to adjust to all the meds. I screamed at him and accused him of trying to poison the emperor.

Carrie tapped her finger on the screen where Dr. Luebke's name appeared. "There he is again," she said. "Just like a bad penny that keeps coming back."

October 17. The staff put up Halloween decorations today. Seems appropriate since I feel like a freak all the time. Yesterday I got the inspiration for a new game, the search for the Holy Grail. I spent all day today working on it. I actually had a version of it done in about eight hours but it's very rough. I want it to be a masterpiece. My problem is that I'm a perfectionist and I'm never satisfied with anything I create. Dr. Luebke says I am too hard on myself and I need to accept my shortcomings. That's easy for you to say, Doc. You're okay, while I on the other hand am totally fucked up.

October 20. Insomnia worse than ever. Dr. Luebke says if I wake up in the night and can't get back to sleep within half an hour I should ring for a nurse and they'll give me another sleeping pill, but the pills make me sick to my stomach so I try to tough it out. Last night I was awake in bed for over an hour and thought I was going to freak out, so I got up and walked around in the hall for a while. It was quiet as a tomb. It was kind of fun. I walked up and down the hall three times and no one saw me. There was a nurse at the main station, but she never noticed me. She was probably asleep. I'll bet I could have escaped if I'd wanted to. I actually considered it—briefly—but I didn't know where I'd go once I left the building. I could go to Laurie's, but I know she'd just bring me right back here. All of my friends have deserted me 'cuz they don't want to deal with a crazy person. So I went back to my room. The illicit adventure must've tired me out because I slept like a baby after that.

"Here's Luebke again," Carrie said. "He's clearly a player in this somehow." Will remained silent. Behind them, Michelle leaned against a file cabinet. Whatever secrets she might have gleaned from perusing the journal, she wasn't tipping her hand.

October 23. Laurie visited. She brought her new boyfriend. His name is Ted and he runs a travel agency. I didn't like him, and I think the feeling was mutual. He was clearly uncomfortable around me and I aggravated the situation by telling him I was William the Conqueror and quizzing him about history and geography. The dumb shit has never even heard of Runneymede or Hadrian's Wall. How can you be a travel agent if you don't know anything about British history? Where the hell does he suggest people go on vacation, Peoria? Laurie was pissed at me. I told her she was wasting her time with that loser. She left in a huff.

October 25. Insomnia has been bad all week. It helps if I get up and walk around. I'm making good progress with the Holy Grail. I've got some dynamite graphics. Once it's finished, I wonder if I could market it. I wish I weren't in a fucking mental hospital. Having a nuthouse as a return address is definitely not a good marketing tool. I'm sure I could sell it to a big company, but they'd only pay

peanuts and then make megabucks putting it out under
their own name. I want to set up my own company so
I'd be able to keep the profits. But how?

October 27. Had a severe panic attack early this morning.
Never had one that bad before and was literally bouncing
off the walls. Nurse Sandow was on duty and called one
of the doctors and got approval to give me some kind of
injection. Then she sat with me until it kicked in. Dr.
Luebke came around later to see how I was doing. I
spoke to him in pig Latin. He finally got so frustrated
with me that he left.

Will chuckled. "Pig Latin, eh? I like that. You're going
to have to introduce me to Scott."

October 28. I'm having trouble coming up with enough
challenges for the final two levels of the game. I want
people to have to really work their asses off to make it
all the way to the end. I wonder if any of my old pals
would help me market it. Maybe I'll try to talk to Ken
Lasure. He wouldn't screw me on the deal.

November 2. It's hard to write this. I'm still shaking so
bad I can hardly type. Two nights ago had the worst
insomnia ever. Couldn't get to sleep at all. Was up and
walking three different times. Last time was around 3:00
A.M. Was coming back to my room when I saw someone
walking the other way. I was afraid of getting caught and
panicked, so I ducked into the doorway two rooms down
from me. I intended to wait for the person to pass by so
I could get to my room, but instead I saw the door to a
room across the hall open and the person went inside. I
only saw them from the back, so I didn't know who it
was but I could tell it was someone taller than average.
I went back to my own room and stood there with the
door cracked open a few inches, looking out. Five minutes went by and no one came back out of the room.

I got really curious then, so I sneaked across the hall
and flattened myself against the wall next to the room
and listened. I could hear sounds, like a bed creaking and

sort of a low moaning. I thought this was odd because I knew the patient in the room was a girl named Katherine who's been in a coma for months. She never makes any noise, so I knew the moaning must be coming from the other person. I knew it was dangerous, but I couldn't help myself. I pulled the door open a crack and saw everything.

Carrie swallowed hard and scrolled down so she and Will could read the rest of the account.

He was fucking her. He was right there on the bed and was humping her a mile a minute. There was no way he could have known I was there because he was too preoccupied.

I thought I was going to be sick, so I went back to my room. I kept looking out, and after about five minutes the door to Katherine's room opened and he came out. He was adjusting his pants. He had his back to me and walked toward the nurses' station like nothing was wrong. Just another shift in the life of Nurse Alessandro Delgado.

Carrie gasped and clapped her hand to her mouth. "Oh, my God!" she exclaimed.

"The son of a bitch!" Will added.

"There's more," Michelle said.

Carrie and Will kept reading.

After that I went into a totally manic state. I wanted to scream and pound the walls, but I was paranoid, afraid Delgado would know I saw him and murder me. It'd be so easy to give me an injection of poison. I didn't sleep at all that night and had a very bad day yesterday. I was totally uncooperative with everyone and they called in Dr. Luebke. I spat in his face. I'm convinced there's a conspiracy here at this damn hospital and everyone is in on it. I trust no one. I'm afraid I may be assaulted next. **November 6.** After a couple of really horrible days I had

calmed down some and finally been able to sleep a little.
The more I kept going over what I thought I saw, I talked
myself into thinking that maybe I hadn't really seen it
after all, that I was just hallucinating from all the medication, since that has happened to me before. So the past
two nights I've been peering out my door to see if there
was a repeat performance. And this morning around 3:00
it happened again. I saw him go into Katherine's room.
It was Delgado. I saw it plain as day. I looked at my
clock radio and timed him. He was in there 11 minutes.
I'm afraid they're going to kill me. I have to convince
Laurie to move me out of here.

Carrie turned and looked at Michelle. "We've read about
two assaults. Are there more?"

Michelle shook her head. "No, the rest of it is basically
a descent into total paranoia, where he argues with himself
over what he saw, who else might be in on it, and what
might happen to him if anyone finds out what he knows."

Carrie quickly scrolled through the rest of the entries
and confirmed what Michelle had just said. "The last entry
is December twenty-second?" she asked.

"Yes," Michelle replied.

"And there's nothing else on the disk?" Will asked.

"No," Michelle said.

Carrie got up from the chair. "Print out a copy of this
right away," she instructed Michelle. "And make a backup
copy of the disk." Michelle immediately slid into her chair
and began following Carrie's instructions.

"This is incredible," Carrie said to Will. She ran her
hands through her hair. "I feel like I'm in shock. Of all
the hospital people we've interviewed, Alessandro Delgado
would be about the last person I'd suspect of doing something like this. He's good-looking, he's articulate. My God,
he flirted with me through his whole deposition. What on
earth would possess someone like that to do such a sick
thing?"

"Who knows?" Will replied. "But the important thing is

we now know about it. And we've got to be very careful about how we document it."

"Poor Scott," Carrie murmured. "Think what this has done to him. He was having enough emotional problems before this happened. It's no wonder he's not made much progress during his time at Jackson Memorial."

"I think the first thing we should do is get Delgado's personnel file," Will suggested. "In order to pin liability on the hospital, we need to show that they knew or should have known he was a bad apple."

"We should also talk to people at Delgado's previous places of employment," Carrie put in. "See if anything shows up on his record there and find out whether Jackson Memorial checked out his background before they hired him."

"We're going to need to talk to Scott's sister," Will said. "Explain to her what we discovered and get her permission to let Scott participate as a witness in the case."

"Maybe we should think about suggesting to her that Scott be moved to another hospital," Carrie said.

"Do you really think that's necessary?" Will asked. "We obviously won't let Delgado know that we're on to him until we've got things firmed up enough so that charges can be brought against him. As long as Delgado's kept in the dark, I can't see where Scott will be in any danger."

Carrie felt a chill come over her. "But what if Scott's right?" she asked, beginning to shiver. "What if other people at the hospital were aware of what Delgado did and let him get away with it or, worse yet, aided and abetted the crime?"

Will closed the short distance between them and put his arm around Carrie. "Then we'll find out about it and nail them, too," he said reassuringly. "This is the big break we've been waiting for. Now we just have to carefully use it to bring Delgado to justice and make the hospital shoulder the responsibility for its role in what happened."

"But what if—" Carrie began.

"Don't worry," Will cut her off. "We'll do it. Together."

Oblivious to the fact that Michelle was still busily working away behind them, he enveloped Carrie in a big hug.

Carrie clung to him gratefully and buried her head in his shoulder. *Together*. It was amazing how wonderful a single word could sound.

Chapter 31

Scott's sister, Laurie Rouleau, was an audiologist at a busy downtown medical clinic. When Carrie called her Thursday morning to say it was important that she and Will talk to her about her brother, Laurie agreed to the meeting with obvious reluctance.

"I suppose you could come around ten-thirty," Laurie finally said. "I had a cancellation, so I could probably spare you a little time then."

"We'll be there," Carrie said.

Laurie was an attractive brown-haired woman in her early thirties. She ushered Will and Carrie into a small office. "I'm sorry if I was short with you on the phone," she apologized to Carrie. "By the time you called I'd already had two difficult appointments with children, and that started my day on the wrong foot. I do a lot of work with kids, and it can be very frustrating," she explained.

"A lot of them are frightened, but instead of showing their fear they turn belligerent. I'm able to establish a rapport with most of them, but some just pretend they don't understand what I'm asking them to do and refuse to cooperate. Just like my brother," she said, sighing. "So, what's going on with Scott that's so important you had to see me immediately?" She looked at them expectantly.

"A while back you gave one of my partners permission to interview Scott," Carrie said. "To determine if he could possibly know anything about who had assaulted our client."

"The comatose woman," Laurie said, nodding. "Yes, I

remember." She furrowed her brows. "Don't tell me Scott was actually able to be of some help?"

"It appears he's going to be of tremendous help," Will replied. "On two separate occasions he saw a man sneak into our client's room in the middle of the night and rape her."

"I don't believe it!" Laurie said. "Scott told you this?"

"Indirectly he did," Carrie answered. She told Laurie about the computer disk and its contents.

"Oh, my God!" Laurie exclaimed. "Is the person Scott saw someone who works at the hospital?"

"Yes," Carrie said. "It's a male nurse."

"What's his name?" Laurie asked.

"Delgado," Carrie replied.

"I don't think I know him," Laurie said.

"He works third shift," Carrie explained.

Laurie shivered and wrapped her arms around herself. "Is Scott in danger? Should I transfer him to a different hospital?"

"He's not in any danger, and we promise he won't be," Will replied at once. "There's no indication that anyone at the hospital knows what Scott saw, and we're going to be sure they don't find out until the nurse in question has been taken into custody."

"When will that happen?" Laurie demanded.

"We're not certain of that yet," Carrie admitted. "Possibly on Monday."

"Monday!" Laurie was clearly upset. "That's four days away. What if something happens to Scott in the meantime?" She put her hands over her face. "I'm sorry. I'm not handling this very well, am I? I'm sure Scott would find my sudden concern for him rather amusing. As I mentioned earlier, dealing with my brother can be extremely frustrating at times. I try to visit him two or three times a week. On one visit he might sit for half an hour and converse rationally and I'll be lulled into thinking he's making real progress. Then the next time I come he'll be ranting about how he's Leonardo Da Vinci and I feel like we're back to square one."

"Has Scott had emotional problems all his life?" Carrie asked.

"Pretty much," Laurie answered. "He was hyperactive as a kid, took Ritalin for a while, but it actually seemed to make him worse. My mom spent a tremendous amount of time with him, and he's been in therapy off and on since age eight, but no one ever seemed to be able to get to the root of his problem. Our parents' death really set him back, and then when he suffered a head injury last fall I had no choice but long-term hospitalization."

"He obviously has a real talent for computer programming," Carrie said. "He let me play the Holy Grail game he developed. When he gave me the disk I assumed there was a copy of the game on it. I couldn't access what was on it, so I put our firm's head techie on the case. She was able to crack the code he developed but said it was the most sophisticated encryption she's ever seen. She said Scott must be a genius to have developed something so intricate."

Laurie smiled. "She really called him a genius? Scott would love to hear that. Of course he wouldn't believe it. Part of his problem is that he's a perfectionist. Nothing is ever good enough; no project is ever considered finished. Scott has had several good jobs in the computer industry, but his bosses always got frustrated with him because the name of the game is speed—turning out a product faster than your competition. Scott could develop dynamite products, but he never wanted to let loose of them and move on to the next project. He was forever tinkering, trying to make them better. That just doesn't fly in that business."

"Having to keep the secret of what he knows about the assault is probably not helping his recovery," Carrie suggested. "Maybe once the nurse has been removed from the hospital, Scott will progress faster."

"I hope so," Laurie said. "So. What's going to happen on Monday?"

"We haven't got all the details worked out just yet," Will said. "But we plan to schedule the nurse to come to our office for a second deposition that day."

"Won't that tip him off that you're on to him?" Laurie asked with concern.

"It shouldn't," Carrie replied, "because we're going to schedule a number of other staff members for second depositions at the same time. We'll tell the hospital's attorneys that there are some questions relating to security that we forgot to cover the first time. Hopefully that won't give anyone cause for suspicion."

"So the nurse will show up at your office and then be arrested?" Laurie asked.

"That's the part we haven't entirely worked out yet," Will admitted. "There is a detective who's been assigned to work on investigating the assault on our client. To date he hasn't done much investigating. He's spent most of his time harassing our client's boyfriend. We're going to talk to the detective and show him Scott's journal. Hopefully he'll believe it's legitimate and agree to be on hand for the nurse's deposition, at which time he can make an arrest."

"It sounds simple enough," Laurie agreed. "Is Scott going to have to testify at the trial?"

"We don't know that yet," Carrie admitted. "That will depend in part on what the hospital does when it finds out about the nurse. We're hoping they'll want to settle the case, in which case Scott wouldn't have to testify. But if they won't settle, we might need him. Would you have a problem with that? Since you're Scott's guardian, we'd need your permission."

"I don't know," Laurie said. "Is a patient in a mental hospital qualified to testify at a trial?"

"We'd have to get a ruling from the judge on that," Will said.

"And you're certain Scott isn't going to be in any danger?"

"We don't believe so," Carrie said sincerely. "He's a very special person, and it took a lot of courage for him to come forward with what he knows. Believe me, I will personally do everything I can to make sure nothing happens to him."

Laurie looked at Carrie earnestly for a moment, then

said, "That's good enough for me. I was planning to visit Scott after work tonight. Can I say anything to him about this?"

"Sure, as long as you do it discretely," Carrie replied. "I'm planning to go visit him myself this afternoon. I'm going to try to have a quiet discussion about what's expected to happen over the next few days."

"Tell him I'll see him later, then," Laurie said.

"I'll do that," Carrie replied. She reached over and patted the other woman's hand. "Thank you so much for what you and Scott are doing. I can't tell you how much it means to us and to our client's family."

Laurie sighed. "I'll admit I'm a little spooked by this whole thing, but you seem trustworthy, and if Scott can help nail that bastard, then I think it's our duty to help any way we can."

"I promise you won't regret it," Carrie said.

Will and Carrie returned to the office at lunchtime. While they'd been gone, Jackie Crabb had been making phone calls trying to track down Delgado's former employers. "The people at the Atlanta hospital were real jerks," Jackie explained. "I ended up having to lie and say that I was a prospective employer calling to check Delgado's references. They finally did transfer me to someone in Personnel, who put me on hold while she claimed to look in his file. When she came back on the line, she said all his evaluations were very good and there were no negative comments from any of his supervisors."

"He was in Atlanta right before coming to Chicago?" Carrie asked.

"That's right," Jackie replied.

"And where was he before that?"

"Vancouver," Jackie answered. "Because of the time difference between here and there I was just able to reach someone and they gave me the name of their personnel director and said she should be in within the hour. Do you want me to call her or would you like to do it?"

"I can do it," Carrie said. Jackie handed her a small slip

of paper. "Patricia Sauter Wilson," Carrie read. "Thanks a lot, Jackie. I appreciate the help."

"You're welcome," Jackie replied.

As Carrie and Will headed back toward their offices, Will asked, "What would you like me to do next?"

"Are the notices of Monday's depositions ready to go?" Carrie asked.

"I'm sure Karen is done with them by now."

"Then why don't you fax those to Charlene Bull? Maybe you should call her first and warn her they're coming. Give her the jive about how we were just reading through the transcripts and discovered we missed a crucial line of questioning with each of those witnesses. And if she bitches about the short notice, just say we're running out of time and need to speed up the rest of our discovery."

"Anything else that needs to be done?"

Carrie hesitated a moment, then said, "Would you mind terribly trying to talk to Detective Clauff? I wore out my welcome with him long ago. Maybe he'll be more cooperative with you."

"No problem," Will said amiably. As they reached Carrie's office, he asked quietly, "Are you still going to be in the mood to go out tonight?"

"Oh, sure," Carrie replied eagerly. In the blur of the previous twelve hours' activity she had almost forgotten their date. There was no way she was going to cancel out, no matter how fatigued she was feeling. "I probably won't want to stay out real late," she said in an effort not to sound too eager, "but maybe we could grab dinner or something."

"Sounds good," Will said. "I'll catch you later."

Patricia Sauter Wilson, the personnel director of Vancouver Memorial Hospital, was very cordial when Carrie reached her. Without divulging the details of the situation, Carrie explained that she was involved in a lawsuit against the hospital where Alessandro Delgado was currently employed. "I wonder if you'd be able to tell me a bit about his work history with you?" Carrie asked.

"Sure," Patricia replied. "If you can hold on a minute,

I'll go pull his file." When she came back on the line, she said, "Thanks for waiting. I've got it. Let's see . . ." Carrie could hear pages turning. "It looks like he worked here for three years."

"Did you know him personally?" Carrie interrupted.

"No, his tenure here was before my time. Besides that, we have a staff of eight hundred, so I'm afraid I don't get the chance to meet everyone."

"Does it look like he was a satisfactory employee?" Carrie asked.

"It seems so," Patricia answered. "There are a number of performance reviews that state he was a hard worker, had excellent skills, good rapport with patients." Carrie could hear more pages shuffling. "Wait a minute," Patricia said. "Here's something."

"What is it?" Carrie asked eagerly.

"A memo from Delgado's supervisor attaching a letter of complaint from a patient's parents. It seems that the parents accused Delgado of sexually assaulting their sixteen-year-old daughter."

"Oh, my God!" Carrie gasped. So Delgado did have a history of assaulting patients. "Was he disciplined?"

"Let's see. It looks like a disciplinary proceeding was started, but then Delgado resigned."

Carrie could feel her adrenaline pumping. "Do you make notations in an employee's file when prospective employers call to check references?"

"I always do," Patricia replied, "but I think my predecessor did it more sporadically."

"Is there any indication that Jackson Memorial called to check Delgado's references?"

"No. When did he start working in Chicago?"

"I believe it was about two and a half years ago."

"That was after I started here," Patricia said, "so if someone had called I would have recorded it."

Carrie squeezed her eyes shut and offered up a silent prayer of thanks. It looked like they finally had some evidence that Jackson Memorial had been negligent in its hir-

ing practices. "Would you be willing to tell me the name
of the family that filed the complaint?" Carrie asked.

"I'm afraid I can't give out that sort of information without approval from our attorneys," Patricia replied. "Sorry.
It's hospital policy."

"I understand," Carrie said. "I may get back to you on
that. But in the meantime you've been a tremendous
help."

"I'm happy to help out," Patricia said. "Good luck on
your case."

As soon as she hung up the phone, Carrie sprinted down
the hall to see Will. "I've got good news," she said as she
walked in his office. She told him what she had learned
about Delgado's tenure in Vancouver.

"That's dynamite!" Will said enthusiastically. "The notices of deposition have been served. Charlene Bull was not
pleased with us, but I got her to calm down. As for your
buddy Detective Clauff, he's out until tomorrow."

"That's all right," Carrie said. "It'll give us a little extra
time to figure out how to present this whole thing to him."
She looked at her watch. It was three o'clock. "I'm going
to run up to the hospital and talk to Scott. I'll be back by
five for sure."

"Give some thought to where you'd like to have dinner,"
Will said.

"I will," Carrie said, smiling.

Two trips here in two days, Carrie grumbled to herself
as she got out of the car and walked to the main entrance
of Jackson Memorial. *I'm starting to feel like I live here.
Not a particularly pleasant feeling.*

Carrie didn't want anyone on staff to notice that she
was paying Scott another visit, so she entered the building
through the side entrance and came up the stairs, just as
she had done the day she first met with Von Slaten. When
she reached the third floor, she opened the door a crack
and peered out. When it appeared the coast was clear, she
hurried over to Scott's room, thankful that he was housed
at the far end of the hallway.

Carrie found Scott alone in his room working away at his computer.

"Queen Guinevere!" he greeted her loudly, but his eyes looked nervous. "You're here to finish the game?"

Carrie pulled a chair up next to him. There was no sense beating around the bush. "Thank you so much for the disk," she said quietly. "It was very helpful."

Scott looked furtively around the room.

"It was very brave of you to come forward with that information," Carrie whispered. "We're going to see to it that the person responsible for hurting Katherine never has the chance to do that to someone else."

Scott began to tremble.

"It's okay," Carrie said, leaning over and putting a hand on his arm. "You don't have to be afraid. No one here knows what you told me. No one will hurt you. You're safe. And I hope that after Monday the person who hurt Katherine won't be around here anymore."

Scott continued to tremble, but he gave a small nod.

"I saw your sister this morning," Carrie said. "She said I should tell you she's very proud of you and she'll stop to see you tonight after work."

Scott nodded again.

Carrie gave the young man's arm another pat. "I know the next few days are going to be rough, but just try to act like nothing happened. It's very important that no one here know our secret. Do you understand?"

Another nod.

"Good." Carrie got up from her chair. "Thanks again, and I'll see you soon."

"Good-bye, Guinevere." Scott gave a small wave as Carrie left.

As Carrie was walking to her car, Dr. Peckham was coming toward the building. "Ms. Nelson, how are you today?" the doctor asked jovially.

"Fine, thanks," Carrie replied. "And you?"

"Just fine. I hear that some of my colleagues are being called back for second depositions," he said. "Is that standard procedure?"

Carrie marveled at how fast news traveled. "Oh, yes," she answered blithely. "It happens all the time. Strictly routine."

"Glad to hear it," the doctor said. "I'll pass the word around that it's nothing to get excited about. You know what nervous Nellies some people are."

Carrie merely smiled.

"Nice to see you," Dr. Peckham said. "Good day."

"Good day," Carrie replied. She briskly headed for her car, eager to get back to the office, finish up some mundane chores, and then enjoy her dinner with Will.

Chapter 32

Back at the office Carrie wrapped up a few loose ends, but by about five-thirty she was feeling physically and emotionally drained and decided to call it a day. After stopping in the ladies' room to freshen her makeup, she walked down to Will's office and found him making some changes in a computer document. "I'm ready for dinner whenever you are," she said, settling into one of the chairs in front of his desk.

"I'll be right with you," Will replied, looking over his shoulder and giving her a warm smile. "I'm almost finished tinkering with this brief."

"You don't have to hurry," Carrie assured him. "I just can't do any more work today. I'm totally wasted."

Within ten minutes Will had completed the work on the brief. "All done," he said, shutting down the computer and stretching. "Any thoughts about where we should go for dinner?"

Carrie shrugged. "I don't care. What sounds good to you?"

"Do you like Italian?"

"Sure," Carrie replied.

"Have you been to Luigi's yet?"

Carrie paused for just an instant. She recognized the name as the place where Madree had seen Will and the infamous "other woman" about four weeks back. She briefly considered making up some excuse why she'd rather go elsewhere, but then she thought, *The hell with it.* If Will wanted to go to a particular restaurant, why should she be a wet blanket just because he might have been there pre-

viously with someone else? After all, Madree had assured
her Will hadn't acted at all lovey-dovey with that woman.
Maybe she really was a former secretary or his cousin
from Cleveland.

"No, I haven't been to Luigi's yet," she said brightly.
"But the *Trib* food critic gave it an excellent review. I'd
love to go there."

Half an hour later they were seated in a quiet booth in
an elegant restaurant where the lighting was subdued and
Frank Sinatra tunes wafted softly from the sound system.

"Have you been here before?" Carrie asked casually as
they perused their menus.

"Yes, I was here shortly after it opened," Will replied.
"I had the scampi in white wine with garlic, and it was
superb. And the bruschetta with goat cheese appetizer was
excellent, too."

"I'm not a fan of goat cheese," Carrie replied. Will
clearly wasn't going to volunteer any information about the
woman who had accompanied him on his previous visit,
and since she couldn't very well come out and ask who
he'd been with, she decided to forget about the past and
concentrate on enjoying the present. "I love veal. Which
of those dishes do you think might be good?"

Two hours later, they were enjoying cups of strong black
coffee and the last morsels of a shared order of tiramisu.
The food and wine had been excellent and the conversation
companionable, although try as they might, they had been
unable to totally avoid talking about the *Buckley* case.

"I hope nothing happens to Scott Rouleau as a result of
his coming forward to help us," Carrie said with concern.

"I'm sure he'll be fine," Will assured her. "In fact, as we
discussed with his sister, it's probably a weight off Scott's
mind to have finally told someone what he saw. In the long
run, it might be beneficial to him."

"I hope so," Carrie said. "I was thinking that I'd like to
call the Buckleys and Todd tomorrow and tell them about
the new developments."

"Do you think that's wise?" Will asked.

"I feel like it'd be dishonest not to," Carrie replied.

"They've been through so much, and up until now we've had nothing to offer them. I think they deserve to finally have some hope that we're going to have a good result."

"I guess there's nothing wrong with that," Will agreed, "but I'd keep the details to a minimum and make sure they understand we haven't hit a home run yet. I've always thought the worst thing you can do a client is to promise something you can't deliver. It's better to be a bit pessimistic. Then if things do work out well they'll be all the happier."

"That's probably good advice, but it seems sort of clinical," Carrie said. "I guess I have a tendency to develop an emotional attachment to my clients, especially if they're people and not corporations."

"There's nothing wrong with that," Will assured her. "That's one of the things that makes you a good lawyer. You obviously put your heart into your work."

"That's what's been such a blessing about working at Ramquist and Dowd," Carrie said, sipping her coffee. "You don't have that god-awful pressure to churn out the billable hours and run cases through like you're working on an assembly line. I still work a lot of hours, mind you, but it's my choice and I get to manage my cases as I see fit instead of having to jump whenever some senior partner hollers."

"I've enjoyed the autonomy, too," Will agreed. "And it's a nice change to be in a firm that's small enough for you to get to know every employee's name, right down to the messengers and the cleaning people. We were so departmentalized at my old firm that I could go for weeks without seeing anyone who didn't work in my wing of the forty-ninth floor. Being part of a megafirm has its perks, but working at Ramquist has made me remember why I went to law school in the first place."

"You should have seen Burt the day he announced he'd lured you away from your old haunts," Carrie said, chuckling at the memory. "Talk about the cat who swallowed the canary. He was ecstatic."

"I must admit that my first meeting with him was a bit peculiar. I've been asked a lot of odd questions in job inter-

views, but Burt was the first person to ask me my favorite
Elvis song."

Carrie laughed. "Which is?"

" 'Jailhouse Rock,' " Will answered. "How about you?"

"Gee, I don't know," Carrie said. "Fortunately Burt
didn't ask me that in my interview." She thought for a
moment. "I guess I'd go with 'Heartbreak Hotel.' Actually,
all of the early songs were good because Elvis displayed
such a natural exuberance. A lot of the later stuff sounded
canned, like he was just going through the motions."

Will had a strange little smile on his face.

"What's the matter?" Carrie demanded.

"Nothing. I was just wondering if there are any other
law firms in the city where the partners sit around and have
serious discussions about Elvis."

"I doubt it," Carrie replied. "In that department I think
Burt definitely has a monopoly on eccentricity."

They had finished their coffee and the waiter had
brought the check. "Are you ready to go?" Will asked.

Carrie nodded. "I'm beat. It's been a long day."

"A lot has happened in the last twenty-four hours," Will
agreed. He took out his wallet and tossed some bills on the
table. "Okay. Let's hit the road."

Will had driven to the restaurant, and so Carrie's car was
still in the building's underground parking garage. The drive
back to the office was quiet. Carrie was glad that she already felt comfortable enough with Will not to feel the
need to talk nonstop.

They reached the garage, and Will pulled into the parking space next to Carrie's car. "Thanks for dinner. I really
enjoyed it," she said.

"Me, too." Will leaned over and kissed her on the lips,
lightly at first, then more deeply.

"I'd better go," Carrie said ruefully when the clinch
ended. "The wine is really making me sleepy. I'll see you
tomorrow."

She got out of Will's car and, using her remote keypad,
unlocked the door on her own vehicle. As she tossed her
briefcase and purse onto the front passenger seat and was

about to get in, Will called out, "Wait a minute. I think you've got a flat tire." He cut the engine on his car and got out to take a closer look.

"Look, both your rear tires are flat," he said, pointing.

"Oh, shit!" Carrie grumbled.

"If you want to call the auto club I'll wait around with you until they come and fix them," Will offered. "Or if you'd prefer, I could give you a ride home and pick you up in the morning and you could deal with it then."

Carrie sighed. She was beginning to feel like the walking wounded. If she called the auto club now it could easily be two hours before they got her back on the road. She needed to go home and get some sleep. "If you're sure you don't mind, I think I'll take you up on the offer of chauffeur service," she said.

Will smiled and put his arm around her. "Smart move," he said. He opened the passenger door for her. "Hop in."

"I think I could get used to this service," she said. *And I know I could get used to having such a nice guy around on a regular basis,* she thought to herself as she settled back in the comfortable leather seat.

Fifteen minutes later, Will pulled into Carrie's driveway. "Thanks again for the lovely evening and for the ride," Carrie said, leaning over and giving him another quick kiss.

"It was my pleasure. Let's do dinner again soon—hopefully when we're both a bit more alert," Will suggested. "And I'll pick you up tomorrow about eight."

"Sounds good," Carrie said.

Carrie and Will went to the police station to meet with Detective Clauff late the next morning. When Will talked to the detective on the phone, he had merely said that he and Carrie would like to meet with him to discuss a possible break in the case. Will told Carrie the detective had clearly sounded doubtful that the two lawyers would have anything useful to add to his investigation. However, he had agreed to meet with them at eleven-thirty.

"I'm glad the auto club was able to fix the flats so promptly," Will said during the ride to the police station.

"Me, too," Carrie agreed. "The guy said the punctures in both tires were clean and deep. I must have run over something with sharp nails sticking out yesterday on the way to work."

"Good thing they make good tires nowadays. Years ago, if you ran over something like that the tires could have blown and you might've lost control of the car."

"Yeah, I'm lucky they went flat in the ramp *and* that I had such a nice chauffeur," Carrie teased.

Upon getting to the station, Will took the lead in explaining about the interviews of Jackson Memorial patients and the recent acquisition of Scott Rouleau's journal. The detective sat impassively, listening to the story. But when Will handed him a copy of the journal transcript, he picked it up, flipped rapidly through the pages without reading any of the entries, and then dropped it on his desk.

"Is this something young Mr. Fleming dreamed up?" Clauff asked, rolling his eyes.

"Of course not!" Carrie shot back. "I'd talked to Scott Rouleau on several visits to the hospital, and he apparently felt comfortable enough to confide in me."

"Why in the world should I believe anything a mental patient says?" the detective asked pointedly.

"Why would Scott make this up?" Will countered. "Where's his motive to lie?"

"How should I know?" Clauff said, throwing up his hands. "He's unbalanced. Maybe it makes him feel powerful to get somebody else in trouble. Maybe he truly believes it happened this way, but the guy is simply not a credible witness. Hell, the two of you are hotshot lawyers. You tell me: Is a mental patient ever deemed competent to testify in a legal proceeding?"

"That's an issue where we'll probably need to get a ruling from the judge on," Will agreed. "But we'll take care of that end. All we're asking from you right now is to have an open mind that Delgado could be the person who assaulted Katherine Buckley."

Detective Clauff continued to look highly skeptical.

"Scott Rouleau went to great lengths to keep this information hidden," Carrie said. "The head of our firm's computer department said she's never seen such a sophisticated encryption before. Scott was clearly frightened by what he witnessed. He struggled with the question of whether he should tell someone about it. He knew I was Katherine's friend, and he must have decided to trust me to use the information to help her and her family."

Carrie paused a moment and looked at the detective earnestly. "I know you and I have had our differences about this case," she said, "but please trust me on this. I truly believe, with all my heart, that everything Scott says in this journal is true."

The detective put his head back a moment and stared at the ceiling, as if trying to decide what to believe. "So what do you want me to do?" he asked. "Interview this witness and get his story firsthand?"

"Not right away," Carrie replied.

"What, then?" Clauff asked, raising his eyebrows.

"We've scheduled a series of second depositions of hospital personnel for Monday," Will explained. "Delgado is up first, at nine o'clock. We were hoping you could be there and hear him testify."

"Don't you think he'll be likely to smell a rat and take off as soon as he sees me?" Clauff asked.

"Well . . ." Carrie hesitated a moment, then plunged forward. "We were thinking maybe we could pass you off as a new attorney in our firm."

The detective laughed heartily. "I get to pretend to be a lawyer? I'm starting to like this idea."

"You never met Werner Von Slaten, did you?" Carrie asked. "We wouldn't want anyone to recognize you."

"No, I only talked to him on the phone," Clauff answered. "So what should I wear for my acting debut?"

"A dark suit would be good," Carrie replied, not sure if the detective was toying with her or not.

"All right," Clauff said. "So I show up in my dark suit and try to look like I fit in at your firm. Then what? This Delgado sounds like a pretty smooth operator. I'm not questioning your legal prowess, but do you really think he's going to break down in the middle of a deposition and confess all?"

"We're not sure what will happen," Will admitted. "But we're hoping that if we start putting pressure on him about his record in Vancouver and then hit him with the allegation that someone saw him in a compromising situation with Katherine, he might give up something."

"At which point I can slap the cuffs on him and take him away," Clauff said.

"Something like that," Will agreed.

Clauff rubbed his hands over his face. "This whole scenario sounds so strange that *I* should probably have my head examined for even considering it, but what do I have to lose? All right, you've got yourselves a deal. I will be in your office at eight-thirty Monday morning, dressed in appropriate lawyer garb. I expect the whole thing to bomb royally, but what the hell—it'll give me several years' worth of new lawyer jokes."

Chapter 33

"**O**n paper it all looks great," Carrie said, pacing the floor of her office on Monday morning. "So why am I so jittery?"

"It'll go fine," Will assured her.

"I'll be so glad when this is over," she said fervently, fiddling with the buttons on her black suit.

Carrie had spent a nervous weekend worrying about how things would go. Because of the apparent rapport she had had with Delgado in his earlier deposition, she would again be handling the questioning. She and Will spent Sunday afternoon at the office going over in meticulous detail the questions Carrie would ask.

Detective Clauff arrived at the office at the appointed hour, looking quite dapper in a black suit and black wing tips. Carrie gave him a folder full of documents and a couple of legal pads to complete the effect of the perfectly turned-out litigator. She had been a bit fearful that the detective would look stiff and out of place and immediately alert the hospital contingent that something was afoot. To her surprise, Clauff managed to act and sound appropriately lawyerly, and no one seemed to question Ramquist and Dowd's new partner, David Carlson.

Carrie intended to start off in a friendly stance, asking noncontroversial questions, then slowly move into a discussion of his background, building into queries about the allegations of rape in Vancouver and then finally hitting him with the charge that someone had seen him assault Katherine.

By 8:55 everyone was assembled except the star witness.

At 9:05, Carrie started to worry. "Are you sure he knew the correct time?" she asked Charlene Bull.

"I'm positive," Charlene replied. "I talked to him on Saturday. He said he'd be here."

By 9:20 Carrie was frantic. Something was obviously wrong. Maybe Delgado had been tipped off—but how and by whom? Scowling, she turned to Werner Von Slaten, who had been sitting quietly on one end of the large conference room table. "You didn't happen to tell him not to come, did you?" she demanded.

"I most certainly did not!" the hospital's administrator shot back. "I resent that remark."

"Why don't you try to call him?" Will suggested to Charlene Bull.

"Fine," Charlene said. She consulted her file to get Delgado's number, then got up and walked over to the phone on the far side of the room. After a minute or so, she replaced the receiver. "It rang ten times. He didn't pick up, and his answering machine apparently isn't on." She returned to her chair. "I don't know what to tell you. I'm really sorry about this. I'm sure I'll be able to reach him later. Could we reschedule him for tomorrow or the next day?"

Carrie couldn't wait until tomorrow or the next day. She needed to know what was going on now. "Do you have his home address?" she asked.

"Yes," Charlene replied. "Why?"

"I think we should all go check on him," Carrie replied. "I'm afraid something might have happened to him."

"This is absurd!" Von Slaten sputtered. "You're making it sound like there's some sort of sinister plot afoot. I'm sure he just forgot or was delayed. Maybe he had car trouble."

Carrie shot Will a desperate look. "I agree with Carrie," he said. "What harm can come from checking on him?"

"What about the other depositions you've got scheduled for this morning?" Charlene asked. "Those witnesses are going to start arriving soon."

"We'll have the receptionist tell them to wait," Carrie said. "We won't be gone long."

"Oh, all right," Charlene finally agreed, no doubt sensing that Carrie wasn't going to let loose of this stupid idea. "Who all is going?"

"I think we should all go," Carrie replied. "You, Werner, Will, David, and me."

"Who's driving?" Charlene asked.

"I have a Cadillac," Von Slaten put in. "I can take everyone."

"Fine," Will said. "Let's go."

The drive to Delgado's near northside apartment took about fifteen minutes. Charlene Bull sat in the front with Von Slaten while Carrie sat sandwiched in the back between Will and Detective Clauff. The detective had been remarkably quiet throughout the entire fiasco, but as they drove Carrie could see him giving her amused looks. *He'd probably like to admit* me *to Jackson Memorial,* Carrie thought morosely.

They all trooped up to the fifth floor of the large apartment complex. Von Slaten first rang the doorbell, then pounded on the door and called out, "Alessandro, are you in there?" but there was no response.

"He's not here," Charlene Bull said.

Standing there in the hallway, Carrie was suddenly overcome with an inexplicable feeling of dread. "Let's get the key from the building manager," she said urgently.

"For the love of God!" Von Slaten spouted off. "This is absurd."

"I'll get the manager," Clauff said. "Wait here."

Within five minutes the detective returned with an obese middle-aged man in tow. "I shouldn't be doin' this," the man grumbled.

"I promise you won't get in any trouble," Clauff assured him. "Just open the door."

The manager complied, and the five people stepped inside Delgado's apartment. The manager lingered out in the hall. As soon as they crossed the threshold, Carrie could see Clauff sniffing the air. Although she couldn't smell anything, she knew this was not a good sign. She looked at Will. For the first time he, too, looked grim.

"Alessandro?" Von Slaten called out. "Anybody home?" He turned to Charlene Bull. "You see, I told you he wasn't here. This was a colossal waste of time."

Clauff was methodically pacing through the apartment. Carrie and Will followed at his heels. The place appeared to be a nicely furnished bachelor's pad. The living room had comfortable seating, a big-screen television, and a quality sound system. The kitchen was utilitarian. There were two plates, one coffee cup, and two glasses in the sink. The bathroom was a bit messy, with a pair of jeans and a sweatshirt thrown carelessly in front of the clothes hamper and two large forest-green towels draped over the shower curtain rod.

Clauff moved silently toward the only closed door in the apartment, obviously Delgado's bedroom. Carrie and Will were still right behind him. In the background Carrie could hear Von Slaten complaining to Charlene about Carrie leading them on a wild goose chase and forcing the hospital to incur unnecessary expenses.

Von Slaten opened the door to the room. A faint putrid odor caught Carrie unaware and she felt herself gagging. Then she looked straight ahead and her knees nearly buckled. On the floor next to the bed lay the lifeless body of Alessandro Delgado. A hypodermic needle and a bottle lay nearby. Clutched in Delgado's right hand was a piece of paper. On it were printed the words, "I AM SO SORRY."

Carrie could feel herself making a sort of choking sound. Detective Clauff was on the floor examining the body. Von Slaten and Charlene had now arrived at the room and peered in. "Oh, my God!" Charlene screamed. "Is he dead?"

"Don't touch him!" Von Slaten yelled at Clauff. "You might contaminate the crime scene."

Clauff shot Von Slaten a disparaging look, reached in his breast pocket, and pulled out his detective's shield. "Everybody out of here," he ordered, "and be careful not to touch anything as you go. Tell the manager to call Homicide."

Will, Von Slaten, and Charlene immediately complied with the detective's order, but somehow Carrie found herself inexorably drawn forward toward the body.

"That goes for you, too," Clauff said in a perturbed tone as he realized Carrie was still there. She stood rooted to the spot, staring intently at the shell of the man who had assaulted and impregnated Katherine Buckley.

"All right," Clauff said more kindly as he turned around and looked Carrie square in the face. "I believe you that this is the guy who raped your client. Are you happy now?"

Carrie managed to gulp and give a small nod.

"Good." The detective gave her the briefest of smiles. "Now get the hell out of here and have your boyfriend get you a glass of water. You're looking pretty green around the gills." He turned back to his work, not bothering to see whether or not Carrie obeyed.

Part III

Part III

Chapter 34

The week following Delgado's death sped by in a blur. Carrie was surprised to find herself having conflicting emotions about the demise of Katherine's assailant.

While she believed that Delgado's crime was both heinous and unforgivable, she couldn't help but feel a tinge of sadness that a young life had ended so abruptly. And at some level she felt cheated that he hadn't stuck around to own up to what he had done and face the legal consequences of his acts.

The Buckleys had been shocked to hear the identity of their daughter's attacker.

"Oh, my God, I can't believe it!" Melody Buckley exclaimed. "He was always so charming and so kind to us."

"At least this means that Todd will finally be off the hook," Ed added. "More than any of us, that poor boy has been through hell."

Like Carrie, Katherine's parents had mixed feelings about Delgado's suicide.

"There's a real sense of relief in finally knowing the identity of the person who hurt Katherine and knowing that he'll never be able to do something like that to another poor girl," Ed Buckley said. "But it can never be a time for rejoicing when a person that age passes on."

"I feel sorry for his family," Melody Buckley put in. "I'm sure they are mourning their loss, just as we mourn for Katherine."

The Buckleys had consented to having fetal tissue samples taken from Katherine's baby, and DNA tests confirmed that Delgado was the child's father. Todd Fleming was quietly exuberant when he heard the news. "It's going to take a while for it all to sink in," the young man said. "But thank you so much, Carrie, for helping clear my name. You can't begin to know what that means to me. It was hard enough for me to try to cope with Katherine's accident. The possibility of criminal charges hanging over me almost drove me over the edge."

For all their earlier wrangling, Detective Clauff had been very generous in sharing the details of Delgado's autopsy with Carrie. The cause of death was a lethal injection of morphine. A bottle of morphine identical to the one found next to the body was missing from the hospital's pharmacy. Delgado's body had also contained traces of cocaine and heroin. A search of his apartment had revealed evidence of regular drug use and possibly occasional dealing.

"It looks like he was an all-around bad hombre," Clauff said to Carrie. "I hate to say it, but his putting himself out of his misery was probably not the worst thing that could have happened. It could very well have spared other victims from Katherine's fate—or worse."

Scott Rouleau and his sister were both relieved to hear about Delgado's death. Carrie had phoned Laurie Rouleau as soon as she'd gotten back to the office after the trip to Delgado's apartment. Laurie had been concerned about her brother's fragile emotional state and had wanted to be with him when he heard the news. Carrie, still feeling responsible for Scott's welfare, met Laurie at the hospital. Again, Carrie was careful not to draw attention to the fact that she was visiting Scott.

Scott had digested the information with quiet equanimity. "Did he know I ratted on him?" he asked after a moment of reflection.

"No, he didn't," Carrie assured him. "In fact, no one at the hospital knows you were our source. The only people who know are the police."

"So he's not dead because of me—at least not directly," Scott said.

"Absolutely not," Laurie said at once.

"You can't blame yourself for what someone else does,"

Carrie said. "Delgado made his own choices, and when he realized he'd been exposed, he apparently couldn't deal with it."

"He was a bad person," Scott said philosophically. "Maybe it's a good thing he's dead."

"Maybe it is," Carrie agreed.

"Now that you know who assaulted your client, does this mean the case is over?" Laurie asked.

Carrie shook her head. "Not necessarily. The hospital might continue to deny liability."

"How can they?" Laurie asked incredulously. "Their employee assaulted a patient on their premises."

"That's true," Carrie agreed, "but they may claim that they had no knowledge of Delgado's sexual proclivities, that he appeared to be a model employee, and that he carried out the assaults so surreptitiously that there was nothing to put them on notice that he was up to no good."

"But don't they have a duty to supervise him?" Laurie asked. "Don't their patients have a right to not be abused by the staff?"

"I think the answer to both of those questions is yes," Carrie replied, "but somehow I doubt that the hospital is just going to admit culpability and write out a big settlement check."

"So Scott's involvement in the case isn't automatically over?" Laurie asked with obvious concern. "It's still possible he might have to testify?"

"I'm afraid I really can't give you an answer to that," Carrie admitted. "I'm going to push hard for a settlement, but I can't hold a gun to anybody's head. The hospital has a right to go to trial and have a jury decide whether or not they're liable. If the trial does go forward, we might need Scott's testimony."

Both Laurie and Scott looked less than thrilled with this possibility.

"But that's not a given," Carrie hastened to add. "It's possible the hospital would be willing to stipulate that Delgado assaulted Katherine Buckley while on duty. In that case Scott wouldn't have to testify and the jury would just have to decide whether the hospital should bear any responsibility for Delgado's actions."

"I don't understand all this legal procedure," Laurie said, shaking her head. "It doesn't make any sense to me. You'd think if a hospital employee committed a crime while on duty the hospital would automatically be liable. How can they possibly claim otherwise?"

Carrie managed a wan smile. "I went into law in part because I enjoy all the nuances, the fact that so few things are black and white. But I'll admit there are times when I'm feeling especially cynical that I agree with you completely. A case like this one *should* be black and white. The hospital *should* be held responsible. It *should* pay Katherine's family for what Delgado did. Unfortunately, it just doesn't work that way."

"I'll testify if I have to," Scott said stoically. "Now that Delgado is dead, I'm not afraid anymore."

"You're very brave, Scott," Carrie said, patting his arm. "And according to the head of our firm's computer department, you've got a real talent for software development. In fact, I was telling her about your Holy Grail game and she said she'd like to see it. She said she knows some people who might be able to help you market it—if you're interested, that is."

Scott's expression immediately brightened. "I wouldn't want to sell it outright. I'd like to retain ownership so I'd get royalties on every sale. Would that be possible?"

"I don't see why not," Carrie said. "Do you have a copy of the game on a disk that I could take along and show her?"

Scott nodded eagerly. "I have one right here." He got up, opened a dresser drawer, and pulled out a disk. "Here it is," he said, handing it to Carrie. "Do you really think this person could help me market it?"

"If Michelle says she's going to do something, you can believe her," Carrie promised him. "I'll give this to her and let you know what she says."

Laurie walked out into the corridor with Carrie. "Thank you for treating my brother like a human being," she said, her eyes tearing up. "If there'd been more people like you in his life he might not be stuck in this damn place."

"Maybe being able to reveal what he knows about Delgado will have a healing effect for him," Carrie said. "And if we can help him market his game, that should help, too. Who knows, maybe this whole tragic situation will yield some good results for Scott. We can hope, anyway."

Laurie gave Carrie a warm smile as she headed for the elevator.

Depositions in the *Buckley* case were halted for a week following Delgado's death. The respite gave Carrie a chance to catch up on work she'd been neglecting in other cases. It also gave her and Will time to formulate a fair settlement offer and present it to the hospital.

"We want to come up with a figure that fairly compensates the Buckleys but at the same time isn't so high that the hospital will reject it out of hand," Carrie said. "Do you have any ideas?"

Will tapped his pen on a legal pad on his desk. "If a jury finds liability, the punitive damage award could be astronomical. Of course, the hospital is going to argue that we'll never win on liability." He closed one eye, mentally tallying up the figures. "I don't know. What if we offered to settle for five million?"

Carrie nodded. "I was thinking something in that ballpark."

"Have you talked to the Buckleys about what they're looking for?"

Carrie shook her head. "This case has never been about money for them. They just wanted to know what happened to Katherine and have the hospital admit responsibility. I'm sure they'd accept any amount that we recommended."

"So we're agreed we make an offer to settle for five?"

"Agreed," Carrie said.

"Where do we stand on finishing up the depositions?" Will asked.

"Assuming we don't settle, we're going to have to focus on proving that the hospital knew or should have known that Delgado was up to some bad acts at work. I'm afraid we're going to have to redepose most of the staff to find out if they knew anything about his activities and if they ever saw him do anything improper with Katherine or any other patients."

Will nodded. "That will take time, and it's already the first of May."

"It can't be helped," Carrie said. "Most of those deps should be fairly short. Look at it this way—at least we don't have to spend any more time on patient interviews."

"Yes, but that idea paid off, didn't it?" Will teased.

"Yes, it did. Thank you for refusing to let me abandon the process in midstream."

"So, have you rethought your position about Luebke being the bad guy?" Will asked, tweaking her just a bit.

Carrie made a face. "Not entirely. I still think there's something shady about the guy. It wouldn't surprise me if he knew what Delgado was up to and looked the other way."

"So you'll want Luebke on the list of people to be redeposed?"

"Put him at the top of the list," Carrie said.

Chapter 35

On a sunny afternoon in early May, Carrie was working on a list of potential witnesses in the housing discrimination case when Tammy rapped lightly on the door and stepped inside the office. Carrie looked up from her file.

"There's a woman in the reception area who's demanding to see you," Tammy said. "I tried to tell her she needed an appointment, but she's insistent that she has to talk to you now."

"Who is it?" Carrie asked.

"Alessandro Delgado's mother," Tammy replied. "She's going back to Miami tomorrow and says she has to talk to you before she leaves town."

Carrie stared at her secretary in disbelief. "What on earth would she want to talk to me about?"

"I don't know," Tammy shrugged. "She won't say. Maybe she wants to apologize for what her son did."

Carrie rubbed her hand over her chin, weighing what she should do. "Oh, all right," she finally said with resignation. "Bring her back here. No matter what she wants, this is going to be very awkward, but I guess I may as well see her."

Tammy nodded. "Just to warn you, she has a pretty thick accent. I had trouble understanding her."

"Great," Carrie murmured.

Several minutes later Carrie found herself face-to-face with the mother of Katherine Buckley's rapist.

Maria Delgado was probably in her early sixties, but she looked much older. Her skin was lined and dotted with age spots. Her gray hair was pulled back into an unfashionable bun. Her black dress had been visibly mended, and she wore black orthopedic shoes. The woman's life had obviously not been an easy one. Carrie immediately felt great sympathy for her.

"Mrs. Delgado, please have a seat," Carrie said cordially. "Would you like something to drink? Some coffee or a soft drink?"

"No," the woman replied.

After a moment of uncomfortable silence, Carrie asked gently, "What can I do for you, Mrs. Delgado?"

"Thank you for seeing me," Delgado's mother said softly, her hands folded sedately in her lap. As Tammy had warned, her speech was heavily accented with the tones of her native Cuba. "I want to say how sorry I am for what Alessandro did. I have four daughters, but he is my only son. He used to be a good boy. I don't know what happened to him. I am so sorry for how he hurt that girl. That was a most wicked thing to do." The woman paused, her chin quivering. "Please tell her family I am sorry."

"I will," Carrie promised, happy that Tammy had correctly ascertained the reason for the woman's visit. "It was very nice of you to take the time to stop and tell me that. I'm sure this has been a very difficult time for you."

"Alessandro was a good boy," the woman repeated, seemingly talking to herself now. "Such a handsome boy he was. His sisters loved to dress him up. He was the youngest, you know. He was their little pet."

Carrie nodded politely, wondering how she could courteously encourage this grieving old woman to leave.

"Alessandro always had a streak of mischief in him," the woman babbled on. "Sometimes he would do things when he knew he should not. But if the girls or I caught him, he would never lie. He would admit what he did and say he was sorry. That was the kind of boy he was."

Just as Carrie's eyes were beginning to glaze over, the bombshell dropped.

"That is why I know he was murdered."

Carrie's head snapped up. "What did you say?" she asked incredulously.

"He would not run away from trouble," his mother said, shaking her head firmly. "That was not his nature. If he did wrong and was caught, he would take responsibility for what he did. My son would never take his own life. Someone must have killed him."

"Mrs. Delgado," Carrie said carefully, "I know Alessandro's death must have come as a huge shock to you, but there is no evidence of murder. Alessandro died of a lethal injection of morphine. The bottle was found on the floor next to him. The morphine had been taken from the pharmacy at the hospital where he worked. And he left a note saying he was sorry." Carrie paused and gave the old woman a kindly look. "Your son wasn't a little boy anymore. He had done something so bad that he wasn't able to forgive himself. I know that is a hard truth, but you have to accept it and move on."

"No!" the force of the woman's exclamation shocked Carrie. "He would not commit suicide! He was murdered!"

Trying to humor her visitor, Carrie asked, "Who do you think could have killed him?"

"A bad person," the mother answered at once.

"What bad person?" Carrie asked patiently.

"I don't know."

"Why are you telling me about this?" Carrie asked. "If you truly think Alessandro was murdered, you should speak to the police."

"I did speak to them," Maria Delgado said, tossing her head. "They were not interested in the truth. They would not listen."

Probably not, Carrie thought. *The police have better things to do than trying to pacify the obviously disturbed mother of a criminal who'd decided to off himself.*

"What am I supposed to do with this information?" Carrie asked.

"You talk to the police," Maria Delgado said at once. "They would pay attention to you."

Don't be so sure of that, Carrie thought, recalling how little heed Detective Clauff had paid to her entreaties that he look for a suspect other than Todd Fleming. Carrie looked at her visitor intently as she considered her options. It looked as though Delgado's mother truly believed her son had been murdered. She showed no sign of departing Carrie's office until Carrie agreed to help her. If Carrie pretended to think her story contained even a modicum of truth, the woman would go home to Miami happy. Carrie hated to give people false hope, but sometimes a few white lies were the only way to handle a delicate situation.

"All right," Carrie said. "I'll talk to the police myself."

"You will make them investigate my son's death," Maria Delgado demanded.

"I'll do what I can," Carrie qualified. "I can't force the police to do anything, but I'll tell them your concerns."

"Then you do your own investigation," Maria insisted. "You find out who killed my son."

"I'm not equipped to do that," Carrie protested. "I'm just a lawyer."

"My oldest daughter, Gloria, is coming here later this month to clean out the apartment," Maria said firmly. "She will help you."

Carrie suppressed a groan.

"You will find out what happened to Alessandro," the woman said regally. "And the person who murdered him will be punished."

"I'll look into it," Carrie said noncommittally. "And believe me, if I see any indication that Alessandro did not take his own life, I will insist that the police reopen their investigation."

"Thank you," Maria Delgado said, getting to her feet, "for seeking justice for my son."

Carrie smiled benignly, all the while thinking, *Your son already got just exactly the justice that was coming to him.*

"I can't believe you told her you'd look into it!" Will chided later that afternoon when Carrie dropped in to tell him about Maria Delgado's visit.

"I said what I did to pacify her," Carrie protested as she paced back and forth in front of Will's desk. "I didn't actually promise her anything."

"You got the poor old woman's hopes up," Will said. "She thinks you're somehow going to exonerate her son. Imagine how let down she'll feel when she eventually learns that sonny boy really was the scumbag everybody says he was."

"Honestly!" Carrie sputtered. "I had to tell her something so she'd leave. I promise I'll let her down very easy when the time is right."

Chapter 36

Two days later, while getting their morning fix of coffee in one of the Ramquist and Dowd break rooms, several of Carrie's colleagues razzed her about agreeing to go to the police to plead Mrs. Delgado's case for opening a homicide investigation into her son's death.

"You really are a soft touch," Terry Payne said. "I thought you only took pity on poor defenseless animals. I guess this goes to show your kindness extends to defenseless old women, too."

"You must be a glutton for punishment," Ann Muchin put in. "I don't imagine the detective welcomed your suggestion with open arms."

"Hardly," Carrie said, taking a sip of the strong hot java. She had paid a call on Detective Clauff the previous afternoon. "Well, Ms. Nelson," the detective had said when he saw her. "I would have expected you'd be out celebrating your great victory. Have a seat. To what do I owe this dubious honor?"

"I haven't won any victory yet," Carrie explained as she parked herself in the chair in front of Clauff's nondescript desk. "The hospital hasn't agreed to settle, so the case is still going on. As to the reason for my visit, I guess you could say I'm just keeping my promise to a poor old woman."

The detective raised his eyebrows. "Something tells me I'm not going to like the answer, but would you translate that into English, please?"

"Sure." Carrie took a deep breath. "Alessandro Delgado's mother is convinced he was murdered, and I promised her someone would look into it."

Detective Clauff stared at Carrie for a long moment, then burst out laughing. "You've got to be kidding. You weren't by any chance smoking some of those funny cigarettes before you came to see me, were you?"

"Of course not!" Carrie sputtered indignantly.

"Then I can only assume that you've been spending so much time around that mental hospital that some of the bad vibes are starting to rub off on you. I already heard Mrs. Delgado's sob story—"

"Yes, she said she talked to you," Carrie interrupted him, "and she also said you didn't believe her."

"Why should I?" Clauff demanded. "Instead of becoming a priest like she wanted him to, her son grew up to be the kind of guy who gets his kicks from having sex with an unconscious woman and does a few drugs on the side. It's impossible for the old lady to square her idealized vision of Junior with reality, so she's in serious denial. It happens all the time with criminals' families. Most of them come to accept the truth eventually. It just takes a while."

"Isn't that an awfully blasé attitude?" Carrie challenged.

Clauff shrugged. "So what if it is? It's my opinion and I'm welcome to it."

"So you're saying you refuse to even consider the possibility that Delgado might have been murdered?"

"Ms. Nelson—"

"Call me Carrie," she said sweetly.

"Carrie. You seem like a nice girl—for a lawyer, that is, but if you don't mind my saying so, you're becoming a regular pain in the ass."

Carrie frowned.

"Nothing personal," Clauff added quickly. "I'll admit I was wrong about young Mr. Fleming. You kept trying to tell me that someone who worked at the hospital assaulted Ms. Buckley, and as it turned out, you were right. I'm a big enough man to admit that I made a mistake. But Delgado a homicide? Not even someone with your vast intellectual skills could convince me of that. In fact, I've never seen a more clear-cut case of suicide in my life."

"So you won't be investigating his death any further?"

"In a word, no."

"Then you won't mind if I check into a few things?"

The detective squeezed his eyes tightly shut, then opened them again. "Oh, you're still here. For a minute there I thought I was having a hallucination. *You* want to check into Delgado's death. Just what do you have in that devious little mind of yours?"

"Nothing sinister, I assure you. One of Delgado's sisters is going to be flying in from Baltimore in a week or two to clean out his apartment. I promised Mrs. Delgado that someone would go over there with her and take a look around. I didn't really think you'd be interested in the assignment. I just wanted to make sure I wouldn't be stepping on anyone's toes or getting in the way of an ongoing investigation by doing that."

Detective Clauff rubbed his palm slowly over his chin. "Since Delgado's death has already been ruled a suicide, there is no ongoing investigation. Ergo, the answer to your question is no on all counts. You won't be stepping on toes; you won't be getting in the way of anything. You also won't be finding jack shit," he added in a much louder tone, "but that's your problem, not mine."

Carrie smiled and nodded. "That's all I wanted to hear. Thank you very much for your time." She stood up and turned to go.

"Hey!" the detective called her back.

Carrie turned around again.

"Just for my own personal edification, you don't actually believe that Delgado's death is anything other than it appears?"

Carrie shook her head. "No, of course I don't. And I tried to tell his mother that. Several times, in fact. But that poor, broken-down old woman—who just lost her only son—can't or won't accept what you and I both know to be the truth. I just couldn't bring myself to be the person who snuffs out her last bit of hope. So I promised her that someone would look into the circumstances of Alessandro's death. I intend to keep that promise. I know as well as you do that nothing will come of it. But in the meantime, Maria Delgado can hold out hope a little bit longer, and when it finally comes time for her to face up to the truth, maybe she'll be stronger and better able to cope with it."

Clauff gave her an amused look, then said, "Be my guest. Make the old lady feel all warm and fuzzy. Then drop me a card when you've slipped her the bad news." He got up and put his hand on Carrie's shoulder. "It's been nice seeing you again. Now scram. I've got real live cases to work on."

Late the following day Carrie got a call from Charlene Bull. "I'm going to be sending a formal letter," Charlene said, "but I wanted to give you the courtesy of a call first. The hospital is rejecting your settlement offer."

"Why doesn't that surprise me?" Carrie asked drolly.

"The board of directors met this morning and discussed the matter at some length. It was their consensus that since there is no evidence that anyone on staff knew or had reason to know what Delgado was up to, a payment to your clients is not justified."

"There was no discussion of a counteroffer?" Carrie probed.

"Well—" Charlene hesitated a moment, then said, "The board didn't feel any payment was warranted under the current state of the evidence. Of course, if that situation changes, they might reconsider. If it's any consolation, I know Dr. Peckham tried hard to convince the board to settle."

From Charlene's tone, Carrie gathered that the young woman had also recommended trying to settle the case. Obviously Von Slaten had been able to convince the board otherwise. *"C'est la vie,"* Carrie said airily. "I guess we'll just continue to forge ahead."

"I guess so," Charlene agreed. "I'll see you tomorrow at the hearing to quash Dr. Luebke's subpoena."

"Right," Carrie said. "That's going to be a royal waste

of time. Why is he fighting so hard to avoid being rede-posed? I can't imagine he's got a snowball's chance in hell of winning."

"I really don't know," Charlene admitted. "Once he hired his own counsel, I was pretty much left out of the loop."

"Well, I didn't like the good doctor from the moment I first met him, and the more of these delaying tactics he pulls, the more it makes me wonder what he's trying to hide."

"I really doubt that he has any untoward motive," Charlene said. "He probably just doesn't like lawyers."

"There are a lot of days I don't like them either," Carrie muttered. "I appreciate the call, Charlene. I'll look forward to getting your letter, and I'll see you in court."

Carrie walked into Judge Little's courtroom at quarter to nine the following morning. Will had a brief due in another case, so Carrie was on her own. It was a hot, muggy day for early May, and Carrie was wearing a black-linen dress with a wide black belt and black-and-white pumps. The humidity made everything feel sticky, and Carrie gave a little yank on the bodice of her dress to move it away from her skin. Although she loved springtime in the Midwest, she did not like this kind of weather. It was downright uncomfortable, and it sometimes spawned severe thunderstorms or even tornados.

Court was not yet in session. As Carrie took her place at counsel table, Judge Little's bailiff, Adrienne Thomas, walked up to her. "Tell your secretary that the dog I got from her is working out just great," the young woman said. "He's a real sweetie."

"Tammy will be glad to hear it," Carrie said. "The only problem is that once she's successfully matched you with one animal, she immediately starts trying to talk you into taking another one."

"One is enough for now," Adrienne laughed. "But if I ever move to a bigger place, I might consider a second one."

Charlene Bull and Steve O'Connor walked into the room several minutes later. Carrie glanced around and was surprised to see that neither Luebke nor Von Slaten was present. "What, no clients today?" she asked the new arrivals.

O'Connor shook his head. "I told Dr. Luebke there was no need for him to come, and that seemed to suit him just fine."

"Werner had a staff meeting," Charlene said.

"This is the first proceeding he's missed since the case started," Carrie commented. "I'm surprised he didn't insist that you videotape it for him so he could watch it later."

Charlene laughed. She was probably just as sick of the hospital administrator's constant presence as Carrie was.

Adrienne Thomas called court into session promptly at nine, and Judge Little took her place behind the bench. "I see we have a motion to quash a subpoena," the judge said. "Mr. O'Connor, you have the floor."

"Thank you, Your Honor," replied O'Connor, getting to his feet. "As the court is well aware, the plaintiffs have alleged various negligence claims against Jackson Memorial, a hospital where Dr. Kenneth Luebke has staff privileges. The plaintiffs' suit does not name any individual physicians as defendants. Dr. Luebke has already given one deposition. He appeared voluntarily for that proceeding and almost immediately the questions posed to him ranged far afield of any issues even arguably germane to this case." O'Connor paused and took a sip of water.

"As the court will see from the portions of the deposition transcript attached to our motion, Dr. Luebke said clearly and unequivocally that he had no knowledge of the identity of the person who might have assaulted Katherine Buckley. Although Ms. Buckley's assailant has now apparently been positively identified, Dr. Luebke had no knowledge of the assaults. It is Dr. Luebke's belief that the plaintiffs are using the discovery process to delve unnecessarily and improperly into the backgrounds of physicians on staff at Jackson Memorial. It has come to Dr. Luebke's attention that the plaintiffs' attorneys have been contacting the doctor's former patients in an attempt to unearth negative information about him."

Carrie frowned. O'Connor was clearly referring to Gwen Starling, the young woman whose mother was convinced her daughter had been assaulted by Dr. Luebke. How in the hell had he found out about that? She couldn't believe Mrs. Starling had tipped him off. So where was the leak? Could it be that the mysterious person who had called to tell Carrie about the Starlings had also told Dr. Luebke what he'd done? That didn't make any sense. Unless the mystery man wanted to make Dr. Luebke sweat.

"Now Dr. Luebke has been served with a subpoena to appear at a second deposition," O'Connor was continuing. "Since Dr. Luebke gave full and complete information in his first deposition, he has nothing further to add on any issue germane to this case, and it appears that the plaintiffs' attempts to force him to sit through another round of questioning are nothing more than a fishing expedition that borders on harassment. For that reason, Your Honor, we respectfully request that you quash the subpoena and release Dr. Luebke from his obligation to appear for the deposition." O'Connor sat down.

Judge Little turned to Carrie. "Ms. Nelson, your turn."

Carrie stood up. "Your Honor, in the past two weeks the plaintiffs have made significant strides in gathering evidence to support the claims against Jackson Memorial. As Mr. O'Connor has already indicated, we have now established conclusively the identity of the person who assaulted Ms. Buckley. That person was a hospital employee. Prior to learning this important information, we had already deposed most of the staff and employees at the hospital. Since we did not yet know the perpetrator's identity, we were obviously unable to focus our questioning on what staff members might have observed about his behavior."

Carrie paused a moment and referred to the notes she had scrawled on a legal pad. "Dr. Luebke should in no way feel that he is being singled out for special treatment. We have sent out notices of second depositions to virtually all persons who testified previously. The only reason we found

it necessary to serve Dr. Luebke with a subpoena rather
than just issue another standard notice of deposition is that
the doctor made it clear at his first deposition that he would
absolutely not submit voluntarily to any further questioning. Under the circumstances we felt we had no choice
but to subpoena him."

Carrie took a drink of water. "In light of the fact that
we still have six weeks in which to complete discovery and
in view of the recently discovered evidence of the assailant's identity, it is crucial that we have the opportunity to
again question the entire staff at Jackson Memorial. We
submit that Dr. Luebke's motion should be denied."

Judge Little addressed Charlene Bull. "Ms. Bull, as counsel for the hospital, do you have anything to add?"

Charlene shook her head. "No, Your Honor. The hospital has no opinion one way or the other on this issue."

Judge Little nodded. "Thank you, counsel. Mr. O'Connor, while I have some sympathy for your client's position,
I am going to deny your motion. As Ms. Nelson pointed
out, the time for conducting discovery has not yet run.
Until it does, the plaintiffs are entitled to make all reasonable efforts to gather information that will assist them in
proving their case. There has been no showing that scheduling Dr. Luebke, or any other staff member, for a second
deposition is being done for purposes of harassment or
delay. On the contrary, Ms. Nelson's explanation about the
newly discovered evidence makes it eminently reasonable
for the plaintiffs to need to ask more questions of persons
who have already been deposed. While that process may
seem burdensome—and to some may even feel like harassment—it is entirely in keeping with our system of
jurisprudence."

The judge turned to address Carrie. "Although I am denying Dr. Luebke's motion, I will take this opportunity to
remind the plaintiffs that while continued discovery is per-
missible, fishing expeditions of any sort are not. If it appears that Dr. Luebke or any other witness is being
subjected to lines of questioning that are not reasonably
calculated to lead to the discovery of relevant evidence,

then I invite counsel for the aggrieved witness to bring the matter before me at once. Are there any questions about my ruling?''

All three attorneys shook their heads.

"Very well," the judge said. "Ms. Nelson, you may prepare an order for my signature." She rapped her gavel on the bench. "This matter is adjourned."

Carrie, Charlene Bull, and Steve O'Connor rode down in the elevator together.

"Looks like you're on a roll, Carrie," Charlene said in a tone that conveyed signs of envy.

Carrie shrugged. "We're just plugging away," she said modestly.

Steve was very subdued. "I guess I'll see you both next week," he said as they reached the ground floor.

When he had headed off toward his car, Carrie said, "I don't envy him. Unless I miss my guess, Luebke is not going to be very pleased with the result, and I suspect he's one of those people who's only too happy to kill the messenger who brings the bad news."

Charlene smiled. "I must admit there have been times when my client—or at least its main representative—gets on my nerves, but I'd be willing to bet that Werner Von Slaten at his absolute worst couldn't begin to hold a candle to Dr. Luebke."

Chapter 37

In light of the flurry of professional activity that had occurred in the two weeks since their dinner date at Luigi's,
Carrie and Will had found little time to nourish their bud-
ding personal life. They had worked in several quick
lunches and one Sunday movie matinee, but they had not
yet had a chance to take their relationship to the next level.
So in the first week of May when Will asked Carrie if she
would like to try a new, highly praised French restaurant
on Saturday night, she jumped at the chance.

Although there were plenty of things she knew she
should be doing at the office, Carrie decided to treat herself
to an entire day off. She slept late, soaked in a hot tub,
and cajoled the manager of her favorite salon into squeezing her in for a facial, manicure and pedicure. The storms
that had been in the forecast all week had not materialized,
and it was still hot and muggy, weather more suitable to
late July than early May.

After spending a considerable amount of time surveying
the contents of all four of her closets and trying and dis-
carding no less than seven outfits, Carrie finally settled on
a simple black sleeveless dress that ended just above the
knee. She would carry a matching black jacket in case the
restaurant was overly air-conditioned. The next problem
was choosing appropriate jewelry from her vast collection.
Deciding that bold but not gaudy was the way to go, she
selected a vintage amethyst necklace, bracelet, and earring
set made in Paris in the thirties.

She slipped into a pair of black pumps, touched up her
lipstick and gave herself an extra spray of Chanel No. 5 for

good measure, then stood back to scrutinize her image in her bedroom's full-length mirror. She pirouetted, tossed her hair back, and winked at herself. Her cat, reflected in the mirror, gazed at her disdainfully from his perch at the foot of her bed.

"I'm being silly, aren't I, Muffin?" she asked, walking over and scratching the animal's head. "Well, that's because I feel happier than I've felt in a long time. In fact, I feel almost"—she searched for the right word—"giddy. And to tell you the truth, I don't know when I've felt like that. Maybe right after I resigned from Henley, Schuman, and Kloss. And that wasn't true giddiness, it was hysteria at the realization that I had no job. Anyway, right now I feel terrific." She gave one more glance in the mirror. "And you know what? I don't look too bad, either, even if I do say so myself." She tickled the cat under the chin. "I'll see you later," she said, then smiled wickedly. "Unless, of course, I get a better offer, in which case you may be on your own for the night."

Since the restaurant was on the north shore, Carrie met Will at his house and he drove from there. "It looks like everybody must have discovered this place," Carrie commented as they pulled into the crowded parking lot.

Inside, too, the restaurant was overflowing. The frazzled hostess informed them apologetically that there would be a very brief wait while their table was reset. Carrie and Will passed the time by looking at the decor, which mimicked a chic bistro in the south of France. As Will was pointing out an amusing vintage French Rail poster, Carrie heard a familiar voice behind her.

"Well, counselor, fancy meeting you here."

Carrie and Will turned and saw Dr. Peckham and his attractive young wife. Justine Peckham was wearing a low-cut white minidress. The doctor had his arm around his spouse's waist, and from his slurred speech and glassy eyes it was readily apparent that he had been imbibing rather liberally.

"You 'member my wife, Justine," Dr. Peckham said.

"Yes, of course," Carrie said, smiling. "Mrs. Peckham, this is Will Rollston."

"Nice to meet you," Will said politely, shaking hands with the woman. "Have you folks already eaten?"

Justine nodded. "It was excellent."

"First-rate," the doctor agreed. He leaned forward and said confidentially, "We're having a little celebration. You see, it's our wedding anniversary. Our seventh." He gave his wife's wasp waist a little squeeze.

"Congratulations," Will said.

"All of their truffle dishes are outstanding," the doctor said. "And if you're interested in a wine suggestion, the '88 Petrus is just superb."

"Thanks," Will said. "We'll keep that in mind."

"So, how's the case going these days?" the doctor asked.

"Gerry, this isn't the place to be talking business," Justine scolded.

"It's still going," Carrie replied noncommittally.

"That goddam Von Slaten!" the doctor said, slapping his thigh with his left hand. "If he knew what was good for him, he'd settle. I've already told the hospital board as much. I'm going to have to find out what the hell's going on. After all, you've got the goods on him."

"Not exactly," Carrie demurred.

"Well, you know whodunit, don't you? What a shock that was—and what a waste. Delgado was a hell of a good nurse."

"Then you never suspected him of taking liberties with patients?" Carrie said, fishing.

"Absolutely not. Could have knocked me over with a feather when I heard. You know," the doctor said, looking Carrie as squarely in the face as his inebriated state would permit, "I've been wondering how you stumbled onto Delgado. That must have been some skillful piece of sleuthing."

Carrie shrugged. "You'd be surprised at all the different sources of information you come across working up a case like this," she said, neatly dodging the question.

"I s'pose so," Dr. Peckham said, nodding. He leaned

forward again. "You know, I tried to slip you a helpful
hint myself."

Carrie looked back at him blankly.

"Delores Starling," the doctor added in a stage whisper.

Carrie's mouth dropped open. "*You* were the one who
called me about Delores Starling!" she exclaimed. "Why
didn't you say it was you?"

"I didn't want to get personally involved," he answered
flippantly. "Anyway, as it turns out, I guess we were bark-
ing up the wrong tree there. Unless—" he said, clearly inti-
mating that he still wondered if Dr. Luebke might somehow
provide a missing key to the *Buckley* case.

"Gerry, we really must be going," Justine prodded.

"Do you have far to drive?" Will asked.

Justine shook her head. "Just to Kenilworth." She took
hold of her husband's arm. "Come on, Gerry."

"Yes, dear," Peckham replied, kissing his wife on the
cheek. "Bon appetit," he said gaily as they turned to go.
"Don't forget—the '88 Petrus."

A short time later, after Will and Carrie had been seated
at their table, Will shook his head in wonder. "That was
a shocker, seeing a distinguished fiftyish doctor stewed to
the gills."

"It's their seventh anniversary," Carrie reminded him
sweetly. "He was celebrating."

Will scanned the wine list, then gave out a low whistle.
"Whoa! Get a load of this. The '88 Petrus goes for three
ninety-five a bottle. And from the way the good doctor was
acting, he didn't stop at one. That is *some* celebration.
Maybe he senses the missus is starting to get the seven-
year itch, and he thought he needed to spend a bundle to
keep her from trading him in for someone younger and
wealthier."

Carrie rubbed her chin with her index finger. "Who
would have thought that he was the one who made that call
telling me about the Starlings?" she mused, not listening to
Will at all. "And from the sound of it, he still thinks
Luebke knows more than he's saying. I wonder if that's
so."

"Like I've said before, it's probably just professional jealousy," Will commented. "Remember, they're both still vying for the chief of staff position."

"Luebke might be the key," Carrie said stubbornly.

"He might," Will agreed. "But you know what?" He lightly kicked her foot under the table to get her attention. "Right now I don't give a damn about Peckham or Luebke or the case."

Carrie looked in his eyes and felt herself turning to mush. "You don't?" she asked weakly.

Will shook his head. "No, I don't. I came here to have a nice quiet evening with you. So, with your agreement, let's call for a moratorium on any more shop talk tonight, okay?"

"Okay," she readily agreed. "You've got yourself a deal."

"Good." Will picked up the wine list again. "Now what do you say we select some liquid refreshment, assuming that the Peckhams didn't clean out the entire wine cellar."

"You don't have to ask twice," Carrie said, smiling.

The food and drink were excellent, the service polished but unhurried, the conversation light and companionable. It was ten o'clock when Will pulled the car back into his driveway. "Could I interest you in some coffee or a nightcap?" Will asked casually.

"Why not?" Carrie answered in the same vein.

Will held her hand as they walked up to the door. It was still warm and muggy, and the wind was blowing fiercely. "It still looks like it could blow up a bad storm," Will commented. He unlocked the door, turned on a light in the entryway, and followed Carrie inside.

Will's dog came out of the kitchen, ambled over to Carrie, and sniffed her hand. "Hi, Floyd. How are you doing?" she asked, rubbing the animal's ears. "We had really good food and didn't even bring you any leftovers. Wasn't that mean of us?"

"He's hardly malnourished," Will laughed. "Have a seat. What can I get you?"

"I don't know. Do you have any Scotch?"

"You bet. I've got Chivas and I've also got a very good eighteen-year-old single malt."

"I'll try the single malt." She sat down on the sofa. The dog lay down on the floor next to her.

"Good choice. On ice?"

"No, neat," Carrie replied.

"Ah, a serious drinker," Will joked.

Will came over and handed her the drink and then sat down beside her. He held up his glass. "To a very nice evening," he said.

"I'll drink to that," Carrie said, lightly clinking her glass against his. She took a sip of the Scotch. "That's good stuff," she said appreciatively.

"Nothing but the best for you."

Carrie leaned back against the cushions and contemplated the *Avengers* poster. "I really like that poster," she said. "We should rent some videos of the show sometime."

"I've got most of the episodes on tape," Will said. "We can watch them anytime you'd like."

"That'd be nice," Carrie said, taking another sip of her drink.

Will put his arm around her. "Would you like to watch one now?"

Carrie turned to face him. "Not really," she answered softly.

Will smiled. "Me either," he said. He set his glass down on the coffee table and took Carrie's drink out of her hand and set it out of the way as well. Then he kissed her, and suddenly watching old videos was the last thing on either of their minds.

Sometime later, when their clothes were in disarray and they were struggling not to roll off the sofa onto the floor, Will asked, "Would you be terribly offended if I suggested moving into the bedroom?"

"I thought you'd never ask," Carrie murmured. "But what will Mrs. Peel think?"

"The hell with Mrs. Peel!" Will growled as he scrambled to his feet and pulled Carrie up next to him. "You're the one I want to make love to."

Once they were in the bedroom, the shedding of clothes was accomplished with minimal awkwardness, and soon Carrie found herself on the cherry fourposter, pulling Will down to her. The actual experience of their first coupling was even better than the fantasies she'd allowed herself over the past couple of months. Will was a wonderful lover, ardent and playful, passionate yet tender. Carrie reveled in the luxuriant feelings he aroused in her and wished they could go on forever.

At the summit of their passion, Carrie suddenly heard a strange noise. "What's that?" she asked, looking around.

"What?" Will asked, still panting from the recent exertion.

"That noise," Carrie replied. "Don't you hear it? It sounds like a siren."

"Oh, my God!" Will said, "I think it's a tornado siren." As he rolled onto his side, the door burst open and in a single bound the dog leapt up onto the bed, whimpering furiously.

"Floyd, no! Get off of here, you big lummox!" Will scolded.

Floyd began to paw furiously at the sheets. Outside the siren was still wailing.

Carrie began to laugh.

"What's the matter with you?" Will asked, clearly overwhelmed by all the sudden activity. "Floyd, stop that! You're going to tear a hole in the sheets."

Carrie laughed harder.

"Do you think we should go to the basement?" Will asked. "And what on earth is so damn funny?"

"I'm sorry," Carrie said, wiping her eyes. "I was just thinking that usually the first time with someone new is awkward and stiff and sometimes not even very good. But this—" She spread her arms as though embracing the whole experience. "This was absolutely terrific! The tornado sirens are just an added bonus."

"So you don't want to go to the basement?" Will asked again.

Carrie shook her head. "Not a chance. I'm not leaving this bed, and you're not either," she said, reaching for him.

"What about him?" Will said, motioning to the oversized canine who had calmed down somewhat after managing to stick his head under a sheet. "Don't you think he's going to be in the way?"

"We'll work around him," Carrie said, sliding down toward the foot of the bed. "I'm used to sharing the bed with a furry animal—although I'll admit mine is quite a bit smaller. Now, come down here and join me."

Will followed her instructions.

"See," Carrie said confidently. "There's plenty of room for all of us. And I'll bet there'd be even more space if you and I sort of doubled up."

"What did you have in mind?"

Carrie rolled over and settled herself on top of him. "Oh, I don't know. How about this?"

"This does it for me," Will agreed, putting his hands on her hips to steady her.

"See what I told you?" Carrie said as she leaned down and kissed his nose. "We all fit just fine."

Chapter 38

After a weekend filled with unaccustomed passion and myriad sybaritic experiences, Carrie arrived at the office on Monday tired yet ebullient. She hated to admit—even to herself—just how long it had been since she'd felt this good.

When she walked into one of the break rooms to get coffee, she couldn't believe her good fortune. Will was there, and he was alone. "Good morning," he said, looking at her with obvious lust in his eyes. "Did you sleep well?"

"Like the dead," Carrie replied as she stood next to him and rubbed his arm. "And I had a lot of room to stretch out. My cat doesn't take up much space."

"Sorry about Floyd's overexuberance," Will said, leaning close to her. "He's afraid of storms and he doesn't like to be alone."

"No problem," Carrie said, smiling. "I hardly noticed he was there."

They could hear someone coming down the hall. They quickly stepped apart and Carrie poured herself a cup of coffee. "So, how was your weekend?" Will asked, trying to sound nonchalant.

"Fine," Carrie replied as Madree walked into the room carrying her coffee cup. "How about yours?"

"Fine," Will replied. "Good morning, Madree," he said, taking a sip of coffee.

"Hi, Madree," Carrie chimed in.

"Good morning," Madree said, surveying the situation.

"Well, see you two later," Will said brightly as he headed for his office.

"So," Madree said casually as she helped herself to some coffee. "You slept with him."

Carrie's jaw dropped. "And just how did you come to that brilliant conclusion?" she sputtered.

"Don't bother trying to deny it," Madree said, waving a well-manicured hand. "It's written all over your face. You're glowing."

"Did I really look that pathetic before?" Carrie asked, brushing a piece of hair out of her eyes.

"No, of course not," Madree assured her. "I'm just more attuned to these things than most people. And I was hoping this might be the weekend you two finally connected. Congratulations!" she said, patting her friend on the arm. "So, how was the sex?"

"Shhh!" Carrie said, looking around frantically to make sure there was no one within earshot. "I'd like to keep this quiet for a while, if you don't mind."

Madree rolled her eyes. "Why? Neither of you is married. And it's not like you need to be ashamed of him. He's a hunk."

"I'd just prefer it if we could have a little time to ourselves to see how the relationship develops before we invite the whole world in."

"That's what I like about you," Madree joked. "You're so refreshingly old-fashioned." She leaned close to Carrie. "So, tell me. How was *it*?"

"*It* was fantastic," Carrie whispered back. "Now I have to get to work."

"You're no fun," Madree scolded. "Oh, go ahead and run off. You know I'll worm the details out of you sooner or later."

Carrie winked at her friend. "Talk to you later. And remember, keep your mouth shut until I tell you otherwise."

Madree stuck out her tongue.

Carrie had just settled into her chair in her office when the phone rang. "Carrie, this is Gerry Peckham," a friendly voice said when she answered. "I hope I'm not calling at a bad time."

"Not at all," Carrie replied.

There was a slight pause, then Dr. Peckham said, "This is a bit awkward, but I'm calling to apologize for my behavior on Saturday evening. I'm afraid I made quite a spectacle of myself."

"Don't worry about it," Carrie said. "You're human. You're entitled to let down your hair once in a while. And after all, it's not every day that a person has a seventh anniversary."

"That's very kind of you," Dr. Peckham said, sounding obviously relieved. "When I came to my senses yesterday and realized the impression I must have made, well, I just had to call. I value your opinion, and I wouldn't want you to think I overindulge like that on a regular basis, because I assure you I do not."

"No problem," Carrie told him. "As far as I'm concerned, your sterling reputation remains untarnished. And don't worry, Will and I have no intention of mentioning the incident to anyone else."

"Thank you, Carrie," Dr. Peckham said. "You're a class act. As I believe I mentioned, I do think this case should settle, and I want you to know I'll do whatever I can to push the board in that direction."

"Thanks," Carrie said. "I appreciate it."

Shortly after hanging up from her talk with Peckham, Carrie got a call from Ed Squiers, the attorney for slumlord Joe Scalerri.

"What can I do for you, Ed?" Carrie asked cheerfully. "Did Scalerri think of some other type of lawsuit to file against my poor, downtrodden clients?"

"On the contrary," Squiers replied. "I was calling to offer your clients a settlement."

"Really?" Carrie asked skeptically. "I suppose your man thinks this whole thing will go away for a measly few thousand dollars."

"How does two hundred and fifty thousand grab you?" Squiers volleyed back.

"What?" Carrie shouted into the phone. "Why the sudden generosity?"

"Let's just say that Joe was involved in a situation yesterday that made him see your clients in a new light."

"What happened?" Carrie asked.

"He went over to the apartment complex yesterday to see if there was any damage from Saturday night's storm," Squiers explained. "As he was inspecting one of the rear entrances to the building, two teenage punks from another building came up behind him. Without any warning, one of them threw a container of gasoline and the other threw a match, turning Joe into a human torch."

"Oh, my God!" Carrie exclaimed. "Was he badly hurt?"

"He would have been if it hadn't been for the fact that Eureka Washington's son Billy was playing outside with two friends. The boys saw what happened, and when Joe panicked and began to run, Billy Washington knocked him to the ground and urged him to roll over. That put out the fire. One of Billy's friends ran inside to call 911. The three boys were able to give police a description of the two assailants, and they're now in custody."

"How's Joe doing?" Carrie asked.

"He'll have to spend about a week in the hospital, but thanks to Billy Washington's quick thinking, he's expected to make a full recovery. In addition to the settlement, Joe wants to give Billy and his two companions a handsome reward."

"I'm speechless," Carrie said. "I never would have believed that Joe Scalerri would voluntarily pay one red cent to settle that case."

"Well, it took a near-death experience to bring him around," Squiers said, obviously relieved that the case was drawing to its conclusion, "but I guess better late than never."

"Maybe Eureka's voodoo worked after all," Carrie murmured.

"What was that?" Squiers asked.

"Nothing," Carrie said, smiling to herself. "This is wonderful news. My clients will be ecstatic. I'll draft the settlement papers and send them over to you later today."

"There's no hurry," Squiers said.

"Oh, yes, there is," Carrie contradicted. "I want this case all sewn up before Scalerri starts to feel better and reneges on this wonderful offer."

The remainder of the week was taken up with new depositions of Jackson Memorial staff members. After the adrenaline rush of discovering the identity of Katherine's attacker, this new round of proceedings soon devolved into an exercise in frustration for Carrie, for no one at the hospital admitted even suspecting Delgado's proclivities for unnatural sexual practices.

Several of the female staff members freely admitted that Delgado was an unabashed ladies' man who liberally made suggestive remarks. But he had apparently never made any physical overtures or done anything that made the women feel at all threatened.

"He was an incorrigible flirt," Dr. Dawn Redding confirmed. "He was always joking around, but I enjoyed his banter. There was nothing sinister about it. And from what I saw, he was a good nurse and his behavior with patients was above reproach."

"He loved to tease us," Mary Sanders, a nurse who had worked with Delgado, reported. "He'd ask those of us who were married when our husbands were going to be out of town so he could come visit. Or he'd tell us to leave the back door to our house open so he could sneak in. It was all in good fun. He never forced himself on anyone. He just seemed to enjoy joking around. He seemed to have a nice way of dealing with the female patients, too. I never saw him do anything improper."

Jackson Memorial's personnel director, Lee Arthur, was not employed by the hospital at the time Delgado was hired. "Who was the personnel director at that time?" Carrie asked.

"That would have been Louis Miku," Arthur replied.

"Have you brought Mr. Delgado's personnel file with you today?" Carrie asked.

"Yes, I have," Arthur answered.

"Are you able to tell from your review of that file

whether or not Mr. Miku checked Mr. Delgado's references before he was hired?''

Arthur paged through the file. "It appears that he did. There is a piece of paper here with the words 'Atlanta' and 'Barbara Baker, pers. dir.' with a check mark next to the name. Under that it says, 'Good skills, Good attendance, Would rehire.' "

"Does it appear that Mr. Miku checked any other references for Mr. Delgado than Atlanta?" Carrie asked.

"On the same piece of paper there is a note that says, 'Vancouver' and a check mark," Arthur replied.

"Is there a name of a person Mr. Miku talked to in Vancouver?"

"No."

"Are there any other notations as to what the person in Vancouver might have said?"

"No."

"So it's not possible to tell from your file whether Mr. Miku in fact talked to anyone in Vancouver or, if he did speak to someone, what they said?"

"It's not possible to tell what they said," Arthur agreed. "I am assuming from the fact that 'Vancouver' is checked off that he did speak to someone there."

"But you don't know that for certain, do you?" Carrie pressed.

"No," Arthur admitted.

"Mr. Arthur, is there anything in your personnel file on Mr. Delgado to indicate that he had been suspected of molesting a young female patient at one of his previous jobs?"

"No, there is not."

"If you were doing a reference check on a prospective nurse employee and were told that the person had been suspected of molesting a patient, would you recommend hiring that person?"

"Objection," Charlene Bull cut in. "Calls for speculation."

"I am merely asking what the hospital's routine personnel practices are under Mr. Arthur's direction," Carrie said.

"You may answer the question subject to my objection," Charlene instructed Arthur.

"You're asking if I would recommend hiring someone who was suspected of molesting a patient?" Arthur asked.

"That's right," Carrie said.

"No, I would not," he replied.

"Thank you," Carrie said. "No further questions."

Dr. Luebke's reconvened deposition took place on Friday afternoon. It was the last proceeding scheduled for the week. Even though Will was going to be doing the questioning, Carrie could already feel herself getting a stress headache in the morning and had to fortify herself with two Advil before the proceeding began.

"I'd like to nail that bastard to the wall," she groused as she paced back and forth in Will's office before during the lunch break. "I'm positive he knows something that could help us. I don't suppose you could beat it out of him."

"I've never found beating a witness to be a very effective technique," Will said wryly. "Just calm down. If I can get some sort of admission out of him, I will. And if not—"

"If not, we'll have to go to trial because the damn hospital won't settle unless we can show that someone knew what Delgado was up to," Carrie said bitterly, flopping into a chair.

"I thought you liked to try cases," Will said. "At least that was your reputation."

"I didn't know you ever paid attention to my reputation," Carrie said somewhat suggestively.

"You'd be surprised," Will said, smiling because his attempts to improve her mood seemed to be working.

"I'm perfectly happy trying cases if there's a need for it," Carrie said, "but it's asinine to try things unnecessarily, and if there was ever a case that ought to settle, it's this one. We know Delgado assaulted Katherine, and we've proved that if the former personnel director had done his job he would have learned that Delgado left his Vancouver job under a cloud of suspicion. What more do Von Slaten and the hospital board need to loosen up their purse strings? Don't they realize a jury could award the Buckleys a whole lot more than the amount we've demanded?"

"They apparently don't care about that," Will said.

"To say nothing of the bad publicity they'll get from a trial. They're damn lucky that so far there's been nothing in the media identifying Delgado as the perpetrator. You'd think they'd want to keep it that way. It's going to be bad for business if all that dirty laundry comes out in the press."

Will glanced at the clock on his desk. "It's time to head down to the conference room. Your buddy Doc Luebke should be arriving any minute now. I'm sure you'll want to give him a warm welcome before I start beating the truth out of him."

Deep down, Carrie had known it was very unlikely that Will was going to get any type of useful admission out of Dr. Luebke, and her suspicions in this regard were confirmed. Steve O'Connor had obviously coached his client well in the art of answering only the question posed and nothing more. The doctor glared at .Will throughout the entire proceeding and snarled monosyllabic answers to most questions.

"Did you ever observe Alessandro Delgado acting inappropriately in his care of Katherine Buckley?"

"No."

"Did you ever observe Delgado acting inappropriately with any patient?"

"No."

"Did any patient ever express concern about Delgado's treatment?"

"No."

"Did the family of any patient ever express such concern?"

"No."

"Did Alessandro Delgado appear to carry out his nursing duties in a professional manner?"

"Yes."

"Did you ever have reason to suspect that Alessandro

Delgado was taking sexual liberties with Katherine Buckley or any other patient?"

"No."

"Did any other staff member at Jackson Memorial ever express concern about Alessandro Delgado's nursing abilities or the way he treated patients?"

"No."

After two hours of this painful process, Carrie felt as if she were going to explode with frustration. Will, too, had finally had enough. "Doctor, do you have any thoughts about Alessandro Delgado that we have not yet covered that you'd like to share with us?"

"No," came the curt and immediate reply.

"Dr. Luebke, are you still in the running for the chief of staff position at the hospital?"

"Objection," Steve O'Connor said loudly. "Irrelevant."

"Are you going to allow him to answer?" Will asked patiently.

"Yes, subject to the objection," O'Connor replied.

"Do you remember the question, Dr. Luebke," Will asked patiently, "or would you like to have it read back?"

"I remember it," Dr. Luebke said in his most loquacious reply of the afternoon.

"And the answer is?" Will prompted.

"Yes," the doctor said, reverting to form.

"No further questions," Will said wearily, dropping his pen on the table.

"Counselor?" O'Connor turned to Charlene Bull.

"I have no questions," Charlene said.

O'Connor smiled. "Then I guess we're through." He got up from his seat, and Dr. Luebke quickly followed suit. In less than thirty seconds they were out the door.

Back in Will's office, Carrie took two more Advil. "Shit," she said, settling into a chair in front of Will's desk.

"I did the best I could," Will said apologetically.

"I know you did," Carrie said hastily. "That wasn't a comment on your abilities. It was a comment on the general frustration I'm feeling about the case."

Will came around his desk, walked behind her, and

began to knead her shoulders. "You're too close to this case, and you've been working too hard. It's only natural that it's starting to get you down." He leaned down and nuzzled her hair. "I have a suggestion."

She leaned back against him. "What's that?"

"Why don't we knock off work early and grab a bite to eat and then go to my place and just hang out?"

"That sounds good to me," Carrie said.

"Maybe we could watch a couple of those old *Avengers* tapes," Will suggested.

"We could do that," Carrie agreed.

"Or I could make sure the dog is secured in another room and we could pick up where we left off last weekend," he said seductively.

Carrie laughed and reached back and ruffled his hair. "That option sounds better yet."

Chapter 39

On the third Sunday in May, Will and Carrie attended Todd Fleming's law school graduation. Ed and Melody Buckley and Katherine's two older siblings were also on hand to see him graduate with honors. Carrie fought back tears as Todd's name was called and he came forward to receive his diploma. She couldn't help but think of the resplendent wedding Katherine had dreamed of that would never take place, the idyllic life the young couple had planned that would never be. When Carrie lost the battle to hold back her emotions and the tears came, Will put his arm around her and she buried her head in his shoulder.

The date for Katherine's C-section had now been set: July 4. An ultrasound had revealed that Katherine's pregnancy was a bit more advanced than the doctors had originally thought. Although Carrie thought the choice of a delivery date was a bit macabre, the Buckleys had insisted that there was no better time for their grandchild to assert its independence by being born. As yet, the fact that the baby's birth date would also be the date of Katherine's death was a subject the Buckleys had not broached with Carrie. The Buckley family's date with destiny was only seven weeks off, and it weighed heavily on Carrie's mind.

Todd's family was also from the Chicago area, and Will and Carrie had been invited to a reception at his father's club. After congratulating the graduate and having a glass of wine, Carrie began to feel claustrophobic. "Let's get out of here," she said to Will in a low voice. "I'm starting to feel kind of woozy."

Will put his arm around her and they departed the reception without delay. "Are you all right?" Will asked with concern once they were outside.

"I'm fine now," Carrie said, taking some deep breaths of fresh air. "I don't know what came over me. All of a sudden I started to feel like the walls were closing in. I didn't mean to leave so abruptly. Do you want to go back inside?"

"Hell, no!" Will replied at once. "It was nice of Todd to invite us, and no offense to him or the Buckleys, but I think we've both had our fill of these people for a while. We need some time to ourselves."

Carrie smiled. "I was thinking the same thing, but I was too polite to say it."

Will hugged her. "I'm glad we're on the same wavelength. Let's do something fun for the rest of the day and make a pact that we won't mention the case until we're back at work tomorrow."

"It's a deal," Carrie said eagerly.

"Good," Will said. "What would you like to do? How about going to a movie? What do you feel like seeing?"

Carrie thought a minute, then said, "There's an Alfred Hitchcock retrospective playing this weekend at a theater in my neighborhood. I think if we leave right now we could just make the beginning of *To Catch a Thief.*"

Will looked a bit skeptical. "You're sure you want to see an old movie? What about the new Steven Spielberg flick?"

"It's not just an old movie," Carrie said. "It's Cary Grant. It's Grace Kelly. It's the French Riviera. It's wonderful dialogue and beautiful costumes."

"Well, if you put it that way—" Will said, throwing his hands in the air. "The hell with Steven Spielberg." He took her hand and they walked to his car. "I just need clarification on one thing," he said as he opened the car door for her.

"What's that?"

"If I agree to go to this movie, which you have no doubt already seen at least twenty times, will you promise that we can make out for a good portion of it?"

"And miss even one shot of Cary Grant?" Carrie asked indignantly. "Are you crazy?" Upon seeing Will's wounded expression, she said, "I'll make you a better offer. If you sit through this movie, which is one of my all-time favorites, when it's over you can come to my place and we'll do all the making out you want."

Will brightened. "You drive a hard bargain, counselor, but you've got yourself a deal."

The following Wednesday, Carrie kept her word to Maria Delgado by meeting her eldest daughter at Alessandro's apartment. Gloria Frank was an attractive dark-haired woman in her early forties. She and her husband owned a small Continental restaurant in Baltimore. She was clearly not happy to have to take time out of her busy schedule to travel halfway across the country to go through her deceased brother's belongings, and she made no bones about the fact that she thought her mother's notions about Alessandro being murdered were daft.

"From the day he was born, Mama always had her head in a hole when it came to Alessandro's escapades," Gloria said disgustedly only moments after she met Carrie at the door of the apartment. "He was a wild kid from the time he was in grammar school. Everyone else knew it and accepted it. But not Mama. She always insisted Alessandro was a good boy and someone else must have led him astray."

"Your mother said Alessandro would never have taken his own life because he wouldn't have been afraid to face the consequences of what he had done," Carrie commented.

Gloria made a spitting sound. "Mama is loco," she said disdainfully. "Leaving somebody else to clean up the mess is exactly what Alessandro would have done." She looked at Carrie and frowned. "Speaking of loco, I really don't understand why you're here."

"I promised your mother—" Carrie began.

"You kept your promise," Gloria said, waving her hand.

"You showed up, didn't you? Now you can go again if you want."

"If you don't mind, I'd rather stay," Carrie said.

"Suit yourself," Gloria said. She surveyed the living room furnishings. "I've arranged to donate most of his things to a church that runs a homeless shelter. They'll come tomorrow and pick the stuff up. The only things I plan on taking with me are a few personal mementos for Mama and my sisters."

"What can I do to help you?" Carrie asked.

"I was going to sort through the things in his bedroom first. I guess you could help with that, if you really want to."

"I do," Carrie replied.

Carrie had to take several deep breaths before she was able to walk into the room where Delgado had died. As soon as she crossed the threshold, her eyes involuntarily went to the spot where she had seen him lying on the floor. There were no outward signs of death in the room, but Carrie still found herself shivering.

"I'll look through the closet," Gloria said. "You take the desk and the computer."

"What am I supposed to look for?"

Gloria shrugged. "How should I know? It was your idea to come here and look for clues that would prove Alessandro was murdered," she said rather sarcastically. Seeing Carrie's face, she realized that her remarks had been a bit hard-edged, and said more congenially, "Use your own judgment. If they look like worthless papers, throw them out. If you see anything that looks interesting, put it aside and I'll go through it later."

Carrie nodded and switched on the computer. After looking through a sampling of files, she commented, "There doesn't seem to be much on here."

Gloria was standing on a chair, checking out the top shelf in the closet. "My guess is he probably spent most of his time downloading porn off the Internet," she said. "Look at this filth." She pulled a handful magazines off the shelf and let them drop to the floor.

Carrie could see the cover of one of them. It showed a couple engaged in oral sex.

"This was my little brother in a nutshell," Gloria said disgustedly. She got off the chair. "I don't want the people from the church to see this stuff. I'm going to see if I can find some garbage bags so we can throw out anything really disgusting."

During Gloria's brief absence, Carrie continued to peruse the computer files. Remembering the windfall she'd gotten from Scott Rouleau's computer, when Gloria returned with the garbage bags, Carrie asked, "Would you mind if I made a copy of these computer files and took them with me?"

"Be my guest," Gloria said, getting back up on the chair and again peering into the depths of the closet. "Oh, God. He's got a whole series of smutty videos." She pitched them out onto the floor. "I think the homeless shelter can do without these."

After copying the computer files onto a disk, Carrie began to go through the desk methodically. As she sifted through the contents of the drawers, she couldn't help feeling like a voyeur. After all, the items she was handling belonged to the father of Katherine's soon-to-be-born child.

In one drawer Carrie found a bank book showing that Delgado had thirty thousand dollars in a savings account. She also found a life insurance policy with a face value of fifty thousand dollars that named his mother as the sole beneficiary. She reported these finds to Gloria, who got down off her chair and came over to inspect the documents.

"I'm amazed that Alessandro was able to save that much money and even more amazed that he ever gave enough thought to the future to actually buy life insurance," she said. "This is very nice. It will make life a little easier for Mama."

Gloria looked at Carrie and smiled for the first time. "Thank you for finding this. I probably would have just thrown everything in the desk into the trash. Maybe there's a purpose in your being here after all." She walked back to the closet. "Well, I think I've found all of the smut in here. Now I'll look through his clothes."

Carrie found little else of interest in the desk. Last year's tax return showed that Delgado had earned forty-two thousand dollars. There were several outstanding credit card bills with small balances and the title to his car, a three-year-old Nissan. She put those documents in a stack for Gloria.

"My brother had excellent taste in clothes," Gloria commented, pulling out a fashionable dark suit. "He had quite a wardrobe—a lot of designer names. I wonder how he managed that on his salary."

"When did you last see your brother?" Carrie asked.

Gloria shrugged. "I don't know. Five or six years ago, I suppose."

"Did your other sisters have much contact with him?"

"No." Gloria pulled a camel hair coat out of the closet. "Some homeless person is going to be awfully happy to get this." She tossed the coat on the bed, then turned to Carrie. "Look, I know we sound like a heartless bunch, ignoring our poor little brother in his time of need. But the truth is, he was bad news from the beginning. Caused our mother all kinds of grief, but she endured it stoically and kept making excuses for him because she finally had the son she'd always wanted. I'm sorry he's dead, and I know how much my mother is grieving. But I can't say I'm surprised that he came to an untimely end, and I'm not going to sit here and wring my hands over him.

"What more can I say? His was a wasted existence."

She walked back to the closet. "Father Francis Xavier is going to love getting all these clothes for the homeless."

"I've finished going through the desk," Carrie said. "I found some family photos and put them here with the financial documents. Otherwise there doesn't seem to be anything of interest."

Gloria nodded. "I think we're done in here. I'll look through the living room. Why don't you check out the kitchen?"

An hour later Carrie opened the last cupboard door in the kitchen. While surveying an eclectic group of coffee cups, much like the collection she had in her own home, she spied what appeared to be a shred of paper hanging down from the top of a shelf. When she reached up to investigate, she discovered an envelope taped to the shelf. Thinking that that was certainly an odd place to store something, she pulled the envelope free and opened it. Inside were two sheets of yellow ledger paper filled with columns of figures. The left-hand column contained six-digit numbers. The next column had what appeared to be dates, and the two right-hand columns contained still more numbers.

As Carrie stood there trying to puzzle out the meaning of her find, Gloria walked in. "I'm all finished," she announced, rubbing her hands on her thighs. "How about you?"

"I'm all done, too," Carrie replied. She held out the sheets of paper. "I found this in an envelope taped to the top of a shelf. What do you suppose it is?"

Gloria took the papers and briefly scanned them. "I have no idea," she said, handing them back to Carrie.

"I wonder why Alessandro would have hidden these papers like that," Carrie said, furrowing her brow.

"He was probably dealing with bookies," Gloria replied. "It could be a record of the dates he placed bets."

"But why would he hide it?" Carrie asked.

"Who knows?" Gloria replied, clearly not interested in the answer. "Maybe he was cheating the bookie somehow. Or maybe he was acting as a bookie himself and cheating his customers by keeping two sets of books. Believe me, Alessandro would have been capable of any of those things." She gave the room a quick once-over to see if there was anything worth taking.

"Would you mind if I took these?" Carrie asked, waving the papers.

"Be my guest," Gloria replied. "I hope you're good at solving mysteries—my brother was a real enigma. Let me know if you ever figure out what it means. My guess is you won't."

As Carrie followed Gloria back out into the living room, she shoved the papers into her purse, next to the computer disk. Gloria had packed up two shopping bags full of personal belongings that she would share with her sisters and her mother. Everything else in the apartment would be donated to charity.

"Thanks for your help today," Gloria said. "I'm sorry if I sounded like a bitch earlier. Even though I don't have any illusions about who and what my brother was, this has been hard for me." She extended her hand.

Carrie gave Gloria's hand a firm shake. "I'm glad I came. Your mother's a good person—and so are you."

Gloria snorted. "I'm not so sure about that. I know Mama will be very happy about what you tried to do, even though you weren't able to prove her murder theory." She took a deep breath, then said, "Listen, this is rather awkward, but I'd like you to convey my family's apologies to your clients and express our sincere wishes that everything works out all right with their grandchild."

Gloria paused a moment and shook her head. "It's all a little hard to comprehend. Alessandro's child is about to be born. My niece or nephew." She paused again and ran her hand over her neck. "I'm afraid I don't quite know how to feel about that."

"Don't worry. I don't either," Carrie admitted. "My clients are convinced that having the child will soften the blow of losing their daughter. While that's not the course I would have chosen, they're at peace with their decision, so who are we to judge?"

"I guess you're right," Delgado's sister agreed.

"It was nice meeting you, Gloria," Carrie said, giving the woman a quick hug. "I'm sorry we couldn't have met under better circumstances."

"Me, too," Gloria said. As Carrie took her leave, Alessandro's sister was standing in the living room looking at the sad remains of her brother's life.

Chapter 40

Carrie's relationship with Will continued to develop, and they spent the first weekend in June at a resort in Lake Geneva, Wisconsin.

"For the first time since the case started, I'm feeling pretty upbeat about it," Carrie said, lying on a chaise lounge beside the pool at the resort.

"I told you getting away for a couple days would do wonders," Will teased as he rubbed sunscreen on his chest and arms. "You kept saying we couldn't spare the time, but aren't you glad now that we came?"

"I sure am," Carrie replied. She leaned forward and kissed him. "Thank you so much for not taking no for an answer."

"You're very welcome," he said, kissing her back.

Although Carrie was still trying not to broadcast the liaison around the office, she had been forced to spill the beans to her secretary because Will had asked Tammy if she could baby-sit Floyd while he was away for the weekend. Tammy already knew that Carrie was going away for the weekend, and she put two and two together.

"I suspected something was going on," Tammy said, wagging her finger when Carrie confirmed that she would be accompanying Will on his weekend getaway. "You haven't seemed to be yourself lately. You've been in too good a mood."

"What is that supposed to mean?" Carrie asked, somewhat offended. "Was I really such a grumpy bitch before?"

"No," Tammy assured her. "But you've seemed happier the last month or so."

"I am happy," Carrie confided. "But I'm a little nervous, too."

"About what?" Tammy asked.

"I don't know," Carrie admitted. "I guess that it won't work out or that I'll jinx it by talking about it too much. Anyway, I'd appreciate it if you didn't make a big deal out of it just yet."

"All right," Tammy agreed. "But I don't understand why you don't want to tell the whole world. After all, almost everyone in the office knows all about your past dating disasters. If I were you, I'd want them to know I was capable of having a successful relationship once in a while."

"Gee, thanks a lot," Carrie said ruefully. "You really know how to boost a girl's ego."

"You're welcome," Tammy replied cheerfully.

Over the course of the weekend, Carrie and Will's relationship evolved into a blend of easy camaraderie and boundless passion. Carrie returned to the office on Monday reenergized and ready to see the *Buckley* case through to its conclusion.

By this time, the formerly relentless stream of depositions in the case had slowed to a trickle. Try as they might, Carrie and Will had been unable to find anyone to corroborate Scott Rouleau's account of seeing Delgado assault Katherine. The hospital remained unwilling to stipulate that Delgado had in fact been Katherine's assailant, in spite of the DNA tests showing he was the father of the child she was carrying. This meant that Scott would have to testify at the trial.

While neither Scott nor his sister was thrilled at the prospect of Scott's continued involvement in the case, they were both resigned to doing whatever was necessary to help the Buckleys prevail in their lawsuit against the hospital. Carrie promised them she would try to avoid naming Scott as her informant until the time actually came for him to testify.

Scott seemed to have made fairly significant strides in his recovery since Delgado's death. He was responding well to a new regimen of medication, and his mood was buoyed by the possibility that Michelle Brud might be able to help him market his Holy Grail game.

To no one's surprise, there was nothing of interest in Delgado's computer files. Carrie had phoned Maria Delgado and told her that there was no reason to believe that Alessandro's death had been anything other than a suicide. Mrs. Delgado had accepted the news with aplomb. Although Carrie kept the sheets of paper she'd discovered in Delgado's kitchen cupboard taped to the wall next to her desk, the entries remained as cryptic as ever, and she doubted that their meaning would ever be revealed.

During the second week in June, Carrie devoted a couple of days to mundane matters such as preparing exhibits for use at the trial. Carrie asked Charlene Bull if the hospital would be willing to stipulate the amount of Katherine's medical bills. Charlene responded that she didn't think that would be a problem. A couple of days later Charlene ruefully called back and said Von Slaten had nixed the idea of stipulating anything and Carrie would have to prove up the amount of fees charged by each doctor.

"I'm really sorry," Charlene apologized. "I guess I should have learned by now not to stick my neck out and make any promises until I've gotten the client's okay."

"It's not your fault," Carrie said, inwardly groaning. The printouts of Katherine's medical bills for the past year filled three large boxes. It was going to be a real pain in the ass going through all of that material. "I hope Von Slaten realizes that this means I'm going to have to question each of Katherine's doctors about what treatment they provided and the fees they charged. That will prolong the trial and cost the hospital more in attorneys' fees, but if that's the way he wants to play, so be it."

"I tried to tell him all that," Charlene confided, "but he didn't seem to care."

"Fine," Carrie grumbled. "The guy's been a Class A jerk every step of the way. Why should I expect him to change his stripes now?" She thought a minute, then said, "I've got an idea. Do you think you could maybe do me a small favor and inform each of the doctors personally what's going to happen? Maybe if they realize that they're going to have to waste time sitting on the witness stand explaining their billing practices they might put some pressure on Von Slaten."

"That's brilliant," Charlene chuckled. "Why didn't I think of that? I'll send out chatty little letters to them all right away."

"Thanks," Carrie said. As she hung up the phone, she glanced over at the three boxes of bills. There wasn't time to wait and see if Von Slaten eventually softened his stance on this issue. She'd have to the assume that she would have to present proof to the jury as to amounts of the bills. She'd need to get one of the paralegals working on that right away.

Two nights later, on a Thursday evening, Carrie, Will, and a number of other attorneys from their office went to a program at the University of Chicago Law School sponsored by the Chicago Bar Association. The featured speaker was the newest appointee to the Seventh Circuit Court of Appeals, a dynamic black man in his late forties. The judge's talk focused on what every lawyer could do to improve the caliber of the nation's legal system as well as the public's image of lawyers. The speech was both articulate and humorous, thought-provoking and inspiring. The audience gave the man a standing ovation and the Ramquist and Dowd contingent left singing his praises.

"Wasn't that a dynamite speech?" Burt Ramquist said enthusiastically as they made their way out to the parking lot. "It's so refreshing to hear that kind of enthusiasm about our profession, especially coming from a judge. It reminds me why I went to law school in the first place."

"I thought you went to law school so you could earn a lot of money," Madree said teasingly.

"That, too," Burt replied jovially. "There's nothing wrong with takin' care of business, darlin'," he said in his best Elvis drawl.

"It was a great talk," Ann Muchin agreed. "I think he's going to be a wonderful judge."

When they reached the parking lot, they all dispersed to

find their cars. Will and Carrie had parked near each other. "Do you feel like stopping somewhere for a drink?" Will asked as they reached her vehicle.

"I don't think so," Carrie replied. "I'm kind of tired. I think I'd like to go home, look through the mail, and then call it a night. After all, we are going out tomorrow, and I need my beauty sleep." She smiled up at him.

"You're doing just fine in that department," Will said. He leaned down and kissed her lightly on the lips. "Okay. Suit yourself. I'll see you in the morning."

"Good night," Carrie said.

It was a warm evening, but instead of turning on the car's air-conditioning, Carrie drove with the windows down. She loved summertime, when everything in the world seemed so very alive, and she enjoyed breathing fresh air, even if the smells of the city were sometimes not all that sublime. She turned the radio to an easy-listening station and enjoyed the short ride home.

She pulled into her driveway and parked the car near the back entrance to her town house. One of her favorite Frank Sinatra tunes was playing on the radio, and she waited for the song to finish before rolling up the windows and turning off the ignition. She got out of the car, opened the rear driver's side door and leaned in to take out her briefcase. As she began to straighten up, a crashing blow landed across the back of her head.

Carrie's briefcase and purse fell to the ground. Although the impact sent her reeling and her knees buckled, she somehow managed to remain on her feet. As she fought to regain her balance, she was struck again, this time between the shoulder blades. She fell to the ground, the wind knocked out of her.

She struggled to catch her breath. She rolled over and brought her knees up in a defensive posture and put her hands in front of her face. There was an interval of several seconds when she hoped that the attacker had left. Then he struck again, this time kicking her in the side with a hard-toed shoe.

The pain was excruciating. Carrie cried out and tried to

grab the attacker's leg, but he was too quick. In swift succession he delivered four or five more kicks. Through her pain, she tried to get a look at the madman's face, but all she saw was a dark blur.

There was another blessed interval where the blows stopped. Carrie tried to move, thinking wildly that she might be able to roll under the car, but then he struck again. He was behind her now and dragged her to a sitting position as easily as if she were a rag doll. While holding her stationary with one hand, he delivered a series of vicious blows to her face with the other.

Carrie had never experienced such agony in her life. She stopped moving, hoping with her last bit of coherent thought that maybe if he thought he had beaten her into unconsciousness he would stop, but the strategy was to no avail. The blows continued, to her head, to her stomach, back to her head again.

Her mind floated. Was she going to die? She felt like she might. She kept her eyes squeezed tightly shut and tried not to react to the continuing punches. On the verge of losing all cognitive function, she couldn't trust her senses anymore. Had the blows finally stopped? Her whole body was in such torment that she couldn't tell.

As she lay motionless on the ground, she could have sworn she heard someone talking. It sounded like nothing more than disjointed words at first, then they became more distinct. "You goddam bitch. You don't learn too easy, do you? The tires and the door were supposed to teach you a lesson, but they didn't. Well, maybe you'll wise up after this. Drop the fucking case—or the next time we meet you're going to be real sorry."

Such strange words, Carrie thought. Her head hurt so badly that she felt like she was spinning. Round and round she went. She was so dizzy. Why was the world spinning like this?

Such strange words. She managed to open one eye. She must have imagined the words because there was no one there. She was all alone. She tried to raise her head and then everything went dark.

Chapter 41

"Carrie? Carrie, can you hear me?"

From far off, Carrie heard a voice calling her. Of course she could hear them, but she was so very tired. Why didn't they leave her alone?

"Carrie." The voice was becoming more insistent. "It's time to wake up now."

She didn't want to wake up. Then she smelled something acrid right under her nose. They knew how to get her attention, those conniving little devils. She opened her eyes, or at least she tried to. Everything seemed to be out of focus. Her left eye didn't seem to be working at all. She blinked her right eye hard and saw faces swimming into view. She was apparently lying down. A man dressed in white was leaning over her. Behind him were Will and Ann.

"Carrie," the man in white said. "I'm Dr. Jon Castro. Do you know where you are?"

Did the man think she was an idiot? "If you're a doctor," she said very slowly because her lips hurt and her tongue felt swollen, "then I must be in a hospital."

"Yes, you are," the doctor said, giving her an encouraging smile. "Do you remember what happened?"

It took a moment, but then everything came flooding back. Carrie nodded. Oh, yes. She remembered. In fact, she'd be willing to bet this was one evening she would never forget.

After lying unconscious in her driveway for some period of time, she had come to and managed, with great difficulty, to crawl inside the house and call Will. He'd had trouble understanding her at first, but as soon as he'd figured out what she was saying, he had urged her to hang on, while he called 911. Then he jumped in his car and raced back downtown. While speeding to her aid, he had phoned Ann, since her apartment wasn't far from Carrie's, and asked her to meet him there.

Ann, Will, and the police had all converged on Carrie's town house simultaneously. Will had ridden to the hospital with Carrie in the ambulance, while Ann followed in her own car. Carrie had blacked out again during the ride. She didn't know what had happened after that.

"Would you like to hear the good news?" Dr. Castro asked.

"Is there some?" Carrie asked.

"Absolutely," Will said.

"You better believe it," Ann chimed in.

"Then I guess I should hear it," Carrie said agreeably.

"Well," the doctor said, "you've got a real shiner there and you have a couple of ribs that are badly bruised and you're black and blue pretty much all over, but there's nothing broken and no internal injuries. You're going to be sore as hell for a while, but all in all I'd say you were very lucky."

"Goody for me," Carrie said.

The doctor turned to Will and Ann. "Is she always like this or is the painkiller I gave her affecting her?"

"She's pretty much always like this," Ann replied.

The doctor turned back to Carrie. "I'm going to leave you with your friends. I have some other patients to check on. We're going to keep you here for a few more hours just to make sure no complications develop, but then you can be released so long as someone stays with you." He patted her hand. "Try to take it easy. I'll check back in a little bit."

As the doctor moved away, Will and Ann moved forward. Each of them took one of Carrie's hands.

"You gave us quite a scare," Ann said.

"That's for sure," Will agreed. "I was never so frightened in my life as during the drive down to your place. I didn't know what I might find when I got there."

"I just wanted to see if you were on your toes," Carrie said. "Can I have some water?"

"Sure," Ann said, handing her a glass with a straw.

Carrie slowly sat up a bit and took a drink. The effort left her exhausted. "Thanks," she said, handing the glass back to Ann.

"There are some people here who'd like to talk to you about what happened," Will said gently. "Do you feel up to it?"

"Police?" Carrie asked.

"Yes," Will answered.

"I suppose so," Carrie said. "I'm afraid I can't tell them much."

"I'll go get them," Ann said.

A short time later she returned with two uniformed officers and Detective David Clauff.

"What are you doing here?" Carrie asked the detective.

"I called him," Will said. "I thought in case there's any possibility of a connection between what happened to you and the *Buckley* case, he should hear about it."

"How are you doing?" Clauff asked.

"I've been better," Carrie replied. "You're not going to laugh at me again like you did the other times I talked to you, are you?"

"I'm not laughing," Clauff said. Motioning to the uniformed officers with him, he said, "This is Sergeant Fisher and Sergeant Patrick. They've got your driveway cordoned off, and as soon as it gets light they'll go over the area with a fine-tooth comb."

"I doubt you'll find anything," Carrie said. "He came out of nowhere and left the same way."

"Can you tell us what happened?" Clauff asked gently.

Carrie recounted the incident as best she could.

"Can you give us any kind of description?" Sergeant Fisher asked.

"Not really," Carrie said. "He seemed big, but then I was on the ground looking up at him the whole time."

"What kind of clothing was he wearing?"

"Long-sleeved shirt and pants, dark colored. Dark brown or black. And black boots with steel toes."

"Did you see his face?" Sergeant Patrick inquired.

Carrie shook her head. "I think it was covered with a stocking or mask of some sort. I couldn't make out any features."

"Will mentioned that when he talked to you on the phone, you said the guy made some comments warning you off the *Buckley* case," Clauff said. "Can you tell us about that?"

Carrie closed her one good eye and took a deep breath. "To tell you the truth, I'm not sure if that really happened or if I imagined it. By that point I really wasn't thinking straight anymore."

"Well, what do you think you heard?" Clauff asked.

Carrie gritted her teeth, trying to dredge up the memory. "Something about my being a stubborn bitch who didn't learn very fast. And that I should have learned my lesson when my car and door were damaged, but I didn't."

"What happened to your car and door?" Sergeant Patrick asked.

"The front door of her town house was defaced a while back," Ann said. "Someone scratched the words 'Stop it' into the door."

"And two of her car tires were punctured last month," Will added.

"Were either of those incidents reported to the police?" Sergeant Patrick asked.

"No," Carrie replied. "I thought the door was scratched up by some punk, and I figured I ran over something that punctured the tires."

"Do you recall the man saying anything else?" Clauff asked.

Carrie swallowed hard, then nodded. "He said I'd better drop the case or the next time we met I'd be real sorry."

"Was the *Buckley* case mentioned by name?" Clauff asked.

Carrie shook her head.

"You just assumed that's the case he meant?" Clauff asked.

"Will and I assume that's the case he meant," Ann said hotly. "What other case could it possibly be? It's been contentious as hell from the word go, and one person is already dead as a result of it."

Detective Clauff sighed. "As I've already explained to Carrie, absolutely all the evidence points to the fact that Delgado took his own life."

"I'm not disagreeing with you on that," Ann replied. "I'm just pointing out that any case that has emotions rising high enough for someone to commit suicide might also have more sinister elements involved."

"Meaning what?" Clauff asked.

"Meaning Carrie has suspected all along that someone at the hospital knew what Delgado was up to," Ann said. "She hasn't been able to find any evidence backing up that theory, but maybe she's right. Maybe she's closing in on the person without even knowing it and he wants to stop her."

The detective rubbed his eyes. It was late. He was tired, and he clearly didn't want to hear any of this. "Any suggestions who this elusive someone might be?" he asked.

"Werner Von Slaten, the hospital's administrator," Will offered.

"Or maybe Dr. Kenneth Luebke, a neurologist who treated Katherine Buckley," Ann suggested. "He's gone to great lengths to avoid having to answer any questions about the case. Maybe he has more to hide than anyone realized."

"What's your opinion of all this?" Clauff asked Carrie.

"I'm not sure I have one at the moment," Carrie admitted. Her head was still spinning. "It still hasn't completely sunk in that I was really attacked."

"The assault must be linked to the *Buckley* case," Ann insisted. "Why else would someone target you?"

"I suppose it could have been random," Carrie said.

"A random attacker tells you to drop a case?" Ann asked incredulously. "How much of a coincidence would that be?"

"What do you think?" Will asked Clauff.

The detective paused before answering, clearly choosing his words carefully. "I don't think this was random," he said. "I think Carrie was clearly the target. The attack was carefully planned and executed, and it was carried out by a professional."

"A professional attacker?" Carrie asked. "I didn't know you could choose that as an occupation."

For the first time since Carrie had met him, the detective looked grim. "I talked to your doctor before we came in here," he said. "I don't want to upset you any more than you already are, but if the blows you received had been just a little harder or a few inches to the left or right, up or down, they could have done very serious damage."

"The doctor said I was lucky," Carrie said fliply.

"Only because the guy planned it that way," Clauff said soberly. "To put it bluntly, the only reason you're not dead is because he didn't want you to be."

"That's pretty blunt," Carrie agreed.

"I don't know what's going on here," Clauff admitted, "but you've obviously rubbed somebody the wrong way. I'll talk to people at Jackson Memorial first thing in the morning and, as I mentioned, the sergeants will look for physical evidence at your house. Beyond that, I'm frankly not sure what to tell you. I take it that dropping this case is not a possibility?"

"Absolutely not," Carrie said resolutely.

"Maybe we ought to think about it," Will said.

"No!" Carrie said, raising her voice for the first time. "I'm not giving in to whoever it is. Ouch!" she exclaimed, feeling a sudden jolt of pain. She grimaced and gingerly touched her right ribs.

"Are you okay?" Will asked with concern.

Carrie nodded. "The painkiller must be starting to wear off."

"Do you want me to look for the doctor?" Ann asked.

Carrie shook her head. "Not right now. I'll try to wait a while."

"Are they letting you out tonight?" Clauff asked.

"Yes."

"It might be a good idea if you didn't go back to your place until later tomorrow, so you don't unwittingly disturb any evidence," Clauff said.

"She can come home with me," Will said.

Clauff nodded. "It might also be a good idea for you not to be alone at night, at least for a while."

"We can take turns staying with her," Ann offered.

"Good," Clauff said. "You might also want to consider getting a big dog."

"I have a big dog I can loan her," Will said.

Clauff smiled. "Well, then, it sounds like you're all set."

A sudden thought popped into Carrie's mind and she sat up. "We have to make sure Scott Rouleau is safe," she said urgently. "If someone truly wants to stop the *Buckley* case, then he's in serious danger because he's our key witness. I think we should call his sister and move him out of the hospital right away."

"Nobody at the hospital knows Scott's our witness," Will reminded her. "We'll talk to his sister tomorrow, but I'm sure he'll be fine."

Detective Clauff leaned down and touched Carrie's uninjured cheek. "Keep an ice pack on that eye," he advised. "The swelling should go down substantially in a couple of days, but it's going to be pretty colorful for a couple of weeks."

"Thanks for coming down here to see me," Carrie said. "I'm sorry if I ruined your night."

"Look at it this way. My night wasn't ruined half as bad as yours was," Clauff answered lightly. "Take care of yourself, kid. I'll be in touch." He and the sergeants took their leave.

"Are you ready for more painkiller now?" Ann asked.

Carrie shook her head. "Hand me that glass of water and then both of you sit down and talk to me. I'm starting to feel a little spooked about this whole thing."

"You got it," Ann said. She fetched the water and Carrie took a long drink through the straw.

"Thanks," Carrie said, handing the glass back.

"What should we talk about?" Will asked.

"Gee, I don't know," Carrie answered. "Did the Cubs win tonight?" She fell silent for a moment, then asked in a slightly quavery voice, "Who could have done this? It's just a case, for God's sake. What could make somebody so angry or so afraid that they'd resort to this?"

"I don't know," Will said, taking Carrie's hand and holding it tightly. "That's what we hope the police will find out."

Carrie stared at the ceiling with her good eye. "I feel like there's something I'm missing, but I have no idea what it is," she said in frustration. "I must have the key to this whole damn riddle and I don't even know it."

"Why don't you try to get some rest?" Ann said. "We can talk about this more later."

"Will you stay with me?" Carrie asked. "I don't want to be alone."

"We'll stay right here," Ann assured her.

"We won't let anything else happen to you," Will said, stroking her hand. "I promise."

Carrie nodded and drifted off to sleep.

Chapter 42

Armed with a prescription for a strong painkiller, Carrie was released from the hospital just as the sun was coming up. Will took the day off to look after her. She was exhausted and went to bed as soon as they arrived at Will's house. She slept quite peacefully until around noon, when she awakened feeling like she had been run over by a steamroller.

She had never realized what hard work getting beat up was. It seemed that every part of her body ached and making even the simplest movements or performing the simplest tasks caused excruciating pain. Determined to do things for herself, she refused Will's offer of assistance and spent fifteen minutes getting from the bed to the bathroom and back again. When she returned to the bedroom and gingerly lowered herself onto the bed, her body was screaming so for mercy that she would have wept except that would have taken more effort than she currently had available.

Will got her another dose of painkiller, and she managed to eat a little soup before dozing off again. When she revived around four o'clock, she could hear Will talking on the phone in the living room. Gritting her teeth, she got up and made her way out there.

"I guess that's to be expected," Will was saying in a grim tone. "We appreciate what you're doing anyway. Talk to you later." He hung up the phone, then noticed Carrie. "What are you doing up?" he scolded.

"I'm not used to lying around doing nothing," she replied, carefully sitting down on the sofa. "I thought I'd try sitting up for a while. Who were you talking to?"

"Detective Clauff," Will replied, sitting down next to her. "He spent the day talking to people at the hospital, but of course no one admits knowing anything about the bastard who attacked you."

"Does that really surprise you?" Carrie asked, managing a smile. "The hospital is scarcely willing to admit that we spelled its name correctly in our pleadings. I didn't expect anyone to admit they hired a goon to rough me up."

Will reached over and took her hand. "I'm so damn mad about this whole thing that I can hardly see straight," he said, looking at her earnestly. "If I knew who did this to you, I swear I'd blow his head off."

"And I probably wouldn't discourage you," Carrie replied.

Will leaned over and gently kissed her on the lips. "Does that hurt?" he asked.

"A little," she admitted. "But don't stop."

They cuddled for a while, then Will said, "The detective says the police are done investigating at your place, so you can go back whenever you want."

"I'd like to go back there tonight," Carrie said.

"Really?" Will asked, surprised.

Carrie nodded. "Muffin will need food, and when I'm feeling down it's just nice to be in my own surroundings. You can stay with me there," she added.

"You're damn right I'm staying with you," Will said forcefully. "And we're taking Floyd with us."

"I don't think Muffin will like him," Carrie protested.

"He'll just have to get used to it," Will said firmly. "Floyd is better than a burglar alarm when it comes to alerting you to strange people prowling about."

"All right," Carrie said, leaning her head against Will's shoulder.

"Would you like something to eat?" Will asked.

"In a little while," she said. "Just sit here with me for a minute." Will put his arm around her and they sat in silence for a time. Then Carrie looked at the poster on the wall and said ruefully, "I'll bet Emma Peel wouldn't have let that guy get the better of her. She would have cut him off at the knees." She ran her tongue around her lips, remembering the attack. "I really didn't even try to fight him off," she said, her eyes filling with tears.

"Don't think like that!" Will said, pulling her close to him. "Remember what the detective said. The guy who did this was a professional. There was nothing you could have done, and who knows, maybe if you'd tried to fight back he would have hurt you even worse." He leaned close.

"Carrie, he could have killed you," he said hoarsely. "What happened to you was horrible, and I know how much you're hurting now, but it could have been so much worse. I could have lost you forever, just when I found you." He put his arms around her and buried his face in her hair. "So please don't talk like that, okay? You're here and you're going to be fine, and that's all that matters."

Carrie was so touched by the sentiment that she found it impossible to speak for a time. When she had recovered herself, she took a deep breath, let it out again, and said, "Well, when you put it that way, I guess maybe things didn't turn out so bad. Now, let's have a little something to eat and then I'd like you and Floyd to take me home."

"You got it," Will said, kissing her lightly.

Carrie and Will spent a quiet weekend at her place. His dog took up residence in the kitchen, while Carrie's cat spent most of his time hiding under her bed.

Will took charge of installing motion-sensitive lights in the driveway. Carrie actually thought he got a bit carried away—the entire block now lit up like a soundstage when a car so much as approached the drive.

"I hope the neighbors don't complain," Carrie said.

"The hell with the neighbors!" Will retorted. "This is to ensure your safety. If anyone bitches about it, I'll set them straight."

By Monday, Carrie was still very sore but was beginning to feel claustrophobic at home and was looking forward to going back to work. Although her eye remained terribly black and blue, the swelling had gone down and her vision had nearly returned to normal. Feeling self-conscious about her appearance, she spent a full thirty minutes staring in the mirror, applying and reapplying her makeup, before Will finally called a halt to her efforts. "Come on," he cajoled. "You look great."

"I sure do," Carrie said ruefully, running her finger over the purple bruise under her eye.

"People are going to be so happy to see you that they won't even notice that. I promise."

"If you say so," Carrie said, finally turning away from the mirror.

"I do," Will replied. "Have you had your pain pill?"

Carrie shook her head. "I'm going to try to do without them during the day. If I start to ache too badly, I'll just take some Advil."

"You're one tough dame," Will said, smiling.

"You're damn right I am," Carrie said nodding. "Now let's blow this pop stand."

The entire Ramquist and Dowd staff seemed to be on hand to welcome Carrie when she walked in the door with Will. When she finally made her way to her office, she discovered it was filled with flowers. "Where did all these come from?" she asked Tammy in amazement.

"Lots of different people," Tammy replied.

Carrie walked around the room examining the cards. There was an arrangement from the firm and a separate one from Burt Ramquist featuring a helium balloon with Elvis's visage. Charlene Bull had sent a large spray of lilies. She smiled up at her secretary as she read all the cards. "This is so sweet," she murmured.

"Everyone was worried about you," Tammy said. "Except maybe Dr. Luebke."

Carrie frowned. "What makes you say that?"

"I guess he was so pissed off about being questioned by the police on Friday that he called Burt up at home and started reading him the riot act. Dona told me about it."

"What did Burt do?" Carrie asked.

"He told Luebke that whoever beat you up was guilty of

attempted murder and if the doctor didn't shut up immediately he would be looking at a harassment charge. Burt told Dona that Luebke slammed the phone down immediately."

Carrie laughed. "Good old Burt."

"Are you going to drop the case?" Tammy asked.

"No way," Carrie answered resolutely.

"But what if the attacker comes back?" Tammy persisted, her voice heavy with concern.

"I can't let myself think about that," Carrie said, sticking out her chin. "I have no way of knowing for sure if the attack really was connected with the case. Everyone assumes it was, but frankly that makes no sense to me. It could just as well have been a psycho—maybe even a former patient at Jackson Memorial—who thinks I'm being too hard on the hospital."

Tammy looked skeptical.

"Look," Carrie said soberly. "Even if what happened to me was somehow related to the *Buckley* case, I am not bowing out. I have too much invested. That case is part of me. I owe it to the Buckleys and to myself to see it through."

"But surely the Buckleys wouldn't want to see you in danger because of them," Tammy said.

"I talked to them this weekend," Carrie said. "Obviously they were concerned about me, but they respect the fact that this is my call. They said they'd love to have me remain on the case if I felt comfortable doing so. I assured them I did, and that's that."

"You're awfully blasé for someone who just got the crap beat out of her," Tammy commented.

"It's either that or fall apart," Carrie said. "And I'll be damned if I'm going to fall apart. So I made up my mind that I would pick myself up and go on with my life as best I could."

"You're the bravest person I know," Tammy said, giving her boss a hug. "I think I'd move to Alaska if something like that happened to me."

"No, you wouldn't, because that would mean the bad guy won. You'd find the strength to deal with it."

"I'd at least get an attack dog," Tammy said.

Carrie smiled. "I have one on loan. I'm not sure h
would actually attack anyone, but he could keep someon
at bay just by sitting on them."

Will renewed the settlement offer with the hospital, bu
it was again soundly rebuffed. The hospital also failed t
budge from its hard line of refusing to admit any wron
doing on Delgado's part. As a result, two weeks after she'
been attacked, Carrie once again found herself in Judg
Little's courtroom, this time seeking an order that woul
allow Scott Rouleau, a person who had been found incon
petent to make decisions about his own welfare, to testif
as a plaintiffs' witness at the *Buckley* trial. Carrie's assau
had only increased her adamancy about keeping Scott
identity secret as long as possible. Thus, Scott was referre
to in the motion papers as patient J. Doe.

"This case just keeps getting weirder all the time," Baili
Adrienne Thomas commented to Carrie and Will as the
settled in at counsel table. "Are you going to come in nex
week and ask that the comatose woman be allowed to te
tify via mental telepathy or something?"

"I don't think so," Carrie replied.

"I hope the case doesn't settle," Adrienne said. "This
going to be the most interesting show we've had in th
court since the four women who thought they were van
pires were on trial for kidnapping twenty different guys an
sucking their blood."

When the case was called, Charlene Bull asked to b
heard on a preliminary matter. "You have the floor," Judg
Little said.

Charlene stood up. "Your Honor, before we get to th
merits of the plaintiffs' motion, the defendants request tha
the name of the patient at issue be disclosed. It is imposs
ble for us to make an intelligent response to the motio
without knowing the patient's identity."

Judge Little nodded to Carrie to respond.

Carrie got to her feet. Her facial bruises had faded to
light yellowish hue, and her ribs had healed to the poi
where she felt only the occasional twinge of pain. Althoug

Detective Clauff had not completely given up hope of finding Carrie's assailant, he admitted that the odds of that happening were slim.

"Your Honor," Carrie said, "maintaining anonymity is necessary for the witness's own protection." She held her head high as she continued. "As the plaintiffs detail in their motion, I was recently the victim of a vicious attack. My assailant indicated that the purpose of the attack was to convince me to drop this lawsuit. It is obvious that I have refused to bow to that pressure. However, if someone is intent enough on bringing this case to an end to be willing to inflict physical harm on me, then I can only assume that that person would also be willing to inflict similar physical harm on our key witness. It is for that reason that we believe it is imperative not to reveal the witness's identity until such time as that person is called to testify at trial." She took her seat.

Judge Little scratched her nose with the end of her pen. "This is a highly irregular request," she said. "It is a tenet of our judicial system that a party is entitled to know the nature of the allegations against him. Ordinarily that means revealing the identity of all witnesses. But, the assault on Ms. Nelson changes the landscape here. Even though I have some misgivings about not allowing the hospital to know the identity of the patient at issue, I find Ms. Nelson's argument about the witness's safety to be persuasive. Therefore, I am going to go along with the plaintiffs' request to withhold the identity of the witness until trial."

Carrie smiled and nodded at the judge.

"Having resolved that issue, I'll turn the floor back to Ms. Nelson to argue the merits of the motion and explain why a person who has been found legally incompetent should be allowed to give testimony in a legal proceeding."

Carrie again stood up. "Your Honor, I will be the first to agree that nothing about this case is usual or routine. The primary plaintiff, Katherine Buckley, is unable to testify in her own behalf. Alessandro Delgado, a former hospital employee and the person who has been proved through scientific testing to have assaulted Ms. Buckley, also cannot testify because he is deceased. The hospital has refused to stipulate that Mr. Delgado was Ms. Buckley's attacker. Believe me, Your Honor, the plaintiffs wish they did not have to impose on J. Doe to testify, but we have no choice. As far as we have been able to determine, Doe was the only witness to Delgado's assault on Ms. Buckley."

Carrie paused and took a sip of water. "As your honor is aware, the law presumes that all persons are competent to testify. While it is true that J. Doe is a patient at Jackson Memorial, that does not automatically mean that Doe is incompetent to testify about what Delgado did. The hospital will, of course, be entitled to argue that Doe was mistaken about what Delgado did, but that argument goes to the weight of the testimony, not to its admissibility. We request that either J. Doe be allowed to testify or the hospital be required to sign a stipulation admitting to what Alessandro Delgado did." Carrie sat down.

Charlene Bull argued that a patient in a mental hospital was, as a matter of law, incompetent to testify as a witness in any type of legal proceeding. "How can anyone argue with a straight face that a mental patient who is under the influence of psychotropic medication is a reliable witness? Not only is what the plaintiffs are suggesting contrary to law, it is bad public policy."

In the end, Judge Little disagreed. "Once again, I find myself fashioning a unique remedy for a unique case. I find the hospital's refusal to stipulate to Delgado's involvement in the case troubling. If the scientific evidence shows what Ms. Nelson has indicated it does, the hospital's position appears to border on being frivolous. As Ms. Nelson points out, the plaintiffs' sole recourse is to call the only eyewitness to the crime. Therefore, it is the ruling of this court that patient J. Doe may testify at trial. Plaintiffs' counsel shall prepare an order for my signature." The judge rapped her gavel sharply on the bench.

Will leaned over to Carrie and patted her hand. "Good job. Looks like we've cleared the last hurdle in the case."

Carrie smiled at him and nodded. "Yup. Next stop: the trial."

Chapter 43

Everyone at the firm was invited to an informal gathering at O'Malley's after work on Friday, July 3, to celebrate Terry Payne's divorce. After months of wrangling, the young partner and his wife had finally reached an agreement giving them joint custody of their two children. Terry was so happy to finally be able to put this ugly chapter of his life to rest that he declared that from five until seven that evening drinks would be on him.

Carrie had insisted that she and Will put in an appearance. "Are you sure you want to do this?" Will asked when Carrie appeared in the doorway of his office shortly after five o'clock. "It's going to be pretty raucous. We could go somewhere a bit more subdued for dinner and then catch a movie."

Carrie knew that Will was concerned about her state of mind, given that the following morning Katherine Buckley's baby would be delivered by C-section and then Katherine's life support would be disconnected. Will had been walking on eggs around Carrie all week, clearly expecting that at some point she might break down. But she had surprised him, nonchalantly going about the business of preparing for the trial, never letting on that anything was bothering her.

"I want to go to Terry's party," Carrie said, looking Will straight in the eye. "I want to be somewhere raucous tonight. I want to be with my friends and have a few drinks and laugh and have a good time."

She walked over and stood behind Will and put her hands on his shoulders. "I know you're afraid I'm going to fall apart because of what's going to happen tomorrow.

We've been dancing around the issue all week. And the truth is that part of me is numb and to some extent I've been operating on autopilot, but that's how I cope with bad things. I force myself to live as normally as possible. That's what I did after I was attacked, and that's how I'm going to get through tomorrow. So let's go and show our support for Terry and then maybe go home and watch some old movies. You don't need to worry about me," she said, leaning down and nuzzling his cheek. "I'll be fine."

Will turned his face up and kissed her. "All right, then," he said. "Let's party."

The lighthearted atmosphere at O'Malley's was precisely the tonic Carrie needed. She and Will ended up joining Terry and several other colleagues for the pub's famous fish fry, and it was nine-thirty by the time they got back to Carrie's place. Will had installed an enormous doghouse in her backyard, after the attack, and Floyd came out to greet them when they pulled into the driveway. They watched Carrie's video of *Some Like it Hot* and then went to bed.

Carrie fell asleep easily but woke up abruptly in the middle of the night. Propping herself up on one elbow, she squinted at the clock on the bedside table. It was three-thirty. Katherine had about seven hours left to live, if you could call the state she'd been in living.

Carrie lay down again. Will was sleeping peacefully next to her. Her cat, which had been sleeping on her side of the bed, woke up, moved closer to Carrie's face, wedged his head under her chin, and began to purr loudly.

Carrie closed her eyes and tried to get back to sleep, but dark images swam before her eyes, making rest elusive. She imagined Katherine's baby crying helplessly for a mother it would never know. She imagined Katherine's lifeless body being transported to a funeral home. She imagined the funeral and the burial. In her mind's eye she saw Katherine's child growing up, asking about its parents. Carrie wondered what the Buckleys would tell the inquisitive youngster. Clearly they would want their grandchild to learn all about its mother, to understand what a loving person she had been. But what, if anything, would they reveal about its father?

The cacophony of dark thoughts left Carrie feeling sorrowful and anxious. She inched backward until she was touching Will. The cat followed her movements so as not to lose contact with her. Will stirred in his sleep and instinctively put an arm around Carrie. She leaned back against him, finding his solid presence reassuring. She didn't know how she could ever have made it through the last month without him. Closing her eyes once more, she finally drifted off to sleep, hoping that this terrific man would remain part of her life for a long time to come.

Carrie and Will got up around eight the next morning. Although neither of them mentioned Katherine and Carrie did not comment about her disturbed slumber, their mood was somber. After having a cup of coffee, they took Floyd for a walk before breakfast. When they returned home, Carrie made Belgian waffles. After they'd eaten they had another cup of coffee while perusing the morning paper and attempting to make light conversation.

"Pat Grove can't use her tickets to Ravinia the first Saturday in August," Carrie told Will. "Do you want to go?"

Will shrugged. "It's up to you."

"I haven't been there yet this season," Carrie said. "And I always enjoy it."

"Then let's go."

"Okay. I'll tell Pat we'll take them."

"Do you want to go over the list of prospective jurors today?" Will asked.

Carrie nodded. "That'd be a good idea. I'm going to work on my opening statement."

"I thought the draft you showed me was great," Will said.

"It's coming along," Carrie agreed. "For me they're always a work in progress right up until the time I get up and start talking to the jury."

"That's the best way to do it. You sound more natural if it comes from the heart."

"This one definitely will," Carrie said softly.

The morning stretched on without any word from the Buckleys. Carrie put fresh linens on her bed and did a couple of loads of laundry. Will repaired a window box on the front of the town house that had been damaged in a storm. Carrie cleaned out the cat's litter box. Finally, at twelve-thirty, the phone rang.

Carrie and Will both stared at it for a moment. "Do you want me to get it?" Will asked.

Carrie shook her head. Taking a deep breath, she picked it up. "Hello. . . . Yes. . . . I see. . . . Yes. . . . All right. Give Ed and Melody our best. . . . I will. Thank you." She gently hung up the phone and turned to Will. "That was Bishop Wilson. Katherine had a daughter. Six pounds, twelve ounces. Healthy and alert, with a few wisps of brown hair. They're going to name her Cassandra."

Carrie paused a moment in an effort to maintain her composure. Clearing her throat, she went on, "Katherine died at 11:52. The funeral will be on Monday afternoon. Bishop Wilson is going to officiate."

Will came over to her and put his hands on her shoulders. "Are you okay?" he asked gently.

Carrie swallowed hard and nodded. "I think so," she answered. "In some ways it's a bit of a relief. At least she's not suffering anymore, and maybe the fact that the Buckleys have their granddaughter will make the pain of losing Katherine a bit easier to bear."

Will pulled her to him. "There's nothing wrong with crying, you know. You don't have to be brave on my account."

Carrie pulled back so she could see his face. "I know that," she said. "And that's very sweet. But you see, I have to be brave for me." They held each other close for a minute, then Carrie said, "Let's have a little snack and then you can listen to my opening statement."

Katherine's funeral service was a celebration of her life. Bishop Wilson, who had known her from birth, offered touching and sometimes humorous reminiscences. In the front row, next to Ed and Melody and Katherine's siblings,

Todd Fleming sat holding baby Cassandra. Carrie and Will sat farther back with Katherine's cousin—and Carrie's old roommate—Amanda Buckley and her fiancé.

Although the service was in some respects painful for Carrie, she also found it to be healing. She understood, perhaps for the first time, that funerals were for the living, to help them find the strength to go on. As the final strains of the choir's last hymn faded and the casket was borne out of the church, the capacity crowd began to file out.

Out on the steps, Amanda, a tall, dark-haired woman, took Carrie's arm. "Do you think there's any chance the case will settle?" she asked.

Carrie shook her head. "We've given the hospital every opportunity to get out of this with some dignity, and they've made it clear they're not interested."

"I just feel so bad that Ed and Melody still have to go through a trial after all they've already been through."

"I know," Carrie agreed. "But they're very resilient. I'm absolutely in awe of how strong they've remained through all this. I don't know if I could have done it."

"Oh, Carrie, we see each other so seldom these days," Amanda exclaimed, fighting back tears. "What a shame we had to meet on an occasion like this. I miss talking to you."

"Me, too," Carrie said, hugging her friend.

After a long moment, Carrie heard Will politely clear his throat. She released her hold on Amanda and looked up at him. "Everyone's heading out," he said. "I think we'd better go to the car."

Carrie nodded mutely.

"Why don't you ride with us?" Amanda's fiancé offered.

"Thanks," Will said. "We'll do that."

He put his arm around Carrie and the four of them walked to the car, ready to follow Katherine on her last earthly journey.

Chapter 44

A week after Katherine died, Carrie spent Saturday evening at the office doing final preparation for the trial, which started on Monday. Will had been with her most of the day, but he left around five to go home and change clothes before going to a bachelor party for a colleague at his old law firm. He had given Carrie strict instructions that when she finished at the office she was to go directly to his house and wait for him.

Carrie found his continued concern for her safety touching but somewhat unnecessary. As the physical scars from the attack faded, she had slowly begun to put the incident behind her. Although she had spent every night since the attack with Will, alternating between their residences, she had regained her confidence and did not think it would bother her to spend a night at her place alone. Because she knew Will would resist that idea, she did not plan to broach the subject until after the trial was over. In the meantime, she had to admit she was basking in the attention.

Carrie had met with Scott Rouleau and his sister several times in the past couple of weeks. Scott was responding well to his new regimen of medication and psychotherapy and was now occasionally able to leave the hospital overnight to stay with Laurie. Carrie had met them at Laurie's home, trying her best to avoid having anyone at Jackson Memorial learn in advance of the trial that Scott was her key witness.

Around eight o'clock, after putting the finishing touches on the questions she wanted to ask in her examination of several witnesses, Carrie turned to a task she had long been

dreading: reviewing Katherine's medical bills. Jackie Crabb
had meticulously sorted the three boxes of papers by medical provider and totalled the amount of fees charged by
each one. This type of minutiae was one of Carrie's least
favorite parts of preparing for trial, but she knew it had to
be done. There was no time like the present. So she picked
up the first neatly clipped stack of papers and began to go
through them.

In a few minutes something on one of the bills caught
her eye. In the top left-hand corner, under Katherine's
name, was a number. 284453. Why did that seem familiar?
Carrie tapped her pen on the legal pad in front of her and
racked her brain. She could swear she'd seen that number
before. She thought hard for a minute, then threw the pen
down and laughed out loud. It was a sure sign she'd been
working too hard when numbers started looking familiar.

Deciding that she needed a can of caffeinated soda, Carrie swung around in her chair, intending to get up and walk
down the hall to one of the break rooms. As she did so,
her gaze fell on the sheets of paper she had removed from
Alessandro Delgado's apartment. She had taped them to
the wall next to her desk, not because she seriously expected ever to be able to break the seemingly mysterious
code, but more as a reminder of all the secrets life held.
As her eyes focused on the small print on the top sheet,
there it was. The same number. 284453.

Now more puzzled than ever, Carrie looked back at the
medical bill. 284453 was Katherine's patient identification
number. Was it a coincidence that the same number
showed up on papers found in Delgado's apartment? Carrie
pulled the sheets off the wall and gave them a closer look.
Katherine's patient ID number appeared not just once but
ten times. All of Delgado's other entries also bore a six-
digit number. Could it be possible that each number on the
sheets represented a patient at Jackson Memorial? And if
so, what was Delgado keeping track of?

Carrie looked more closely at the entries bearing Katherine's ID number. In the first, to the right of the number,
was the notation "07/25." To the right of that were the

numbers "1500" and "300." To the right of the next entry
bearing Katherine's ID was written "08/24," "1800," and
"450." The tenth entry read "05/12," "2400," and "600."
Carrie figured that the second column represented dates.
May 12 would have been a week before Delgado died.
What could the numbers in the last two columns stand for?
She contemplated the question for a moment, then the obvious answer popped into her head. Money. The last two
columns must represent dollar amounts.

Carrie thought back to Gloria Frank's surprise at her
brother's ostentatious lifestyle, his closets full of designer
clothes, and his hefty bank account. Gloria had doubted
that Delgado could have managed to maintain that level of
comfort on his nurse's salary. Her take on the situation was
that her brother had probably picked up some extra income
by dealing drugs. But maybe it wasn't drug money that had
lined Delgado's coffers. Maybe the money had come from
overcharging insurance companies for care received by patients at Jackson Memorial.

Carrie frowned as she thought through the logistics of
how such a scheme might have worked. It was unlikely
that Delgado could have single-handedly bilked insurance
companies unless he somehow created a phony identity for
himself as a doctor and then cashed the checks. That scenario was doubtful, since she had to assume that insurance
companies—or their computers—would be smart enough to
catch on to a bogus doctor. So how else could the scam
have worked?

Well, Carrie thought, what if Delgado had helped a doctor pad his bills and in return had received a cut? That
would explain those last two columns. The larger number
could represent the amount the patient's bill was padded,
and the final column could represent the amount of kick-
back Delgado had received. Now only one question remained. Which doctor's fraud had Delgado been aiding?
She had a good idea of the answer to that question.

Carrie quickly pawed through the pile of documents until
she came to Dr. Luebke's bills. Flipping through them, she
searched for any indication that it was Luebke whom Del-

gado was fronting for. It didn't take her long to see that
the evidence showed no support for that idea. There was
nothing the least bit remarkable about Luebke's bills. Disappointed but still believing she was on the right track,
Carrie methodically worked her way through the bills of
all of Katherine's other doctors. One by one she tossed the
stacks of bills onto the floor next to her. Dr. Redding, Dr.
Neumann, Dr. Morrow. There was nothing at all unusual
about any of them.

"Oh, no," Carrie said aloud, a sudden feeling of dread
welling up inside of her. Her heart now pounding, she
flipped through the rest of the stacks until she came to the
bills representing Dr. Peckham's treatment of Katherine.
Jackie Crabb had put the total for each doctor on a yellow
Post-it note on top of the stack. Carrie swallowed hard as
she looked at the figure representing the amount Dr. Peckham had charged for treating Katherine Buckley. It was
three times as large as the next highest total.

Carrie was breathing hard now, and her throat felt con-
stricted. She thought of Peckham's trophy wife, his expensive sports car, his house in Kenilworth, the bottles of
Petrus he had downed like water. Then she thought back
to how she had been assaulted within twenty-four hours
of the time Charlene Bull had informed all of Katherine's
former physicians, including Peckham, that the amount
and nature of their medical bills would be an issue at
trial. Was the timing of the attack mere coincidence?
Carrie doubted it.

She sat frozen in her chair for a moment, feeling unable
to move. Then she brought her hand to her mouth in a
gesture of horror as a chilling thought came to her. If Peckham had paid to have her viciously assaulted in order to
warn her off the case, what might he do to Scott Rouleau
in order to derail the trial for good? Carrie flipped through
her Rolodex, then snatched up the phone.

"Come on, dammit, answer," she hissed, as Laurie Rouleau's phone rang over and over. After seven rings, an answering machine picked up. At the beep, Carrie spoke
urgently into the phone. "Laurie, this is Carrie Nelson. It's

about nine o'clock Saturday night. I just learned something that makes me fear for Scott's safety. I'm going to the hospital now to check on him. I'll call you again later. 'Bye.''

Hanging up the phone, she frantically searched through the phone book until she found the number for the bar where Will had said the groom's friends would be feting their pal. That call was answered by a harried bartender. After she shouted Will's name into the phone several times, the bartender reluctantly agreed to have him paged. Carrie spent several anxious minutes on hold, exhorting Will to please be there. But when the bartender came back on the phone, he said gruffly, "Sorry. Somebody said they left about a half hour ago."

"Did anyone hear them say where they were going?" Carrie asked urgently.

"I have no idea," the bartender answered. "Sorry."

Carrie disconnected from that call, then dialed Will's home phone number. When his machine picked up, she left a brief message saying that she was going to Jackson Memorial to check on Scott and that if she hadn't called back by the time Will got home he should come looking for her. She slammed the phone down, got up, grabbed her purse, and headed for the parking ramp.

On the brief drive to the hospital, Carrie gave little thought to what she was going to do when she got there and even less to her own safety. As far as gaining access to Scott, she was counting on the fact that the hospital had not bothered to beef up its security precautions even in the light of the Buckleys' lawsuit and that one of the side doors would be open. Once she got up to Scott's room, she'd have to think of a way to lure him out of the hospital without scaring him to death. Maybe she could tell him Laurie had managed to get him a last-minute overnight pass and Carrie had been sent to fetch him. She nodded to herself. Yes, that should do it.

It was completely dark, with only the smallest sliver of moon in the sky by the time Carrie pulled into the hospital's parking lot. She briefly considered leaving the car at the far end of the lot, nearest the street, but then abandoned the idea. It would be safer for her and Scott if she parked closer to a door so the two of them wouldn't have so far to walk once they exited the building. With her heart in her throat, she pulled into a space near the west door. Then, taking a deep breath, she cut the engine, got out of the car, and quickly headed for the building.

Moving rapidly but trying not to run for fear of calling attention to herself, she walked to the west side entrance. She hesitated just a fraction of a second, then pulled on the door. When it opened easily, she momentarily closed her eyes and murmured a silent prayer of thanks. She walked inside and then moved stealthily up the stairs to the third floor. When she reached the landing, she took a couple of deep breaths, then opened the door a crack and peered down the hall. The coast was clear. She quickly crossed the hall to Scott's room.

I made it, she said to herself as she put her hand on the door handle. *Thank God. I made it.* She was so pleased with herself that her face bore a slight smile as she opened the door and slipped into the room. As soon as she was inside, the smile vanished. Scott Rouleau was sitting in a chair by his desk. Next to him stood Dr. Peckham, with a snub-nosed revolver pointed directly at Scott's head.

"Why, Carrie," the doctor said with a humorless smile of his own. "How very nice to see you. Come right in and join us."

Chapter 45

For a fleeting instant Carrie contemplated making a mad dash back out the door or screaming at the top of her lungs to attract attention. Dr. Peckham quickly disabused her of that notion by saying in an authoritarian tone, "If you attempt anything in the way of heroics, I will kill both you and Scott instantly. Do I make myself clear?"

Carrie swallowed hard and nodded.

"Good," Dr. Peckham said, waving the gun at her. "Now come over here where I can see you. Pull that chair over and sit next to Scott."

Carrie did was she was told. As she sat down, she asked Scott softly, "Are you all right? Has he hurt you?"

"He doesn't know who I am," Scott said in an agitated tone. "I am King Tut, Ruler of all Egypt, and this usurper dares order me around like a common peasant."

"It'll be okay," Carrie said, reaching over and patting Scott's hand reassuringly. She felt sorry for him. The poor kid hadn't been this irrational since the first time Carrie had met him. Peckham had probably set Scott's recovery back by months—assuming, of course, that Scott survived this ordeal and was able to make a recovery.

"No touching each other!" Peckham ordered. "Move your chair away from his," he directed Carrie.

Carrie again complied with the directive, sneaking a peek at her watch at the same time. It was ten minutes to ten. She wondered how long it would be before a nurse or an aide next made rounds. Again Peckham seemed to read her mind.

"The nurse made the last check of the evening at nine

o'clock," he said. "No one will be coming back until seven tomorrow morning. And unfortunately at that time they'll discover that this patient didn't make it through the night."

"I am a god. I am immortal," Scott babbled. "No mere earthling can harm me."

"We'll see about that," Peckham said angrily.

"Yes, we will, earthling," Scott shot back. "Soon you will be going to the next dimension."

"Shut up!" Peckham ordered.

"Scott, please," Carrie said in a soothing tone. She racked her brain trying to think what she might be able to do to defuse the situation. With Scott in this mental state, Peckham was apt to lose patience and kill them both. Maybe if Carrie could get Peckham talking he would see the futility of his scheme. Or if that was too much to ask, maybe she could at least delay the scheme's implementation long enough to give Laurie Rouleau or Will or someone else a chance to come to their rescue.

"How did you find out Scott was my witness?" Carrie asked conversationally.

"It took a fair amount of detective work on my part," the doctor admitted as he paced back and forth in the small room. "You were quite clever in keeping his identity secret. But I bribed the other patients with expensive chocolates and other treats and eventually one of them was able to tell me that it seemed you and your colleagues had interviewed Scott more times than you'd interviewed anyone else. So I put two and two together." Peckham smiled, obviously quite pleased with himself.

"I assume you knew about Delgado assaulting Katherine," Carrie said.

"Of course." Dr. Peckham waved the hand holding the gun dismissively. "Probably almost from the beginning. You see, one night last summer I was called in to see a new patient. After I got him settled into his room, I thought I heard a sound coming from Katherine's room, so I walked in there to check. And lo and behold, I found Alessandro in flagrante delicto with her."

The doctor put his head back and rolled his eyes, remembering the sight. "I don't know who was more shocked, me or Delgado. I guess it was probably a draw. I walked out and left him to finish his business and then summoned him to my office the next morning. He obviously thought his career here was over. He was very contrite, said he had appetites he couldn't control and that nubile female patients were simply too much for him to resist."

"Patients?" Carrie repeated. "You mean Katherine wasn't the only woman he raped?"

"Oh, my, no," Peckham replied. "There were a variety of others, all the rest of them conscious and to some extent happy to participate in the activity. But Katherine was his favorite. Apparently her unique mental and physical state made her an ever-available receptacle, so to speak, for our young friend's ardor."

Carrie was unable to suppress a shudder of revulsion. "That's disgusting!" she exclaimed.

Peckham merely shrugged. "We all have our little peccadilloes, don't we? Anyway, Alessandro clearly expected that I would not only have him fired but also turn him over to the authorities. He was pleasantly surprised when he learned that I had no intention of doing either—provided he did me a favor in return."

"He helped you defraud insurance companies by padding the patients' bills," Carrie put in.

Peckham's face lit up. "You *are* a smart girl. Bravo."

"But why did you need Delgado's help?" Carrie asked. "If you'd filed the claims on your own, you would have been less likely to get caught, plus you wouldn't have had to share the money."

Peckham gave a small smile. "I needed assistance because I am notoriously inept with any type of paperwork and when it comes to computers I am a virtual Luddite. You see, insurance claims are filed electronically. I didn't know how to file them myself, and I couldn't trust my own office staff to help me out, since they have a disgusting penchant for honesty. What I needed was an accomplice who was conversant with medical jargon and not technologically challenged. Alessandro and I were a match made in heaven."

"So he helped you pad the bills and then you cut him in on part of the booty."

"Right again," Peckham said. "Alessandro and I shared a passion for the finer things in life, and we both needed a little extra help to attain them."

Carrie frowned. "But surely you must earn a very handsome income from your practice. Why did you need more money?"

Peckham laughed heartily. "My dear Carrie, you are so naive. Allow me to enlighten you. Yes, it is true that I make what by most people's standards would be considered a very respectable income. However, most people do not have a first wife bleeding them dry in alimony, two teenage children in hideously expensive private schools, and a second wife with tastes that require a king's ransom to support." Peckham paused for a moment. "So you see, it really was imperative that I boost my income, and padding some insurance bills a bit seemed to be the best way to accomplish it."

"And since Alessandro had expensive tastes, too, he was only too happy to help you out," Carrie said.

"That's correct," Dr. Peckham said. "Alessandro was a recreational drug user, and for a time he had attempted to supplement his income with a bit of dealing, but that really wasn't his cup of tea. There was too much risk involved and besides, it required him to dirty his hands. He was far better suited to white-collar crime."

"How much of a cut did you give him?" Carrie asked.

"It varied from patient to patient but generally around twenty to twenty-five percent," Peckham answered.

"What exactly did he do to help you?"

"A variety of things. He helped me choose the patients whose bills we would adjust. We picked them quite selectively. We obviously couldn't fudge everyone's bills. Katherine was an ideal candidate. She had first-rate insurance coverage, and since she required round-the-clock care her bills were already quite high. I figured no one would notice if we added on a little more." Peckham paused a moment, then added almost wistfully, "Of course, I never counted on her getting pregnant."

"That must have been a horrible shock," Carrie said.

"It certainly was," the doctor said. "I couldn't believe Delgado would be so stupid. I assumed he was at least using condoms."

"Did you and Delgado work out a strategy after the news of Katherine's pregnancy broke?" Carrie inquired.

"Of course. He was understandably nervous, but I told him if he kept his mouth shut—and stayed away from Katherine—he should have nothing to worry about because there was no proof of who had carried out the assaults. I figured that in the absence of any proof, the judge would dismiss your case and neither of us would have anything to worry about."

"You underestimated me," Carrie said brashly. "I found out who the rapist was."

"Yes, unfortunately you did," Peckham agreed. "And poor Alessandro went ballistic. The night he found out you were onto him, he phoned me in a complete panic. I told him to calm down and said I'd come over and we'd discuss it. When I got there, he was seething with rage. He said if he was going down for the assaults, then I was going down with him for insurance fraud." Peckham paused a moment, then said almost wistfully. "Of course I couldn't allow that to happen."

"So you killed him," Carrie said coldly.

Peckham slowly nodded his head. "I'm afraid I had no choice."

"How did you do it? I can't imagine he just stuck out his arm and allowed you to inject him with morphine."

"Now you're the one who's underestimated me," Peckham said. "I came prepared. I suggested that he and I have a drink to calm our nerves. I spiked his drink with a fast-acting sedative that knocked him out within ninety seconds."

"Why wasn't that found in his blood?" Carrie demanded.

Peckham smiled. "Because I chose my poison wisely. By

the time I moved him into the bedroom and administered the fatal dose of morphine, all traces of the first drug had already left his system."

"You're a cold-blooded monster," Carrie spat out.

"That's not true," Peckham said. "I tried my best to convince Von Slaten to settle the case, and when that didn't work, I did everything I could to warn you off, but you simply wouldn't take the hint. I employed a professional to tamper with your car and your front door. Finally, in desperation, I was forced to have you roughed up and given a more direct warning. I was astounded when even that didn't get you off the case. I guess that goes to show that some people are just slow learners."

"You tried to frame Dr. Luebke," Carrie said.

"I didn't really try to frame him. I just wanted to divert attention away from Alessandro and me."

"How did you know about Gwen Starling?"

"When we first met, Ken Luebke and I were quite friendly. He confided in me that one of the most difficult times of his career was when he formed an inappropriate, but platonic, romantic attachment to a young patient."

"He didn't assault Gwen Starling?"

"No."

"What about the malpractice actions that have been filed against him?"

"Nearly all doctors have had their share of malpractice suits," Peckham said. "You of all people should know that folks sue at the drop of a hat. I think Ken's insurance company had to pay nominal damages in one case and the rest were dismissed."

"So there's nothing untoward in Dr. Luebke's past?"

"Not that I'm aware of," Peckham replied. "It's just that he's a self-righteous pain in the ass. I'm going to make a far better chief of staff than he ever would."

"Do you really think you're going to get away with three murders *and* be named chief of staff?" Carrie asked incredulously.

"My dear Carrie, I am certain of it."

"I have to go to the bathroom." Scott Rouleau, who for

the past half hour had been sitting quietly in his chair, now spoke up loudly.

"Keep quiet and sit still," Peckham barked back.

"I have to go bad!" Scott said insistently.

"I told you to shut up!" Peckham exploded.

"I have to go," Scott said, sounding on the verge of tears.

"For God's sake, let him go," Carrie urged.

Peckham scowled, then said to Scott harshly, "All right. You have ninety seconds. If you're not out in that length of time, I will shoot Ms. Nelson in the head. Do you understand me?"

Scott's eyes grew wide and his head bobbed nervously up and down.

Peckham pointed at the bathroom with his gun. "Go on. Remember, I'm timing you."

Scott scurried into the bathroom and slammed the door behind him.

As the doctor stared at his watch, Carrie shifted nervously in her chair and glanced at her own timepiece. It was nearly eleven. Her energy was lagging, and she didn't know how much longer she could keep the madman talking. If she and Scott were going to survive, she was afraid she was going to need to take some affirmative action to save them, but what?

"Ten, nine, eight, seven . . ." Peckham was counting off the remaining seconds. "Hurry up." Carrie heard the toilet flush, and then Scott came back into the room just as the doctor counted, "Two, one." Peckham glared at Scott. "All right. You had your break. Now get back in your chair."

Scott complied without protest.

"Does Justine know what's going on?" Carrie asked.

For the first time that night, Peckham's face softened. "Of course not," he answered. "She's completely innocent of any wrongdoing. I did it for her, you know. A few years ago I once suggested that we think about moving to a smaller house, and she became so distraught that I had to sedate her." Peckham paused and his lower lip seemed to tremble. "So you see, I had to do whatever I could to maintain the standard of living to which she is accustomed. My beautiful Justine. She's an angel."

Carrie wondered what the angel would think if she knew she'd driven her husband to larceny and murder. "I'm sure if you leveled with her about your money crunch she'd be happy to scale back her expenses," Carrie said. "Why don't you talk to her about it?"

"There's no need to talk to her," Peckham said, his voice taking on a manic sound. "She has no need to know about any of this. Things are going to continue just the same as they always have. I know what I'm doing. I'm in control," he said, his dementia now coming through loud and clear and making the words ring hollow. "I'm going to be named chief of staff in another six weeks. That will bring in extra money, so I won't have to continue the insurance scam." He began to pace wildly back in forth in front of Carrie and Scott.

"How are you going to explain Scott's demise?" Carrie challenged.

"Heart failure," the doctor replied without hesitation.

"And what about me?" Carrie demanded. "It'd be quite a coincidence if I just happened to be visiting Scott and I keeled over, too."

"Oh, I have other plans for you," Peckham replied ominously. "They won't be finding your body for a long time."

A wave of pure terror came over Carrie, but she clenched her jaw and fought to maintain her composure.

"I'm getting tired of all this chitchat," Peckham said. "I think it's time to move forward with my little plan." Still pointing the gun at his hostages with his right hand, he reached into his jacket pocket with his left and pulled out a syringe and a vial of milky-looking liquid.

"What's in there?" Carrie asked.

"Something to make our friend go to permanent beddie-bye," Peckham replied. His surgeon's hands were very agile, and he rested the vial on his thigh and removed the protective sheath from the syringe.

Carrie watched the proceedings with mounting horror. Then, just as the doctor was about to plunge the needle

into the liquid that would end Scott's life, Carrie launched
herself off her chair and grabbed for the vial. At the same
instant, to Carrie's utter amazement, Scott jumped out of
his chair and lunged for the gun.

The doctor was so stunned by their sudden outburst that
he loosened his grip on both objects. Carrie grabbed the
vial out of his hand and flung it at the wall, smashing it to
bits. Scott kneed him in the groin and was able to wrest
the gun away. As the doctor went down on his knees in
pain, Scott pointed the gun at his head.

"Keep him right there," Carrie shouted. "I'll go for
help." She ran to the door and flung it open, intending to
sprint down the hall to the nurses' station. Instead, she ran
into the waiting arms of Detective Clauff. Behind him were
several uniformed officers.

"Oh, thank God you're here!" Carrie exclaimed to the
detective as the uniformed officers went inside the room
and took charge of Dr. Peckham. "I'm so glad Will got my
message and called you."

"Will didn't call me," Clauff responded.

"He didn't?" Carrie asked, perplexed.

Clauff shook his head and Carrie turned. Scott Rouleau
was standing in the doorway, a big grin on his face. "You
know computers are my life," Scott said in a voice that
sounded completely rational.

Carrie nodded, not understanding what that had to do
with their miraculous rescue.

"Well," Scott went on, "a couple days ago I had an allergic reaction to one of my meds that caused my feet to
break out in an ugly rash. I'm supposed to soak them in
Epsom salts three times a day to help clear it up. Just
before Dr. Peckham came in I had been in the bathroom
soaking my feet. I had my laptop with me and I never
brought it back out. So when I was in there a little while
ago, I E-mailed the police station for help."

Carrie broke out laughing and threw her arms around
Scott. "This is the second time your computer expertise has
saved the day," she said, giving him a big hug. "After I've
calmed down from the events of this evening, I want you

to give me some lessons. It's obvious you can get the same results with computers as some people do with kick boxing."

Scott laughed and hugged her back. "You've got yourself a deal," he said.

Epilogue

Local Hospital Names New Chief of Staff
By Gail Wolfe, *Chicago Tribune* Staff Writer
Dr. Kenneth Luebke has been named the new chief of staff at Jackson Memorial Hospital. The announcement was made today by Werner Von Slaten, Jackson Memorial's administrator. Dr. Luebke, a neurologist who has been on staff at the hospital for nine years, will replace Dr. Robert Morrow, who is retiring. Dr. Luebke will assume his new duties on September 1.

Carrie handed the newspaper to Will, who was sitting on the other side of her desk. He skimmed the article and nodded in satisfaction. "Good for Dr. Luebke," he commented. "I'm happy for him."

"Me, too," Carrie agreed. "Peckham very nearly succeeded in railroading him in order to claim the top job for himself."

"I wonder how Peckham is enjoying his stay in jail. It must be quite a comedown from his palatial digs in Kenilworth."

Carrie made a face. "If you ask me, his current lodgings are much too good for him. Come to think of it, torture would be too good for him."

"I think Illinois outlawed torture as a form of punishment some time ago, but if it's any consolation, I doubt he'll be getting out anytime soon."

"That definitely is a consoling thought," Carrie agreed. "He can claim insanity till he turns blue, but I'd bet money that no jury will find him insane, and with my testimony and Scott's, he'll be spending the rest of his miserable life behind bars."

"Good place for him," Will said. He leaned back in his chair. "The Buckleys were certainly pleased when they picked up their settlement check yesterday."

Carrie smiled. "They did look happy, didn't they?" After learning about Dr. Peckham's complicity in Delgado's regular assaults of Katherine, Carrie and Will upped their settlement demand to eight million dollars, and the hospital paid it without a peep of protest. "I hope now they'll be able to start moving on with their lives."

"Cassandra is a lucky little girl to have grandparents who love her so much," Will commented.

Carrie nodded.

"When does Scott get to leave the hospital for good?" Will asked.

"This weekend," Carrie replied. "He's going to be staying with Laurie for a while, until he gets reoriented to life on the outside. He'll be pretty busy now that Michelle hooked him up with someone who's going to market his Holy Grail game. She thinks he has a really bright future."

"I'm glad things worked out for him," Will said. "And I'm especially glad he had the presence of mind to summon help. I don't know if I'll ever be able to forgive myself for leaving you alone that night."

"No one could have ever predicted Dr. Peckham was the bad guy," Carrie said. "Besides, you did call home around eleven, and you came rushing to the hospital as soon as you heard my message."

"Yeah, but by the time I got there you'd already been rescued," Will said ruefully. "On the mad dash over there I was imagining myself as your knight in shining armor and there I was, upstaged by someone who thinks he's King Tut."

"He doesn't really think that anymore," Carrie said. "All that stuff's in his past."

"Anyway, I have a lot of guilt over that incident," Will went on.

"I see," Carrie said seriously. "Do you have any ideas how you might work through that?"

"I do have one idea," Will said.

"What's that?" Carrie asked innocently.

Will reached into his jacket pocket and pulled out an envelope. "I just happen to have in my possession two round-trip tickets to San Francisco, leaving this afternoon. I'm told the atmosphere there is quite therapeutic."

"Two tickets, eh?" Carrie said. "Have you decided who you're taking with you?"

"That's a tough decision," Will said, getting up and coming around Carrie's desk. "What are you doing this afternoon?"

Carrie reached up and put her arms around Will's neck. "I'm leaving for a week in California with the nicest, sexiest guy I've ever met."

"You'll have to introduce me to him sometime," Will teased.

"No way. He's too good to share with anybody. I'm keeping him all to myself." Carrie pulled him down into a lingering kiss.